SPANISH DAGGER

SPANISH DAGGER

SUSAN WITTIG ALBERT

THORNDIKE
CHIVERS

This Large Print edition is published by Thorndike Press, Waterville, Maine, USA and by BBC Audiobooks Ltd, Bath, England.

Thorndike Press is an imprint of Thomson Gale, a part of The Thomson Corporation.

Thorndike is a trademark and used herein under license.

The text of this Large Print edition is unabridged.

Other aspects of the book may vary from the original edition.

Set in 16 pt. Plantin.

LIBRARY OF CONGRESS CATALOGING-IN-PUBLICATION DATA

Albert, Susan Wittig.
  Spanish dagger / by Susan Wittig Albert.
    p. cm. — (A China Bayles mystery) (Thorndike Press large print mystery)
  ISBN-13: 978-0-7862-9672-9 (hardcover : alk. paper)
  ISBN-10: 0-7862-9672-0 (hardcover : alk. paper)
  1. Bayles, China (Fictitious character) — Fiction. 2. Women detectives — Texas — Fiction. 3. Herbalists — Fiction. 4. Texas — Fiction. 5. Large type books. I. Title.
  PS3551.L2637S63 2007b
  813'.54—dc22
                                                 2007012870

BRITISH LIBRARY CATALOGUING-IN-PUBLICATION DATA AVAILABLE

Published in 2007 in the U.S. by arrangement with The Berkley Publishing Group, a member of Penguin Group (USA) Inc.
Published in 2007 in the U.K. by arrangement with The Berkley Publishing Group, a division of Penguin Group (USA) Inc.

U.K. Hardcover: 978 1 405 64198 2 (Chivers Large Print)
U.K. Softcover: 978 1 405 64199 9 (Camden Large Print)

Printed in the United States of America on permanent paper
10 9 8 7 6 5 4 3 2 1

The mystery story is two stories in one: the story of what happened and the story of what appeared to happen.
— Mary Roberts Rinehart

It's possible to solve a mystery and still not know all the answers.
— Terence Faherty, Prove the Nameless

ACKNOWLEDGMENTS

A great many people helped with this book. For help with the papermaking aspects, I'm grateful to the members of the Yahoo! papermaking list (especially Gin Petty, Beth Heesacker, and Velma Bolyard) for their encouragement and inspiration.

For the facts regarding the operations of the Texas regional drug task forces (now largely disbanded), thanks go to Nate Blakeslee for his riveting book, *Tulia: Race, Cocaine, and Corruption in a Small Texas Town,* and to the Texas ACLU for its comprehensive reports of abuse and scandal, "Flawed Enforcement" and "Too Far Off Task."

For her careful reading of the manuscript and her help with the botanical information, I am happy to thank Alice Le Duc, Ph.D., Director of Education, The Sarah P. Duke Gardens at Duke University.

For their encouragement, good cheer, and

help with herb facts, I am grateful to members of the Essential Herbal Internet Group, with special thanks to Dr. Tamara H. Hunt, who introduced me to agave nectar.

For having the wisdom to enter and the good luck to win the Story Circle mystery character raffle, congratulations go to Melissa Grody, together with my thanks for her enthusiastic cooperation in shaping the character who bears her name in this book.

A mystery series, especially a long-running series like this one, wouldn't be possible without the encouragement of a supportive editor and publishing team. Special thanks go to Berkley editor Natalee Rosenstein, who has guided these books from the beginning; to her assistant, Michele Vega; and to Catherine Milne in publicity. I couldn't do it without you.

And as always, thanks and thanks again to Bill, husband and writing partner, who is always generous with his ideas, suggestions, computer support, and hugs.

A NOTE TO THE READER

To a novelist, writing books in a series presents all sorts of interesting challenges and opportunities. Characters can grow and change, becoming more complex, more interesting, and more problematic with each book. Settings and their histories can be deeply explored. Themes can be developed and explored, in major and minor keys, from book to book. And books can be linked by plots, as well. One story line might be introduced as a subplot in one book, developed as a major plot in another book, and wrapped up in a third. I've especially enjoyed playing with this technique, for some stories are simply too complex to be told in one telling.

The story of China's relationship to her father — complex, multilayered, and full of ambiguity — seems to me to deserve an extended telling. So *Spanish Dagger* carries forward and develops a tale that began in

9

Bleeding Hearts, with China's discovery of her connection to Miles Danforth and the letters Robert Bayles wrote to Laura Danforth. It will be continued and more or less concluded in *Nightshade,* although I think it is true that stories that affect us deeply, such as the discovery of a father's secret life, are never quite concluded. Family stories like these shape our lives in ways that we often don't discover for many years. They can come back to haunt us for decades — at least, this has been true in my own family, and perhaps in yours, as well.

I realize, of course, that connected books impose certain demands on readers. Some people may not be able to read them in order, for instance, while others may be frustrated by a conclusion that doesn't quite wrap up the full story, and may be impatient for the next installment. There's danger for the author, too, who risks being accused of leaving a "dangling plotline." But for me, the potential enrichments of an extended tale are worth the extra effort it takes to write and read them. For you, too, I hope.

And before we leave you to get on with the story, China and I also want to remind you of one important thing. Don't use any herb medicinally or therapeutically until you do your research. Plants are "natural," yes.

But that doesn't mean they are always safe.

Susan Wittig Albert

CHAPTER ONE

"Spanish dagger" is one of the many folk names for that striking, statuesque plant, *Yucca glauca*. A member of the genus *Agave* and one of the most common herbs of the Southwest, Spanish dagger can be seen along roadsides, in pastures and meadows, and across the arid plains. A plant of great and varied utility in many native cultures, it has supplied food, drink, medicine, clothing, footwear, and even construction materials to peoples throughout the Americas.

It's possible to solve a mystery and still not know all the answers. It's possible to know in detail what happened to Colin Fowler and Lucita Sanchez last week. It's possible to know how it was done, and even who did it, and why. But knowing an answer to any question doesn't mean that you know *the* answer. And knowing the truth doesn't mean that there's no unfinished business. There are always pieces of the puzzle that don't quite fit, threads of story that can't be neatly tied, answers that can't be matched with the questions that still linger.

In other words, one mystery leads, inevitably and inconclusively, to another. The best we can hope for is a break in the clouds, a brief lifting of the fog, an interim solution and the promise of some sort of temporary and momentarily satisfying clarity.

It's a tough world, a crazy and chaotic world, this world we live in. But it is very good to be alive. And what happened in Pecan Springs this past week certainly reminds me of that indisputable fact.

"Gosh, China," Carole said warmly, "this is a great place."

She looked around the spacious room, with its beamed ceiling, white plastered walls, and fieldstone fireplace, then glanced toward the kitchen on the other side of the counter island. "It's absolutely perfect for a workshop. And this terra-cotta floor will clean up easily." She grinned. "Making paper is a messy business, as I'm sure you know."

I knew. I'd never been able to make paper without ending up with puddles of water

14

and pulp on the floor. I opened the sliding glass door and we went onto the wooden deck. It was shaded by a large live oak tree, its April green leaves fresh and glistening in the afternoon sun. "We can set up the beater and drying racks out here," I said. "And another table, if we need it."

"Perfect," Carole said approvingly. "How many folks have enrolled?"

"Twenty, with six on the wait-list."

"Then we've definitely maxed." Carole pushed her gold glasses up on her nose. "I like to be able to spend at least ten minutes with each person. When there's more than twenty, somebody gets shortchanged."

We went back inside, where I picked up Carole's suitcase. "Let's take a look at your bedroom." I led the way down the hall, past the bathroom. At the bedroom door, Carole pulled in her breath.

"Lovely," she exclaimed. "China, this is perfect! I'm going to love it here."

I hoped so. I've invested a great deal of time and thought in the decorating project and love the way it's turned out: an antique four-poster bed made up with lavender-scented sheets and covered with a Texas Star quilt and a scattering of pillows; a polished mahogany dresser and rocking chair; a red and blue braided rug on the gleaming oak

15

floor; wood shutters at the windows; even a small television set and VCR. And since the cottage is at the very back of the lot, away from the street, there's almost no noise — except, of course, for Miss Lula, the yappy little dog, as old and crotchety as her owner, who lives on the other side of the alley.

If you didn't know, you'd never guess that Thyme Cottage was built as a stable, in the long-ago days when everybody in Pecan Springs had at least one horse. It sits under a large pecan tree behind the two-story stone building that houses my herb shop, Thyme and Seasons, Ruby Wilcox's Crystal Cave, and Thyme for Tea, the tearoom that Ruby and I own together. The fully equipped kitchen and spacious main room (fancifully called "the Gathering Room") make the cottage a great place for all sorts of workshops and classes. The newly decorated bedroom, which looks out onto the gardens that surround the building, enables me to rent the cottage as a bed-and-breakfast when it's not otherwise scheduled. I've been getting quite a few rental requests lately, because the place is listed in the new *Pecan Springs B&B Guide.*

This week, Thyme Cottage was doing double duty: Carole Gaye, who lives and works near Taos, would be teaching a papermaking workshop and staying in the cottage. Carole is an accomplished paper artist with a national reputation, and always in demand as a teacher. I was only able to get her because she's a friend of Ruby's, so I was glad the accommodations pleased her.

I showed her the bathroom, then asked, "What else do we need to do before Saturday's workshop? Do you have everything you need?"

"Most of it," Carole said. "I'll set things up on Friday, but since tomorrow's only Thursday, I'm taking the extra day to relax. There is one thing, though. If you know where to find a few yucca plants, I'll collect some leaves. Yucca makes great paper, and since it's easy to find in this area, I want to show people how to work with it."

"Sure," I said. "There are quite a few yuccas along the railroad tracks. If you'll come to the shop about eight thirty, we can drive over there." I'm usually at the shop just after eight, which gives me time to get a few things done — sweeping, dusting, even some garden work — before customers start showing up at ten. Owning your own business has plenty of plusses, but sleeping until noon is not one of them.

Carole nodded. She was about to say

something else, but she was interrupted by the sound of the front door opening and a loud "Yoo-hoo!"

"We're coming, Ruby," I yelled, and we went back down the hall to the Gathering Room, where, with bubbly squeals, Ruby and Carole — friends since they met at a yoga retreat a couple of years ago — fell into an enthusiastic embrace. With Ruby was our new partner, Cassandra Wilde, carrying a tray laden with breakfast goodies: fruit, juice, and a couple of Cass' famous gingerbread waffles. Cass had also included a small pitcher of dark agave nectar for the waffles. It's made from the heart of the wild agave plant and is higher in fructose than sugar-based syrups or honey. Good for anyone who needs to watch the sugar. Carole would definitely not go hungry.

If you were here with us, you could meet everyone in person, but since you're not (and since you may be new to Pecan Springs and in need of an orientation), I'll take a few moments to tell you who we are. You've met Carole Gaye already — she's the diminutive one, wiry and sturdy, with muscles developed from years of pounding plant fiber and toting buckets of pulp. Her attractive gray hair is cut like a boy's, and she's wearing gold granny glasses, khaki slacks, a

18

neatly tucked-in black tee, sneakers, and not a smidgen of makeup.

The willow-slim, very tall gal (six feet plus-plus in her wedgies) is Ruby Wilcox, business partner and best friend. Makeup, yes, lipstick and eye shadow and liner as dramatic as any queen of the Nile. Hair in springy ringlets the color of fresh carrots. Eyes, blue, green, or brown, depending on her choice of contacts and eye shadow. Green today, complementing her springtime outfit: calf-length cropped linen pants in a flowery yellow print, a loose buttercup yellow tunic over a mustard yellow tee, straw sandals, and a saucer-sized sunflower pendant with matching sunflower earrings. Ruby in full bloom, fully outfitted for her working day.

Ruby's Crystal Cave is the only New Age shop in Pecan Springs, which shouldn't be a surprise, since small-town Texans don't usually go ga-ga over tarot, incense, crystal balls, the I Ching, astrology, and spirit channeling. But Ruby, who teaches everything from Understanding Your Birth Chart to The Path of Rune Wisdom, has a loyal and loving following. Last Saturday, she taught a daylong class called Learning from Your Inner Teacher, which has something to do with trusting that part of yourself that is unconsciously plugged in to the Cosmic Switchboard. The Gathering Room was packed with women, whose devotion to Ruby makes many male Pecan Springers nervous. Good ol' boys have a tendency to view Ruby as an Alien Being. The idea that their wives and daughters might tune in to something other than *Fox News* or *As the World Turns* gives them the fidgets.

Ruby and I have been close friends for a long time, and I can testify that there are plenty of fascinating contradictions stowed away behind that in-tune-with-the-universe facade. Yes, she's intuitive, so intuitive that it's often spooky. She can scan your stars and tell you things about yourself that you haven't yet discovered, and she can coax the Ouija board to tell more tales than a Baptist snitch in a Methodist choir.

But when it comes to business, Ruby is ruthlessly pragmatic. She knows to the penny how much cash flowed through the register at Thyme for Tea — her brainchild — last month. She can also tell you how many new clients we added to Party Thyme, the new catering service, locally (and humorously) known as Ruby's "traveling circus." She proposed starting that little enterprise because she had the idea that people who enjoyed their visit to Thyme for

Tea might be happy to hire Party Thyme to cater their next big garden party.

And she's been right, by golly. Thanks to her firm and capable management, Thyme for Tea and Party Thyme are turning a healthy profit. Ruby may look like and act like a card-carrying member of the Ya-Ya Sisterhood, but there's an admirable brain beneath those bouncy red curls and an iron fist in that yellow velvet glove.

Cassandra Wilde — in the kitchen, stashing Carole's breakfast goodies in the refrigerator — turned our duo into a trio when she joined our enterprise this spring. Cass is blonde and bountiful and proud of it. "Sassy, brassy, and size twenty-two," she coos seductively. "Wanna see my love handles, sweetie?" Her sense of style and color is as outrageous as Ruby's, and since there's some eighty pounds more of her than there is of Ruby, the effect can be . . . well, a little overwhelming. If you prefer shrinking violets, Cass' in-your-face attitude will not win you over. On the other hand, her cooking will. Guaranteed.

Ruby and I met Cass six or seven months ago on the set for *A Man for All Reasons,* a local amateur theater production. After opening night, she came to us with a bright idea: a personal chef service called the

Thymely Gourmet that would be an extension of Ruby's other two bright ideas. That is, people who enjoyed the food at Thyme for Tea and subsequently engaged Party Thyme to cater their garden party would be happy to hire the Thymely Gourmet (that's Cass) to put a dozen splendid dinners in the freezer. After giving the proposal some thought — and giving Cass a trial run in the kitchen — we said yes, and we two became we three.

Although I was initially skeptical about the Thymely Gourmet, I have to admit that the concept is a winner. Cass herself — a gifted cook who was recently certified as a personal chef by the American Culinary Foundation — is definitely a dynamo. She has no Off button, her cheerfulness rarely wanes, and if you watch her too closely, you'll get dizzy. Cass' Thymely Gourmet has become, as Ruby puts it, "the third ring of our circus." And even I have to admit that having Cass as one of the ringleaders makes the circus a lot more lively.

Which leaves me. I'm China Bayles. I'm five-four in my Birkenstocks, a bit on the hefty side (although I'm on a campaign to lose some weight). My hair is brown with a streak of gray, my nails usually have garden dirt under them, and I don't have an ounce of interest in fashionable clothes: jeans, tees, and tennies, that's me. I was a criminal attorney in Houston before I moved to Pecan Springs, single, on the scary cliff of forty, and desperately soulweary. I was sick of playing games — the sort of dirty pool everybody has to play to make the justice system work — tired of fighting and clawing my way up the ladder, and ready, oh, more than ready, to lead a kinder, gentler, less combative life.

So I opened an herb shop, planted a garden around it, and began collecting girlfriends. A few years into my new incarnation, I took a deep breath and said yes to a former Houston homicide detective named Mike McQuaid, whose marriage portion included his gun collection; his melancholy basset hound; his son, Brian (now fifteen); and Brian's spiders, snakes, and lizards, who have staked out free-range privileges throughout our house. These collaborations have been challenging, since privacy, autonomy, and personal independence are high on my list of personal priorities. But I've managed, in spite of the difficulty in adjusting to Brian's geckos and McQuaid's guns — McQuaid is the name I used when we met on opposite sides of a legal issue, and it's stuck. It's been a good marriage, too, if a little scary sometimes, such as the day McQuaid announced that he was quitting his second career (as a professor in the Criminal Justice program at Central Texas State University) in order to hang out his shingle as a private investigator.

Gulp. Ruby tells me I think too much and too logically about the possibilities, such as not being able to make the mortgage payments. She says I need to let go and listen to my Inner Teacher. But my Inner Teacher is also worried about the mortgage payments, especially because McQuaid's last case was the rare book theft he investigated for Jeremy Paxton in March. We have now arrived at late April without a client, which is why I take heart when Ruby shows me our healthy bottom line. Two risky business ventures in one family is two too many. But by this time, Cass has finished in the kitchen, Carole and Ruby have caught up, and I am glancing at my watch. It is nearly five, time to help Laurel close up both shops.

"I hate to be a spoilsport," I said, "but I've got company coming for dinner tonight." I was not looking forward to the occasion, but it could no longer be put off. There were questions that had to be answered. Old questions, maybe some new questions, none of which had any answers, at least as far as I was concerned.

"I guess that means you can't join Ruby and Cass and me for an early supper," Carole said regretfully.

"I'm afraid so," I said.

"I'll have to take a rain check, too," Cass said. "The Thymely Gourmet is serving an out-of-this-world dinner to a pair of prospective clients. Well-heeled clients, I am happy to say."

Ruby made a face. "I'm sorry, but I can't do supper, either, Carole. I've got a personal problem. Two personal problems, actually."

"Only two?" I teased. I already knew about one. Ruby's boyfriend had stood her up the night before, and she was fretting about it.

Actually, it is no longer accurate to say that Colin is Ruby's boyfriend. She was madly in love with him for months — and when Ruby is in love, it's a passionate, wholehearted, hang-on-to-your-hat, over-the-top affair. She takes a deep breath, closes her eyes, and steps into the void, plunging into total free fall without so much as a bungee cord while her friends look on, wringing their hands in helpless dismay.

But in early April, after months of feeding

the eternal fire of hope with scraps of poor excuses, Ruby decided that Colin would never be able to give her what she wants: love, commitment, and a future together. So she told him she was turning down the flame, for which I have to give her a great deal of credit. Who among us is capable of actually ending a love affair, even when it falls pitifully short of our great expectations? I know what it cost Ruby to put some distance between herself and Colin and to assert her independence. I deeply admire her for stepping back from the brink of what was beginning to look like a toxic situation. And to give Colin credit, he agreed that breaking up was the right thing to do — with just enough regret to allow Ruby to feel he really did care, after all, but not enough to make her think she might have been just a tad too quick to push the eject button.

But "distance" does not necessarily mean closure, and while Ruby is no longer extending those hopeful invitations to dinner-plus-sleepover at her house, she is still accepting Colin's occasional evening-out invitations, on a just-friends basis. Not a good idea, if you ask me. Having been there and done that, it is my personal opinion that when a love affair dies, it ought to stay dead.

Definitely, decidedly dead. If it threatens to rise again, it ought to be treated the way you'd handle a vampire — by plunging a dagger into its heart. Trying to resurrect it as a friendship can only extend the pain.

But as usual, Ruby is doing things her way. Or not, as the case may be. Colin had planned to drop in about ten last night to pick up a box he had left in her keeping, then stay for soup and sandwiches. He didn't show up, and she's been fretting all day. I feel for her, of course. It's no fun to be stood up, even if you've made up your mind that your heart is no longer in love. But failure to show up for a date was one of Colin's less agreeable habits, and Ruby ought to be used to it by now. His unreliability is one of the reasons — but only one — that I am not his biggest fan.

"What's the *other* problem?" I asked.

Ruby's shoulders slumped. "My mother."

"You can't solve your mother in one evening," Cass said sympathetically. "What's she done now?"

Ruby's mother lives at Cedar Summit, a retirement village in Fredericksburg, about an hour's drive from Pecan Springs. Under the best of circumstances, Doris is not the kind of person you want to spend time with. She always wears a sour expression, as if life

27

has not gone according to her expectations and plans; understandable, given the fact that no matter how much willpower and muscle you exert over events and people, you can't dictate how everything turns out. Doris has definitely given it her best shot, though. Ruby was nineteen when she found out she was pregnant — the same week the baby's father was killed in Viet Nam. When Ruby started to show, Doris packed her off to a home for unwed mothers in Dallas and insisted that the baby be given up for adoption, even though Ruby desperately wanted to keep her. It was years before Amy came back into her mother's life, and Ruby still mourns all those lost decades.

It is a sad irony that, in the last few months, Doris the supercontroller has been losing her grip. She gets lost, she misplaces her door key and her checkbook, she forgets appointments, and she has morphed into a kleptomaniac with a passion for scarves — and not your ordinary, dinky dime-store scarves, either. A couple of weeks ago, the security guard at Dillard's stopped Doris from waltzing out the door with a pricy alligator bag stuffed full of hand-painted silk scarves. Doris claimed that she'd merely forgotten to stop at the cash register to pay for the bag and its contents, but the security tapes told a different story. And when Ruby started snooping around her mother's apartment, she found silk scarves hidden in the closet, in drawers, in the refrigerator, in the oven. The conclusion is clear: Doris is losing her marbles. Or, as the colorful Texas expression has it, she's a few peaches short of a pie.

"What's happened now?" Ruby repeated in a depressed tone. "It's not pretty. I got a call from Melanie, the administrator at Cedar Summit. Maybe you remember that Mom can't drive her car any longer — she lost her license after she ran into that school bus last spring. But her car is still in the parking lot until we decide what to do with it. This afternoon, she took the keys from the board in the office, and when the guard wouldn't let her drive out of the compound, she locked herself in the car."

"Oh, dear!" Carole exclaimed. "Is she all right?"

"Right as rain," Ruby said ironically. "Melanie called a locksmith and they got her out within the hour. But she was . . . well, her language was even worse than it was after the car wreck." She shook her head. "The school bus, the shoplifting, and now this — it's clear that Mom has some serious problems. Melanie is insisting that we move her into a supervised unit. She wants to schedule a psychiatric evaluation, as well. I talked to Ramona — my sister, who lives in Dallas — and both of us agree. I'm driving to Fredericksburg tonight to tell Mom what has to be done."

Poor Ruby. Doris was not going to leave her apartment willingly. She wouldn't take kindly to "evaluation," either. "If you have to stay overnight," I said, "don't worry about the shop or the tearoom. We can cover for you here."

"I can stop by and feed your cats in the morning," Cass volunteered. "Call if there's anything we can do."

"Thanks," Ruby said. "I'll phone if I can't make it back." She gave us each a hug, trying to smile, but her worried look didn't disappear. If I knew Ruby, it wasn't the shop or Doris that was bothering her. It was Colin Fowler, and for a fierce instant I hated him for causing her pain, for treating her as if she didn't matter.

I straightened my shoulders. Where Colin is concerned, there is nothing I can do for Ruby except hope that she will stop seeing him altogether. And I certainly couldn't help her cope with Doris. Anyway, I had my own relatives to deal with tonight, and I sure as hell wasn't looking forward to it.

CHAPTER TWO

LEMON-MINT TEA CONCENTRATE

Lemon balm gladdens the heart, warms
the stomach, and cheers the sad and
melancholy.
— Polish proverb

Fresh herbs: mint, lemon balm, lemongrass,
lemon verbena, 2 quarts water

Gather and rinse about four cups of fresh
herbs. Chop mint, lemon balm, and lemongrass. Strip the leaves from the lemon verbena and discard the stems. Bring water to
a boil in a nonreactive pan. Add herbs,
cover, and remove from heat. Steep for 10
minutes. Strain and refrigerate. Dilute two
to four times, depending on the strength
you prefer. Serve over ice, garnished with
slices of lemon and sprigs of fresh mint.

"Brian is having dinner at Jake's house,"

McQuaid said, peering into one of the grocery bags. "They're working on their science project."

"That's good," I said decidedly. Jake is Brian's girlfriend of some months' standing. The kids have had more than their share of trouble in the past few months, after the high school football coach, a man whom their friends idolized, was shot. They had nothing at all to do with the shooting, but they were both on the scene and both were in a highly compromised situation. It was a tragedy for the whole town, and some of the kids at the high school — some Pecan Springs football fans, too — still blamed them. I was glad that Brian was gainfully occupied for the evening. He didn't need to be faced with any more uncomfortable situations, especially in the family.

McQuaid frowned. "I hope you remembered the salmon." He was in charge of the grill tonight, and salmon is one of his favorite things to cook.

I enumerated the items as I set them on the kitchen counter. "Salmon for the grill, and some fresh ginger for the marinade. Yellow squash, zucchini, plum tomatoes, onions, mushrooms — also for the grill. Potatoes. Salad fixings. Strawberries and whipping cream." A container of soup and a loaf of herb bread were thawing on the counter, and I had made some concentrate for Leatha's favorite lemon-mint iced tea before I left for the shop this morning. All I had to do was marinate the salmon and veggies for the grill, make a salad, and mix and bake the shortcakes. Everything easy. Everything under control.

Everything except me. McQuaid caught the expression on my face, put down the package of salmon fillets, and pulled me to him. Ruggedly good-looking, my husband has dark hair, steely blue eyes, and a twice-broken nose. But best of all, he's six-feet-something, with broad shoulders and narrow hips, and comfortable in his body. Nothing rocks him, nothing knocks him off-balance. When he holds me, he is steady and strong and solid as an oak, the kind of man you can rely on when the world turns upside down.

"Hey, babe," he said softly, kissing my ear. "Don't sweat it. They'll get along — at least, they'll be civil. Leatha is your mother. And Miles is your brother, for Pete's sake. They're civilized. There won't be any violence."

I pulled away. "Half brother," I corrected him testily.

Robert Bayles, my father, had begun his

long-term liaison with Laura Danforth before he married my mother, and Miles was the result. The affair had been going on for three decades when my father drove his blue Cadillac through a bridge rail and down a steep embankment, where it burst into flames, some sixteen years ago. An accident, my mother and I had been told. Something much more sinister, my half brother believed, after reading some letters his mother had saved. Miles was a lawyer, and lawyers love answers much more than questions. He wanted to get to the bottom of the mystery — if it had a bottom.

After reading the letters for myself, I had to agree that the idea seemed plausible. But sixteen years is an eternity in law enforcement. As far as Houston Homicide was concerned, this wasn't even a cold case. It was an automobile accident. Period. Paragraph. End of story. It would be impossible to get the matter reopened. If Miles wanted to dig around in the ugly past, that was his business. But I had told him to deal me out. I have a husband, a son, and a business to tend to. I am busy getting a life. I would be just as glad if Miles Danforth went away. Far away.

He didn't, of course, and now he was about to get what he asked for: an evening with Leatha, McQuaid, and me — the whole fam-*damn*-ily, as McQuaid's easygoing father puts it with a chuckle. But Miles wanted more than a good meal and pleasant conversation. He intended to talk about the way Dad died. If there was a better recipe for an uncomfortable dinner party, I didn't know what it was.

I learned who Miles Danforth was just two months ago, around Valentine's Day. It was a shock, for I had lived my entire life believing that I was an only child — and all of a sudden, I wasn't. I had a brother. As teenagers we hung around Stone, Bayles, Peck, and Dixon, my father's law firm. Then, he was just Buddy, a slim-hipped, dark-haired kid with sexy eyes and a lazy, heart-thudding smile, whose mother was my father's secretary. I already half-suspected that there was something going on between Dad and Buddy's mother, but it wasn't any of my business. I respected Laura Danforth's ability and admired her directness, and to be brutally honest, I looked up to her more than I did my alcoholic mother. Maybe that was one reason for the major crush I had on Buddy the summer I was fourteen. I had no idea he was my father's son.

Neither did he. Miles — the nickname was

abandoned when he got his law degree — had learned the truth only a short time before I did, from the love letters and photos he found after his mother died. If the discovery was a shock for me, it must have been a massive earthquake for him, a volcanic eruption, a cataclysmic rearrangement of his entire universe. Although his father — our father — paid his college and law school tuition and even gave him his first job, Dad had never acknowledged that Miles was his son. It must hurt like hell.

I could sympathize, because Dad never really acknowledged me, at least not in any way that mattered. In all the years of my life with Robert Bayles, we shared only one close father-daughter moment: he took me to a shooting range, taught me to load and fire a gun, and gave me a 9mm Beretta. I still have the gun, and the memory. But now that I think about it, it wasn't exactly a father-daughter moment, was it? It was the sort of thing a father might do with his son. Had he taken Buddy to the same range? Had he given him a Beretta, too?

And what about Leatha? At first, I thought I wouldn't tell her about Laura and Buddy. It would be unendurably painful to learn that her husband had deceived and betrayed her, from the day she became a bride to the night she became a widow. Even worse, he had fathered a son, the son she hadn't been able to give him. My mother had been a fragile Southern belle who sought comfort and solace in bottles of bourbon. Would this send her looping out of control, destroy the happiness and stability she had worked so hard to achieve?

But after a week's reflection, I knew I had to tell her. The past had been shadowed by too many secrets, too much deception. It was time to let in the light, to put all the old lies behind us. Anyway, the Leatha I knew now was different from the Leatha I knew then. Her second husband, Sam, was supportive and loving, and she was building a new life, far away from Houston. She had confronted other tough challenges and remained steadfastly sober. I could trust her to handle it.

It wasn't easy, of course, and I wound up blurting it out, rather than breaking the news gently, as I'd intended. She said she had suspected for years that Dad and Laura Danforth were having an affair, but she hadn't known that her husband had fathered Laura's son. Knowing hurt. Knowing re-opened all the old wounds and brought up the buried pain of the past. She wept and I wept, and we wept together — healthy, at least for me. I don't cry easily, or about trivial things. The tears seemed to exorcise the last stubborn devils of my old anger toward Leatha for turning to alcohol instead of taking care of me.

But she wasn't ready to meet Miles. He had invited McQuaid and me — and Leatha — to have dinner with him at one of Austin's best restaurants. McQuaid and I had accepted, and reciprocated by inviting him and his daughter Caitlin, a remote and silent child, to our house for barbecue. We'd invited Leatha, too, but she refused. On both occasions, Miles said nothing about Dad, and I hoped his silence on the subject meant he'd given up the idea of digging into the past. Whatever the truth of the matter, trying to get the investigation reopened was a waste of time. And when I told McQuaid about the letters and about Miles' suspicions, he agreed with me. McQuaid knows the Houston police department inside out. There wasn't a ghost of a chance that a sixteen-year-old traffic accident would be turned into a cold-case murder.

That had seemed to be the end of it — until a couple of weeks ago, when Miles called again, saying he wanted to meet Leatha. I relayed the message, and she agreed, on the condition that we meet at our house for a casual, quiet evening. She wanted to get it over with, to put it all behind her, she said, and I could hear the resignation in her voice. I hadn't told her about Miles' hidden agenda. If I had, she probably wouldn't have agreed to come. And I wanted to get it over with, too.

Now, McQuaid's arm tightened around me, pulling me against him, and his lips brushed my cheek. "Y'know, I like Miles, even if he is a lawyer — and obsessed with this stuff about your dad. He's a pretty good guy, as brothers-in-law go." He looked down at me, his blue eyes light. "Half brothers-in-law, I mean. Nothing like Sally's brother Rodney, thank God. That guy was something else."

McQuaid's laugh rumbled deep in his chest. I chuckled, and suddenly my perspective shifted. Sally was his flaky first wife, Brian's mother, and the mention of her and her tattooed, ponytailed, Harley-riding brother reminded me that families these days are nothing like the symmetrical packages we once held dear: two parents of the same race, religion, and ethnicity; two children, an older boy and a younger girl; and an equal number of grandparents lined up on either side, smiling. Now, families are like a big garden salad. Mom and dad —

sometimes a single parent, sometimes a dad-mom pair or two moms or two dads — are tossed together in a large bowl with a bunch of kids of varying parentage. Flighty ex-spouses, itinerant former and current in-laws, and grandparents of varying ethnic and racial identities are sprinkled around like sunflower seeds or garbanzo beans. In that context, there was nothing very weird about my father's illegitimate son having dinner with his half sister, his half brother-in-law, and his dad's widow. I might as well lighten up and go with the flow.

In the beginning, my fears about the evening seemed to be exaggerated. We had dinner on the screened back porch, looking across the lush green grass of the yard to the pale green leaves of the mesquite on the other side of the stone wall. The April evening was cool and lovely, the spring flowers generous, the woods lively with the calls of nesting birds. Leatha, coifed and manicured and carefully dressed in sage green silk patio pants, a matching silk shirt, and the pearls my father gave her the Christmas before he died, was her most elegant and composed Southern self. Gracious and interested, she told Miles to call her Leatha, asked about his mother's last illness, cooed over photographs of his ten-year-old daughter, and — when she learned that his wife had been killed in a boating accident a few years before — sympathized with him about the challenges of being a single parent. You would never know that he was the son of the man who had caused her so much heartache.

For his part, Miles — dark-haired, bearded, casually dressed in khakis and a sport shirt — was intelligent and interesting, his father's charming savoir faire tempered by his mother's genuineness. He kept us smiling with amusing stories about Zwinger, Brady, Brandon, and Danforth, the prestigious Austin law firm in which he was a partner. If Leatha saw any resemblance between him and Robert Bayles (as I certainly did), she kept it to herself.

McQuaid, equally casual in jeans and a red polo shirt, livened the party with his usual bluff hospitality, responding to Miles' stories about the law with his own tales of close encounters in the law enforcement business. Thanks to his expertise at the grill, the salmon and veggies were delicious, nicely complemented by the soup, salad, and hot herb bread. And even Howard Cosell, McQuaid's crotchety old basset, was on his best behavior. Having enjoyed a surreptitious bit of salmon and potato, he

41

settled himself just inside the screen door for an after-dinner doze, propping one wary eye open in case a squirrel came around. Howard is at war with the squirrels.

The hard part came when we were finished with the strawberry shortcake and I had poured our second cups of coffee. The sun had set and twilight filled the shadowy yard, so I lit an oil lamp and put it on the table. As I sat down, Miles stirred his coffee, cleared his throat, and opened the subject I knew he had come to discuss.

He was tense and apologetic. He didn't want to cause any unnecessary pain, but he felt compelled to clear up several mysteries about Uncle Bob's death. That was the name he had always used as a kid growing up, he explained to my mother with a disarming, disingenuous frankness — the name he felt most comfortable with. It irritated me — why not call a spade a spade? — but Leatha only nodded, and in a way, I was relieved. "Uncle Bob" distanced us, somehow, from the nearer and more disquieting kinship we shared.

"Actually, I wouldn't know any of this," he went on, "if it hadn't been for some letters my mother kept." He glanced at me, and then at McQuaid, as if for support. "China and Mike have seen them, and they agree with me. For weeks before he died, Uncle Bob was convinced that somebody was trying to kill him."

There was a moment's silence. Leatha stared at Miles over the flickering oil lamp. "Trying to *kill* him?" Incredulous, she turned to me. "That can't be true. Can it, China?"

"That's what he thought, Mother." I reached for her hand. "Of course, that doesn't necessarily mean that he *was* in danger." I squeezed her hand and let it go. "People imagine all sorts of things."

"I don't think Uncle Bob was imagining anything," Miles said with a thin smile, and began his story, as if it were a summation to a jury he was trying to persuade. I didn't need to listen. I already knew what he was going to say.

Among the papers Miles found after his mother's death had been fourteen letters from my father. The first eight or ten were informal and chatty, written while Dad was out of town on various business trips. They were full of references to cases that had long since been settled, to people I didn't know, to Buddy, who had been working for Stone and Bayles, but had — with Dad's help — gone on to another firm. They weren't love letters in the usual sense, but I could read love in every line: tenderness, affection, warmth. Each ended with "You have all my heart, Laura — Bob." For me, that single short phrase had shone a new and different light on my father, explaining nothing but revealing a great deal. He had led two different lives: in one, he was an adulterer without compunction or conscience; in the other, he was a caring and devoted lover. It made me wonder how many other secret lives he had led.

But it was the later letters that Miles was talking about, those written just a few weeks before Dad died. He was working on behalf of someone he called simply K, with no mention of the legal issues at stake or any explanation why the case was taking him to so many different places. In one letter, written from Denver, he gave Laura the file numbers of several documents, telling her to copy them and put them into a safety deposit box she was to rent under an assumed name. In another, from Miami, she was to make an appointment with someone named Gregory and arrange for a flight to Washington. She was to say nothing to anyone, not even Buddy.

The last two letters were the most troubling. He wrote from Washington, where he had seen Gregory. He had also taken out a large life insurance policy in Laura's name, keeping it separate from his estate. "You need to start looking for another job," he wrote. "Don't wait until this is over."

The last letter, written in Dallas the week before he died, was terse, brusque. Laura was to quit Stone and Bayles, move out of her apartment, and go to San Antonio for a month. The last few sentences were chilling: "If something happens to me — I should probably rather say 'when' — you are not to make or encourage any sort of investigation." If she did, her life would be in danger, and Buddy's — and Leatha's and mine, as well. "I want your promise on this, Laura," he wrote. "It may be the most important thing you ever do for me."

Leatha listened to all of this, her eyes wide, her cheeks shadowed. "He was afraid," she whispered wonderingly, "and I never knew." She put her fingers to the pearls around her neck. "He didn't breathe a word."

"He didn't want you to know, Leatha," McQuaid put in quietly. "He cared about you and China. He wanted to keep you completely out of it."

I gave him a grateful look. I could tell by the softening of my mother's mouth that she believed him — or wanted to.

Miles went on, his voice tense but dispassionate, almost flat. "Mother always insisted that Uncle Bob's death was no accident, but she would never tell me what made her think so. After I read the letters, I understood. He doesn't mention death threats, but he obviously knew he was a target."

"Death threats," Leatha murmured. "Well, Bob always was a little paranoid, not without cause, I suppose. I never knew any of the details — he was always tight-lipped about what went on at the office. But I do know that the firm represented some . . . well, some pretty unsavory characters."

"Unsavory" was an understatement. What I didn't know growing up, what I had learned once I became a lawyer myself and a member of the Houston legal community, was that Stone and Bayles had built their practice on scandal-ridden Texas politicos, on oil and energy deals, on questionable land transactions. They and their clients played for high stakes in high-risk, winner-take-all games. Maybe that was why my father didn't invite me to join his firm when I got out of law school. Maybe he wasn't proud of what he was doing and didn't want me to see the kind of cards he was dealing. He had invited Miles, however, perhaps with the thought that Stone, Bayles, Peck, and Dixon might add one more name to the roster: Danforth. My brother — my half brother — probably knew a lot more about the firm's unsavory dealings than I did.

Miles leaned forward, his eyes dark and intent on Leatha's face. "To tell the truth, I'm pretty lost just now. I was hoping you might remember something that could give me a clue as to the direction I ought to take. A name, a case, something Uncle Bob might have said to you — anything that might help me."

"Clue?" Leatha asked. "Direction?" Puzzled, she appealed to me. "What's this about, China?"

"Miles is investigating Dad's death," I said flatly.

"Investigating!" she exclaimed, both brows shooting up. She straightened her shoulders. "Why, that's ridiculous! It's been sixteen years, for heaven's sake! Anyway, it was an accident." She turned back to Miles. "It was an accident," she repeated firmly. "The police said so."

"Perhaps you can remember something that might help," Miles persisted, as if she hadn't spoken. "Please think back. Maybe he left some papers at home, or in a safety deposit box. Maybe there was a computer. Perhaps you still have it."

Leatha was shaking her head. "He always kept his papers in his briefcase. He'd bring them home to work on, but he took everything back to the office. The only safety deposit box was the one where we kept my jewelry. And that was before everybody had a computer at home. Why, Bob never even learned to type." Her chuckle was barbed. "He always said that's what he paid Laura for."

Miles didn't seem to feel the sting. "Then maybe he mentioned a name. How about Miriam Spurgin? Did she ever come to your house to talk to Uncle Bob?"

Leatha shook her head. "I don't remember anybody by that name. At least, I'm certain she didn't come to the house." She smiled tightly. "We only entertained mutual friends."

"How about Max Vine? Did Uncle Bob ever mention him?"

"No." Leatha frowned. "Who are these people? And what do they have to do with Bob?"

"They were reporters for the *Houston Chronicle*." Miles' voice was hard. "They're both dead."

"Oh," Leatha said, with a little shrug. "Well, that's too bad. But I still don't see why you're asking me about them." She sniffed. "Bob hated reporters. He always said they were too nosy. They'd do anything for a story. He would never have anything to do with reporters."

On the step, Howard Cosell grunted, snuffled, and closed both eyes, giving up on squirrels. Somewhere deep in the woods, an owl called, and the oil lamp flickered. I regarded Miles' shadowed face.

Two dead reporters. So this was the reason for tonight's discussion. Not very compelling, on the face of it. But maybe there was more.

"You said they were dead?" McQuaid asked, with professional interest. "How? When?"

"Miriam Spurgin was struck by a vehicle in a parking garage three weeks before Uncle Bob died. Hit and run. Neither the driver nor the vehicle was ever found, of course." There was a taut resonance in Miles' voice, and I felt a sudden chill. "The next week, Max Vine's car blew up."

McQuaid was frowning. "Blew up? I think I remember that case. I was on Homicide at the time. It was a professional job. Killed a kid, too. Right?"

"Yes." Miles' mouth was a thin, flat line. "Vine, an investigative reporter, was taking his daughter to school. The bomb blew them both to kingdom come." His voice took on a metallic edge, and I thought of his own daughter, Caitlin. "The girl was only twelve."

"That was Jim Hawk's case," McQuaid said thoughtfully. "It got to him — the girl, I guess. He put a lot of work into it, but I don't remember that it was ever solved. Bombings are tough, because most of the evidence is blown to bits. The forensics are better now than they were sixteen years ago, though. If it had happened today, Jim might've cracked it."

Suddenly, Miles gave him a sharp look. "You're telling me that you *know* the investigating officer, Mike?"

McQuaid's grin went lopsided. "Hell, yes. That was my department. I knew everybody. Of course, I haven't been around the shop for a while," he added. "Lots of new faces, I'm sure. Jim is retired now, but we're still buddies."

Yeah. Once a cop, always a cop. McQuaid had gotten out of the business, but the business hadn't gotten out of him, which was why he'd left full-time teaching for investigative work. The thrill of the chase was a lot more invigorating than grading undergraduate exams.

Miles was looking at my husband with a

new kind of awareness. I could guess where this was going, and I wasn't sure I liked it. "This is irrelevant," I protested, for the record. "Dad's car — that wasn't a bomb."

Miles looked back at me. "What was it, then?"

"Yeah," McQuaid said, intrigued. He glanced from me to Leatha. "What was it? I don't think I've ever heard the details."

I poured myself another cup of coffee. I *knew* where this was going, and I definitely didn't like it.

"He hit the guard rail." Leatha's voice was carefully steady. "He'd been drinking — he wasn't legally drunk, but he'd had a couple of martinis. The car went down a steep embankment and turned over."

I pressed my lips together. She was leaving out the graphic details. The Caddy had been doing seventy. It careened into the rail, went airborne, flipped, and pancaked, wheels up. My father never had a chance. He was crushed to death, dead before the car burst into flames. I identified the body, to spare my mother the horror.

"That's the official story," Miles said.

"I don't see how it could be anything else," Leatha replied reasonably. "The driver of the car behind him saw what happened. He said there wasn't anybody else involved.

Bob just suddenly lost control and veered off the road. In case you're thinking he might have been forced off the road," she added pointedly.

Miles' mouth tightened. "Do you know what happened to the car? Afterward, I mean."

Leatha frowned. "I never asked. I didn't want to know." She bit her lip. "Bob was very proud of that Cadillac. It was only a few months old. I don't think he'd driven it a thousand miles."

"The car went to the police compound," Miles said steadily. "The state accident investigator took a look, saw what he expected to see, and filed his report with the cops and the insurance company. The Cadillac was towed to the scrap yard." He paused. "That's where my mother found it. She bought it and had it hauled away before it could go to the crusher."

"Your mother did that?" I asked in surprise.

"Well, that was silly." Leatha's voice was thin and querulous. "That car killed him. Why would she be so sentimental about it?"

"It wasn't sentiment," Miles said. "She —"

"Hauled away where?" McQuaid interrupted tersely, leaning forward.

"I have no idea," Miles said, throwing up his hands. "The paper trail is fragmented and sketchy. There isn't much to go on, and I'm certainly not an experienced investigator. But it looks to me like maybe she rented a garage and had the car towed there."

"A garage!" Leatha scoffed. "How ridiculous. If it wasn't sentiment, what was it? Surely she didn't intend to *sell* it. The car was a total loss."

"She wasn't interested in selling it," Miles replied evenly. "She had those letters. She didn't think his death was an accident, and she wanted to preserve the evidence." He paused, with a glance at McQuaid — a hopeful glance, it seemed to me. "The car may still be there. I intend to find it and have a look at it."

"Why in the world would you want to do *that?*" Leatha demanded. She appealed to me. "Don't you think that's ghoulish, China? I hope you won't want to see it."

"There where?" McQuaid said, trying not to sound eager, and I knew that he was halfway hooked already. "Houston?"

"I don't think so." From the relief in Miles' voice, I could tell that he knew, too. He was no longer in this alone. "There's a receipt for the purchase of the car, and a tow truck receipt that shows the number of

53

miles hauled. Doesn't look to me like Houston." As a final appeal, he added, "I'm sure you've done lots of investigations like this, Mike. You must have some ideas. I'd be grateful for any help you'd be willing to offer."

I got up and began to clear the table. Howard got up, too, and came over to see if he could help. "When you've got some concrete information," I said in a business-like tone, trying to stave off the inevitable, "I'm sure we'd be glad to know. In the meantime —"

"In the meantime," Leatha said loftily, "I fail to see why Laura Danforth — whom I always thought was a sensible person — would keep a totally wrecked car for sixteen years. Sixteen years!" She narrowed her eyes at Miles, and malice sharpened her tone. "Morbid. Utterly, completely morbid. What did she do? Light candles and incense on it every year on his birthday?"

I added McQuaid's empty dessert plate to the stack. "Mother," I said, "you're missing the point." Not quite true. She was inten-tionally, deliberately avoiding the point. "Mrs. Danforth kept the car because —"

"And I cannot understand why," she went on, her voice rising, "either you or China would have any interest whatsoever in find-

ing that old wreck. You are intelligent young people with plenty to keep you busy. Your father has been dead for sixteen years. I should think you would want to bury the old fool and get on with your life, rather than obsessing over a silly old Cadillac."

"Mother!" I exclaimed.

But it wasn't any use. Having worked herself into a state of righteous indignation, Leatha pushed her chair back. "Don't use that patronizing tone of voice to me, China Bayles," she said bitterly. She flung her napkin down. "You always know it all, just like your father. And you, too." Standing, she glared at Miles, then at me. "The two of you are a pair. You're both exactly like *him,* full of logical explanations and legal arguments and big words." She swallowed her tears with an audible gulp. "Thank you for the dinner, China and Mike — it was very nice. Good night."

I put down the stack of plates. "Wait, Mother. I'll walk you to your car."

"Don't bother." She lifted her chin with dignity. "I believe I can find it. It's right out there in the driveway, you know. Not hidden away in some old garage."

The screen door banged behind her. I started to follow, but McQuaid put out his hand. "Let her go, China," he said softly.

"She just needs a little time, that's all. This whole thing has been hard on her. Phone her in the morning — I'm sure she'll feel better then."

"You're probably right," I said reluctantly, and sat back down again. Leatha spun the tires on gravel as she drove off down the drive. Howard Cosell flopped onto the floor, the owl called again, and the first firefly of the season flickered against the screen. "More coffee, anybody?"

McQuaid stood and picked up the stack of dessert plates. "Miles and I have a few things to discuss. You're welcome to join us, China, but we'll understand if you don't want to be involved." He balanced two cups on the stack, and added some silver. "Hey. It's time to break out the hard stuff." He grinned at his brother-in-law. "What's your pleasure, Miles? Brandy? Bourbon? Scotch?"

Miles returned the grin, visibly relaxing. "Bourbon," he said. "Neat."

"I'll put the dishes in the dishwasher," I said stiffly, and began to clear the table.

The job took longer than it usually does because I dawdled. I knew what they were talking about out there, and I didn't want to hear it. When I finally finished and went out on the back porch, they were just winding things up. Miles stubbed out his cigarette and stood.

"Great," he said. "I'll put a retainer check in the mail tomorrow." He glanced at me. "Mike and I have agreed —"

"I know," I said briefly. McQuaid hadn't had a paying client for several weeks, and the bank account was looking thin. My half brother might as well help us pay the mortgage, my Inner Teacher wisely observed. All things considered, I should keep my mouth shut.

"Good," he said. "I'm glad you're on board." He turned back to McQuaid. "I can't say how grateful I am, Mike. I didn't come here with the object of hiring a private investigator, but I'm glad that's how it turned out. You're experienced. You know that police department. You'll get the job done faster and better than I could."

"Yeah. Well, we'll see," McQuaid said gruffly. "No guarantees, but I'll give it my best shot."

Miles turned to me, half-smiling. "I hope you don't think I pulled a fast one, China."

I did, actually, but it would have been churlish of me to say so. I shrugged. "McQuaid is his own boss. I don't interfere in his business decisions."

"True words," McQuaid agreed, putting

an arm around my shoulders and giving me a squeeze. "But I wouldn't take the job if China was opposed." He looked down at me. "I don't hear you saying no."

"Would it do any good?" I countered. "Would it do one single ounce of good? A scintilla, an iota, even a smidgeon of —"

"Thanks for the dinner," Miles put in hastily. "It was great. Terrific. Really."

McQuaid dropped his arm. "Any time," he said, the genial host. They shook.

Miles hesitated, still looking at me. "I don't want to impose, China, but I wonder if I could bring Caitlin down to spend a weekend sometime. You know, she really loved it when we were here for your barbecue."

Somehow I had missed Caitlin's enthusiasm. She was a shy, quiet child, and had hung on to her father as if she was afraid to let him out of her sight — which I could understand, I suppose. She had lost her mother, something that must have been terribly traumatic. I wasn't sure how she would manage a whole weekend without her dad or how I would manage a whole weekend with an uncommunicative child. *Maybe it would be good for her,* my Inner Teacher suggested. *And good for you, to give a little.*

I sighed. "Sure. We can do that. Just give

us a little advance warning."

Miles smiled. "I'll definitely do that. Thanks again." He gave me a brotherly hug, lifted his hand to McQuaid, and disappeared into the dark.

"Well," McQuaid said heartily.

"I don't want to discuss it." I picked up the glasses.

"I wish you wouldn't be that way," McQuaid said, taking the glasses away from me. "I was hoping you'd want to get involved. After all, he was your father."

"I am not being *any* way," I said, and took the glasses back. "And I definitely do not want to get involved."

"Sure thing, sugar," McQuaid said pleasantly. "If that's the way you want to play it." He looked around for the dog. "Hey, Howard. Come on, buddy. You need to make a pit stop before bed."

Grrr. I looked after him. He wasn't going to argue with me? He wasn't going to try to persuade me?

Tch-Tch, my Inner Teacher said in a disapproving tone.

CHAPTER THREE

Whether growing in its native setting or as an invited guest in flower beds, the yucca is an impressive plant, both formidable and beautiful in appearance. On its tall, sometimes branched stem, sharp-pointed leaves radiate in a cluster, and out of this daunting green arsenal arises the showy flower stalk with its masses of creamy white bell-shaped blossoms.

Elizabeth Silverthorne,
Legends & Lore of Texas Wildflowers

"I hope your dinner party was fun," Carole said as she climbed into Big Red Mama the next morning.

The sun was climbing over the trees, the morning was cool and bright, and we had already stowed Carole's collecting equipment — buckets, gloves, clippers, and a bottle of mosquito repellent — in the back of the van. Mama is short, fat, and basically red, with psychedelic yellows, greens, and blues swirled over her sides. Ruby and I originally intended to repaint her a sedate green, with our name in professional-looking letters, but the longer we put it off, the more comfortable we got with Mama's vintage hippie-wagon look. She may look her age, but so do we. We love her as she is.

"Definitely not," I said, backing into the alley. And it wasn't surprising that when I called my mother that morning she hadn't wanted to discuss it. I suspected that it would take awhile for her to simmer down. "How was your evening?"

"I found a terrific place to eat," Carole said happily. "An old Texas roadhouse called Beans. The owner's name is Bob — he's a real character. I like his golden retriever, too. He wears a red bandana and a leather saddlebag filled with bottles of beer. The dog, I mean," she added, to clarify, and I laughed.

"That's Bud. Short for Budweiser. Sometimes people send him to the convenience store for cigarettes. He brings back the change, too. And Bob serves up the best chicken-fried steak in town." I negotiated the turn onto Crockett. "In fact, we're heading in that direction right now. The yucca we're looking for grows along the railroad behind the restaurant." I slowed to avoid a kamikaze squirrel. Mama does not like to step on small animals. "Heard anything from Ruby this morning?"

Carole made a face. "She called around seven thirty. She's pretty upset. Things didn't go very well last night, apparently. Her mother thought she might be having a heart attack, so Ruby spent the night at the hospital."

"That's no surprise," I said grimly. "Whenever something unpleasant comes along, Doris has a heart attack. She'll probably have three or four more before this is over. Ruby doesn't fall for it, but what can you do when your mother begins to shriek bloody murder and clutches her chest with both hands?"

"Poor Ruby," Carole said. She gave me a sidelong glance. "She asked me if anybody had heard from Colin yet. I wasn't sure what to say, but I guess the answer is no. Yes?"

"Yes," I said tersely. I shifted into high gear and Mama rattled cheerfully along, glad to be out and about in the spring sunshine. "It's not the first time he's stood her up, but it's the first time he's been seriously out of touch."

"From something Ruby said," Carole

remarked delicately, "I gather that you don't think he's right for her."

"It's complicated," I said, hanging a left. I was reluctant to talk to Carole, whom I haven't known very long, about Colin, whom I don't like very much. Unfortunately, I knew more about Ruby's former boyfriend than Ruby did. I even knew his real name. But I was sworn to secrecy. I couldn't tell Ruby what I knew, which meant that I couldn't tell Carole.

At that moment, a police car pulled ominously alongside Big Red Mama. The blue bubblegum-machine light went on and the officer motioned us over to the curb.

"Oh, no!" Carole exclaimed in rueful dismay. "What have we done? We weren't going over the speed limit, were we?"

"Not a chance," I said, braking and pulling over to the curb behind the squad car. "Mama's too smart to break the law where she's likely to get caught." I rolled down my window and stuck my head out. "Morning, Smart Cookie," I called to the uniformed officer who was climbing out of her squad car and coming toward us. "Haven't you got anything better to do than flag down law-abiding citizens?"

"Smart Cookie?" Carole let out her breath in relief. "She must be a friend of yours."

"You bet. A good friend." I grinned. "She's the chief of police. She's good at that, too."

"She's the *chief?"* Carole said, blinking admiringly. "Wow. I can hardly believe it."

This is the usual response to Sheila Dawson, who is a gorgeous blonde with lavender eyes, delicate features, and a to-die-for figure that can't be disguised by her starched blue police uniform. But don't be deceived. Whether she's wearing her gun on her shapely hip or tucked into her Gucci, Smart Cookie is all cop, all the time. Although right now, she sounded more like a worried friend than a cop.

"I hear that Ruby's mom had a heart attack," she said, after I had introduced her and Carole. She folded her arms on Mama's open window. "How is she?"

Pecan Springs is a small town and gossip zips around at the speed of light. Ruby's trials and tribulations were probably on the tip of everybody's tongue. But gossip doesn't always tell the whole story. "Not to worry," I said comfortingly. "Doris will be okay. With her, heart attacks are a habit."

"One of those, huh?" Sheila rolled her eyes. "I had an aunt like that. She cried wolf so many times that people stopped listening — until the day she had a real heart attack

64

and died."

"It happens," I said. "But it's Ruby we need to worry about, not her mother." I gave Sheila a scrutinizing look. "Colin didn't show up for their date night before last, and he hasn't been heard from since. I don't suppose you've seen him, have you?"

Sheila frowned. "Of course not."

There's a story behind this innocent-sounding exchange, and the sooner it's told, the quicker you'll understand what's going on here. Sheila was acquainted with Ruby's friend Colin (whose real name is Dan Reid) when they worked with the Dallas Police Department. Back then, the two of them were . . . well, not to put too fine a point on it, they were lovers. Sheila has been understandably unwilling to share this information with Ruby, but she has insisted to me that she was never very serious about their relationship. For one thing, Reid and his wife, while separated, had not yet divorced. For another, a serious involvement would have gotten in the way of Sheila's work. And since I know for a fact that Smart Cookie has always been more serious about her law-enforcement career than about eating, sleeping, or sex, I have no reason not to believe her.

Dan Reid, aka Colin Fowler, was an

undercover narcotics agent assigned to the Dallas PD's Organized Crime Division, which must be like wading barefoot and waist-deep through raw sewage. As Sheila tells it, Reid had a tendency to freelance — he was something of an outlaw — and didn't always keep in touch with his street supervisor and his boss at the OCD. He was a first-class investigator, and his work led to more arrests than anybody else's in the division.

But outlaws don't generally follow the rules, and they almost always threaten the powers that be, which is how Reid got himself into serious trouble. Shortly after Sheila moved to Pecan Springs to become chief of security at Central Texas State University, Reid was arrested and charged with tipping off a low-level distributor named Mario, who was about to be busted for dealing. Mario fled, but not far enough. His body was found the next week, floating in Lake Worth, just below the bridge on State Route 199. Reid was charged with hindering apprehension, a third-degree felony that's good for two to twenty. He got three years. He served one.

When he was released from prison, Reid took a new name — Colin Fowler — and began a new chapter in his life. Newly divorced, he moved to Pecan Springs and opened Good Earth Goods on the town square, where he sells environmentally friendly stuff. Colin wears the jagged edge of rebelliousness just barely visible beneath good looks and a friendly, trust-me personality, which may be part of the reason he was good at his undercover work. Ruby met him just a little over six months ago and fell in a major way.

I realize that this bare-bones version of Dan Reid's life and career makes him sound like a bad actor and I'm sorry, for there are a number of interesting ambiguities here. I certainly have some sympathy for an undercover cop who has been risking his life for months, maybe years, patiently hand-feeding a few small fish, hoping they'll give him a line on the bigger sharks swimming out there in the sordid sea. I can understand how Reid must have felt when he heard that Mario was slated to go down, and why he might have decided to tip him off, especially if he suspected that there was something funny going on in his division. Unfortunately, this is sometimes the case, for there are more corrupt cops in the world than you want to know about. It was entirely possible that somebody higher up in Reid's chain of command was swimming with those bigger fish whose names Mario was about to cough up. If Mario and Reid were both out of the picture, it would be business as usual for the dealer-distributor and his cop buddy. And if you think this scenario is far-fetched, just read the newspapers a little more carefully. Official corruption is an inevitable part of the war on drugs, and the biggest casualty of the war may be our faith in law enforcement.

As I said, I didn't much like Colin Fowler, but in a perverse way, I had to admire Dan Reid. What's more, I'm sure that Ruby — who likes to think of herself as a grown-up Nancy Drew — would be thrilled to find out about Colin's ex-undercover ex-life. But she isn't going to hear it from me. I promised Sheila, who told me all this in exchange for a pledge of locked lips. Neither she nor I wanted to influence Ruby, one way or another.

Sheila pushed her cop cap back on her head. "Where are you two headed?"

"We're out to steal some yucca," I said. "Carole's teaching a paper-making class on Saturday, and she covets a couple of buckets of leaves from those plants along the railroad track."

"Steal it? The railroad company ought to pay you to take that stuff." Sheila looked doubtful. "You're telling me that you make *paper* out of it?"

"Oh, yes!" Carole exclaimed. "Yucca fiber makes wonderful paper — strong, flexible, lovely texture and color. Come and take a look when the class is over."

"I will if I can," Sheila said.

I doubted that she'd do it. She's putting in sixteen- and eighteen-hour days right now, and doesn't have much free time. In fact, we haven't had a girls'-night-out for several months, and recently, it's been impossible to catch her for lunch. Even when we're together she often seems to be somewhere else. Something about the job must be giving her trouble. I don't blame Smart Cookie for being so totally preoccupied with her work that she doesn't have time for her life. I know about that, for there have been times when I've been too busy for friends. But that doesn't keep me from missing her and wondering, often sadly, whether we will ever be as close as we once were.

Now, she stepped back from the van and raised her hand in a friendly salute. "Have a great day, guys."

"We will," Carole and I chorused in cheerful unison.

Had we but known.

■ ■ ■ ■

If you think of yucca as a plant that grows only in southwestern deserts, you'd be wrong. This spiky plant, which belongs to the genus *Yucca,* in the Agave family, has an enormous distribution, ranging from the Atlantic (*Yucca filamentosa*) westward to the Pacific (*Y. whipplei*), and from Canada (*Y. glauca ssp. albertana*) south into Guatemala (*Y. elephantipes*). There are some fifty species native to the United States and thirty more to Mexico and Central America, some tall, some short, and all with starbursts of sharp, spiny leaf tips, sometimes at the base of the plant, sometimes near the top of a stalk. If you're looking for yucca, you'll probably find a native in your neighborhood. And where it's not native — the Atlantic northeast and the Pacific Northwest — it has escaped from people's gardens and hightailed it for the wilderness, so you're likely to find it growing there, too.

Texas is home to about twenty species of yucca, in a variety of sizes and shapes. The smallest is Arkansas yucca (*Yucca arkansana*), which produces thigh-high clumps of spiny, flexible leaves and head-high spikes of heavy, waxy flower bells —

striking in a garden. The largest is soaptree yucca (*Y. elata*), which has a thick, strong trunk and can grow to thirty feet high when left to its own devices for a century or so. All these yuccas share the common names Spanish dagger, Spanish bayonet, and Adam's needle, the reason for which you will understand if you ever get jabbed by one of its stiff, spiny points. This morning, I was taking Carole to the sprawling colony of twisted-leaf yucca (*Y. rupicola*) that thrives in the rocky caliche soil along the Missouri Pacific Railroad. She'd find all the leaves she wanted: new, pliant leaves; stiff, mature leaves; and dead leaves, brown and half-decayed. Each makes a different paper — different color, different texture, different weight. She could mix and match to her heart's content.

We turned at Beans Bar and Grill, which is located in the building between Purley's Tire Company and the Missouri Pacific Railroad, across the street from the old fire house, recently converted into a dance hall. I pulled through the parking lot and steered Mama down a narrow dirt track beside the tracks, along a row of straggly desert willows and poverty weed. You may not think of railroad tracks as being the prettiest places in the world, and usually they're not.

But native plants sometimes survive along the railroad right-of-way when they are grazed or plowed out of existence elsewhere, and that's what has happened here. Since this was April, the six-foot embankments were strewn with spring wildflowers: blue-bonnets, scarlet paintbrush, red and gold Indian blanket, and drifts of bright yellow coreopsis, like spilled sunshine. Sadly, the embankments were also strewn with the usual vacant-lot litter: newspapers, empty liquor bottles, beer cans. The Herb Guild has talked about adopting this space and making it into a pocket park — which is not a bad idea. With several small Xeriscape gardens, a few gravel paths, and some regular attention, this could be a very pretty space.

I stopped under a mesquite tree, its pale green leaves spreading a feathery umbrella that would shade Mama from the morning sun. Carole and I got out, unloaded the buckets and other gear, and started off. We were headed toward a sizable colony of yucca on the south side of the tracks. It had been a warm spring and the plant was already in bloom, with four- and five-foot spikes of white and pale green pendulous flowers, tinged with purple. They have the distinction of being pollinated by only one creature: the female yucca moth. No moths, no pollination; no pollination, no fruit. It's as simple as that.

"Beautiful, beautiful," Carole muttered. She was gazing covetously at the leaves and totally ignoring the stunning flower stalks.

"Oh, but look at the flowers," I urged. "Aren't they gorgeous? And they're a delicacy, too. You can chop up the petals and use them in soups and salads — or fry them like fritters. I've never tried pickling the buds, but people do. The fruits come along later in the year, and the local Indians roasted them in hot ashes, like potatoes, and ate them. Or they dried and pounded them into flour, or fermented them into booze and —"

"Stop already," Carole commanded. She handed me a pair of gloves and clippers. "You cut those green leaves. I'll get the brown ones. We don't need a lot — just fill the bucket, that should do it."

We worked in companionable silence for a few minutes. It would have been impossible to move through the dense colony without getting thoroughly spiked, so we moved around it, cutting here and there as we went. My bucket was full when I straightened and caught sight of a heap of old clothes, half-visible among the spiny clumps.

I gave the offending heap a fierce scowl. "I wish people wouldn't litter," I said peevishly. "Maybe, if we turn this into a park, they won't be so quick to dump —"

I stopped. Something about the heap of clothes didn't look right. Stepping carefully, I saw a sneaker, then the stretched-out leg of a pair of jeans. And then I realized what I was looking at. A man, sprawled facedown in the yucca, his face half-hidden by one arm, flung up. He was out cold.

Carole wrinkled her nose. "Somebody did too much celebrating at Beans last night, I suppose. He couldn't have been sober, or he wouldn't have been walking through this patch of yucca. It's murder."

"Maybe he was walking along the railroad tracks and fell down the embankment," I said. "And he could be passed out on dope, not booze." Small towns are no longer the safe havens from drugs that they used to be. Pecan Springs is located on the I-35 corridor, which carries drug traffic from the Mexican border to San Antonio, Dallas, and points north. I reached for my cell phone. "Well, we can't just go away and leave him here — he'll get heatstroke. I hate to call the cops because they'll just throw the poor schmuck in jail. But at least he'll get medical care, if that's what he needs."

But while I was punching 911, Carole had ventured into the yucca. With an effort, she pulled the man onto his back. What I saw made me gasp and drop my phone.

The man was neither drunk nor drugged. His red shirt was soaked with dark red blood.

He was Colin Fowler, and he was dead.

"Poor Ruby," Carole breathed, wrapping her arms around herself and shivering, although the temperature was already pushing eighty. "She may have broken up with him, but I'm sure she still cares. What in heaven's name are we going to tell her?"

We were watching a team of Pecan Springs police going over the crime scene with tape measures and cameras — slowly, because the needle-sharp leaves of the yucca plants were making their work painfully difficult. EMS had arrived and the medics were standing by. But they had turned off the emergency lights on the ambulance and were in no special hurry. There was nothing they could do for Colin. Anyway, they had to wait for the justice of the peace, who is required by Texas law to certify every unattended death, whether it happens in a hospital, at home, or in the middle of a yucca patch.

"I guess we have to tell her the truth," I said grimly. My heart had slowed from a hammer to something like a reasonable pace, but my mind still refused the reality of Colin's death. It had reminded me, like a sock in the stomach, that we only think we are in control of our lives. I hadn't liked the man, or trusted him, but that only made it worse.

Carole looked away from the scene. "I think *you* have to be the one to tell her, China."

"Yeah. But I sure as hell don't want to do it over the phone. When you talked to her this morning, did she say when she was coming back?"

Carole shook her head. "It's up in the air. Her sister is driving down from Dallas to help. They have to move their mom's stuff into an assisted living unit, and she wasn't sure how long that might take." She paused, frowning. "There was something about her grandmother, but I didn't quite catch it."

"That's Grammy," I said. "Doris' mother. She's a wonderful old lady — must be eighty-something, but she's sharp enough to win every Scrabble tournament she enters. She and Doris live in the same retirement village." I paused, considering. "Sounds like Ruby might have to stay in

76

Fredericksburg for a while, which is not all bad. There's nothing she can do here, anyway. The autopsy will take several days, and the body won't be released until —"

I stopped. There was a hand on my arm, and I turned to see Sheila.

"I'm glad you found him, China." Her voice was thick and her lavender eyes were dark with pain, reminding me that she and Colin — Dan — had been lovers. "I hate to think of him lying here for days and days, nobody knowing or caring. I —" Her voice broke and she tried to blink back the tears.

I fought off the impulse — a powerful one — to gather Sheila in my arms and hold her while she cried. She may be a cop, but there's a human being under that uniform, and humans hurt when someone they've cared for is murdered. However, a pair of young uniforms were watching her curiously, and she had turned so they couldn't see the pain that was written on her face. Sheila is a pro, and when she's on the job, she's nothing but a pro. She obviously didn't want her officers to know that she had any personal connection to the dead man, or that this was anything more than a routine investigation.

So I cleared my throat and spoke with all the composure I could muster. "Carole and

I were trying to decide what to do about telling Ruby. I was saying it might be better to hold off until she comes back. She's got her hands full with her mother. She doesn't need the trauma of —"

"Hey!" An urgent male voice hailed us from a short distance up the tracks, and all three of us turned. "Hey! What's happening? Somebody die?"

It was the press, Johnny-on-the-spot. More specifically, it was Hark Hibler, the editor of the Pecan Springs *Enterprise*. Technically, Hark is my boss, since I edit the paper's weekly Home and Garden page. My copy is usually late and whenever I meet him, I have a tendency to feel like a freshman who hasn't handed in her English homework. But Hark wasn't looking for me. He had a camera in one hand and a notebook in the other, and he was closing in on us at a gallop, his dark hair flying, the just-gotta-know juices rushing through his veins, and the irresistible urge to *report* written all over his face.

I wasn't surprised to see him. The *Enterprise* building fronts on Alamo Street but looks back on this stretch of railroad track and vacant lots. He probably glanced out his office window, noticed the commotion, and came to have a look. That's life in a small town. You can't hide a thing, especially a dead body — although I thought it sadly ironic that this particular body had lain more or less in plain sight for some time without anyone noticing. How long? It was likely that Colin didn't show up for his date with Ruby some thirty-six hours ago because he couldn't. He was already dead, or about to get that way.

Hark wasn't headed for us. He was zeroing in on Colin's body, which was lying faceup now, as Carole and I had left him.

"Fowler!" he gasped, astonished. "My God! I figured him for a dead doper! But it's Colin Fowler!" He raised his camera to snap a quick picture, but Smart Cookie was quicker.

"Drop it," she yelled, and before he could react, she had closed the distance and seized the camera.

"What the hell do you think you're doing?" Hark bellowed, then saw who it was and turned down the volume. "What's wrong with a photo? It's just for the record. You know I won't print it."

It's true. The *Enterprise* is a family newspaper — although it isn't as squeaky-clean as it was when old Arnold Seidensticker was both editor and publisher. Arnold always insisted on scrubbing the dirt off the news

79

before it appeared in the paper, which made Pecan Springs seem like the cleanest little town in Texas. This was a perfectly misleading picture, of course, for Pecan Springs has never been the cozy retreat from the realities of human greed and violence that the Chamber of Commerce likes to pretend that it is. Hark owns the paper now, and prints more of the truth. But not always all of it, especially when special handling is required. Photos of dead people definitely fall under the "do not print" rule. No matter how many corpses the children of Pecan Springs see on TV cop shows, they won't see any in our local paper.

Sheila wasn't taking any chances. "No photos," she repeated grimly, handing the camera to one of the cops. "You got that, Hibler?"

Hark heaved a heavy sigh. "I got it." With a look of mingled pity and distress, he took in the blood that soaked Colin's shirt. "What's your best guess, Chief?"

"He's dead. That's my best guess."

"No, I mean when and how."

Sheila's mouth tightened. "No comment."

"Stabbed, looks like. A deep jab in the chest. Bled to death." He shook his head. "Last night?"

"No comment."

Hark is persistent. "Robbery, maybe. Did you check his wallet?" He frowned, something registering. "Hey. That's a shoulder holster he's wearing under that shirt. But it's empty. You find the gun?"

"No comment," Sheila snapped. "I mean it, Hark. When I have something definitive to say about the investigation, you'll be the first to know. Until then, lay off the questions." Her voice was low, gritty. "Just lay the bloody hell off."

"You don't need to jump down my throat," Hark said with offended dignity. He pushed his dark glasses up on his nose. "I'm a newspaperman, remember? It's my job to report the news. And murder is definitely news."

I went over to join the conversation, such as it was. The *Enterprise* comes out twice a week now, so there couldn't be any story until Saturday. We don't have a local TV station, and the San Antonio and Austin stations probably wouldn't do anything more than mention this killing. Of course, once the boys at the Nueces Street Diner heard that Colin Fowler was dead, it would be all over Pecan Springs quicker than you can say "boy howdy." But if we could keep the story off the front page of Saturday's paper, the news might not get to Fredericksburg for a while.

"Listen, Hark," I said quietly. "It would be good — really, really good — if we could spare Ruby, at least for a few days. Her mother's not very well, and she's trying to hold things together in Fredericksburg."

At the mention of Ruby's name, an expression of deep concern crossed Hark's face. He and Ruby dated before Colin came on the scene, and for once in Ruby's life, a man had cared more for her than she'd cared for the man. In fact, Hark had told me once that he'd hoped to marry her, and I confess to wishing that their relationship might turn into something permanent. He reminds me somehow of Garrison Keillor — sloping shoulders, soft voice, a perennially rumpled personality. He's not very exciting, maybe, and he certainly doesn't have any of Colin's barely disguised bad-boy attraction. But while thrills and chills may be what you want for the short term, comfort, reliability, and trustworthiness count most in the long haul. And now that he's lost some fifty pounds and grown a dark mustache, Hark is not at all bad-looking.

"I can't kill the story," he said finally. "But I can put it where it won't be noticed — much. But that's just for the Saturday edition," he added hastily. "Tuesday, it'll be front page. After all, Fowler owns a business here. He's a member of the Chamber. He —" His eyes went to the body and he seemed to flinch. "Damn. I didn't like the man, but . . ." His voice trailed off.

"You didn't like him?" Sheila asked sharply. "Why not?"

I knew it wasn't an idle question. Hark has a nose for a story and keeps his ear to the ground. And at any given time and on any given subject, he always knows twice as much as he can print. Sheila was hoping that he'd picked up something that might lead to Colin's killer.

Hark slid her a cautious glance. "Let's just say I didn't think the best man got the girl."

"Ah," Sheila said, getting the point. She eyed him. "Nothing else? What do you know about his friends, his business associates?"

"Only what everybody else knows, I suppose," Hark said with a shrug. "He opened his store not quite a year ago. I interviewed him for the paper, but he was pretty evasive. I couldn't get much out of him about his past. Where he lived, what he'd been doing before he came to Pecan Springs, that sort of thing. Odd, though. He wasn't anxious for me to run his photo. I couldn't figure that one out. Usually, people with a new business want all the publicity they can get from us."

I was watching Hark, and not entirely comfortably, either. In my days as a lawyer, I learned to smell lies. I could sniff one now, although maybe it wasn't quite a lie. But Hark knew something, I'd bet. He had a lead that he planned to follow up on his own. A lead that might take him to a story.

Smart Cookie eyed him, smelling what I smelled. But she only said, in the most pleasant voice she had used so far, "If you can keep a lid on this for twenty-four hours, I'd be personally grateful, Hark."

"Oh, yeah?" he asked, raising one darkly ironic eyebrow. "How grateful?"

She ignored him. "Forty-eight would be even better. And if you hear anything around town, let me know. Okay?"

"I'll do what I can," Hark said guardedly. He stuck his notebook into his back pocket and put out his hand. "Camera?"

"Give the man his camera," Sheila said to the cop, who handed it over.

"The world has come to a pretty place," Hark muttered, "when the press can't do its job without pressure from the police to suppress the story."

"You're not doing it for the police, Hark," I reminded him gently. "You're doing it for Ruby."

"Yeah," he said. "Ruby." He gave me a hopeful look. "Suppose I'll get points for this?"

I shrugged. "Maybe."

"I doubt it," he said ironically.

"Yeah," I said. "Me, too."

Then a car door slammed and we all turned. Maude Porterfield, the justice of the peace, had arrived at the crime scene, and things were about to happen. I said hello to Maude and good-bye to Sheila and Hark, then stood for a moment looking bleakly down at Colin's body, wondering whether I should say some sort of small good-bye for Ruby, or even for myself.

But it was too late for that. For Colin, no more hellos, no more good-byes, just a long, dark night.

Chapter Four

Margaritas are traditionally made with silver tequila, which is produced from the blue agave (*Agave tequilana*), a stately plant with long, stiff leaves, each defended by a row of sinister teeth and a needlelike tip. This well-armed relative of the yucca thrives in an arid climate in volcanic soil. In the Tequila region of the state of Jalisco, Mexico, where much of the blue agave is commercially grown, the fields cover the slopes of two extinct volcanoes. The word *tequila* may be derived from the Náhuatl Indian word for volcano, which seems somehow fitting.

If tequila isn't your cup of tea, consider the agave's healing properties, much prized in folk medicine. The macerated pulp from the heart of the plant has been used as a compress for wounds, infections, chapped lips, sunburns, and rashes. The fresh leaves are an effective emetic and have also been used to treat intestinal disorders. And if you don't have any fresh agave leaves handy, tequila is said to have the same therapeutic properties. *¡Salud!*

Sadly, Carole and I gathered up our cargo, and I took her back to the cottage so she could start processing the yucca we had collected. It was already after ten, so I had to hurry to open the shop.

I was still shaken by what had happened this morning, but as usual, I felt better the minute I opened the door and stepped inside. Thyme and Seasons isn't very big, but it's stuffed to the rafters with things that look pretty, smell delightful, and are good for you, and I find it as soothing as a summer afternoon in the garden. The century-old building that houses the shop is constructed of native Texas limestone, with pine plank floors and cypress rafters. The shop's stone walls are covered with herbal swags and wreaths, while bundles of herbs and braids of garlic and peppers hang from the ceilings. The wooden shelves are loaded with large jars of bulk herbs, bars of handmade soaps, packages of herbal cosmetics, bags of potpourri, vials of essential oils, bottles of herbal vinegars, boxes of fragrant herbal teas, and books about herbs and gardening. The aisles and corners are crowded with baskets of dried plants and flowers — tansy and sweet Annie and celosia, salvia and yarrow and goldenrod. The sweet, spicy scents were so heartwarming I just wanted to close my eyes, let them flood through me, and wash away the horrible sights I had seen this morning.

But there wasn't time for that. Cass arrived to open the tearoom, and a minute later, our friend Melissa Grody came in to help with Ruby's shop. Missy is a pretty strawberry blonde with gold-framed glasses and a soft, sweet-sexy voice that reminds her friends of late-night hotline voices. She's been studying for her entrance test into the nursing program, and we all have our fingers crossed for her. She has a special interest in herbal remedies, so maybe she'll find a way to use that in her nursing career.

Missy and Cass both know Colin and were appalled when I told them what had happened. "I can't believe it," Missy murmured sadly. "How is Ruby going to deal with this, along with everything else?"

"Who's going to tell her?" Cass asked, and both of them looked at me. "It ought to be done today, before she finds out by accident."

I was saved by the bell. A pair of ladies

came in looking for presents for a bridal shower, and ended up buying a whole trousseau of herbal soaps and cosmetics. For the next hour, I was so busy with customers that I barely had time to think, which was definitely not a bad thing. When I finally surfaced, I discovered that my brain had been working on the problem while my hands were busy. So I called McQuaid and asked him to meet me for lunch. He suggested Miguel's Cantina, a dark, dusty place with very loud Tejano music, where you can sit at a table in the back room and talk without being overheard.

I agreed. Miguel makes the best margaritas in Pecan Springs. It wasn't noon yet, but Missy agreed to watch both shops, and I took off. I was ready for anything that would lift my spirits.

McQuaid was killing time with a two-day-old copy of the *Enterprise* when I arrived. There was a large plate of cheese-covered nachos in the middle of the table. An enticingly salt-rimmed margarita (most people's favorite way to drink tequila) was waiting at my place, and a bottle of Dos Equis sat in front of McQuaid. He folded up the newspaper as I sat down.

"What's up, babe?" McQuaid's voice — a

deep baritone that resonates with male strength and authority — is one of the things I love about him. He raised his beer. "*Salud.* Everything going okay?"

"Not exactly," I said unsteadily, and reached for my frosty drink. "*Salud.*" I saluted, sipped, and put the glass down, meeting his eyes. "Carole and I found Colin Fowler this morning, along the MoPac tracks, behind Beans. He was dead."

McQuaid coughed. "Dead!" he managed, when he could get his breath. "You're joking."

"I wouldn't joke about something like that." The cosmic Chicano music of Los Lobos came through the loudspeaker, the guitar fast and loud. I leaned forward and put both elbows on the table. "Okay, McQuaid. It's time to come clean. I need to find out how you know Colin Fowler. Dan Reid, that is."

"Dan . . . Reid?" He frowned. "What makes you think I . . ." He stopped. "Sheila," he said. "She told you."

"She told me that much. And *you're* going to tell me the rest." We had been through this a time or two. McQuaid, who learned a long time ago that keeping secrets might be essential to staying alive, had always maintained that he'd never laid eyes on Colin until the guy showed up in Pecan Springs and began dating Ruby. I had the feeling that this wasn't the whole story, but there hadn't been any special reason to pursue it. Now I was going to find out the truth of the matter.

"And when you've told me what you know about him," I added, "I'll be glad to tell you how he died."

McQuaid's mouth set in a stern line. "What I know about him is confidential," he said. "It's police business."

"My, these nachos look good," I said pleasantly. I picked one up, flicked off a jalapeño seed (those things are hot!), and popped it into my mouth. I closed my eyes, exaggerating my pleasure. "Oh, yum." Sometimes male strength and authority have to be countered by female canniness.

"How did he die?" McQuaid growled.

I opened my eyes. "What do you know about him?"

There was a silence.

He smiled, showing white teeth. "You tell first, hon."

I smiled, too. "I don't think so, dear."

"Welcome, señor, señora." The waiter, young and diffident, appeared at my elbow. "May I take your order, *por favor?*"

I glanced at my watch. "Oh, gosh, just

look at the time. On second thought, I don't believe I can stay for lunch." I pushed my chair back, picked up my bag, and got to my feet. "Sheila told me to stop by the police station and see if there were any developments in —"

"Sit down," McQuaid said, in his steely cop voice.

"*Señor?*" asked the waiter nervously, glancing at the third chair.

"Not you," McQuaid said. "Her." He looked at me. "Sit down, China. Please." To the waiter, he said, "I'll have the usual. And bring me another drink."

"*Pérdon, señor,*" the waiter said humbly, pencil poised. "I'm new here. What is the usual, *por favor?*"

"*Numero siete. La señora* will have *numero ocho.*"

"I am so sorry," I said regretfully to the waiter, "but *la señora* must leave." To McQuaid, I added, "I'll see you at home tonight, dear." I paused, considering. "No, on second thought, I may not make it home until late. But there's some leftover casserole in the fridge. Just stick it in the microwave. Oh, and don't forget that Brian has a soccer game at six thirty. His clean shorts are in —"

"For Pete's sake, I'll tell you what you

92

want to know!" McQuaid roared. To the waiter, he said, in a level voice, "The *señora* will have number eight." To me, he said, "Sit down."

"Promise?" I asked.

"Promise," he said, and I resumed my seat. *"Siete y ocho, pronto,"* said the waiter. *"Muchos gracias."* He fled.

"I'm so glad you reconsidered," I said sweetly. "Now, how is it that you came to know Dan Reid?"

"Blackmail," McQuaid muttered. As he saw me push back my chair, he added hastily, "It was in Houston, just before I left the department. At the time, he was working undercover with the Dallas PD. In the Organized Crime Division."

"Tell me something I don't already know," I said, raising my voice over the soulful strains of Ruben Ramos singing "Es Demasiado Tarde."

McQuaid gave me a resigned look. "Did you know that he got a year for tipping off an informant who was about to be arrested? The informant was murdered."

"But only a year," I remarked pointedly. "Odd that he didn't get more, especially since the informant ended up dead."

"Exactly," McQuaid said, with a wry twist in his voice. "And listen to this. About four months after Reid was sentenced, his supervisor was indicted on multiple charges of conspiracy, money laundering, mail fraud, wire fraud — the whole nine yards. He shot himself before he could be brought to trial."

I raised my eyebrows. "Ah," I said. The picture was becoming clearer.

"Yeah. But his suicide didn't save the skins of the dozen or so dirty cops who were also indicted, most of them for protecting drug deals and escorting shipments of cocaine. They got what was coming to them. Fifteen to thirty." I could hear the satisfaction in McQuaid's voice. There's nothing he hates more than police corruption.

"Reid's sentence," I said. "It was very light. Too light — especially in comparison to the other sentences." I'd seen that sort of thing before, and knew what it suggested. "He might have flipped," I said — admitted corruption and then agreed to finger other cops in return for a lighter sentence. "Or maybe he was working undercover for somebody else. For the FBI, maybe. Or the DEA."

This sounds convoluted, I know: an undercover cop ostensibly tracking down drug dealers while he is secretly working for an outside agency, the Federal Bureau of Investigation or the Drug Enforcement

Administration, to finger the crooked law enforcement officers who are part of the ring. But that's about the only way bad cops can be caught and convicted. McQuaid himself had had a similar — and dangerous — assignment with the Texas Department of Public Safety a few years before, and got pretty badly shot up when the arrest didn't go the way he expected. He no longer uses a cane, but he limps sometimes when he's tired. I like to think that the episode put an end to his days of derring-do, but I know I'm fooling myself.

"There was plenty of speculation about that," McQuaid said. "Sending Reid to jail might've been a way of making him look like a bad cop and legitimizing him for another undercover assignment. It's been done — but of course that's only a guess. He could just as easily have been a crooked cop who flipped."

I looked at him. "Why didn't you tell me this when Ruby first starting dating this guy? Good cop, bad cop, either way, he was bad news. She could've been in danger."

"And I was going to swear you to secrecy?" He gave a scornful chuckle. "Get real, China. If I told you, and you told her, it would've whetted her appetite. It's the danger factor. Makes a guy look like a super-stud."

I made a face, but I had to admit that he was right. We sat back as the waiter came to the table bearing our food: chipotle enchiladas with spicy black beans and rice and another Dos Equis for McQuaid, an *ensalada de nopalites* and iced tea for me. *Nopalites* or *nopales* are the green pads of the prickly pear cactus, carefully stripped of their spines. They're cubed, blanched, chilled, and tossed with thin-sliced red onions, corn, tomatoes, mild chile peppers, cilantro, feta cheese, and vinaigrette for a light, spicy salad. Grilled chicken is not traditional, but Miguel adds it anyway. I heartily approve.

When the waiter had gone, McQuaid added, "I didn't discuss any of this with Reid, if that's what you're wondering. I didn't even let him know that I recognized him. If the man was guilty, he served his sentence — light as it might be — and deserves the chance to get on with his life. If going to prison was part of the job — creating a new cover story, maybe — I wouldn't want to get in his way."

I picked up my fork, wondering what it must be like to spend a year in jail as part of your job assignment. Not very pleasant, and dangerous, to boot. I thought of the dozen dirty cops, whose time in prison was definitely not a job assignment.

"Do you think it might have been a revenge killing?" I asked thoughtfully.

"Because he cooked a baker's dozen of corrupt police officers? Yeah, sure. That's happened before. Cop rats out buddies in return for a light sentence, cop ends up in a box." McQuaid attacked his enchiladas with cheerful enthusiasm. "Okay, it's your turn," he said, his mouth full. "How did it happen, China?"

My turn. I put down my fork, seeing Colin's face. A nice face, with a strong mouth and wary, watchful eyes. Whatever I thought of the careless way he had treated Ruby, he had always been decent to me. And now he was dead.

"He was stabbed in the chest." I frowned, thinking of what I'd seen. "Up under the ribs. Got his heart, most likely. He was wearing a shoulder holster, but the gun was gone."

"Weapon? Witnesses? Was it a robbery?"

"No witnesses — yet. Not a robbery, either. He had a couple of fifties in his wallet, and credit cards. The cops were still looking for the weapon when I left the scene." It was a knife, obviously, but they

97

wouldn't know what type or how it was used until the autopsy report came down, which might take awhile. Adams County is too small to have its own medical examiner. Victims' corpses are sent to Bexar or Travis, whichever has the shorter waiting list. Since those are big counties, with plenty of crime, the waiting list can be pretty long.

"Knifed." McQuaid dug into his beans. "Doesn't sound like a cop. Cops prefer guns. On the other hand, the killer might have wanted to be up close and personal. Wanted to look him in the eye while he shoved it in. Hate can do that." He looked up at me and his glance softened, something just occurring to him. "My gosh, I didn't even ask. How's Ruby taking it, China?"

"Ruby doesn't know yet." I pushed my salad away, my appetite suddenly gone. "She's in Fredericksburg, trying to cope with her mother." I told him about Doris locking herself in her car and then having a heart attack. "I'm hoping we can keep Ruby there for a while — keep her in the dark. Maybe the police will find out who killed him before she gets back."

"They won't," McQuaid said matter-of-factly. "You know that as well as I do. No witnesses, no weapon, no apparent motive — and too many possibilities, given the guy's background. It could've been some-body taking revenge for what happened in Dallas. Could've been connected to a cur-rent assignment. Could've been connected to his business. It could even have been a disgruntled ex-wife or girlfriend." He gave me a look. "Any local enemies that you know of?"

I shook my head. "But that doesn't mean anything. To tell the truth, I only knew him through Ruby. She would have a much bet-ter idea of who —" I stopped.

"Yeah," McQuaid said in a practical tone. "Ruby was closer to him than anyone else in town. She's the one who's most likely to know whether somebody local had it in for him, or whether he's had any recent com-munications with people from his past. Sheila's going to want to talk to her, sooner rather than later." He put out his hand, took mine, then let it go. "I know you don't want to do this, China, but you can't put it off. Somebody's going to have to tell her. You don't want the cops to do it, do you?"

I shook my head numbly. My salad, which had looked so tasty just a few moments before, was now distinctly unappetizing.

There was a pause while McQuaid ate the last of his refried beans. "After all that, I don't suppose you want to hear what I did this morning." It was a statement, not a question.

"Why not?" I motioned to the waiter to bring me a to-go box. I wasn't hungry now, but I hate to see a good salad go to waste. "So what did you do this morning?"

He put his elbows on the table and gave me a steady look. "You said last night that you didn't want to hear about it. Still feel that way?"

Oh, that. So McQuaid was already in hot pursuit of my father's hypothetical killer. I might have known. I was about to tell him he could keep his activities to himself, when my Inner Teacher spoke up. *You do want to hear about it,* she reprimanded me sternly. *Don't pretend you don't.*

I frowned. I had enough to worry about with Colin's death, and Ruby. Why should I —

Because, said my Inner Teacher, with irrefutable logic.

I sighed. "So what did you find out?"

Good girl, my Inner Teacher said approvingly.

McQuaid relaxed. "I talked to Jim Hawk. He remembered the car-bomb case very vividly. He couldn't tell me whether there have been any later developments in the investigation, but he's agreed to dig up the case file for me. He thought he might have kept some notes about the stories Max Vine was working on, although at the time, he didn't uncover any significant leads."

"And the other reporter? Spurgin? The hit-and-run victim?" If I was going to hear about one reporter, I might as well hear about the other. I doubted if there was any connection between the two of them and my father, but —

"That wasn't Jim's case, but he's going to pull that file, too. He said he'd phone tonight, late. If he turns up anything interesting, I'll drive to Houston tomorrow to take a look. I might drop in at the *Chronicle,* too, while I'm there. I used to know a few of the reporters there."

"Lotsa luck, babe," I muttered ironically. Sixteen years is even longer in the newspaper business than it is in law enforcement. But newspapers probably maintain more complete morgues. If McQuaid happened to know the right people, and the right people were interested in his questions, he might even get access to Vine's and Spurgin's research notes. Newspapers have a tendency to hang on to stuff a lot longer than your average human being.

The waiter appeared at my elbow with a to-go box and a worried look. "The salad was fine," I told him reassuringly. "I just don't feel like eating right now." I spooned the *nopalites* into the box, closed the lid, and stood up. "I may not get home from Fredericksburg until late this evening. Please don't forget about Brian's soccer game." Pecan Springs was playing San Marcos in what was sure to be a hot contest.

"Where'd you say his clean shorts are?"

"In the dryer. And make sure he finishes his English paper after the game. It's due tomorrow." Brian loves to do his science homework, but he always manages to put off writing his English papers until the very last minute.

McQuaid looked up at me. "I'm glad you've decided to tell Ruby, China. It'll be easier for her, coming from you."

I picked up my box. Easier? I didn't think so. But I didn't have any choice, did I?

No, said my Inner Teacher gently. *You don't.*

CHAPTER FIVE

Like its relatives in the genus *Agave,* yucca is high in saponin, the natural detergent found in many plants. (In Latin, *sapo* means soap.) Saponins seem to function as part of the yucca's immune system, something like a "natural antibiotic" that protects the plant from disease and keeps it healthy. Native Americans used yucca to wash themselves and their clothing, as well as to treat various illnesses. Now, scientists who study these plant chemicals are discovering that saponins can help to fight fungal infections in humans, combat viruses and microbes, and enhance the effectiveness of vaccines.

I checked in with Cass and Missy to make sure things were under control, stopped to answer a customer's question about planting lavender (add sand and gravel to the soil for good drainage — don't overwater), and suggested to another that if she was worried about deer having her landscaping for lunch, rosemary or the silvery herbs, especially the artemisias, would be a much better bet than antique roses. Unfortunately, deer feel about roses the way I feel about hot fudge sundaes. They're somewhat less enthusiastic about roses with thorns, but even a few sharp stabs won't stop them when they're hungry.

Then I went to the cottage to tell Carole that I was going to Fredericksburg. I found her in the kitchen, working with the yucca we had gathered that morning. She had chopped the fresh leaves into one-inch pieces and was cooking them, with washing soda, in a large stainless steel pot on the stove. She put down the wooden stirring paddle, and I saw that the cooking pot was covered with foamy, meringuelike suds.

"Soap?" I asked, frowning, and then realized what was happening. Yucca is rich in saponin, which makes it a natural cleanser. In fact, one species of yucca is called "soap-tree." Carole could probably do her laundry with that yucca stew and have enough cleaning power left for a bath and shampoo.

Carole turned off the burner under the pot. "I'll go with you, China. You don't have to do this alone."

Regretfully, I declined. Now that I had accepted the responsibility of telling Ruby the horrible news, I didn't think it was fair to share the burden. "I'll be back this evening," I said. "Let Cass know if you need anything."

"Need anything?" Carole rolled her eyes. "You're kidding." She opened the fridge and I saw a dish of lasagna, a salad, and a slice of mint chocolate cake. "Those gingerbread waffles were to die for. And now this!"

"Ah," I said, and grinned. "The Thymely Gourmet strikes again." From behind my back, I produced the to-go box. "And here's another offering. *Ensalada de nopalites.*"

"Oh, Lord." Carole put it into the refrigerator. "If you guys keep plying me with food, you may not be able to get rid of me."

"Stay as long as you like," I said cordially. "But only until next Tuesday."

Carole cocked an eyebrow. "Next Tuesday? What happens then?"

"The cottage is rented to a lady who is flying down from Chicago for her daughter's wedding," I said. An herbal wedding — a large and elaborate one, with the ceremony at the First Baptist Church and the reception at the Springs Hotel. Thyme and Seasons was providing the herbs, and Party

105

Thyme was doing catering. The next couple of weeks were going to be very busy, which is good. Being busy is a necessary prelude to making money, which is a necessary concomitant to putting groceries on the table and paying the utility bills.

Especially if your husband is an underemployed private eye.

As it turned out, I didn't get away from Pecan Springs right away. Not wanting to see Ruby unless I had the latest information, I stopped at the police station to find out from Sheila if there had been any new developments that I could share with Ruby.

I found her hunched over a gray metal-topped table in the cafeteria, her lunch spread out in front of her: a vending-machine Cello-wrapped turkey-and-cheese sandwich, a large bag of Cheetos, and a can of cherry Coke. I averted my eyes. For Sheila, this is a comfort-food meal. I don't know how she does it, but she can eat two or three of these a day without gaining an ounce. Heaven only knows what the insides of her arteries look like.

"Anything new in Colin's case?" I asked, pulling out a chair. Sheila has gotten touchy about sharing information, so when she slanted me a questioning look, I added, "I'm going to Fredericksburg to tell Ruby what happened. If there's anything you can tell me, I'd appreciate it."

There was, but not much, and Sheila was able to give it to me between sandwich bites. A neighborhood canvas had turned up a witness, a kitchen worker at Beans who was taking garbage out to the garbage bin shortly before ten on Tuesday night. He had heard somebody yelling bloody murder in the general direction of the railroad tracks. He had been afraid to investigate or call the cops ("Hey, ya'll don't 'spect me to git involved in no killin', do ya?"). Still, the report helped to fix an approximate time of death, and confirm that Colin was killed where we found him. If there were other witnesses, they hadn't turned up yet. And there was still no sign of a weapon. Sheila was about to go over to Colin's house to supervise a search, and *no* (in answer to my unvoiced question), I could not go along. It was police business.

But yes, Sheila thought it was a good idea for me to tell Ruby what had happened. "She's got to know. You can help her deal with it." She shook out the last cheesy crumbs of Cheetos into the palm of her hand and licked them up.

"She pulled the plug on the relationship,

you know," I said quietly. "She finally decided it wasn't going anywhere, so she called it quits."

Not looking at me, Sheila wadded up the bag, made a ball of it, and tossed it into the trash can. "No, I didn't know. Recently?"

"Three weeks ago. She was seeing him occasionally, but he was no longer invited for overnights."

"Poor Colin," Sheila said dryly. "Must've come as a shock that she'd throw him out of bed. He always thought he was God's ordained ambassador to deprived womanhood. Not to speak ill of the dead," she added, and her voice became sad again. "He was a good man, in his way. When he loved you, you were his and he was yours, for at least, oh, thirty seconds."

I leaned forward on my elbows. "McQuaid just told me about the Dallas cops. The ones who got fifteen to thirty, the supervisor who killed himself. Have you picked up anything that would suggest that this might be a revenge killing?"

Sheila shook her head. "Nope. *Nada.*" She didn't quite meet my eyes.

I sat back. The chief might know something, but she wasn't telling me. Police business. And then I remembered something. "Uh-oh," I said. "Rambo."

"Rambo?"

"Colin's Rottweiler. He probably hasn't been fed since Tuesday. He must be ravenous. If you're sending somebody over to Fowler's place, tell them to be prepared for the dog." I said this without any intent to manipulate, I swear to God — although the minute the words were out of my mouth, I saw their potential.

Sheila looked doubtful. She has been bitten several times and has developed a phobia about attack dogs. Rottweilers are at the top of her do-not-call list. "Actually, I was headed over there myself." She hesitated, not wanting to admit that she's a chicken where big, possibly dangerous dogs are concerned. "Do you know this animal, China? Is he aggressive?"

I have not been personally introduced to Rambo, although I have heard Ruby say that his bark is worse than his bite. However, I could see where this might lead. I put on my concerned-for-the-safety-of-my-friend look, shook my head gravely, and lied through my teeth.

"Sure, I know the dog. And yes, he's definitely an aggressive animal." How wrong could I be? Aren't all Rottweilers known for their ungovernable urge to chow down on the postman, the neighbor's kids, and your arm? "Even Colin was a little uneasy around him," I added for good measure. "He only kept him because he's a super watchdog. Guess he figured that nobody would have the guts to come on the property if Rambo was on the job."

I could see her considering the problem. "I'd send the animal control officer, but he quit last week, and I don't have the money to rehire." She gave me a cautious look. "I don't want to put you in any danger, China, but since you know this animal, maybe you'd be willing to go over there with me. Do you think you could handle him?"

"I suppose I could," I said, feigning reluctance. "I could try. Although," I added, rubbing it in just a little, "I wouldn't want to intrude on police business."

"You won't," Sheila said firmly. "Remember that you're there just to handle the Rottweiler. Until the place is released, it's a crime scene. I don't want you poking around. No snooping. Okay?"

"Snoop?" I was indignant, my motives impugned. "How can I snoop when I'm trying to keep a crazy dog from eating my favorite police chief?"

Smart Cookie shuddered.

Colin had lived in a two-bedroom frame on

Oak Street — a small house with a narrow front porch, a yard that contained a couple of scrappy desert willows, and a low hedge along the walk. It wasn't far from I-35, and the vibrating hum of traffic was a steady monotone beneath the courting chorus of a male mockingbird. He was doing his spring-fling thing at the top of a utility pole, launching himself into the air just as he reached a crescendo in his symphony of stolen songs.

Sheila and I went around to the back, where Colin had apparently been doing some landscaping. Three spiky yuccas and a handsome *Agave zebra* were still in their five-gallon black plastic nursery pots, waiting to be set into the ground. I was a little surprised to see them. Colin hadn't struck me as the gardening type. But then, gardeners are everywhere, in all disguises, and yuccas and agaves have an architectural quality that makes them a strong addition to many gardens, especially attractive to men. To tell the truth, I thought a little more highly of Colin, now that I could see he had an interest in plants.

Sheila pulled on a pair of thin plastic gloves and tried Colin's keys until she got the right one, while I took note of the chain-link run and domed doggie igloo beside the garage. It was sheltered behind a large red-tipped photinia bush in glorious bloom, its blossom clusters as large as saucers. I could hear the Rottweiler on the other side of the door, growling and snarling. He was on his hind legs, his claws scrabbling at the door. I could hear his jaws snapping. I could almost hear his teeth clicking, picture the drool dripping.

"I hope you know what you're doing with this dog, China," Sheila said ominously.

"So do I," I said under my breath. I shivered. Why had I thought my experience with an elderly basset would qualify me to control a Rottweiler? Why hadn't I thought to bring a leash? Or a muzzle? Or something large and heavy to beat off this vicious dog? Or —

But when Sheila cautiously opened the door and we jumped to one side, Rambo had his own high priority, and we were not it. He practically knocked the two of us over as he rushed down the steps, raced to the nearest bush, and hiked one hind leg with a nearly audible sigh of relief. I had no idea that Rottweilers had such a large capacity. While the dog was taking care of his long-overdue business, I opened the fridge and found a pack of hot dogs. I filled a bowl with water and carried the bowl and the hot dogs to the dog run.

By the time I got out there, Rambo was finished peeing and had gone to the farthest corner to do the other thing, his back modestly turned, his eyes blissfully closed. I waited until he had finished, set the water bowl in the run, tossed the hot dogs after it, and closed the gate as the dog raced in for the kill, as though they were baby bunnies. I stood for a moment, watching him wolf down weenies. There must be some dry dog food in the house. I'd see that Rambo had enough to tide him over for a few days, and I'd give some thought to finding a new home for him. Maybe there was a Rottweiler Rescue somewhere in the area.

After putting myself into imminent peril just to get a peek inside the house, I was disappointed. The rooms were spartan, with no special effort at decoration, but every-thing — even the bathroom — was neat and scrupulously clean, unusually so for a man living alone. There were a couple of yellow puddles and a smelly pile, testimony to Rambo's distress. But otherwise, it just felt empty, vacant, almost as if it had never been truly occupied. There were no personal touches, no photographs, no ghosts.

More to the point, there was no evidence of a struggle and the place had not been tossed. Sheila and her team would make a meticulous search of the drawers, the closets, and the file cabinet in the bedroom. If there was a computer, they'd take it, and any disks they could get their hands on. They would confiscate and study the usual personal stuff — phone bills, checkbooks, bank statements, safe deposit records, address books, and messages on the answering machine — for possible clues to his killing. But now that I had seen the place, I was willing to bet that if Colin had something significant to hide, something that might be a motive for his murder, he wouldn't hide it here. Even if I had been inclined to snoop, there wouldn't be anything to find, although I did note, just for future reference, that the kitchen window was unlocked.

I located a fresh can of Alpo and a suitable plastic dish, and fed Rambo, who did not seem all that aggressive at the moment. In fact, he looked downright sad and lonely and scared, as if he were wondering what was going to become of him now that the guy who dished out his doggie food and took him for his two-a-days had disappeared. I petted him gingerly, promised to put in a good word with whoever was in charge of recycling Rottweilers, and secured the gate.

I was examining the potted yuccas and wondering if Sheila would let me adopt them when I noticed a piece of paper protruding from under a pot. I tilted the pot and squatted down to read what was penciled on the paper. The handwriting was small and careful, almost like printing. "Call, please. There's been a change in plans. L."

L? I frowned. Who was L? A friend? A girlfriend? A rival to Ruby? The paper appeared to be the corner of a torn scrap of envelope. Not wanting to leave prints, I picked up a twig and carefully turned it over. On the back — the top left front of the envelope — was part of a logo, printed in green ink. It was torn, and all I could make out were parts of two letters, one a curly *S*, the other a loopy *N* or an *M*, artistically intertwined. It was vaguely familiar but I couldn't recall where I had seen it. I turned the envelope over again and resettled the pot. This was police business. No point in advertising that I had been snooping when I promised I wouldn't.

Sheila came around the house from the front, where she had been stringing crime-scene tape. "What've you found?" she asked, seeing me standing beside the potted yucca, looking down at it.

"Dunno." I motioned. "A piece of paper." I watched as Sheila bent down, turned up the pot and read the note. "Anything interesting?"

"Maybe." She replaced the pot and straightened. "What about the dog?" Smart Cookie might be a very good friend, but she is also a very good police officer. She wasn't going to tell me about L's efforts to contact Colin about the change in plans. It was now an official police secret.

I nodded toward the run. "He'll be okay where he is until somebody figures out what to do with him. Seems like a friendly guy." Glancing at my watch, I said, "If I'm going to drive to Fredericksburg, I'd better get on the road."

Sheila pursed her lips, thinking. "Listen, China, I know how hard things are for Ruby, with her mom and all. But would you tell her that I need to talk to her when she gets back? She may know something that could help in the investigation. I'd drive over to Fredericksburg and interview her myself, but the City Council is voting on the department's budget this evening. I'm asking for new staff positions and some body armor, and if I'm not there to defend the requests, those jerks will cut it."

"Body armor?"

"Yeah. Would you believe? I can't require my officers to wear vests because we don't have enough to go around." She turned down her mouth. "Not enough people, either. I need to send somebody over to Colin's shop to check it out, but I don't have an extra officer. I'm glad it isn't high priority."

I shook my head sympathetically. Sheila is always arm wrestling the council for something — more officers, better equipment, more overtime — sometimes successfully, often not, since crime fighting isn't at the top of the council's agenda. The town fathers and mothers would rather think of Pecan Springs as a cozy, comfortable place where jaywalking and double-parking are the worst offenses, so Sheila is often reduced to begging. She hates that part of the job. "It sucks," she says. "But it comes with the territory."

However that may be, it left me with an interesting opening, which I took, of course. "Ruby may not be able to come back for a couple of days, depending on how bad her mother's situation is. If that's the case, do you want me to see what she can tell us about Colin's friends, enemies, etcetera?"

Smart Cookie's brow furrowed. I could see what she was thinking: that I was trustworthy (more or less), that my legal experience made me a competent questioner, and that she could double-check the information with Ruby later. "I don't suppose it can hurt for you to get some background," she said finally. "Yeah, sure. Go ahead, China. See if she has any information we don't. And give me a call if you pick up anything I should know."

From Sheila's point of view, it wasn't optimal, but it was the best she was likely to get, at least until Ruby came home.

CHAPTER SIX

According to an Oxford University study, *Ginkgo biloba,* a popular herbal remedy, could improve brain function in people with early signs of dementia.

Researchers reviewed thirty-three placebo-controlled studies of ginkgo over twenty-six years, involving people with dementia or cognitive impairment. Some studies found that ginkgo boosts peripheral and cerebral circulation, improves the uptake of glucose, thins the blood, and has anti-inflammatory and antioxidant properties. Compared with placebos, the herb improved cognition and mood and emotional function in people with dementia.

"Overall there is promising evidence of improvement in cognition and function associated with ginkgo," the reviewers concluded.

AltHealth News, December 31, 2002

Fredericksburg is some sixty miles west of Pecan Springs. To get there from here, you take Route 306 across the steep, cedar-clad hills of Devil's Backbone, stopping at the overlooks to enjoy the views of the rugged terrain, once known as Comanchería, or Comanche country. The Comanches were a fierce nomadic tribe, mounted on mustang ponies and armed with guns obtained by bartering buffalo hides with the Wichita Indians on the Red River. They were given their name by the peaceable and settled Utes, who called them Komántcia, "enemy," or, literally, "anybody who wants to fight me all the time."

When 306 bumps into U.S. 281, you turn north for about thirty miles, through Blanco to Johnson City. At the stop light, where the highway makes a Y, turn left — that's west — on U.S. 290, and drive past the Lyndon Baines Johnson National Historic Park, where you can see the Johnson Settlement and catch a bus for a guided tour of the LBJ Ranch.

During April and early May, 290 is always crowded with bluebonnet traffic, even on weekdays: SUVs, vans, chartered buses full of senior citizens. The bloom had peaked the week before, but the roadsides were still thickly carpeted in blue, brightened with patches of deep maroon winecups and yellow huisache daisies. The afternoon sun was bright and the sky was cerulean blue, a perfect background for the children posing for the obligatory baby-in-the-bluebonnets photo, an annual phenomenon along this stretch of road. Farther west, at Wildseed Farms (the largest wildflower farm in the nation and well worth adding to your itinerary), the tourists were strolling through acres of Indian paintbrush and scarlet poppies, so beautiful that they will break your heart.

But I barely noticed the traffic or the cute babies buried to the chin in bluebonnets. I was trying to think how I could tell Ruby that Colin Fowler had been murdered, and wondering how much of the Dan Reid story she had to know. McQuaid's information — about the suicide and the dozen crooked cops — helped to clarify the situation somewhat. The tale McQuaid had related would make Colin look like a hero in her eyes, and might soften the blow, if only just a little. I would tell her what I knew — except the part about Colin's relationship to Sheila. That would hurt, and it had no relevance. This answered the question of what I would tell her, but it failed to address the question of how. I was still puzzling over that when I reached Fredericksburg.

The town of Fredericksburg was settled in the 1840s and '50s by German immigrants who landed at Corpus Christi and made their way overland to New Braunfels, and then to this new town, named for Prince Frederick of Prussia. Each settler was given one town lot and ten acres of nearby farmland. They built their cabins of cypress logs, and after surviving the cholera epidemics and Comanche raids that filled the next few years with bitter misery, they replaced those makeshift homes with more permanent dwellings: sturdy *Fachwerk* houses constructed of upright timbers, the spaces between filled with chunks of squared-off limestone covered with a coat of mortar. You can still see those houses as you drive along Main Street, or West Austin or West San Antonio. Many have been expanded, and some have been converted into attractive antique shops, boutiques, and biergartens. But you'll recognize them. Those crafty Germans built their distinctive houses to last, and they have long outlasted their builders.

Cedar Summit, the retirement village where Ruby's mother and grandmother live (in separate apartments, because they get

122

along about as well as two fighting roosters), is on the south side of town. Its architecture echoes the dominant German style, with independent and assisted living units in two-story buildings clustered around neatly landscaped courtyards, and a nursing facility nearby. It is an undeniably pretty place, an enclave from the hustle and mess and confusion of real life. But this artificial segregation always seems somehow sterile to me, and sad, as if these older people have removed themselves — or been removed — from most of what's lively and interesting and real. I hope my retirement (if I ever do retire, which I doubt) does not include a retirement community, or if it does, that the community is open to the world around it, not closed off or shut away.

I parked in the lot, located Doris' ground-level unit, went up to the oak-paneled door, and knocked. After a moment, Ruby opened the door. I was startled at her appearance. Her delicate, triangular face was bare of makeup, the gingery freckles stood out across her nose, and her frizzy red hair was piled untidily on top of her head and secured with an orange Scrunchy. I rarely saw her without at least lip gloss, and she looked young, vulnerable, bruised. She had on jeans and an oversized black T-shirt printed with silvery signs of the zodiac, and she was wielding a blue feather-duster. Her expression was harried, but when she saw me, she broke into a wide, happy grin.

"China!" she exclaimed in delight, and some relief. "What are you doing here?"

"Who is it, Ruby?" came a querulous voice. "Is it Ramona?"

"It's China, Mother," Ruby said, over her shoulder. "You know China Bayles."

Of course Doris knows me. We've often had dinner together at Ruby's house, and she has been in my shop on numerous occasions. I wouldn't say we were friends, exactly, but —

"China?" Doris said peevishly. "What kind of heathen name is that?" A fuzzy pink blanket over her feet, she was stretched out on the sofa in the cluttered living room. "Where is Ramona? What is keeping that girl? I thought she would be here by now. Doesn't she know how sick I am?"

I was startled by the thin reediness of Doris' voice, and by the fact that she didn't appear to know who I was. "How's her heart?" I asked in a low voice.

"Ticking like a clock. It's her mind that's not working." Ruby gave her mother a worried look. "I knew things were bad, but it's much worse than I thought."

"Speak up," Doris commanded in a petulant tone. "I can't hear you. Ramona, is that you, Ramona? Where have you been, you naughty girl? I've been in the hospital, you know. Is my mother with you? If she is, tell her to go away." She waved her hand dismissively. "She doesn't care about me. She never cared."

"Hello, Doris," I said, going toward her with as much enthusiasm as if I were advancing on a cranky old lioness. "It's China. China Bayles. I'm sorry you're having trouble with your heart. I hope you're feeling better."

"I am not at all well," Doris said, enunciating carefully. She propped herself on her elbows, peering up at me. "Who are you? You're not from that wretched Social Services, are you? If you are, you can just go away again. I told them I'm perfectly well." Her voice rose shrilly. "Ruby, why are you letting all these people come around and bother me? Where is Ramona? Why doesn't she come? Doesn't she know I nearly died last night?"

"I told you, Mom," Ruby said patiently, straightening the pillow on which Doris was lying. "Ramona will be here as soon as she gets her car back from the shop. Another day or two, probably."

It was obvious that Doris was in a bad way. Her gray hair, normally curled and coifed into a stiff, blue-rinsed cap, was wispily disarranged and patches of pink, peeling scalp showed through. She had lost so much weight that the flesh flapped loosely from the bones of her arms, and her eyes were deepset and frantic. She had always dressed carefully and prided herself on an immaculate appearance, but today she was wearing a dingy yellow muumuu with a cascade of coffee stains down the front. House slippers with the toes cut out peeked from beneath the blanket.

I glanced at Ruby, startled. I'd known that Doris was having problems, but from a distance, they had seemed funny. Up close, the situation was tragic: difficult enough for Doris, but perhaps even more difficult for her daughters. And now Ruby had to deal with Colin's death, on top of everything else. I tried to swallow the lump that was suddenly, painfully huge in my throat. How was I going to tell her?

Ruby motioned with her duster. "I've made some coffee," she said, and led the way to the kitchen, where she closed the door and leaned against it wearily.

"I just hope I can last until Ramona gets here on Sunday," she said. "I've explained to Mom that she's moving to a new apartment tomorrow morning, but I don't think she understood." She waved her duster around the kitchen. "As you can see, she has to have help, and better supervision. She can't take care of herself any longer."

I followed her glance. The kitchen, small, nicely arranged, and furnished with sleek appliances, was a wreck. Dirty dishes were piled on the counter and in the sink. Food had been spilled on the stove and the floor, and the table in the tiny breakfast nook looked as if it hadn't been cleaned off for a couple of weeks.

"Gosh, Ruby," I exclaimed. "How awful!" Awful for Doris, who had always been so compulsively neat that she wouldn't permit a pillow to be out of place on the sofa. And horrible for Ruby, who had to arrange her mother's care.

"I finally got the bathroom decent," Ruby said, dropping her duster on the counter. She rolled her eyes. "You can't believe the mess it was in. Worse than cleaning up after a dozen kids. And scarves — expensive scarves with the price tags still on them. So far I've found thirteen. I'm putting them together, by store, so I can take them back."

She opened the cupboard, took down the last two clean cups, and poured coffee. "I was thinking of you this afternoon, China, and wondering whether there is such a thing as herbal therapy for dementia."

"You might try ginkgo biloba," I said cautiously. "There's been some promising research on that lately. Let's ask Laurel and see what she recommends." Laurel Riley, who helps out in my shop, recently completed her certification as a Master Herbalist with an emphasis on herbal medicine. She would be up-to-date on the research. I thought of something else. "Lavender will help, too — it has a strong calming effect. It's been used for centuries to treat hysteria and anxiety. Mix ten or twelve drops of essential oil in a half-cup of carrier oil — almond or apricot oil are good, or olive oil, if she's allergic to nuts. Use it as a massage oil. You can put lavender oil in her bath, too, or on her pillow, or in a scent diffuser."

"That sounds good," Ruby said gratefully. "It might work for me, too." She turned, handing me the cup. "I didn't expect to see you today, China. Is everything okay at the shops?"

"Sure," I said, with a hollow heartiness. "Laurel and Missy have everything under control, the way they always do. Cass is keeping a dozen balls in the air, as usual. And Carole is cooking the yucca we collected this morning." I looked down at my cup. I would have gone on, but I couldn't. It was as if my brain's electrical apparatus had shorted out, leaving me without the ability to formulate words.

Ruby pushed a stack of newspapers — the Fredericksburg *Standard* — off the seat in the breakfast nook. "Well?" she prompted, sitting down and leaning her elbows on the table. "You didn't drive all the way to Fredericksburg just so my mom could yell at you." She frowned, and anxiety puckered her forehead. "It's not Amy, is it? Or baby Grace?" Amy is the daughter who came back into Ruby's life after Doris insisted that she be adopted. Grace, just four months old, is Amy's child, and Ruby adores her. "Don't tell me something's happened to my girls!"

"No, of course not," I said, waving away her concern. "The girls are fine." I sat down across from her and took both her hands. Whatever plan I'd concocted on the drive to Fredericksburg had gone completely out of my mind. Clumsy, brutal, I blurted it out.

"It's Colin, Ruby. He's dead."

"Dead!" Ruby pulled her hands away, her eyes going wide, her mouth crumpling. There was a silence, then: "No!" she wailed. "No, he can't be. Not Colin!"

The next few minutes were utterly awful. Ruby dropped her arms into a patch of congealed oatmeal on the table, cradled her head, and sobbed as if her heart would break. I came around the table and slid onto the bench beside her, putting my arm around her shoulders and pulling her close, murmuring comforting sounds. From the living room, Doris called, even more peevishly than before, "Ramona, why are you crying? Ruby, make Ramona stop crying. Sounds like a sick goat. Hurts my head to hear it!" Neither of us answered her.

At last, Ruby raised her head, her eyes brimming with tears. "How?" she whispered. "Was it a car wreck? I kept telling him he drove too fast, but he'd never listen." She knitted her fingers together to keep them from shaking. "He never listened to me at all."

I got up and stood, looking down at her. My lips were stiff and frozen and I felt hollow inside. "He was . . . he was murdered," I managed finally. "Carole and I found him beside the railroad tracks, behind Beans. It was this morning, when we went to get some yucca for the workshop."

"Murdered!" Ruby cried, horrified. "China, you can't — it can't be!" Her voice rose, out of control. "No! I don't believe it.

I won't! It can't be true!"

"Ramona!" Doris shrilled. "Ramona, stop that horrible noise this minute! Ruby, make that girl stop her bawling! What are the neighbors going to think?"

I sat down on the other side of the table and took Ruby's hands again. They were cold as a December day. "It's true," I whispered. "I am so sorry, Ruby. He was . . . he was knifed. Night before last, probably."

"Knifed? Oh, my God." Her voice was weak and shrill. "But who — Who could have done it, China? Why?"

It was an opening, and I seized it, thinking that rational talk might distract her for a moment. "Sheila thought you might have some ideas, since you knew Colin better than anyone. She's hoping you can fill in some of the blanks."

"But I didn't really know him," Ruby said disconsolately. "Colin was the most secretive man I've ever met. In the six months we were together, we didn't talk about much of anything except his business or mine, or music or the art scene. Of course, he was interested in politics and current affairs, and he liked to talk about what he was reading. Our conversations were always interesting, but not . . . well, personal." She pulled down her mouth. "Except when I was talking about me. I did that a lot, you know. To encourage him."

"He didn't tell you *anything* about himself?" I guess I wasn't surprised. When I was single, the men I went out with had lots to say, but we rarely got past externals. The talk somehow kept us apart, rather than bringing us together. And Colin had more to hide than most men.

She shook her head sadly. "That was what finally made me decide we'd never have a real relationship, China. You can't love a man who's a total mystery."

"How about people he knew before he came to Pecan Springs?" I persisted, thinking about the dirty dozen. "Did he talk much about them?"

She shook her head. "He said he was starting over. He was trying to forget the past. I got the idea he'd been in the military, but I couldn't —" She gave me a despairing look. "I couldn't keep nagging him about it, could I? He had to want to tell me on his own, because he trusted me. Not because I pushed him." She pressed her palms together, steadying her hands. She was talking to herself now, as much as to me. "I didn't want him to dwell on what had happened in his past — I just wanted him to share. I wanted him to *want* to open up and let me in. That's not so wrong, is it?"

"Of course not," I said gruffly. "It's not wrong at all." Love has to be based on intimacy. It's impossible to trust somebody you don't know, or be intimate with a man who keeps himself totally private and out of reach. And not knowing the truth about somebody you've let into your life can put you in danger. But things were bad enough already. I didn't want to go there. "His parents," I said. "Did he ever mention his parents?"

"They're both dead, I know that much. He didn't have any brothers or sisters. There's nobody left in his family. At least that's what he said." Ruby got up and found a box of tissues on the counter and sat down again.

"How about his ex-wife?" Ruby knew he'd been married. She had mentioned it to me once.

"She was a nurse, or maybe a doctor's receptionist — something like that. They didn't have any children." She took out a tissue and a purple silk scarf came with it. "Oh, *hell,*" she muttered. "Another one." She folded the scarf and put it down on the only clean spot on the table. "Or if they did have kids," she added disconsolately, "he didn't tell me." She blew her nose on the tissue.

I thought of the note I'd found under the pot in Colin's backyard. "What was his wife's name?"

"I don't know." She blew her nose. "I don't know where she is, either. He said they didn't keep in touch."

I took a breath. It was probably time to tell her. "I don't suppose he mentioned what he did before he came to Pecan Springs?"

She shook her head mutely. Her lips were trembling.

Another breath. "Then I'll tell you what Sheila and McQuaid told me," I said, and related the story of Dan Reid, ex-cop, ex-con, ex-mystery. I didn't try to transform him into a hero, but as I talked, Ruby's mouth stopped trembling, her shoulders straightened, and she became calmer. The story was allowing her to redefine him as a hero — a mythic definition, certainly, without any basis in provable fact. But I couldn't object as long as it brought her some comfort, as long as it gave her a way of explaining what seemed so terribly inexplicable.

"So he was in undercover narcotics," she breathed eagerly, when I finished. "That's why he wouldn't talk to me about his past. He couldn't!" Her eyes widened as she took the idea a step further, down the same dark path I had gone. "Maybe he was undercover for the FBI, or for one of those drug task forces!" And then one more step. "Do you suppose he was killed by one of the cops who went to prison? To get even, I mean."

"It's possible." I told her what McQuaid had said. "Cops who rat out their fellow cops make good targets."

"But I thought there was a witness protection program," she protested.

"He wasn't a witness," I said. "At most, he was an informant. Witnesses testify in public, so everybody knows who they are. That's what puts them in danger." But I knew that Sheila would check with the U.S. Marshals Service in San Antonio, where the Western District has its office. The marshals run WITSEC, the Witness Security Program. If Colin had been under their protection, she would find out. And in the process she might also find out the truth of what had happened in Dallas.

I got on with it. "What about the people Colin hung out with in Pecan Springs, Ruby? He owned a business — he must have had friends, associates, maybe even a partner. Who were they?"

She lifted her shoulders and let them drop. Her voice was flat. "No partner, at least none that I'm aware of. He knew the people who have businesses on the square, and he went to the Chamber of Commerce meetings. He had suppliers, of course, and customers. There must be a mailing list somewhere. Oh, and a college student who worked part-time in the shop." Her mouth twisted wryly. "But he always said he preferred being a loner. That way, he'd know who he could trust."

I wondered briefly how in the world Ruby had managed to stay connected to this man for the five or six months the relationship — such as it was — had lasted. But down deep, I knew the answer to that: Colin's remoteness had probably been part of the initial attraction. That's happened to me. Mystery makes some men seem dangerous, sexy, alluring. But somebody had known him, at least well enough to leave that note. "Was he acquainted with anybody whose name begins with the letter *L?*"

Ruby frowned. "*L?* What makes you ask that?"

"Ramona?" The kitchen door opened, and Doris shuffled into the room, clutching the fuzzy pink blanket under her chin like a child. "Ramona, where is Ruby? Somebody has to tell her about the car. Some horrible woman stole my car yesterday and locked herself into it. The police had to come and —"

Ruby got up and put her arm around her mother's narrow shoulders and turned her back toward the door. "You can stop worrying about the car, Mom," she said comfortingly. "It's all taken care of. Let's go back and lie down. Remember what the doctor said? You need lots of rest, especially with our big move coming up tomorrow." She was speaking in the artificially cheerful tone that people use to invalids and small children. "It's going to be a big day, remember? You're getting a brand-new apartment! Won't that be fun? And somebody will be there to help you out and make sure you get your medicine."

Doris scowled. "I can't understand what's keeping Ruby. That girl never does what she promises. She said she would bring me some chocolates and —" The door swung closed behind the two of them, cutting off her petulant complaint.

I sat for a few minutes, finished my coffee, and rinsed out my cup in the sink. A team of hardworking ants was diligently transporting a treasure trove of bread crumbs across the counter, skirting a puddle of chocolate-chip ice cream that had melted and solidified. I turned around as Ruby came back into the room, pulling off her Scrunchy and running her fingers through her loosened hair. She looked very tired.

"What about Grammy?" I asked. "Does she know what's going on here?"

Ruby frowned. "Grammy has been in Dallas for the past month, with Ramona. She and Mother don't get along, you know, and she said she needed to get away. Maybe she saw what was happening and felt she couldn't cope. She's eighty-five." She gave me a harried look. "What about Colin's arrangements, China? You see how things are here. I can't go back to Pecan Springs until Ramona comes. And maybe not even then, depending on —"

"Don't worry about coming back right away," I said comfortingly. "Missy can help. We'll manage."

"Yes, but —"

"Stop worrying. The autopsy report won't be back until Monday or Tuesday, and they won't release the body until the middle of the week. I —"

I broke off, feeling like a jerk. I shouldn't have mentioned the words *autopsy* or *body*. Ruby's eyes were glazing with tears.

"I tried to stop loving him," she said, half

gulping the words. She stood in front of the window over the sink, looking out at the pretty green courtyard beyond, where a pair of elderly people, a man and a woman, progressed slowly along a sidewalk. The man, gray-faced and frail, was hunched over an aluminum walker. The woman had her hand on his shoulder, guiding him with a loving touch. "It's been hard, but I did, mostly. I've been forcing myself to get used to the idea that Colin and I weren't going to grow old together, like that couple out there." She shook her head sadly. "Now I *really* have to do it. Get used to it, I mean. Get a life without him. He's gone for good now, and there's no tomorrow. Not for us. Not even for him." The tears spilled out of her eyes and ran down her cheeks.

"You're strong," I said. "This thing with your mom is awful. Colin's death is even worse. But you're the strongest person I know, Ruby. You'll make it. You'll be okay."

I wasn't just saying this to make her feel better. Ruby might temporarily lose her bearings, especially when her heart is involved, but she's a whole lot tougher than she looks. She has survived a philandering husband, an ugly divorce, and the unexpected reappearance of the daughter she had given up for adoption. She survived breast cancer. She'll survive this — not without pain, not without scars, but she'll survive.

She took another tissue, wiped her eyes, and blew her nose. "Lucita," she said, and threw the tissue into the trash.

I frowned. "Lucita?"

Her voice was harder, and there was an edge to it. "You were asking whether Colin knew somebody whose name begins with an L. Yes, he did. He knew a woman named Lucita."

"Ah," I said.

Ruby pulled a paper towel off the roll, and when she did, the whole roll came down and bounced across the floor. I went to pick it up and saw, sticking out of one end, a green and white scarf. Wordlessly, I folded it and put it with the purple scarf.

Ruby rolled her eyes and used the towel to attack the ants trekking across the counter. "A month or so ago, I was in Colin's shop. He was out back, checking in a UPS delivery, and I was watching the counter for him. A woman phoned. She said her name was Lucita." Ruby's mouth tightened and her eyes held a hurt look. "She sounded like she knew him pretty well. And she was really urgent about talking to him."

Poor Ruby. Jealousy is a sword. But who

hasn't been pierced by it? Who could blame her? "Did she say what she wanted?"

Ruby took down another towel, wet it, and went after the remaining ants, then after the patch of solidified ice cream, scrubbing with a vengeance. "She just kept saying that she had to talk to him."

"Did she leave a number?"

"Yes. She said it wasn't her usual number and she didn't think he had it. She wanted him to call her back as soon as he came in. I wrote the number down, and when he finished with the delivery, I told him about it."

"Did he call her?"

"Not while I was there. He just sort of shrugged it off, like it wasn't important." She threw the paper towel away, opened the cabinet under the sink, and got out a bottle of spray cleaner. "But then, that was the way he always was," she said, spraying the countertop. She picked up a sponge. "He was so private. Lucita could've been a very significant other and he wouldn't have let on. Especially to me."

Lucita. It sounded Hispanic. "Did she have an accent?"

"Oh, yes. Very south-of-the-border. A cigarette voice. Seductive. Sexy." She was scouring the counter now, hard. "What's all this about an *L* name? Why are you asking?"

"Sheila wanted to have a look at Colin's house before she sent her investigators in. She didn't much like the idea of going in there when she heard about the dog. So —"

"Rambo!" Ruby whirled, her eyes widening. "Omigosh, China! The poor puppy! I'll bet he hasn't had anything to eat for days!"

Poor puppy? "He's fine," I said. "I gave him a package of weenies and a can of dog food for dessert and put him in his run. There must be a Rottweiler Rescue in Austin or San Antonio. I'll call around and see if I can find somebody who will come and pick him up."

"No way," Ruby said emphatically. "Rambo needs a good home. He needs somebody who understands him. Somebody to love him." She lifted her chin in a defiant gesture. "*I'm* taking him."

"You?" I was surprised. "But he's a Rottweiler, Ruby. He's as big as a house. Bigger. He'll eat your cats! He'll eat *you!*"

"Oh, pooh," Ruby scoffed, swiping the sponge across the counter. "Rambo is a great big sissy. He won't bother the cats — he's afraid of them."

I stared at her, incredulous. "That monster muscle dog is afraid of a little-bitty *pussycat?*"

"And thunder, and loud motorcycles. Rambo has lots of phobias. But underneath it all, he's a very sweet Rotti, and very well trained. Colin got him from somebody who trains scent-detection dogs. And yes, I'm taking him. Colin would want me to." She pressed her lips together with that familiar I-have-a-mission look. Having failed to convert Colin to a life of love and commitment, she was going to redeem his dog.

Who am I to argue with one of Ruby's missions? "Okay," I said. "If that's what you want."

"But I can't get him right away. Can you go over to Colin's house and feed the dog and take him for walks until I get back?"

"Yeah, I guess," I said slowly. "Sure, I can do that." Once I got over my initial surprise, it didn't seem like such a bad idea. Rambo needed somebody to take care of him, and Ruby needed somebody to take care of. And if it didn't work out — if the dog wasn't the cream puff she thought — there was always Plan B. Rottweiler Rescue.

Ruby came back to the subject. "*L.* Why did you ask about *L,* China?"

"I was waiting for Sheila when I looked down and saw a piece of paper sticking out from under a pot near the back door." I repeated the text from memory, not exactly, but close. "I didn't tell Sheila I read it," I added. "I had more or less promised I wouldn't snoop."

"It must be the same person who called the shop," Ruby said. She rinsed off the sponge and threw it into the sink.

I paused, frowning. "You said you wrote down the phone number. Where?"

"On the calendar next to the cash register. One of those page-for-every-day things."

I thought. "Was Colin in the habit of leaving the pages on the calendar, or did he tear them off and throw them away?"

"He always left them on, in case he wanted to look back over —" She stopped. "The number is still there, China. I'm sure of it. I wrote down the name, too. Lucita."

"But Lucita might not be the same person who wrote the note," I said. "And even if she is, she may have had nothing at all to do with Colin's death." In fact, it's unusual for a woman to knife a man — unless he's sleeping and she stabs him in the back. A man who is awake and on his feet is usually capable of taking a knife away from a woman.

"I'm aware of that," Ruby said impatiently. "But something tells me that this is important. You need to go by the shop on your way home and get that phone number, China."

"I do not need to do that," I replied firmly. "The shop is locked, and I am not the sort of person to break and enter. It's bad for my reputation. Anyway, investigating the shop is Sheila's job. The police have probably already taped it off and —"

"Of course the shop is locked," Ruby interrupted, "but you don't have to break and enter. I have a key. Colin always said that if something happened to him — if he was in a wreck or sick or something — somebody ought to be able to get in." She opened a drawer, pulled out a towel, and began to dry her hands. "Well, something has happened to him, and I need to get in and find that phone number. But I can't leave my mother right now, so it's up to you. I'll get the key."

"Ruby," I said, "you are drying your hands on a silk scarf."

Ruby wadded the scarf and threw it into the sink. "Who the hell *cares?*" she snapped, and left the room.

I scowled. This wasn't the first time Ruby had insisted that we embark on a harebrained scheme. There was the time she'd talked me into driving out to Carl Swenson's place in the predawn dark to investi-

145

gate his greenhouse, which turned out to be full of a stunningly healthy crop of marijuana. We were still there when the cops arrived. Or the afternoon when her Inner Guide had led the two of us into the basement of an abandoned school in the little town of Indigo, where we stumbled over a very dead body. Or —

I stopped. While the greenhouse expedition had nearly gotten us arrested, and finding the body in the basement had been a truly horrifying experience, the end results had been positive. If it hadn't been for Ruby, somebody would have gotten away with murder.

"Here's the key," she said, coming back into the room. She put it into my hand. "Do it tonight. Then call me and tell me what you found."

"I really think I ought to tell Sheila about Lucita's phone call," I said cautiously. "It's not a good idea for me to —"

"You can tell Sheila about it *afterward*," Ruby said. "If you tell her before, she'll go find the phone number and we won't know what it is. What's more," she added reasonably, "telling her about the phone call means that you have to tell her that you snooped. If you hadn't read that note, how would you know to ask me if Colin knew anybody

146

whose name begins with *L?*"

I hesitated. Nancy Drew Wilcox had a point. Of course, Sheila wouldn't arrest me for snooping. She would probably only give me a lecture. But still —

"Go around the back," Ruby said. "The key opens the alley door. There's an alarm keypad on the wall to the right. The code is nineteen sixty-three." She paused, frowning. "At least, that's what I think it is. To keep the alarm from going off, you have to put in the code before you open the door."

Alarm? I blinked. "Really, Ruby, I don't think I ought to —"

"I'm pretty sure it's nineteen sixty-three. That's the year Kennedy was killed, right? Or was it 1962? Anyway, when you get in, go through the back room and into the front of the store. The calendar should be on the counter right next to the register. Go back about a month. I think it was a Thursday. Or maybe a Friday." She puckered her forehead, thinking. "I'm sure it was Friday, because we went to Krautzeheimer's afterward and had the Friday-night special." Her eyes clouded. "That was the night I told him I didn't love him anymore. It was a lie, and he knew it, but it was the best I could do." She pressed her lips together. "If I had known he was going to be murdered —"

"I don't think going into the shop is a good idea," I said.

"But it's the only idea we have," Ruby cried passionately. "And I have a stake in this, China! I loved Colin, and in some ways, I'll probably keep on loving him for a long time. I don't want to leave this to the cops, but I can't do it myself because I can't leave my crazy mother." She fixed her gaze on me, and it was fierce. "I'm counting on you, China Bayles. Don't you let me down."

I didn't want to argue with her. And anyway, the idea of getting that phone number seemed to have given her a different energy. Maybe it gave her a sense of control. The comfort of doing something, anything. I put the shop key into the pocket of my jeans. I would give it to Sheila and tell her about Lucita's urgent call and the phone number on the calendar. She could put two and two together and come up with *L,* and I would be off the hook.

Ruby took my silence for assent. "Good," she said firmly. "I'm glad you agree with me. And don't forget to call me when you've found it. I won't go to sleep until you do."

"Ramona!" came a shrill cry from the living room. "Ramona, where are you? Call Ruby right now. Tell her I have to go to the hospital. I'm having a heart attack!"

"Oh, lordy," Ruby breathed, letting out a long, weary breath.

"I'm so sorry," I said inadequately. I looked up at the clock. It was time I was starting for home. "When do you think you'll get back to Pecan Springs?"

"I don't know. Not tomorrow, that's for sure. Tomorrow I have to move Mother to the other apartment. Maybe I can come home when Ramona gets here on Sunday. We'll just have to see how things are."

"I wish you didn't have to go through this right now," I said.

"So do I." Her shoulders slumped. "It's hell to get old, isn't it? And it's hell not to."

She closed her eyes, and I knew she was thinking of Colin, who was never going to get any older than he had been the day before yesterday, when somebody had put a knife into his chest.

CHAPTER SEVEN

According to the Oxford English Dictionary, the herb hemp, cultivated for its use as a fiber, oil, and medicine, was also known as neckweed and gallows-grass. A "stretch-hemp" was a person worthy of the gallows, and "to wag hemp" was to be hanged.

I did not intend to stop at Colin's shop — at least, that's what I told myself as I drove back to Pecan Springs. It's not kosher to barge into an active police investigation, and it definitely isn't a good idea to make an unauthorized entry into a shop with an armed alarm system. All I had to do was phone Sheila at home and tell her what Ruby had told me. She'd take over from there and the matter would be out of my hands.

But Sheila was defending her requests for staff positions and body armor at the City

Council meeting tonight. She wouldn't have a chance to search Colin's shop until tomorrow, unless she had done so already. And Ruby was right about one thing. Once the police were involved, it wasn't very likely that we'd pick up any information about the progress of the investigation. If I needed proof of that, all I had to do was think back to the way Sheila treated the note under the yucca pot. If I hadn't peeked, I wouldn't have known that someone named L wanted urgently to see Colin, and I wouldn't have mentioned it to Ruby, who would not, therefore, have remembered that a woman named Lucita had insisted on talking to Colin and had even left her phone number.

With all this running through my mind, I made a bargain with myself. If Sheila and her investigative team had already marked the shop off-limits as a crime scene, I would be a very good girl. I would drive straight home, phone Ruby, and tell her that we were out of luck, because I was disinclined to cross a police barrier. If, on the other hand, there was no crime-scene tape — Well, that was a different story, wasn't it?

Before I left Doris' apartment, Ruby had sent me for takeout sandwiches and salad, and I had made a quick run out to the Fredericksburg Herb Garden, the area's premier herb emporium, where I bought some lavender oil for Doris. While I was there, I also bought some dried chamomile, skullcap, passionflower, lemon balm, and valerian — sedative herbs that have been used for centuries to ease anxiety, reduce irritability, and settle the nerves. They wouldn't cure Doris' dementia — no herb could do that — but they would calm her down so that both she and Ruby could get some sleep.

When I got back with the food, we set the table and brought Doris in to eat — not a very pleasant meal, since she was stuck in a continuous loop of muttered accusations and confusions between Ruby and the absent Ramona. After we finished, I wrote down directions for using the herbs to make tea and left Ruby at the door, looking so fragile and wounded that I wanted to cry. But I summoned my most cheerful grin, gave her a hug, and assured her that everything would be okay.

Would it? As I got in my car and drove off, I had my doubts. The prognosis for Doris' illness probably wasn't good. Ruby had suffered two terrible tragedies, both at the same time. It was more than anyone could be expected to bear.

With all the delays, the sun was dropping

into the west by the time I left Fredericksburg. It was almost dark an hour later, when I got back to Pecan Springs. During the day, the courthouse square is full of tourists, out for a pleasant hour of shopping in stores where they don't have to walk a couple of miles of aisle to find a sweet little souvenir for Bitsy and Betsy back home. Vera Hooper, the town docent, leads them on guided tours of the historic buildings around the square. They take pictures of the pink granite courthouse (the oldest in this part of Texas), peek into Mueller's Antiques and Fine Crafts, and drop in at the Sophie Briggs Historical Museum to gawk at Miss Briggs' famous collection of ceramic frogs and the boots Burt Reynolds wore in *The Best Little Whorehouse in Texas.* And on top of the tourist traffic is layered the usual business traffic of a county courthouse, the central hub of Adams County's affairs. It's usually hard to find a parking space on the square, and Mae Belle Battersby is kept busy collecting coins from the meters and issuing parking tickets to any soul intrepid enough to double park.

But come sundown, things change, and tonight — a weekday night — was no exception. Up the hill and a few blocks closer to the Central Texas State campus, the evening was just beginning to get revved up. Down the hill, toward the railroad tracks, the bars and grills and dance halls were kicking into action. And over on I-35, the shopping malls were no doubt jammed with customers. But there were only two or three cars in the Nueces Street Diner parking lot, Krautzeheimer's German Restaurant had already closed, and the only signs of life on the street were a wandering pair of elderly tourists looking for their lost B&B, and the swarm of Mexican free-tailed bats making their nocturnal exodus from the attic of the old brick building that also houses the town's Parks and Utilities Department (as good as a cave, as far as the bats are concerned). A typical small-town courthouse square on a warm spring night.

I made a sedate double loop around the square, slowing to a crawl on the second pass in front of Colin Fowler's Good Earth Goods. It's a small store, wedged into the block between Mueller's Antiques and Bluebonnet Books, with the usual glass display windows full of merchandise on either side of a central door. I looked for the bright yellow crime-scene tape that should be stretched across the front, but it wasn't there. A Closed sign was hung on the door, and a small bouquet tied with a yellow ribbon was propped on the pavement against it. Colin's death might not be common knowledge yet, but somebody knew and cared enough to send flowers. Lucita, maybe? I parked, left the car running, and checked to see if there was a card. There wasn't.

But just because the cops hadn't posted the front of the store didn't mean that the back was clear. I made a right turn onto Crockett, and then another right halfway down the block, into the narrow graveled alley that runs behind the stores. I drove past the back doors and mini-Dumpsters that belong to the Ben Franklin Variety Store, the Bluebonnet Bookstore, and Mueller's Antiques, counting so that I knew where I was.

The hand-lettered sign on the fourth door was barely visible in the deepening twilight. It was the rear door of Colin's shop, and sure enough, there was *no* yellow tape. Sheila had said it wasn't high priority. It looked as if the crime-scene team wouldn't be here until morning.

Well, heck. There was nothing stopping me from getting that phone number. After all, I had a key, a possibly viable code for the alarm, and explicit permission from Ruby — who had explicit permission from

Colin — to enter the building. What more did I want? An invitation? I made a quick left into the empty parking lot next to the First Baptist Church and parked under a large pecan tree, next to a blue Mercury with BOOK 1 vanity plates. Darla McDaniel's car. Darla, who went to high school with Ruby, owns Bluebonnet Books, on the other side of Colin's shop.

I reached under the seat and felt around until I found the flashlight McQuaid insists I keep there. Still looking for excuses, I told myself that if the batteries didn't work, I couldn't go in. I didn't want to stumble around in the dark in an unfamiliar store, and I didn't want to turn on the lights. Somebody walking past the front of the store might think I was a thief and call the cops.

The flashlight worked. With a sigh, I took it, got out, and locked the car. There were several other cars in the lot and from the direction of the church came the sound of a tinny piano and a warble of high soprano voices singing "Unlock the Gate and Let Me In." The Baptist choir, under the baton of Mrs. Reedy, practicing for the Sunday service. As invitations go, it sounded pretty explicit to me. But I had to hurry if I intended to get my business done and get out of here before they finished.

There was a single dim security light in the church lot, but the alley itself was shadowed. I jumped and caught my breath when an orange tabby cat leaped from a garbage can, knocking off the lid with a noisy clatter. I reached the back door of Colin's shop and took the key out of the pocket of my jeans. I stuck it into the door and stopped, remembering the alarm. What was the code? Oh, yes: 1963 — or maybe 1962. I punched in the numbers, then turned the key, holding my breath. I felt a surge of pure relief as the door swung open into a chill darkness. There was no clanging alarm. All that could be heard were the opening strains of "Nearer My God to Thee." I hoped it was not an omen.

I stepped into the back room, locked the door behind me, and turned on the flashlight, shining it around to get my bearings. The small stockroom was filled with shelves stacked with merchandise and cardboard boxes piled everywhere. In one corner was a table, topped with a computer and monitor, a green light glowing eerily. I shivered. Colin had been the last person to operate that computer, and he was dead. But like the house, this place seemed to harbor no ghosts, restless or otherwise. It was chilly and dark, but the shadows that lurked in the corners belonged there.

Opposite the alley door was the door to the front of the store. I went to it, turned off the flashlight, and opened it cautiously.

There was a small security light in the wall above the cash register, but the front part of the store was palely lit by the streetlight that shone through the shop windows. The shop looked pretty much as it had when I was last here with Ruby. It was filled with merchandise designed to appeal to environmentally aware consumers and to the college kids at CTSU. There were books about how to save the environment, neat displays of environmentally friendly lightbulbs, recycled rubber and plastic stuff, nontoxic cleaners, biodegradable detergents, and racks of chic hemp clothing, as well as hemp bags and backpacks, hemp hats and sandals, hemp twine and yarns, hemp bath and body products, and hemp foods: hemp coffee, hemp pasta, even (swear to God) hemp brownie mix.

There is an irony here, of course. You can legally sell all of these hemp products in the United States, but you'd better not try to grow the stuff to produce them. Hemp was criminalized, along with marijuana, back in the 1940s. It can be grown in many countries, including Canada, but if you try to grow it in your herb garden, the DEA can come along and pop a pair of handcuffs on your gardening gloves.

I thought about this irony as I made my way behind the counter, keeping to the shadows, and an uncomfortable idea began to take shape in my mind. Hemp and marijuana — both of them called *Cannabis sativa* — are siblings. When I first met him, Colin was already an active member of the local Legalize Hemp movement, which picked up steam a couple of years ago. For decades, would-be hemp growers have tried to get the plant decriminalized, and Legalize Hemp organizations have sprouted all over the country, hoping to achieve what Canadian growers achieved some years back: the right to grow the plant legally and harvest the benefits thereof.

Cannabis sativa — hemp — might not be on the list of all-time favorites for those who think of herbs as lovable little plants that add flavor, fragrance, and spice to our lives. Hemp is a multi-use herb, an environmentally benign plant whose fibers, oils, leaves, and seeds have been used by humans for many thousands of years. Hemp ropes made commerce possible, and hemp sails and rigging took ships across trackless oceans.

Hemp paper is stronger than paper made from trees and can be farmed more sustainably and profitably than forests. Hemp has been turned into long-wearing carpets, fine textiles, nutritious cooking oil, durable motor oil, sturdy construction materials, nontoxic paints, and more. And if the truth be told, the pressure to continue criminalizing hemp comes mostly from the companies whose products it might supplant, for it has been scientifically demonstrated that this branch of the *Cannabis* family doesn't contain enough THC — the psychoactive chemical in marijuana — to get anybody high. You can smoke industrial hemp from now until next Sunday and you'll still see the world in the same old boring way.

But now I had to wonder whether Colin's support of hemp might have had something to do with his death. Had he made some powerful enemies in the movement, or outside of it? Or maybe hemp wasn't the only *Cannabis* that interested him. As Dan Reid, he had certainly been involved with drug distribution networks. In fact, he'd been convicted for alerting a drug dealer who was about to be arrested. Maybe Reid had served his time, gotten out of jail, and decided to cash in on what he knew by becoming a dealer himself. It was an unpleasant thought, especially because of Ruby. I pushed it to the back of my mind as I got on with what I had come to do, but I had to admit the possibility.

I was standing beside the cash register, and there was enough light to see that the calendar Ruby had described was not on the counter. *Rats.* I had made all this effort for nothing. I knelt down, turned on the flashlight, and began to search the shelves under the counter. Finally, just as I was ready to call it quits, I found the darn thing, pushed behind some empty plastic bank bags. I sat cross-legged on the floor with the flashlight in my hand and the calendar on my lap and began turning the pages.

Last Friday, nothing. Two Fridays ago, nothing. And then, three Fridays ago, I found it: the name *Lucita* and a local phone number, written in Ruby's scrawly hand-writing. I tore out the page for December 25 — Colin wouldn't be here for Christmas — found a pencil, and copied it down.

I was putting the calendar back where I'd found it when I heard the sound of the back door opening. Someone — someone who had a key and knew the alarm code — had just come into the back of the store. My breath caught, my blood ran cold, and the hair rose on my arms. I couldn't get to the front door without being spotted, and the unknown intruder — the person who had killed Colin? — was blocking the back door. I had to find someplace to hide, and fast. I thrust the calendar page into the pocket of my jeans, turned off the flashlight, and made for the nearest refuge: a rack of hemp shirts and pants hanging at the far end of the counter, near the front door. Breathless, I sank down on the floor behind the rack and pushed the garments apart just enough to see who was coming through the door to the back room.

But whoever it was — a slender figure, dressed in black — did the same thing I had done: opened the door and slid along the wall silently, keeping to the shadows. The figure reached the counter, stepped behind it, came as far as the cash register, and stopped, reaching for something on the shelf. Then the figure did something to the register, hit several keys, and the cash drawer came open with a metallic *ping.* A hand went into the till. I was caught between wanting to stop the thief and not wanting to be discovered — or tackle somebody who was better armed than I.

But then a car passed by on the street and its headlights flickered across the thief's face. A girl's face. A girl still in her teens.

I stood, pushed the clothes apart, and stepped forward, shining my flashlight full on her face. "What the hell do you think you're doing?" I demanded, in my deepest, meanest, most threatening voice.

It had the desired effect. She gasped, shrieked, and threw a dozen bills into the air. "Don't shoot!" she cried, putting up her hands and backing against the wall. "Oh, please! Don't shoot!"

"You've got a lot of nerve, stealing out of the register," I growled. "How did you get in?"

"I . . . I used my key," the girl whimpered. She had a bouncy blond ponytail, plastic-rimmed glasses, and a bad case of acne on her forehead. Skinny as a rail, she couldn't have been any more than eighteen or nineteen. "And I'm not stealing, honest, I'm not! Mr. Fowler owes me for two full Saturdays and a Monday night. Twenty hours. Somebody told me he got killed and I . . . I didn't know how to . . ." She swallowed. "I've found another job, but I really need the money. I was afraid that if I didn't get over here, I wouldn't be able to get it."

I should have guessed. The college student who worked for Colin. "What's your name?"

"Marcy," she said breathlessly. "Marcy Windsor . . . I've worked here for the last three months. I didn't punch a clock or anything like that, and Mr. Fowler always paid me out of the register, instead of writing me a check. So I was afraid I couldn't . . ." Her voice trailed away.

Out of the register, huh? Which meant that Colin wasn't withholding taxes or Social Security. Oh, well. It's a common enough evasion among small businesses, and it didn't involve a large amount of money. The girl was right. If she went through the usual channels, she'd end up without a dime. I had to admire her for having the gumption to come looking for her money, but I wasn't about to let her know that.

"So you thought you'd just help yourself," I said with a dry chuckle.

"He owes me, doesn't he?" she demanded defensively. "But there aren't any records, and I can't prove it. So I thought —" She frowned and held up her hand, shielding her eyes from the light. "Hey, just a darn minute. Who are *you*? What are *you* doing here, in the dark? Are you a cop? Why were you hiding behind —"

"How much does Mr. Fowler owe you?"

"Eight dollars an hour for twenty hours. A hundred and sixty dollars altogether. But I owed him seven dollars and thirty cents for lunch, which makes a hundred fifty-two seventy. He was supposed to pay me on Monday night, but —" She stopped. "You're not a cop, are you? I bet you don't have a gun. Who *are* you? Are you a friend of Mr. Fowler's? What are you —"

"Okay, Marcy," I said. "Find a piece of paper and write down your full name, address, and phone number, and the amount you're taking out of the register. Then put the key on the counter and pick the money up off the floor."

She stared at me, her eyes widening behind her glasses. Someday, after the acne, she was going to be a very pretty girl. "You mean, I get to take it?"

"You earned it, didn't you?" There was no point in a college kid getting tangled up in the settlement of Colin Fowler's business, which could go on for months. She might as well take the money and run. But not before I asked her a few questions. "Did Mr. Fowler ever mention a woman named Lucita?"

Marcy looked uneasy. "Lucita? Well, maybe. I know I've talked to her. She phoned a couple of times."

"Do you know her?"

"I never met her, if that's what you're asking." The girl bent over and picked up the bills from the floor. "She was a bookkeeper, or something like that. The calls were about some . . . some plants Mr. Fowler was supposed to pick up."

"Plants?" I thought of *Cannabis.* "Any special kind of plants?"

She tucked the money into her fanny pack, adding some coins out of the till. "I don't know. Just plants, I guess." She straightened up, not quite meeting my eyes. She knew more than she was telling, I was sure of it. But I'd let it go for now. I could talk to her later.

I took the calendar page out of my pocket and handed it to her. "Name, address, phone number, please," I said, nodding to a cup of pens on the counter. I watched as she wrote it all down, so fast that I knew she wasn't making it up.

She handed the page back to me. "Do they . . . do they have any idea who killed him?"

"Do you?"

She shook her head numbly. "I can't even imagine it. He was . . . strange. But nice. Easy to work for. He never hassled me about . . . stuff."

"Did you ever hear anybody threaten him? Did you ever witness any arguments?"

"Arguments?" She pulled her brows together, hesitating. She started to say something, stopped, and started again, on what I thought was a different track. "Well, I heard Mr. Fowler and Mr. Mueller arguing about the roof. It leaks pretty bad, and Mr. Mueller is supposed to fix it."

"Wilford Mueller, from the antique shop next door?"

"That's the one." She nodded distastefully. "He owns this place. Mr. Fowler was trying to get him to repair the leaks. Mr. Mueller kept putting it off, even though it's in the lease that he's responsible. They had a few heated discussions about that."

I'd bet. Wilford Mueller, who owns half the block, has a reputation as an unpleasant landlord. There had been some real trouble last year, when he tried and failed to get some of his other property rezoned. I wasn't surprised to hear that he and Colin had had their differences. "Other than that, did you ever see or hear anything that might suggest that somebody wanted to kill Mr. Fowler?"

"Not . . . not really." She bit her lip, and I wondered if she was going to tell me what was on her mind. But whatever it was, she filed it away. I'd have to come back for it later. "This was a quiet place to work. Nothing exciting ever happened, and Mr. Fowler was very nice, always polite and friendly. I

167

couldn't believe it when I found out he was dead."

"That makes two of us," I said quietly, remembering the still figure sprawled in the yucca, like a scene from a TV cop show. I took one of the store's business cards, turned it over, and wrote my home phone number on the back. "If I have other questions, I'll call you. And if you think of anything else, call me." I handed the card to her. "Now, go on, scoot. Get out of here."

She scooted, in a hurry, anxious to be gone. I waited until I heard the alley door close, gave it a few minutes more, then made my way through the back room and out. Full dark had fallen, but Mrs. Reedy and her choir were still at it, having moved to a thrilling arrangement of "God Moves in a Mysterious Way" in which the basses and tenors were doing most of the work.

I was closing the door behind me when a low, husky voice spoke out of the darkness, making me jump.

"Is it true?" the voice asked breathlessly. "Don't tell me it's true!"

I turned to see Darla McDaniel, her bulk enveloped in a purple crocheted shawl. She was wearing a red hat decorated with purple feathers. Darla is the Rodeo Queen of the Cowgirl Girlfriends, the local Red Hat chapter. She had just come out of the Blue-bonnet Bookstore's back door, a large box of books in her arms.

"Is what true?" I asked cautiously. Because of her association with the Cowgirls, Darla has a finger in every pie in town. She might have been talking about anything, from a scandal involving Mayor Pauline Perkins to the rumor that Constance Letterman was selling the Craft Emporium, next door to my shop.

But Darla was talking about Fowler. "I heard that . . . that Colin was . . . murdered," she said breathlessly. She set the box of books on the ground and pulled the shawl tighter around her, shivering slightly. Her loose gray dress, printed all over with large purple and red hibiscus flowers, hung straight down from her sizable breasts to her thick ankles. Darla and Ruby went to Pecan Springs High School together, and both were on the same cheerleading squad. They were also both in love with the same high-school quarterback. Darla had worked very hard to marry the guy. But he turned out to be a bad bargain, the marriage was a bummer, and Darla has resented Ruby ever since — for not trying harder, I guess.

Darla pulled down her mouth in a pitying smile. "Poor Ruby," she said. "I understand that she and Colin were . . . involved." She made *involved* sound like it was Ruby's dirty little secret. "This must be very hard on her, with her mother in such a precarious mental state."

Oh, for pity's sake. Darla McDaniel is one of Pecan Springs most notorious tale-tellers. If she knew that Ruby's mother was having difficulties, everybody else in town knew it, too. And whether Hark put Colin's death on the front page of the *Enterprise* or buried it on page six, they no doubt also knew all about it, and how he had died.

I paused. The choir had stopped singing, but Mrs. Reedy filled the silence, tremulously demonstrating a difficult soprano passage. It wouldn't hurt to ask Darla a few questions, since her bookstore was right next door to Colin's shop, and since she is such a dedicated snoop.

"I wonder," I said, "whether you might know who Colin's friends are." I paused. "At the Chamber of Commerce, maybe?" Darla had been the Chamber secretary for four or five years.

"Friends?" If she wondered why I was interested, she didn't let on. "Well, not at the Chamber. He wasn't the kind to hang around and trade chitchat after the meetings. He was always very businesslike, which didn't make him terribly popular." She tilted her head to one side. "If you know what I mean."

I knew. To win friends and influence people in the Pecan Springs Chamber of Commerce, you have to be one of the good ol' boys, even if you're a good ol' girl. Colin was neither.

"Still," she added hastily, condemning with faint praise, "Colin wasn't a bad man. Not at all. He paid his Chamber dues on time, and his assessments — which is more than you can say for a lot of folks. When I asked him for a donation to the United Way, he was very generous. And he helped out at the Merchants' Pancake Breakfast last month, when the flu bug was going around and all our flapjack flippers called in sick."

"Gosh," I said in a genial tone, "I'm sorry I missed that. I would like to've seen Colin Fowler flipping flapjacks."

There was a silence. Mrs. Reedy had stopped singing, and the piano moved into the crashing notes of "Onward Christian Soldiers" as the choir girded its figurative loins to go out and do battle with the unwashed ungodly.

"But I'm afraid Mr. Fowler did have an enemy or two," Darla went on, tucking a stray strand of hair behind her ear. "He and

Wilford Mueller were always going around and around about the roof, which Mr. Mueller had got his back up about. And there was an argument with another man, just last week."

She bent to pick up the box, then put a hand to her hip. "Oh, dear," she said faintly. "My sciatica is acting up something fierce. I've been taking painkillers, but they make me groggy. Maybe you know something that would help. Some herb or another. "

"You might try Saint-John's-wort," I said. "People have been using it for centuries to treat their sciatica." I bent over and hoisted the box. "If you've got a bad back, you really shouldn't be carrying anything heavy, Darla. Let me help."

"Oh, would you?" she cooed. "China, you are such a *sweetie.* My car is right over there, in the lot." She rummaged in her large straw handbag for the keys as I carried the box to her Mercury. She opened the trunk and I put it in. "Why do you suppose the choir has to practice that hymn?" she asked plaintively. "Don't they already know it?"

"Maybe it's one of Mrs. Reedy's favorites," I said, closing the trunk. "You mentioned an argument," I added. "Was it recent?"

"Last week sometime." She considered. "But maybe argument isn't the right word. It happened in this very spot. Reverend Berry lets the merchants park here during the week. We don't have a lot of our own, and the meters are so expensive. I've been trying to get the Council to buy that vacant lot on the other side of Lila Jennings' diner and turn it into a parking area. But the mayor says Chief Dawson wants some new armored vests for the police department, and the city can't afford both." She made a face, indicating displeasure with the city's priorities. "Really, you'd think the police could get along with what they have, wouldn't you?"

"I guess it depends on your priorities," I said. Getting Darla McDaniel to the point is like trying to herd cats. "What were you saying about the argument?"

She adjusted her shawl. "Well, they weren't yelling or anything, so maybe it was more like a serious discussion. I'd never seen the other man before, but I wondered if he might be a police officer. He wasn't wearing a uniform, but he had that look."

"What look?"

She shrugged carelessly. "Oh, you know. Blond, crew-cut, clean-shaven. A Boy Scout. Big, burly shoulders. Big hands. Held himself very straight."

Very straight with burly shoulders and big hands was definitely a cop look. "What were they discussing?"

"Money." She leaned closer, an eager, conspiratorial look on her face. "The man said Colin owed him."

"How much?"

She pulled back, offended. "For heaven's sake, China, you know me better than that. I don't eavesdrop on private conversations. It isn't any of my business how much Colin Fowler owed anybody." She tossed her head. "Besides, they stopped talking when they saw me."

I suppressed a smile. "I just thought perhaps the man might have mentioned an amount. Or maybe he said something like, 'You owe me,' like maybe Colin owed him a favor."

Darla looked dubious. "I don't think it was a favor. His tone was sort of threatening. But you're right. The way he said it sounded like it was . . ." She stopped.

"Like payback time, maybe?"

"Yes, that's it, exactly!"

Payback time. I wondered if the blond, burly man was a friend of one of the Dallas Dirty Dozen. "And you didn't hear anything else?"

"No, that's all." She frowned. "I really hope Ruby's going to be all right. The shock of Colin's murder, together with her mother's situation —" She looked at me, her eyes bright and inquiring. "How is her mother, by the way, China? One of my Red Hatters told me that there was a problem at Dillard's — something about Doris forgetting to pay for some scarves and an alligator bag?"

I refrained from rolling my eyes. Here in Pecan Springs, the grapevine rivals NASCAR for speed and Google for comprehensiveness, and some of the subcultures — the boys at Beans, the Red Hatters, the herb guilders — move the gossip even faster. But Fredericksburg is sixty miles away, for Pete's sake. You'd think there'd be a few roadblocks in the information superhighway.

"She forgot to stop at the cash register on the way out," I said. "Sometimes older people don't always remember the details."

"Oh, absolutely," she trilled in a tone that made clear that she didn't believe me but that it was perfectly okay with her if we both pretended. She opened the car door and slid in. "Please tell Ruby my prayers are with her at this difficult time," she added in a saccharine voice. "If there's anything I can do — anything at all — be sure to let me know."

"Oh, I will," I lied, and waved as she drove away.

A moment later, I was back in my car. I thought for a moment, then pulled the calendar Christmas page out of my pocket and picked up my cell phone. I punched in the number I'd copied from Ruby's note. On the fourth ring, an answering machine clicked on.

"You have reached the Sonora Nursery," a woman said. "Our regular hours are eight to six, Monday through Saturday. We're closed on Sunday. We can't take your call right now, but if you would like to leave a message —"

I clicked off the connection. Well, there it was, the answer to a couple of sizable questions. Sonora, which is located on the east side of Pecan Springs, specializes in plants from the Southwest, South America, and Mexico, like the blue-green agave, *Agave tequilana,* that I bought from them when they first opened. This succulent has long fleshy leaves with sharp-pointed tips. When it's about five years old, it puts up a fifteen-foot stalk that is topped with yellow flowers. The mother agave is diligently putting out litters of pups — agave offshoots — which I have potted up and offer for adoption to friends and customers. In fact, I had several nice-looking pots sitting beside my garage, just ready to go.

Sonora used to be owned by Wanda Rathbottom, who called it Wanda's Wonderful Acres. My first connection with Allan and Betty Conrad — Sonora's owners — came through Wanda, who asked me to give them my opinion about their chances for succeeding as nursery owners in Pecan Springs. That was a couple of years ago, before they bought the place, while they were still debating whether to open a nursery here or in Brownsville, where Allan had managed a greenhouse for a local grower.

Here's the story — the part of it that I know, anyway. Wanda had gotten into some serious financial trouble and had to sell her Wonderful Acres or lose everything to the bank. The Conrads were interested, but worried that it might be bad luck (or bad judgment) to take over a failing business. In a couple of serious, extended discussions during which I got to know the couple pretty well, I assured them that Wanda's business failure had nothing to do with poor location or lack of customers, actual or potential. She failed because of her own bad management, pure and simple. It was not quite the message Wanda intended me to give them, but it was the truth, as least as I saw it.

The Conrads listened, came back with some questions, and then bought Wanda out. They gave the Wonderful Acres a complete makeover and their venture, called Sonora Nursery, has become a great success. They've brought in some interesting, hard-to-find plants, especially agaves and yuccas, which are among their specialties. They advertise widely and the place, which always looks terrific, attracts crowds of customers. I didn't know anybody by the name of Lucita who worked there — as a bookkeeper, according to Marcy — but they've hired quite a few people recently. Lucita was probably new.

Sonora was closed now, of course. I could drive over there in the morning and poke around, although Lucita no longer seemed like much of a lead. That handsome agave and those potted yuccas I'd seen in Colin's backyard — it was dollars to doughnuts that they came from Sonora. The calls from Lucita and the note, too, on an envelope with what I now recognized as Sonora's logo, were probably related to his purchase of the plants. Maybe he had charged them, and she called to verify the account. Or maybe his check had bounced, and she called to let him know. I smiled wryly at Ruby's jealousy of a potential significant other and my eagerness to make something out of nothing. So much for *Cannibis.*

I turned the key in the ignition. This had taken longer than I thought, and it was time to head home. Besides, the choir members were starting to come out of the church. If I sat here any longer, somebody was bound to come up and tell me how sorry she was to hear that Colin Fowler had been murdered and ask whether Ruby's mother had stolen any more scarves lately.

CHAPTER EIGHT

Damiana is an herbal shrub that grows throughout Mexico, Central America, and the West Indies. It produces yellow blossoms and small, sweet-smelling fruits that taste like figs. The botanical name for the plant, *Turnera aphrodisiaca,* reflects its traditional use as an aphrodisiac. A Spanish missionary first reported that the Indians of Mexico made a drink from the damiana leaves, added sugar, and drank it to enhance lovemaking. It has also been used to treat depression and anxiety, as well as diabetes and a variety of intestinal and respiratory ailments. It is commercially available as a liqueur. The dried leaves can be brewed as a tea.

Two hours later, McQuaid and I were upstairs in our bedroom, getting ready for bed. He and Brian had been late coming home, because when the soccer game was over, they had gone with Blackie Blackwell — the Adams County sheriff and McQuaid's longtime fishing and poker buddy — to San Marcos to look at some antique guns for sale. Now, Brian was staying up late to finish his English paper (under the sleepy supervision of Howard Cosell), and McQuaid was in an exultant mood, having added a valuable Remington 1889 open-hammer shotgun with twin twenty-eight-inch barrels to his gun collection. McQuaid takes his guns seriously.

He pulled off his plaid shirt. "How did Ruby handle the news about Fowler?" he asked, tossing the shirt into the hamper. We have come a long way from the early days of our live-in relationship, when I'd threaten to nail his used underwear to the floor unless it was properly disposed of.

"It was a killer," I said, pulling off my jeans. "To make things worse, she has to move her mother to an assisted-living apartment tomorrow. Her sister can't get to Fredericksburg to help until Sunday, so Ruby has her hands full. Which I guess is a good thing," I added, unbuttoning my blouse. "I'm sure it would be a lot harder for her if she had to sit around and think about things." Of course, Ruby would never just sit around and think. If she were here, she would be obstructing justice as much as possible — another reason to be glad that she was stuck in Fredericksburg.

"Any developments in the investigation?" McQuaid's eyes lightened as he watched me take off my blouse. He hasn't been a cop for several years and is now allied with the tribe of private investigators, many of whom don't have much respect for the police. But McQuaid still has a cop's elitist ideas about who is qualified to poke around a crime scene, and I am not one of the anointed. I had already decided against telling him about my after-hours drop-in visit to Good Earth Goods.

However, he didn't seem terribly interested in the investigation just now. He was more interested in investigating me, an interest I was more than willing to encourage. I put my arms around his waist, leaned against his chest, and raised my lips for his kiss. He unhooked my bra, put his hand on my bare breast and whispered huskily, "I want you, China. God, I want you."

I returned his kiss with an unrestrained passion that testifies well to the health and sexual vitality of this marriage. We were still engaged in this mutually satisfying enterprise when the phone rang.

"Drat," I muttered.

"It's probably Jim Hawk," McQuaid said. "Don't go away — I'll call him back." One arm still around me, he reached out to snag the receiver. "Yo, buddy," he said. Then he rolled his eyes and handed the receiver to me. "For you," he said shortly. "Ruby." He went into the bathroom.

"Yo, buddy?" Ruby asked.

"Man talk for 'What are you up to tonight, pal?' How is your mother?"

"Much quieter, thanks to the lavender and the herbal tea," Ruby replied. "I made up a clean bed and put some of the lavender oil on her pillow and in her bath, too. She drank a cup of tea — chamomile and passionflower — and she's finally gone to sleep. Thank God. Let's hope it lasts." She paused. "Did you find Lucita's telephone number?"

"Dang," I said. "I knew there was something I was supposed to do."

"China!" Ruby wailed disconsolately. "Don't tell me you didn't —"

"I did, I did," I said hastily. I glanced toward the bathroom. McQuaid had shut the door and turned on the shower, but I lowered my voice anyway. "I had to hunt for the calendar, but the phone number was just where you said it was. I checked it out. It's the Sonora Nursery. Lucita turns out to be the bookkeeper there. Apparently Colin was buying some plants." I didn't say anything about my *Cannabis* suspicion since it was now entirely moot — just another false lead. "He probably didn't pay his bill, or there was a question about his account, something like that."

"She's a bookkeeper?" Ruby asked, surprised. "How'd you learn that?"

"I got it from Marcy."

"Marcy?" Ruby was mystified. "Who is *she?* How does she know about Lucita?"

I related the tale of the ponytailed ex–shop clerk who had dropped in to raid Colin's cash register. At the end, I added, "According to Marcy, Colin and Wilford Mueller were feuding about the roof. Apparently, Mueller refused to make the repairs Colin thought were necessary. Do you know anything about that?"

"Colin mentioned it," Ruby replied. "He was pretty angry about it. In fact, he was threatening to take Mueller to court and force him to live up to the terms of the lease." I could almost hear her frowning. "Wilford Mueller is a terrible old man, China. Do you remember what he did to Winnie Hatcher last year?"

"What he was *alleged* to have done," I reminded her dryly. "If you will recall, Mueller was never charged with the crime."

Wilford Mueller had petitioned the city council to give him a zoning variance on a rental property on the east side of town, and Winnie Hatcher — who is always outspoken about environmental concerns — cast the vote that kept him from getting it. For a small man, Mueller can make a lot of noise, and when he flew into a rage and began screaming swear words it took three guys to hustle him out of the council chambers. The next morning, Winnie got up to find the word BITCH painted in large red letters on the front of her house, and a gallon of red paint spilled across the porch floor. Unfortunately, nobody saw Mueller doing his dirty work, and he was smart enough not to leave any forensic evidence. The police hauled him in for questioning, but when he maintained his innocence and there was no proof to the contrary, they had to let him go.

"I think you ought to talk to Wilford Mueller," Ruby said decidedly.

"I think Smart Cookie ought to talk to him," I said. "It's her case, you know. She's got the leverage to pry out what he knows, if anything. She can threaten him with jail — I can't." I paused. "We've got another lead for her, too." I told Ruby about the guy with the cop haircut that Darla had seen arguing with Colin in the First Baptist parking lot.

"Darla isn't very trustworthy," Ruby cautioned. "She sees what she wants to see."

"So does everybody else," I said. "We'll let Sheila sort that one out, too."

"But you're going to find this Lucita person and talk to her," Ruby pressed.

"I really don't think that's necessary. Lucita was probably trying to get in touch with Colin about his account, or something like that. It's not worth —"

"Oh, but it *is*," Ruby insisted. "I have the strongest feeling that you should talk to this person. It's *important*."

I don't usually need any special encouragement for a visit to Sonora, and I've learned to respect Ruby's hunches, even when they don't make any sense. Anyway, it wouldn't do any good to say no, or even maybe. Not when she insists. "Okay, okay. I'll go."

"Thank you." She sounded relieved. "I can't explain why this matters. It just does. But there's something else, China, maybe even more important. I remembered it when I was getting a carton out of the closet for Mom tonight. Colin left a box at my house awhile back." Her voice became bleak and sad. "He was coming over to pick it up the night he was killed, but he never got there."

"Yes," I said slowly. "I remember your saying that." Of course, at the time, it was only a mention-in-passing, without any special significance. But that was before Colin was killed. Now, it mattered. Or maybe it mattered. "The box is still there, I suppose."

She took a breath. "Yes, on the shelf in the guest-room closet. An old shoebox."

"What's in it?"

"Pictures, he said. But of course I haven't gone through them," she added hastily.

"You haven't?" I was surprised. Ruby is not widely known for her self-restraint.

"Well, I might have peeked, just a little," she conceded. "It was only photos of guys on a hiking trip in the jungle. But now I wonder whether there's something else in the box, something I missed." Her voice cracked. "Anyway, Colin is dead now. Somebody murdered him. And I think we ought to know more about those photos, don't you? Maybe there's a clue to his killer."

"Maybe."

"Good. I'm glad you agree. So why don't you go over to my house right now and get it? You've still got a key to my front door, don't you? You can look at the stuff there, or take it back home with you, whichever."

"Right now?" I glanced down at my mostly naked self. "Sorry, Ruby. That's out of the question. The only place I'm going is bed, with my husband. Anyway, I don't think it's so urgent that —"

"Of course you don't," she snapped. "You always think that the police are going to solve a crime, and that ordinary people shouldn't get involved because it's obstruction of justice or something like that. But deep in your heart, you know better, China Bayles. You've seen this happen before. The police are okay when it comes to collecting DNA and fingerprints and hair and all that technical forensic stuff, but they're not so good at finding out why people do things, or figuring out what's going on behind closed doors."

Ruby had a point, sort of. But before I could remind her that it was the "technical forensic stuff" that persuaded juries, she was going on, and getting more and more steamed up as she went.

"Anyway, I am definitely *not* going to invite the police to go and search my house, especially when I can't be there. They'd have to get a search warrant, wouldn't they?" Before I could say yes, she added, "And they might get the idea that they could search just anywhere — in my undie drawers or my medicine cabinet."

I chuckled. "They couldn't get a search warrant for your undie drawers, Ruby. Anyway, I need to know why —"

"Because there could be a clue to the killer in that box!" Ruby exclaimed heatedly. "What more reason can you want?"

"That isn't what I meant," I said patiently. "I'm curious about why Colin left those photos with you in the first place. There's plenty of storage room at *his* house — enough for a shoebox, certainly. What did he say about it?"

She didn't answer for a moment. "Why?" she repeated slowly. "Let me think." There was another pause. "I don't remember that he actually said *why* he was leaving them with me. He just said he wanted to and I said it was okay. Sort of no big deal, at the time." She whuffed out her breath. "If you won't go tonight, I guess tomorrow morning will do. First thing. But when you go, you may need to push on the front door, or bang on it or something. It's been sticking, and I haven't had time to get it fixed."

"I thought I was going to talk to Lucita first thing tomorrow," I objected.

"Right after that, then." There was a moment's silence, and when she spoke again her voice was heavy with grief and edged with anger. "I just want to find out the truth, China. I have to know what happened, and why. Somebody murdered him. I have to know *who*."

"I understand," I said penitently. Of course she was upset — who wouldn't be? It wouldn't hurt me to do what she asked — in the morning, though. Not tonight. "I'll go to Sonora and then to your house. But I really need to take —"

"And you'll call me as soon as you've learned anything?" she persisted.

In the background, I heard a door open, and Doris' querulous voice. "Ramona! Who is that you're talking to? If it's Ruby, tell her she has to get over here, right now. I don't understand why she doesn't come. I'm having a heart attack — doesn't she *care?*"

Ruby managed a small laugh. "I guess we need another cup of tea."

I abandoned what I had been about to say: that I intended to take Sheila or one of her officers with me to get that box. It might contain nothing but family photos or something equally innocuous, or it might contain evidentiary material. The O. J. Simpson case demonstrated that the evidence trail can be as important as the evidence itself, and we were definitely talking chain-of-custody here. A smart defense attorney can get evidence thrown out or discounted if he can show that it might have been tampered with somewhere, somehow, by some unknown person. I know. The custody card is one I've occasionally played myself. I wasn't going to load the deck against the prosecution.

"Fix the tea, dear," I said soothingly. "Drink some yourself, and then go to bed and get some sleep. It won't do your mother any good for you to fall apart." We said good night.

As I put down the phone, McQuaid came out of the bathroom, toweling his dark hair. He was still damp, butt naked, and very sexy. "How is she?" he asked.

"Sad. Angry. Trying hard not to lose her cool with her mother. Doris is in pretty bad shape." I went to him and put my hands on his shoulders, thinking how lucky I was that we were here together. "Yum." I kissed him. His lips were cool. They tasted like soap. "Yum, yum."

He put his arms around me and pulled me against him. "I'm glad your mother isn't losing her marbles," he said, nuzzling my neck.

"Or yours," I replied. I shivered as he blew into my ear. "Although there's always tomorrow." Doris had seemed to be all right just a few weeks ago, and now —

"No, there isn't." McQuaid made a lecherous sound deep in his throat. "There's only tonight, woman." And with that, he scooped me up and dropped me onto the bed.

"Tarzan," I said, pulling him down on top of me.

"You bet," he growled.

We had just got to the best part when the phone rang.

"Good grief," I said with resignation. "Ruby's probably thought of something else she wants me to do."

McQuaid said something disgusting and reached for the phone. He handed it to me. "Tell her you'll call back later."

I spoke blurrily into the phone. "McQuaid says I'll call back later."

"Come again?" asked a surprised voice, strong and assertively male.

I refrained from replying that I hadn't quite had time to come the first time and thrust the phone into McQuaid's hand. "It's not Ruby."

McQuaid sat up. "Yeah? Oh, Hawk." His voice warmed. "Hey, buddy. What'd you find out?"

Jim Hawk, Houston PD, Homicide Division, retired. There was a silence as McQuaid listened intently. I could hear a man's deep, resonant voice, but couldn't make out any of the words. But that was okay. I didn't want to. This was that business about my father — a mystery that I was content to leave unsolved.

"Oh, yeah?" McQuaid said with interest, when the man finished speaking. "What about Spurgin?"

Another silence, more listening. And then, "They were both working on the same couple of stories, huh? I guess that means I'd better drop in at the *Chronicle* and talk to Murray, if he's still there. He is? Well, that'll certainly simplify things."

A longer pause, McQuaid beginning to grin. "Hell, yes, Hawk, if you're interested. I can ask, but I can't guarantee that the client will ante up for an additional investigator."

The grin got wider as Hawk said something else. "In that case, welcome aboard, buddy. It'll be great to work with you again, too. I can get there by ten thirty. I'll swing past your place and pick you up." And with that, he hung up the phone and turned eagerly to me.

"Hawk pulled both the Vine and the Spurgin files this afternoon. Turns out that the cold-case team took a look at both of the cases last year and dug up some interesting connections in the stories the two journalists were working on. The team couldn't find enough to warrant reopening the cases for a full investigation, but at least we're not starting from scratch. Luckily, Clyde Murray is still at the *Chronicle.* If I suggest that there might be a story in this, he may let me have a look at the reporters' notes. And Hawk wants to work on the case gratis, for old time's sake. He's a good man, and he's on the ground there in Houston. Might save me a few trips."

"Peachy keen," I said, folding my arms across my bare breasts. "Go get 'em, Chief."

He leaned on his elbow, looking down at me, one dark eyebrow quirking. "Hey. You're mad at me."

"I am not mad."

"Yes, you are. You're pouting." He touched my lower lip, which was only slightly protruding. "See that? That's a pout. But it's pretty. Kissable, too." He bent down and kissed it lightly.

I put my arms around his neck. "I'm not pouting."

He kissed me again, with greater dedication. "You're mad because I took your brother's case."

"Miles is not my brother. He's my *half* brother."

He kissed my throat. "Your half brother.

Your rich half brother, who can afford to hire a PI who hasn't brought in a paycheck lately." He kissed my breast. "Now, where were we when the phone rang?"

I took his hand and moved it to the right place. "There," I said. "That's where we were."

There were no more interruptions.

I dreamed about my father that night. In my dream, I am walking along the freeway where he died. It is dark, and raining, and I am wondering what I am doing out here by myself, without a jacket or umbrella, on such a wet, chilly night. A car, my father's blue Cadillac, roars past me fast, so fast the tires are smoking, like a cartoon car. And then it takes off — *ZOOM* — and sails over the guardrail, down the embankment, cartwheeling end over end until it reaches the bottom and bursts into a savage bloom of flame. I stand dispassionate and staring, thinking how sad it is that I can't cry, can't feel anything at all. And then Buddy is beside me, in the leather jacket and tight jeans he wore when we were teenagers, and he is crying, huge, ugly sobs that come from his gut and tear the night open. I think how odd it is that he can cry and I can't, and then the sky is split by a shriek of a siren so fierce that it shakes me.

When I awake, my face is wet with Buddy's tears.

CHAPTER NINE

BREAKFAST TACOS, SOUTHWEST STYLE

1 pound ground pork sausage
2 cloves garlic, minced fine
1 tablespoon balsamic vinegar
2–3 teaspoons chile powder
4 eggs
1 teaspoon ground cumin
1 green onion, chopped fine
1 Roma tomato, diced
1 cup diced cooked potatoes
salt and pepper to taste
8 ounces grated Cheddar cheese
8 flour tortillas
salsa

Fry sausage with garlic, vinegar, and chile powder until brown. Push to one side of the skillet. Beat eggs with cumin, onion, and tomato. Cook egg mixture in the skillet with the sausage, stirring until softly set. Add potatoes and mix all together. Add salt and pepper to taste. Warm flour tortillas in oven or microwave. Fill with sausage/egg/potato mixture. Sprinkle with cheese and roll tightly. Serve with salsa. Can be refrigerated or frozen and reheated in the microwave.

On spring mornings, McQuaid and I usually take our breakfasts onto the back porch, where we can enjoy the fruity scent of the Zepherine Drouhin rose that climbs the trellis and watch kamikaze hummingbirds looping-the-loop around the feeders. But this morning we were all in a hurry. McQuaid was going to Houston, so he was up by six and gone by seven, snatching the egg-sausage-potato taco I'd microwaved for him as he dashed out the door. He was barely out of sight when Brian clattered down the stairs, wolfed his taco, grabbed his books and overnight bag — this was the weekend of the Science Club's field trip to Lost Maples State Park — and made his usual last-minute beeline for the seven-ten school bus. Howard Cosell watched mournfully from the steps as his favorite kid disappeared down the lane. With his buddy away, Howard's school-year weekdays are blank, bleak, and boring, with nothing to do but nap and keep an eye out for obstreperous squirrels.

I went back upstairs, dressed hurriedly — it doesn't take long to put on yesterday's jeans, a Thyme & Seasons tee, and my favorite khaki vest with button-down cargo pockets — and phoned Sheila to tell her I was on my way to her house. Then I dropped four wrapped tacos in a bag and went out to the white Toyota that replaced my little blue Datsun, which I literally drove to death. I didn't intend to do any more digging into Colin's murder without discussing it first with Smart Cookie and getting her blessing. It's only in mystery novels that an amateur sleuth goes merrily off on her own investigation, risks death to nab a very nasty killer, and hauls him or her to the nearest police station (under citizen's arrest), where she is congratulated by the cops and the district attorney for correcting their investigative errors, tying up all their loose ends, and reestablishing order in the world.

It doesn't work that way in real life, and it shouldn't. Citizen arrests are fraught with peril and loaded with legal liability. Being sued for wrongful arrest, assault, or stalking can be an unpleasant, expensive experience. What's more, I keep my bar membership current, which makes me an officer of the court, which leads me to be conservative when it comes to things like evidence tampering and breaking and entering. I hate to run afoul of the law when it's not absolutely necessary.

The forecast predicted storms by evening, but the morning was cool, bright, and breezy. The sun was just coming up when I swung onto Sheila's street. She lives in a pretty, old-fashioned frame house with a wooden front porch swing, a white picket fence around a large yard, and a giant pecan tree out front that routinely produces enough pecans to keep the neighbors in pies all winter long. After she moved in, Ruby and I helped her Xeriscape her yard with rosemary, salvias, lantana, yucca, red-hot poker, daylilies, native grasses, and yaupon holly — plants that thrive with no extra water and almost no tending. In return, Sheila gave us each a big sack of pecans. She doesn't have the time to bake pecan pies or cope with prima donna plants that fall into a deep sulk when they don't get the attention they crave.

The chief was still in her pink silk pajamas, with a toothbrush in her hand. "It's a good thing you called," she said groggily, when she answered the doorbell. "I forgot to set the alarm clock." She rubbed her eyes with the back of her hand. "No telling how long

I would have slept if the phone hadn't rung."

"I hope you're hungry," I said, holding up the bag of tacos and heading for the kitchen. "I'll make coffee while you get dressed."

When she reappeared, nattily dressed in her blue and gray uniform and her blond hair scooped into a roll at the back of her head, the coffee was ready, the orange juice was poured, and the tacos were steaming from their three minutes in the microwave. I had even taken a minute to slip out the back door and snip a few daisies for the center of the table.

"Hey, nice," she said, casting an admiring eye over the table. She unwrapped a taco, added a hefty jolt of hot sauce, and tasted it. "Every bit as good as McDonald's."

"Better," I said, trying not to sound offended. "It's homemade, with low-fat sausage and no extra salt."

"Everybody needs salt," she replied in a matter-of-fact tone. She finished the first taco and added hot sauce to the second. "So you talked to Ruby yesterday? How did she handle it? Is she okay?"

"It was tough," I said bleakly. "Brutal. She had already resigned herself to losing him, but not this way. Nobody wants to do it like this."

"Of course." Sheila's face was grim. In some people's hearts, there's a place for everyone they have ever genuinely loved, no matter how long ago or how little. Surely, she must have many of the same feelings Ruby had, although they might be muted by time and distance and by the presence of other lovers in her life. But if that's what was in Smart Cookie's heart, she was not going to share it with me. Instead, she asked a cop's question, in a cop's hard voice.

"Did Ruby have any information that might shed some light on his murder?"

I matched her tone, starting with the most important item. "Colin left a shoebox in her guest-room closet. He was coming to pick it up the night he was killed. She's commissioned me to go and get it. I think you should come along."

"A shoebox?" She frowned. "I take it that it's not full of shoes."

"Photos, according to Ruby. If you're busy, send somebody else. If this turns out to be evidentiary material, you'll need a chain-of-custody —"

"I know what I need," she said crisply. "I'm just trying to remember what's on the calendar for today. I've got to be somewhere shortly, but it shouldn't take more than an hour. Will nine thirty be okay? I can meet you there. We can get into Ruby's house?"

"I've got a key." I picked up my orange juice. Nine thirty would give me time to get the box, then head for Thyme and Seasons. After all, I do have to work for a living, and the shop opens at ten. "There are a couple of other things," I added, "neither very important. I understand from Ruby and from Colin's part-time shop clerk that a woman named Lucita called him occasionally." I knew from the glint in Smart Cookie's eye that *L*-word had clicked, although I had cleverly avoided mentioning that I had read the note under the yucca pot. "She's a bookkeeper at Sonora."

"Sonora Nursery? Here in town?"

I nodded, wondering if she was making the connection to the logo on the envelope. "I also picked up some reliable gossip about Colin and Wilford Mueller, who have reportedly been at it hammer-and-tongs about a roof that needed fixing. And Darla McDaniel mentioned that she saw Colin having some sort of set-to with a guy in the First Baptist parking lot — a blond guy, big, burly, with a crew cut. He looked to her like a cop."

She frowned. "Like a cop?" I could see the wheels turning. Sheila knew about Colin's past history. If I could add two and two and come up with a dirty dozen, so could she. Was this a friend of the Dallas cops, looking for revenge?

"Like a cop, according to Darla. You might want to talk to her about it and see if she can give you a better description."

I paused, considering the peril I was in. For obvious reasons, I hadn't planned to tell Sheila that I had gone to Colin's shop. What I needed now was a distraction, to keep the chief from asking the next logical question: How had I managed to learn all this stuff in just over twelve hours? Something popped into my head and out my mouth before I gave it a second thought.

"Oh, and Ruby says to tell you that she intends to adopt Rambo."

As a distraction, it certainly worked. Sheila's eyes widened in alarm. "Ruby wants to adopt that monster? Take him to live with her?" She shuddered violently. "That's nuts. She doesn't know what she's saying."

I shrugged. "I guess she has a soft spot in her heart for orphans. Or maybe she wants to honor Colin's memory by taking care of his dog. Anyway, she asked me to go over there and feed and walk him, and I agreed."

"Well, I can think of better ways to honor Colin," Sheila retorted tartly. "A wreath at the cemetery, for instance. Wreaths don't bite. Wreaths don't leave big piles of dog poop in the yard." She shook her head. "I don't want to be unsympathetic, China, but if Ruby is going to do this idiotic thing, she has to do it right away. The neighbors are complaining about the barking, and they're terrified of that Rottweiler. He's dangerous."

"She can't pick him up," I said, frowning. This distraction was proving to be a problem. "She's stuck in Fredericksburg until Ramona comes on Sunday — and even then, she might not be able to get away. Doris is in pretty bad shape."

"Then I'll send somebody to get the dog and take him to the shelter," Sheila said flatly.

Sometimes I don't know what gets into me. In this case, maybe it was sympathy for a dog who was left all alone, through no fault of his own. I heard myself saying, "Don't do that, Sheila. I'll take him. It'll only be for a few days."

"You are as crazy as she is," Sheila said. "What about Howard Cosell? That Rottweiler will eat him up and won't even burp." Howard, who positively dotes on Smart Cookie, is the only dog she can tolerate. "Anyway, you ought to ask McQuaid before you make a commitment like this."

I shrugged. "Howard will pretend Rambo doesn't exist." Maybe. "McQuaid won't care." Much. "And Brian will be thrilled." Absolutely. In fact, I could count on Brian to keep Rambo happy and occupied evenings and weekends. The rest of the time, the dog could stay in Howard's dog run. Howard doesn't like to use it because it keeps him from chasing the squirrels.

"It's your funeral," Sheila said. There was a paper napkin on the table and she pushed it toward me. "Write down the names you mentioned, if you don't mind." She paused. "Especially that part-time clerk. Name, please, and address, if you know it. I'll want to talk to her."

Rats. The diversion had been good while it lasted, but it had reached a dead end. When Sheila talked to Marcy, she would find out about our nighttime encounter in Colin's shop. She'd probably think there were other things I hadn't told her, too, which would not make her happy. I'd better come clean right now and save us both a lot of trouble.

I put on my best mea culpa look. "I apologize, Sheila. I wasn't going to tell you this because I knew it would only complicate matters. The truth is that I was in Colin's shop yesterday evening, and I happened to —"

"In Colin's shop?" Sheila squawked, her jaw going slack. "What the *hell* were you doing there, China? That's a crime scene! You were trespassing! You were —"

"I was *not* trespassing," I said, in my firmest, most lawyerlike tone. "The shop was *not* posted as a crime scene, I made sure of that. There were no notices, no yellow tape. And there was nothing inside but merchandise." Well, almost nothing.

Sheila gave a disgruntled nod. "We had a domestic abuse case that escalated into a shooting yesterday afternoon, over on Dunbar Road. We were still working Colin's house and I needed some people at Dunbar. We never got to the shop." She gave me a sour look. "You know, if you weren't such a good friend, I'd arrest you for breaking and entering. In fact, I might do it anyway."

"I don't think so," I replied. "Ruby gave me her key *and* the alarm code and asked me to do a case-related errand for her, since she couldn't be here to do it herself."

Sheila eyed me. "Case-related?"

"A woman named Lucita had phoned the shop when Ruby was there. The call seemed urgent and personal, and she jotted the phone number down on Colin's shop calendar." I smiled disarmingly. "You know Ruby and her intuitions. She got the idea that you should know about it, so she gave me her key and asked me to get the number."

"Did you?"

"Yep." My leather shoulder bag was on the table and I pulled out the calendar page. "However, I seriously doubt that the woman had anything to do with Colin's death. I think she was calling about some plants he bought." I copied the Sonora number onto the paper napkin. "Oh, and the alarm code is nineteen sixty-three," I said, writing that down, too. "You don't want your people setting it off."

Sheila gave me a pointed look. "The clerk?"

"Marcy Windsor. Here's her address and phone number." As I wrote, I added, "She dropped by the store last night to pick up the back pay that Colin owed her — a hundred fifty-two seventy, which I let her take out of the register. She's the one who told me that Lucita works at Sonora."

"Hell's bells," Sheila muttered, looking at the napkin I handed her. "Why is it that you always know *everything?* And you always know it before anybody else."

"I don't know who killed him," I said gloomily. "Do you?"

"Not yet," Sheila replied, low and fierce. "But I will, damn it."

I wanted to ask her whether the search of Colin's house had turned up anything useful or interesting — drugs, a big stash of cash, a little black book full of names — but she was wearing her poker-player's face and I knew I wouldn't get anything out of her. If her cards were any closer to her vest, they'd be in her bra.

Sheila looked at the clock, pushed back her chair, and stood up. "I've got to go. I'm supposed to talk about safety to Jackie Barnes' third-graders over at Torres Elementary. It's just around the corner, but I'll be late if I don't hurry."

"You go on," I said. "I'll clear the table and lock up."

Nodding, she took her cop cap off the peg. "See you at nine thirty, at Ruby's."

I rinsed off the plates, put them in the drainer, and locked the door after me. I had a whole hour before I had to meet Sheila — time to go to Sonora and poke around. Talking to Lucita was probably a waste of effort, but I could at least verify my conclusion that her calls to Colin had to do with his account. And I could tell Ruby that I had acted on her hunch, which would make her happy. Anyway, I'm always glad to have an excuse to go to the nursery.

I get a rush from cultivating a successful relationship with a new and unusual plant. Our gardens are like our houses and neighborhoods: most of us are more comfortable with things and people and plants — maybe *especially* plants — that we've known for a long time. We're reluctant to accept something new and different, especially when what's available is a seedling or immature plant and we're not exactly sure what kind of care it requires or how big it will be or what it will look like when it grows up. It's not that we're prejudiced or narrow-minded, of course. We're just slow to accept something new. Our imaginations need to be educated.

Which is why display gardens are so valuable. A nursery can place mature specimens of exotics into a lovely setting that shows gardeners how the plants will look in *their* backyards. And that's what Allan Conrad and his wife, Betty, have done. They've landscaped the front part of their nursery so extensively that it looks like a botanical garden. It's a treat for me to walk around and admire their work. Learn from it, too. Some of the things I've learned (well, copied, if you want the truth) have shown up in my display gardens at Thyme and Seasons — although I couldn't begin to afford the landscaping the Conrads have done. Compared to them, I'm operating on a shoestring.

When you come through the gate at Sonora, the first thing you see is a large circular garden, some thirty or forty feet in diameter. In the middle is an eight-foot waterfall that plunges down a wall of rough limestone and into a shallow pool surrounded by showy clumps of exotic grasses; a tall, wooly Argentine saguaro cactus; several mature Mexican bamboo palms, still bearing a few bright red berries; and a monkey puzzle tree (*Araucaria araucana*) that looks like it might be at home on the African veldt, in the company of lions. The taller, bulkier plants are set off by ferns, cycads, cacti, and yuccas, all attractively and naturalistically arranged, their pots hidden by logs, rocks, and foliage.

The central garden isn't all, of course: another large garden features drought-tolerant plants that thrive in the kind of dry heat we have in the Hill Country — agaves and prickly pear and aloes, interplanted with a dozen varieties of yucca among large rocks, set off with an attractive gravel mulch. Sonora specializes in yuccas. They grow some, import many from Mexico, and distribute them to other nurseries. They also sell them on the Internet, and orders for potted yuccas arrive from and go out to all parts of the country. More power to them, I say. The Conrads' success is testimony to the transformative power of the American dream: it's possible to put your knowledge and skills to work, and succeed even beyond your furthest hopes.

Somewhere just inside the gate, I usually run into Allan Conrad with a watering wand in his hand, paying watchful attention to his plants — a good idea, considering the fact that they represent a sizable investment. Allan is a short, heavyset man with brown eyes, dark hair, and a thick dark mustache, who always wears a plaid shirt, jeans, and a white straw hat. When we were discussing the purchase of Wanda's nursery, I learned that he got his start in his father's nursery in Phoenix, where he met and married Betty, a pretty Mexican-American with a couple of young kids. She was born in Brownsville, a sprawling Texas town on this side of the Rio Grande, across from its Mexican sister-city, Matamoras.

After several years, the Conrads moved from Phoenix to Brownsville, where Betty wanted to raise her children. Allan got a good job with a wholesale grower who imported and distributed plants from Latin America and began learning more of the aspects of his trade. An experienced plantsman, he often returns to Mexico, taking long and arduous trips through the forests and mountains looking for exotic plants that might be cold-hardy enough to survive in American landscapes and gardens. He brings back seeds and cuttings and propagates the plants, with the hope that some of them will be interesting and adaptable enough to find an American market.

And they have — at least, that's the way it looks from the outside. Sonora has become the most successful nursery in the area — in all of Central Texas, actually. I've often wondered how they do it, given the notorious difficulty of making a success of the nursery business. The advertising, the facilities, the nursery stock, the labor — everything costs twice as much as you think it's going to. You need an enormous amount of capital to make it all work.

Allan hasn't done it by himself, of course. Betty, a slender, sweet-faced woman with a certain air of innocence about her, works in the garden and at the cash register, as well as managing the family home, a small house directly behind the greenhouses. The nursery and the children keep her so busy that she doesn't have much time for herself, but I invited her to join our local herb society and she's been faithful about attending the meetings — helpful, too, since she knows so much about the native plants of the Southwest. And I gave her a hand with a minor legal matter having to do with one of her employees. No biggie, but she was grateful and I was pleased to be able to do something useful for her.

Allan and Betty have other help, as well. Every day after school, you'll find Betty's two teenaged children, Ricky and Jeannette, hard at work in the greenhouse. A bright, energetic boy of seventeen, Ricky says he wants to be a plantsman like his stepfather; Jeannette, one of Brian's classmates, is hoping to major in botany when she goes to college. Sonora is a family business.

The nursery is separated from the parking lot by a pink adobe fence, with a double wooden gate in the center, painted an electrifying blue. The gate was still closed, latched but not locked, but since it was after eight, I knew they were open. I lifted the latch, pushed open the gate, and walked past the central garden, where the waterfall was splashing into the pool and several bright red cardinals had flown in to enjoy an early-morning splash. I could see a few workers moving around at the back of the garden, but the place was so quiet, I thought everybody must be in the greenhouses — a lovely place to be on a cool morning.

When the nursery belonged to Wanda, the sales area and shop were located in a dilapidated red barn with a leaky roof. The Conrads tore down the barn and replaced it with an attractive adobe structure with blue-painted trim and a red tile roof, much more in keeping with Sonora's Southwestern theme. The adobe houses the garden shop, the checkout counter, and the office, which is where I was headed.

Actually, I was just as glad that I hadn't run into Allan or Betty. All I wanted to do was find Lucita and confirm that her phone calls to Colin had to do with those potted yuccas in his backyard. Then I could call Ruby and reassure her that Lucita was not a Significant Other. And when I met Sheila at Ruby's to pick up that box, I'd tell her that Lucita was not a Person of Interest, so she wouldn't have to send an officer out here to do an interview unless she had reason to think otherwise. Which she would, most likely. Smart Cookie doesn't take anybody's word for anything — certainly not mine.

The door to the shop was closed and when I pushed it open, I found that the low-ceilinged room was deserted and dim. The lights hadn't been turned on yet, and I paused just inside the door to let my eyes adjust. In front of me was the sales counter and cash register, the wall behind it hung with photos of the Sonora staff. There was Allan at the grand opening, with his trademark white straw hat pushed back on his head, cutting the ribbon strung across the gate. Betty and the two kids, faces shining, standing beside one of the large, rare agaves their father had brought back from a trip. The greenhouse workers, the garden crew — all looking happy and proud to be a part of a successful enterprise. There was also a certificate from the Chamber of Commerce: Sonora Nursery, a rising star in the constellation of Pecan Springs businesses.

I looked around. The small shop was crowded with merchandise, but attractively so: shelves stacked with ceramic pots, racks crowded with books and small tools, corners piled with bags of potting soil and amendments. The air had a pleasantly dusty smell, the smell of dried earth. But there was something else, too — a coppery undertone, ripe, rich. It was a smell I recognized, and a tsunami of apprehension suddenly swept over me.

"Hello," I called urgently, raising my voice. "Anybody here?"

As if in answer, a door opened somewhere at the back of the shop. A woman's voice — Betty's, I thought — said, "Lucita! We've been waiting for you. Did you forget that we're meeting in the —"

The rest of the sentence was swallowed by a frightened gasp. There was a scuffle of footsteps, a moment of silence, and then a shrill, ear-piercing shriek.

The sound jarred me into action. I strode around the end of the counter toward the office door, which hung slightly ajar. I pushed it open and stepped through. Betty, still shrieking, was backed up against a wall, staring in horror at the still form of a heavy-set, dark-haired woman who was sprawled beside an overturned office chair in a litter of papers, a scattering of coins from an empty cash box, and a lake of thick, congealed, copper-scented blood. Her arms were flung out, her torso and thick legs were twisted, and one shoe was off. Her face, frozen in its final grimace, was gray-white, the color of dirty paper. It was turned to one side, toward me. I bent down and reached for the pulse at the woman's wrist.

But it was a futile gesture. I knew she was dead.

Her throat had been slashed.

CHAPTER TEN

Long, long ago, while the earth was yet young, the creatures of the day and the creatures of the night got into a dispute. Day creatures, favoring the bright, clean light of the sun, when everything was clear and understandable, wanted day-all-the-time. Night creatures, loving the moon and the stars and ambiguity and things that go bump in the dark, wanted night-all-the-time. They decided to have a contest to see who would win the right to dictate to the universe which it would be: continual day or continual night.

The game went like this. The day creatures and night creatures took turns hiding a piece of sacred yucca root in one of four moccasins, with the other side guessing which moccasin held the yucca root. They began playing at sunrise one morning and ceased playing at dawn the next day, with the customary lying and cheating and drinking and fun along the way. They played all day and all night, and you'd think that one side or the other would have prevailed.

But as the second day's sun rose, they had played to a draw. Exhausted, they had to admit that neither side could win. The game had taught them that both light and dark are an irrevocable part of the divine plan, and that no creaturely effort can change this settled arrangement.

Traditional Navajo story

I don't know what excuse Sheila gave to Jackie Barnes' third-graders, but she pulled up in the Sonora parking lot, the siren wailing, about fifteen minutes after I made the 911 call. By that time, I had secured the two doors to the garden shop, stationed an employee at the front gate to turn away customers, and was riding herd on a small group of eight frightened, silent employees. I had my arm around Betty, who was still sobbing. She was scared, too. I could feel her trembling.

A few minutes later, Sheila strode toward me, her eyes dark, her mouth set in a crooked line. At her heels were two uniformed officers, a man and a woman; a third stayed behind to replace the temporary gatekeeper.

"Where's the victim, China?" she demanded in an I'm-not-believing-this tone.

"In there," I said, nodding toward the garden shop. "In the office, at the back." I met her eyes and said distinctly, "Her name is Lucita Sanchez. She's the bookkeeper."

Sheila's voice hardened. "The one who phoned —"

My sharp nod cut her off. There was no reason to broadcast the information that we were aware of Lucita's connection to Colin, and every reason not to. If one of the huddle of wide-eyed workers behind me already knew, he or she would be at the top of the suspect list.

"I see," Sheila said grimly. She didn't ask how it was that I happened to be present at the second murder scene in as many days, but I knew she'd demand an explanation later.

Betty, her brown eyes red and streaming, moved forward, and I dropped my arm. "Lucita Sanchez was . . . she moved up here from Brownsville the middle of March," she said, in a small, hopeless-sounding voice. "I can't believe . . . My husband is going to be so upset that something like this could happen here. So upset!"

"I'm very sorry," Sheila said, sounding as

221

if she meant it. She looked from me to Betty. "Were you the one who found her?"

"Yes," Betty said. She swiped at the tears with the sleeve of her denim shirt. "Me and China." She made a stab at an introduction. "My friend China Bayles. She came in about the same time I did. It was . . ." Her voice broke. "It had to be a robbery. The cash box was empty, just a few coins left. But why they killed her, I don't know. There wasn't much — most of our sales are credit cards or checks. And Lucita would've given them anything they wanted."

Sheila gave me a quick glance, and I nodded shortly. It was true that the cash box was empty. But robbery wasn't the motive. I'd bet my boots on that.

Sheila turned back to Betty. "And you are —" she prompted.

"Betty. Betty Conrad. My husband, Allan, and I own this place. He's in San Antonio, and won't be back until later today. We were having a staff meeting in one of the greenhouses. Lucita was late, and I went to the office to get her. That's when I found —" She choked.

"Thank you, Mrs. Conrad," Sheila said gently. "I know how hard this must be for you. I'll want to talk to you in a few minutes, and to your husband, as soon as he gets back. And to everyone else who was here at the nursery last night and this morning." She nodded to the female officer, then swept her glance over the group. "This is Officer Ward," she said, in an authoritative tone. "She will take your names and some preliminary information and find a place where you can wait until we interview you. It may take some time, but we'll make it as quick as we can." She turned to me, motioning briefly. "Ms. Bayles, come with me."

"Yes, ma'am," I said meekly, and followed, feeling as if I were being summoned out to the woodshed.

In the shop, Sheila turned to me, her fists on her hips, scowling darkly. "I assume that you came here to talk to Lucita Sanchez — even though you told me not an hour ago that she had nothing to do with Colin's murder. So what's the deal, China?"

"I didn't think she did," I protested. I held up my fingers in the Brownie oath. "I came because Ruby made me promise I'd talk to her. I hate to disappoint Ruby, especially now that she's having such a tough time with her mom. I had an hour to kill before you and I met to pick up Colin's box, so I came over here."

At the mention of the box, Smart Cookie's mouth tightened. "I'll have to send somebody else to Ruby's house with you. I can't leave here right now." She looked at me. "You know these people, I assume. The Conrads? The employees?"

"I'm one of Sonora's customers. Betty belongs to the Herb Guild and I gave her some help on a small legal matter, so I know her better than I know Allan. I had several conversations with them when they were thinking of buying this place. They're both hard workers, creative, energetic. They've got good ideas, and Allan seems to have experience and strong connections with growers. He's innovative, too. You need all that, in their line of business. They're making a success of this place when Wanda Rathbottom couldn't." I paused. "I don't know any of the others. I never met the victim."

"Do you have any idea how the Sanchez woman might have been connected to Colin?"

"Not a clue," I said. "Last night, I was guessing that her calls had to do with some purchases he made at Sonora. Those yuccas and the agave in Colin's backyard came from here." From her mystified look, I gathered that she hadn't noticed the potted plants, even though she'd been standing right beside them. "You might start by checking the company records to see whether he had an account here. If he didn't, we'll know that she had another reason to call. I —"

The door opened and the crime-scene team leader came in, armed with a large black duffle bag and a camera tripod. And at that point, my cell phone rang, in one of the pockets of my vest. I flinched. Brian had programmed the ring tone so that it gave me the cheery assurance, "The Eyes of Texas Are Upon You" — not exactly the right theme music for a murder scene. Sheila shook her head, turning away as I took out my phone.

It was Ruby. "Did you try to call, China?" She was breathless. "I've been outside running around, but I'm anxious to hear. What did you find out? What did Lucita tell you about Colin?"

More cops — the rest of the crime-scene team, I guessed — crowded into the small shop, and Sheila began to give them instructions. I stepped into a far corner and faced the wall, speaking as quietly as I could. "Lucita couldn't tell me anything, about Colin or anybody else."

"Why not?" Ruby asked. "And why are you whispering?"

"Because she's dead. And I'm whispering

because there are about a dozen cops in this room."

"Dead!" Ruby cried. "Oh, my God!" She gave an audible gulp. "How . . . how did she die?"

"Somebody slashed her throat," I said grimly. "Betty found her. I arrived about five seconds later."

"Slashed her throat! How horrible!" There were a few seconds' silence as Ruby digested the news. "She was killed because she was involved with Colin. I know it!"

"It's possible," I said cautiously. "But if you're imagining a romantic involvement, I can set your mind at rest. Lucita wasn't exactly a come-hither type. But we shouldn't count out some other connection."

Ruby sounded bewildered. "But what other connection could there be?"

Sheila had stopped talking to her team and was looking in my direction.

"I really need to hang up, Ruby." Belatedly, I thought of something. "How's your mom this morning? Any better?"

"She's disappeared," Ruby said flatly. "She walked out of the house while I was in the shower, and I've been out looking for her ever since. I've called the police."

"Walked out? Oh, God, Ruby, I'm sorry!"

"I know," Ruby said, resigned. "Heaven

only knows where she's gone." She pulled in her breath. "But it's not as bad as finding somebody with her throat cut. Are you okay?" Without waiting for my answer, she hurried on, "You're going over to my house, aren't you? Be sure and call me when you've found the box. But don't call Mom's number — I'll probably be out looking for her. Call my cell phone."

"I will," I said. "Good luck." I cut the connection and went back to Sheila, who interrogated me with her eyebrows. "Ruby," I replied.

"She okay?" Sheila asked.

"She's lost her mother. As in wandered away," I added hastily, when Sheila looked shocked. "She walked out the door while Ruby was taking her shower. But don't worry. Fredericksburg's finest are on the case."

Sheila gave her head a pitying shake and turned toward the office. I put my hand on her sleeve. "Don't forget that you're going to send an officer with me to Ruby's house." Now that Lucita Sanchez was dead, I was feeling rather urgent about that box. And the morning was wearing on. I had to get moving.

Sheila gave me a look that said she was too busy to think about another thing. "Stop by the station on your way through town," she said. "I'll call and find out who's available." She motioned brusquely to the crime-scene team leader. "All right, Kathy. Bring your guys and come on — we've got work to do."

The Pecan Springs Police Department has moved out of its cramped quarters in the basement of the building that houses the Parks and Utilities Department and the town's famous flock of bats, and into another building, catawampus across the square. I parked, got out of the car, and was about to dash inside when I was met by Mae Belle Battersby, Pecan Springs' peerless meter maid and traffic officer. She was zipped and buttoned and belted into her polyester police uniform, which was tight enough to make her look like a plump, pink-cheeked sausage.

"Mornin', Miz Bayles." Mae Belle hailed me, raising her cap jauntily above her gray curls. "I hear we got us an important assignment."

"We have?" I asked in surprise.

"We cert'nly have," she said, with a cheerful relish. "Chief radioed not five minutes ago. Talked to me person'lly. Said I'm s'posed to go some'eres with you to fetch somethin', and I'm supposed to keep an eye on it. Said you'd give me the scoop on the way."

I didn't hesitate. Mae Belle may be a few minutes past prime time, but she has been a valued employee of the Pecan Springs Police Department for at least a decade and knows her way around town blindfolded. And whether she is emptying the parking meters into her two-wheeled coin collector pushcart or writing traffic tickets for those who are overparked or double-parked around the square, she takes her work with complete and utter seriousness. As a witness to the collection of Colin's box, she would do as well as any other police officer, and better than several others I could name.

"Well, great," I said. "Let's take my car. I'll bring you back on my way to the shop." It was pushing nine fifteen and the shop is supposed to open at ten, so I'd have to hustle.

"Heck, no," Mae Belle said, beaming proudly. She jingled a set of car keys. "Chief said for me to take a squad car. I don't get a chance to drive one of them babies very often, and I ain't goin' to miss out. No sirree bob. And I'm gonna run that bubble-gum machine on top, too."

"I don't think the chief would want you

to —" I began.

"She said to make it snappy, so that's what I aim to do," Mae Belle said. "Come on, Miz Bayles. Time's awastin'. We got us a job to do!"

Which is why I arrived at Ruby's house in a squad car with the light flashing and siren wailing, and marched up the steps to Ruby's front door closely escorted by a stern-faced uniformed officer of the law, arms akimbo and police gear belt rattling. It was unfortunate that we were walking up to Ruby's front porch at the very moment that Mrs. Wauer, Ruby's neighbor, opened her front door to let Oodles — a fat, white miniature poodle with a sequined collar and a blue bow over each ear — out on the porch. A folding baby gate was stretched across the steps to keep Oodles from going AWOL.

Mrs. Wauer is pushing eighty, and even though she is frail and bent almost double from osteoporosis, she has a shrill voice and a pair of lungs that would be the envy of a marine drill sergeant. Ruby says she talks loud because she used to live on a farm in East Texas and got in the habit of talking to humans at the same decibel level she used to call the cows and pigs. I think she talks loud so that all the neighbors can hear, even those who are watching *Desperate House-*

wives with their windows closed and their air conditioners running.

"Well, if it isn't China Bayles!" she bellowed, as I put my key into Ruby's front door. "And Mae Belle Battersby. Mae Belle, hon, you're lookin' awful pert in that uniform. How's Lester these days? That ol' boy feelin' any better?"

Mae Belle pulled her mouth down. "Lester's not so good, Miz Wauer. It's his ankles. Swelled up like balloons." Lester is Mae Belle's husband, who seems to be on permanent disability. Mae Belle supports not only him, but also a pair of young grandchildren currently living with them.

"That's because he don't get out enough, Mae Belle," Mrs. Wauer said sternly. "You got to get up off your lazy ol' buns and walk, ever' day. Me, I do three laps of the backyard, fair or foul." She looked fondly down at Oodles. "Oodles laps, too, don't you, baby?"

Oodles, thus directly addressed, ran twice around Mrs. Wauer and gave a flurry of intelligent barks.

"He says laps are good for us," Mrs. Wauer translated with satisfaction. "Good for Lester, too." She raised her voice another notch, as if I were standing three doors down the block and were hard of hearing to boot. "China, what d'you hear from Ruby? How's her poor old mother?"

"About the same," I bellowed back, turning the key.

"She steal any more of them silk scarves from Dillard's?" Mrs. Wauer cried. "Mae Belle, you heard about that? Doris went and got herself in trouble with the law."

"Well, that's not exactly what happened," I said, lowering my voice. Mildred Ewell, who lives across the street, had come out on her porch. It was a beautiful morning, but she was wearing her usual red plastic raincoat and green rain hat and carrying a blue-and-white-striped umbrella, furled. Mildred likes to be prepared. "It's a rather unfortunate situation, and —"

My voice was drowned out by Oodles' yaps. He has not liked Mildred Ewell since she smacked him on the rump with a newspaper. Poodles have a long memory.

"Oh, it's a pity, all right," Mrs. Wauer said, with a shake of her head. "Poor old Doris. Couple of sandwiches short of a picnic, is what I hear." She pressed her thin lips together. "Comes of livin' like a canary in a cage, shut up in that place. I told her that, when she fixed it up to move over there. I told her it was a good way to go batty, which is what she's gone and done. Nuttier'n a jaybird at pecan harvest." She looked down at her poodle. "Isn't that what you hear, Oodles?"

But Oodles didn't answer. He was jumping up and down, snapping his teeth and telling Mrs. Ewell that if she didn't go straight back into her house, he would leap off the porch and sink his needlelike fangs into her ankle.

Mrs. Ewell paid no attention. She had unfurled her umbrella against the glare of the morning sun and was marching down the walk, obviously intending to join our conversation. Feeling that Mae Belle and I had better get inside before the whole neighborhood turned out to discuss Ruby's mother's mental condition, I pushed at the door. It was unlocked, but it seemed to be stuck. Ruby's house is an old Victorian with lots of gingerbread. Something always needs repair.

"Best place for old folks is right next door to their kids," Mae Belle remarked sagely. "Miz Bayles, you need a hand? Them old doors ain't always too cooperative."

"Ruby goin' to stay over there at her mother's for a while, is she?" Mrs. Wauer persisted, as Mildred Ewell came across the street, ignoring Oodles, who had gone into attack mode and was flinging himself at the folding gate. Mrs. Ewell is ten years younger than Mrs. Wauer, and gets around much better. She's also the editor of the Herb Guild's newsletter and a regular customer at Thyme and Seasons — not someone I want to antagonize.

"Good morning, China," she said, raising her voice over Oodles' furious yaps. "I see that Ruby has not gotten around to fixing her front door yet. I offered to send Chester over to help, but she said no."

Mrs. Ewell's son, Chester, a bachelor, is all of fifty-five years old, weighs about two hundred pounds, and has lived with his mother all his life. He's been sweet on Ruby ever since she moved in. I could guess why she hadn't taken Chester's mother up on the offer of help, but I could hardly say so.

"She probably thought she could fix it herself," I said apologetically, giving the door another hard push. "Ruby is independent that way."

"We are all in need of help at some times in our lives," Mrs. Ewell remarked knowingly. "That's what neighbors are for — to help. Chester could be a big help to Ruby, if she'd only let him. I've never been impressed by all that female liberation. Let the men help, is what I say."

"I'll be glad to help with that door," Mae

Belle offered. "Don't look like it wants to budge."

Lunging against the gate with increasing ferocity, Oodles offered to escort Mrs. Ewell back home.

"Speaking of fixing," Mrs. Wauer yelled, "tell Ruby I said that man came last night and fixed her meter. He said she wanted it done."

"Fixed her meter?" I repeated blankly. "Water meter? Gas meter? Electric meter?"

"I don't know, now do I?" Mrs. Wauer replied loftily. "All I know is, it's in her guest room. You'd think a meter would be in the basement, or the garage or out back somewhere, so's it's easy to get to when it needs fixin'. But no, this meter's upstairs."

The guest room. Beginning to feel urgent now, I put my shoulder to the door and pushed, without any luck. "How do you know he was a meter man?" I asked, pushing again.

" 'Cause I asked him," she replied. "And 'cause he was wearing a khaki meter-man uniform, and a brown cap with a bill, like a baseball cap, and he had a clipboard and a big key ring with lots and lots of keys. Oodles and me was doing our last lap about dark last night, when he went up to Ruby's back door. I told him she wasn't at home, and he said in that case, he'd go right on in, which he did. I asked him who he was and he said he was from the electric company and they'd had a report of an overload on her meter. O' course, if he hadn't told me, I would've gone straight to the phone and called the police." She cast a glance at Mae Belle. "Right, Mae Belle? That's what you're s'posed to do, isn't it? Ask folks to 'dentify theirselves."

"That's right, Mrs. Wauer," Mae Belle said reassuringly. "You call the police. We'll be here quicker'n you can say hop toad." To me, she said, "You oughta let me try that door, Miz Bayles. You just ain't big enough."

"I could send Chester," Mrs. Ewell offered, as Oodles, bouncing up and down on his hind legs, barked furiously.

"Okay, you try," I said to Mae Belle, who outweighs me by thirty pounds. "But just lean on it. Don't break it if you can help it." To Mrs. Wauer, I said, "How did he get in? And how did you know that the meter is upstairs?"

"Guess he had a key. He sure had a bunch on his belt, anyhoo. I figgered he had a right. And I know the meter's upstairs 'cause my kitchen window looks out on Ruby's stair window. I seen his flashlight, goin' up the stairs."

Keys on his belt. Just because a door has a lock on it doesn't mean that it is secure. Most locks are generic enough to be unlocked by one of several different master keys. "What did he look like?"

Mrs. Wauer looked doubtful. "Like your ordinary meter man, I s'pose."

"He had blond hair," Mrs. Ewell put in, "cut real short, like he was in the military, and big shoulders. I know because he came to my house first," she added in an explanatory tone. "He had Ruby's address written down on his clipboard, but it was wrong. When he said he was looking for Wilcox, I sent him across the street." She smiled thinly. "I believe in being helpful."

Blond hair, cut short. Big shoulders. I thought of the man who had confronted Colin in the First Baptist parking lot. The man who had come to collect what Colin owed him.

There was a solid *oomph!* Mae Belle had put her shoulder to the door.

"Did you see the vehicle this man was driving?" I asked Mrs. Ewell.

"A blue van," she said promptly. "It was parked right out front. It —"

But at that moment, Oodles' gate collapsed under his repeated attacks. He rushed down the steps with a wild energy, teeth bared, six pounds of furious poodle.

"Oodles, you naughty boy!" cried Mrs. Wauer. "You come back here, right now!" But Oodles was giving chase to Mrs. Ewell, who danced backward, defending her ankles with her open umbrella, using it like a medieval shield. I would have liked to see who won, but at that moment, there was another *oomph!* and a *thud.* The door had flown open.

"Don't think it's busted," a victorious Mae Belle reported cheerfully. "But you tell Miz Wilcox she oughtta have Chester give it a look real soon. It's stickin' in the frame somethin' fierce."

But I was already pushing past her, taking the stairs two at a time. "Come on," I yelled over my shoulder, and Mae Belle barreled up the stairs behind me. I took a right at the top of the stairs and ran into Ruby's guest room. The closet door was standing open, and the top shelf was bare. Colin's shoebox was gone.

"Aw, hell," I said disgustedly.

"What does that mean?" Mae Belle asked, putting her hands on her hips.

"It means that what we came for is gone." The blond, burly man with a crew cut had come to collect whatever Colin owed him — at least, that was one hypothesis. "The

238

Eyes of Texas" tinkled in my shoulder bag. I pulled out my cell phone.

"We found her!" Ruby said triumphantly.

"Oh, good," I said, mouthing, "It's Ms. Wilcox" to Mae Belle. "You must be relieved. Where was she?"

"In her car," Ruby said. "She took the car keys off the board in the office — again — and locked herself in the car. Again. Triple A came out and unlocked her." She raised her voice over a sudden commotion in the background. "The moving men are here. They're taking her furniture to the new apartment, and she's a bit upset about it."

That was an understatement. I could hear loud thumps and bumps and Doris, using some very unladylike language.

"I've got to go," Ruby said, sounding harried. "She's arm wrestling the moving man for a lamp."

"Wait!" I said. "I've got something to tell you. About Colin's box."

"Oh, good," Ruby said. "You got it. Well, I'm glad something went right this morning."

"But it didn't go right. Somebody let himself into your house last night — somebody from the electric company, Mrs. Wauer says. He knew the box was in the guest room closet. He took it." I glanced around.

"He doesn't seem to have taken anything else, or done any damage."

"Took it?" Ruby echoed, nonplussed. "But why? Who? How did he get in?"

"I think it was the same man that Darla saw with Colin in the church parking lot," I said. "Mrs. Wauer said he had a bunch of keys. He probably had one that fit your back door lock." I paused. "Did Colin have a key?"

"Yes, but he wouldn't — And why in the world would somebody from the electric company want a box of photos?" Ruby asked, in a dazed-sounding voice. And then, answering her own question: "Because he wasn't from the electric company! And because there was something else in the box. A clue to Colin's murder! China, you've *got* to find that man. And that box!"

"Yeah, right," I said dryly. "Piece of cake. Listen, Ruby. I told Sheila that you're planning to adopt Colin's dog, and she said you needed to pick him up right away, so he doesn't run amok and eat all the neighbors. And I said —"

"But I can't pick him up!" Ruby wailed. "He's there, and I'm here, and my mother —" There was a loud *bang!* in the background.

"You don't have to pick him up. I told

Sheila I'd go over to Colin's and get him. I'll take him to my house."

"Oh, good," Ruby said, relieved. To her mother, she said, "Yes, Mom, just wait. I'll fix it." To me, she said, "You're sure it will be okay with McQuaid? I wouldn't want to —"

"It'll be fine," I said briskly. "But I can't pick up the dog until lunchtime. I've got to go to the police station and get my car, then go to the shop and open up." I checked my watch. "And I have just ten minutes to get there."

"Don't worry, Miz Bayles," Mae Belle said, putting a comforting hand on my shoulder. "We'll get there in a jiffy. I'll put on the siren for you."

On the way, I called Sheila and let her know that Colin's box was gone, taken by a burly blond meter man with a crew cut, driving a blue van. I won't tell you what she said. She was definitely not happy.

Chapter Eleven

China Bayles' Texas Tarragon Vinegar
Texas tarragon is another name for Mexican mint marigold (*Tagetes lucida*), which Southern gardeners like to grow as a fragrant, anise-scented substitute for tarragon.

Fill a quart jar half full of fresh Mexican mint marigold leaves, washed, drip-dried, and bruised with the back of a spoon. Cover with apple cider vinegar, add a lid, and let set in a dark place for several weeks, until the flavor has developed to suit you. Strain and rebottle. Add to mayonnaise, or mix with honey, mustard, and crushed garlic for a tangy vinaigrette.

Cass had already come in and was doing her morning thing in the kitchen of the tearoom, banging pots and pans and whistling. Missy had opened the Crystal Cave and was dusting Ruby's shelves while she listened to whale songs. And Carole Gaye was waiting for me when I unlocked the door to Thyme and Seasons and turned on the lights.

"How is she?" she asked worriedly. "How's Ruby? How did she take the news about Colin?"

"It was hard, but she'll survive." I propped the door open with a ceramic frog filled with aloe plants. As the morning sunlight flooded in, I tied my khaki Thyme and Seasons apron over my jeans and pulled the cash drawer from its hiding place under the counter. "But her mother isn't well at all. Looks like Ruby will have to be in Fredericksburg for a few more days." I put the drawer into the cash register and adjusted the tape.

While I was doing this, Missy came in through the door that connects Ruby's shop to mine. I hated to alarm either of them by telling them what had happened at Sonora that morning, but they'd probably hear about it, one way or another. I got the broom, and while I gave the floor its morning sweeping, I told the story, as briefly and with as little gore as possible.

Missy stared at me, wide-eyed. "Ohmi-god," she whispered, when I'd finished.

"What an awful thing, China!"

"Do you have any reason to think the two killings are related?" Carole asked anxiously.

"The police may be working on that theory," I said evasively, hanging up the broom. "But if you don't mind, I would really like to forget about it. Sheila's in charge, and I've done what I can. It's all up to the cops now."

The bell over Ruby's shop door tinkled, and Missy went back to tend her customer. I picked up my feather duster and began to flick dust off the book rack. "Anyway, there's plenty to keep us busy," I went on. "How's the workshop prep coming along? Do you need any help? Are we all set for tomorrow?"

"I think we're fine," Carole said with an understanding glance, and did her part to change the subject. "I'm enjoying your guesthouse, China. I had a wonderful night's sleep." She glanced around. "And this morning, I've been wandering through your gardens — I love them. I love what you've done with your shop, too. It feels so wonderfully peaceful here." She bent to sniff a bar of fragrant soap, then straightened up, a concerned look on her face. "But there's something I meant to mention to you. Yesterday evening, a delivery man knocked at the door of the guest house and asked for Ruby's address. We tried to look her up in the phone book, but it turns out that she's not listed."

"She went unlisted last year." I frowned. "A delivery man? What did he look like?"

"A big guy, tall, big shoulders." Carole used her hands to demonstrate. "Blond hair, buzz-cut. Very polite."

Oh, hell. The meter man. Why was I not surprised? "Did you give him her address?"

A guilty look crossed her face. "I did. I wrote it down on his clipboard for him. But afterward, I realized that the address I gave him was wrong. Whatever he was delivering, he probably left it across the street. Please tell Ruby that I hope I haven't caused a problem."

"I'll mention it to her," I said. "But don't worry about it." There was no point in going into the whole story. At least now we knew how the meter man got to Mrs. Ewell's house.

Carole nodded. "I got up early this morning and pulled some yucca paper from the plants we gathered yesterday. The sheets are drying now. At lunchtime, maybe you can come back to the cottage and take a look."

"I'd like to, if there's time," I said. "But I've got to do something about Ruby's dog."

"Her dog? I didn't know she had a dog."

"She didn't," I said. "But she does now. She's adopting Colin Fowler's Rottweiler, and I have to go pick him up. He's going to stay at my house until she gets back."

"A Rottweiler!" Carole exclaimed. "But they're vicious! Back home, Rottweilers are on the dangerous dog list. They're banned. People can't keep them."

"Wait a minute," I said, frowning. "*All* Rottweilers are banned? The entire breed?"

She nodded earnestly. "If I remember right, the list also includes Dobermans and pit bulls — really aggressive dogs. I hope Ruby will have second thoughts."

"But surely not *all* of the dogs of those breed ought to be banned," I protested. "That would be like . . . well, like ordering all the Smiths to move out of Pecan Springs, just because some guy named Smith got jailed for putting down too many beers on a Saturday night and going after his mother-in-law with a hammer." I paused, seeing other intriguing difficulties in this. "And what if the dog's mother was a Doberman and his dad was a loose-living Labrador? Who decides whether a mixed-breed dog is on the list? And what does it cost to enforce a law like this?"

I have to admit that my reaction was probably colored by the fact that I have a certain amount of ingrained antagonism toward laws that seem to be discriminatory. Carole, however, was not concerned about what was to me full of potential injustice.

"All I'm saying is that Ruby needs to be careful," she said, concerned. "And you, too, China. Rottweilers are big dogs."

"Thanks. I will," I promised, trying to sound grateful. I knew that Carole was only trying to keep Ruby and me from making a well-intentioned mistake.

As she left, Khat sauntered in and announced that he could handle a Rottweiler with one paw. Khat — Imperial Top Cat and Sovereign Chief of Security at Thyme and Seasons — weighs in at seventeen pounds, about twice the size of your ordinary skimpy Siamese. When I adopted him, his name was Pudding, but Ruby (whose favorite sleuth is Kao K'o Kung, star of the Cat Who Mysteries) renamed him Khat. He may not read backward or like to talk to ghosts, but he can definitely tell time: on his clock, it's always five minutes past time to eat. I scratched him between his dark ears, assured him that he's the best security officer in town, and sent him out to the kitchen to ask Cass for a little something to tide him over until lunch.

The next half hour was nice and busy, exactly the kind of busy you like to be when you own your own shop. Carolyn Marshall purchased two bottles of Texas Tarragon Vinegar, one for herself and another for a housewarming present, and Edna Fisher called to find out if she could get enough fresh mint from my garden to make mint juleps for seventy-five guests, for the Kentucky Derby party she was planning. Edna always thinks ahead, and a good thing, too. Fresh mint goes fast during Derby Week.

I had just finished helping Carl Hudson pick out a dozen two-inch potted basil plants — lemon basil, Purple Ruffles, Thai, cinnamon, and sweet Genovese — when a largish shadow darkened the door. I looked up to see Hark Hibler.

"Thanks, Carl," I said cordially. "Good luck with your basil." I handed him the plastic tray loaded with plants and held the door open for him. As he left, I turned to Hark. "Hey, Hark. What's up?"

It was bound to be something serious. The *Enterprise* may be a small newspaper, but it keeps Hark on the go, checking out the City Council's front-burner controversies, going to junior high basketball games, editing the write-ups submitted by Bible study groups, book clubs, garden clubs, and Brownie

Scout troops — not to mention writing editorials and occasionally tracking down real news. He doesn't have time for casual drop-ins and he doesn't shoot the breeze unless he's aiming at a story. I thought back to my suspicion of yesterday morning: that Hark had some bit of information about Colin Fowler that he wasn't ready to share with Sheila, some sort of lead that he intended to follow up on his own. I wondered if he had managed to dig up a connection between Colin and Lucita Sanchez. If he had, I definitely wanted to hear about it.

But he didn't mention Sanchez. Instead, he leaned his elbows on the counter. "How's Ruby?" he asked in a low voice. "I understand her mother is having mental problems." He gave me a sympathetic look. "Buggy as a bullbat, is what I hear."

If you're from Texas, you probably know that a bullbat is a nighthawk, a small brown bird that is remarkable for its wildly erratic flying and high-pitched chatter as it goes after flying bugs. I smiled wryly, since that's a pretty good description — and not really unkind — of what was happening to Doris.

"I guess you could call it that," I said. "Ruby is coping courageously. Her sister,

Ramona, will be there on Sunday to help out, so maybe she'll be able to get home then."

Hark nodded, relieved. "Tell her I'm thinking of her. I hope things get better, ASAP."

"Sure." I smiled, liking his concern. Ruby could do with some of that. "I'll tell her, Hark."

He looked down. "Must be pretty hard on her, dealing with her mother and . . ." His fingers played with a piece of paper on the counter. "And with Fowler's murder. Both at the same time, I mean. Sort of a double whammy."

"Yeah," I said. It was time to prompt him. "You didn't come over here to talk about Ruby, though. What's on your mind, Hark?"

He straightened up. "I thought you might be interested in a couple of things I picked up recently." He gave me a look that I couldn't read. "About Fowler."

I thought so. "What about him?"

He pulled down his eyebrows. "Well, it's like this. I've been working a story for several weeks. A big story, one that's going to upset some pretty important apple carts here in town."

"Oh, yeah?" I was definitely curious. "Tell me."

He looked secretive. "I'm not ready to break it yet. But I think you might be able to help. A couple of weeks ago, one of my sources told me that Colin Fowler's real name was Dan Reid, and that he came from Dallas." He glanced at me to see if this registered on my face. When it didn't, he went on. "Seems that Fowler or Reid, or whatever you want to call him, was an undercover cop in Dallas, until he was busted for tipping off a drug dealer who was about to be arrested. He did a year in jail. That's where he was before he moved here and set up shop."

I was noncommittal. "So? What's your point?"

Hark looked a little deflated, as if he had expected more reaction to what should probably have been a jaw-dropping, damning revelation. "The point is, did Ruby know about Fowler's background when she was going out with him? This is completely off the record, of course," he added, half-apologetically. "It's just something I need to know, China. It's for me. It's got nothing to do with the story."

I thought about this. Colin was dead, and Ruby had to get on with her life. Hark cared about her, and he'd never given me any reason to think he'd do anything that wasn't in her best interests. His motive for asking probably had more to do with his heart than with his nose for news.

"No, Ruby didn't know it," I said truthfully. "But I did. I told her the whole story last night, when I told her that he was dead. It was news to her."

Hark looked pleased. "Well, that's good. Good for Ruby, I mean. I always knew that she had a good head on her shoulders." Without giving me time to ask what he meant, he went on. "My source also told me that there was something dirty going on in the Dallas PD while he was there. Not long after Reid went to jail, so did several other cops."

"A dozen," I amended.

He raised an eyebrow. "So you know."

"And there was one suicide," I added, just to keep the record straight. "That was Mc-Quaid's information, anyway. He didn't know Reid personally, but he was acquainted with the Dallas situation."

Hark's mouth twitched. "And does Ruby know about that part of it?"

"She does now." I paused. "Of course, nobody's saying whether there was any real connection between Reid and those dirty cops. They're all just guessing, including McQuaid. But maybe you've heard something I haven't." I eyed him.

"Well, I have." He thought about it briefly, then said, "Can I trust you to keep it under your hat?"

I considered. I don't take promises of confidentiality lightly. But in this case, since the issue was related to Ruby . . . Anyway, he looked as if he were bursting to tell me. If it was that good, I didn't want to miss out. "Yeah," I said.

He leaned closer and lowered his voice, as if he were afraid the shop might be bugged. "My source tells me — on good authority — that Reid and Sheila Dawson had a flaming affair back in Dallas, which resulted in Reid getting a divorce. And that when he was killed, they were still pretty good friends." He shook his head sadly. "*Very* good friends, as a matter of fact. Behind Ruby's back."

My heart dropped into my shoes. A rumor like that flitting around Pecan Springs was only going to hurt Sheila, not to mention Ruby. But I wasn't about to let on to Hark. I put on a nonchalant look.

"Is that all? If it is, I can tell you, flat out and final, that it's not true. Sure, Sheila hung out with him when they were in Dallas. But not here. And not behind Ruby's back. Ain't so, Hark. Believe me."

"Actually, I do," he said. "The behind-the-back bit, anyway. It's not like Sheila. But if they were lovers before, it compromises her investigation, don't you think?"

I folded my arms. "I don't see how."

He hesitated. "She could be . . . personally involved."

"We're all personally involved when it comes to murder," I said starkly, remembering Colin among the yucca, Lucita lying in a litter of bloody papers. "But Sheila Dawson is a professional. Whatever her connection to the victim, she'll do her job. No compromises, no personal axes to grind, just top-notch police work. You've been covering her for a couple of years now. You ought to know her well enough to know that."

Hark had an odd look on his face. He was telling me only a part of what he knew, or thought he knew, which amounted to the same thing. This in itself was worrisome. Hark is a reliably good guy, and even if he was on the trail of a delectably juicy story that had BREAKING NEWS written all over it, he wasn't going to smear Sheila — and he would never in the world do anything to hurt Ruby. But if the story about Sheila and Colin was making the rounds out there in gossip-land, it was bound to rear its ugly head in one public forum or another, with potentially disastrous consequences. Yes, definitely worrisome.

"Sure, sure," Hark said, in a conciliatory tone. "And of course I don't intend to run anything about it. I was hoping you might be willing to give me some insight into Reid, just for background. You knew the guy. What was he like, personally, I mean? Was he —"

The phone rang, just as I was about to tell Hark that he could take his personal questions and buzz off. It was McQuaid, calling from Houston to let me know that he had found a cache of interesting information at the newspaper and had decided to stay overnight so he and Jim could follow up on a couple of promising leads. I took the phone and stepped out the front door, out of Hark's hearing.

"It turns out that your father —" he began.

"Somebody else got murdered here," I broke in, feeling that Lucita's death was more urgent than a sixteen-year-old traffic accident.

"Murdered?" he squawked.

Filling him in on what had happened that morning took a few minutes — it's not the kind of thing you can summarize in thirty seconds — and then he had questions, most of which I couldn't answer, since they were cop questions, and I had no idea where the investigation was or where it was headed. When I had done my best to deal with that, I stepped back inside the shop, and then I thought of something else I ought to let him know about.

"We've temporarily adopted a dog," I said in an offhand tone, putting the emphasis on temporarily. "I'm going to put him out in Howard's kennel for a couple of days. Okay?"

"I guess," he said. "Yeah, sure." He became distracted. Speaking to someone else, he said, "Just put those papers over here, and I'll get to them right away. Thanks." To me, he added, "I've had some stuff sent up from the morgue." He paused. "A dog, you said? What kind of dog?"

"Ruby's dog."

Hark, who was browsing the nearby bookshelf, glanced up and raised an eyebrow.

McQuaid rustled some pages. "Oh, yeah?" he said absently. "I didn't know she had a dog."

"She adopted Colin's dog."

"Oh," McQuaid said. More rustling pages. "What kind of dog did you say it was?"

"A Rottweiler," I said with some reluctance, remembering my conversation with Carole. "His name is Rambo. He's a really nice dog, really," I added, in a reassuring tone. "A very nice dog. He was trained by somebody who trains police dogs."

"A Rottweiler!" Hark said, abandoning all pretense of not listening. "Ruby's taking on a Rottweiler? That's crazy!"

"A Rottweiler!" McQuaid exclaimed, suddenly wary. "Jeez, China, are you sure you know what you're doing? What if he goes after Howard Cosell?"

"He won't," I said, with more confidence than I felt. "He's a civilized Rottweiler. A Rottweiler with self-restraint."

"A self-restrained Rottweiler." Hark snorted scornfully. "There's no such thing. Especially if his name is Rambo. Bet he has his own bandolier."

"Hark, hush," I said. I was going to tell McQuaid that Rambo was afraid of cats and thunder, but I stopped. If I laid it on too thick, McQuaid wouldn't believe me. Anyway, I wasn't sure I believed it myself. Rambo didn't look like a dog who was afraid of thunder.

"I don't know, China," McQuaid said. "I'm concerned about Howard. Rottweilers are big dogs, aggressive and temperamental. And poor old Howard's getting pretty slow.

He could never defend himself against an attack."

"It's just until Ruby gets back," I argued. "I'll keep the dogs apart."

"Yeah," McQuaid said, darkly. "Well, okay. But if there's any trouble, Fowler's Rottweiler is going to the boarding kennel, faster than you can say 'heel.' And it's your job to keep that animal away from old Howard. I am holding you personally responsible."

"Yessir," I said, refraining from clicking my heels and saluting. "Good luck with your investigation." I hung up the phone.

Hark returned to the counter and leaned on it. "Getting back to what I was saying. My source told me something else about Reid."

"Oh, yeah?" I said cautiously.

"Yeah. I understand that Reid was here in Pecan Springs doing undercover work for the FBI. It's about police corruption."

"Corruption!" I yelped. I wasn't faking it. I was genuinely astonished. "You've got to be kidding. In this little town?"

But the minute the words were out of my mouth, I knew how foolish they were. It's only in novels that small towns are pure as a snowfall on Christmas Eve and their public officials as blemish-free as a newborn baby. In real life, it's a very different story.

Anywhere there's money, there's greed. And anywhere there's greed, there's the potential for corruption.

Hark chuckled grimly. "News to you, huh?"

"News to me," I admitted. Not welcome news, either.

But after my first astonished rejection of the idea, I had to admit that it was entirely possible. When the City Council appointed Sheila as the new chief of police a couple of years ago, she inherited a police department that had been in the hands of Chief Bubba Harris for twenty-some years. At the time, it had been a small department, and Bubba ran a very tight ship. Officially and publicly, there had been only one scandal while he was in office: a rogue cop who set up his own private speed trap behind a billboard on the road to Wimberley. He collected a pocketful of change before he ticketed the wrong guy — Bubba's cousin — and ended up in jail himself.

But it was entirely possible that something much more serious had been going on behind the scenes during those years, either in the department or on the Council, and that Smart Cookie had found out about it. In fact, maybe that was what had been bothering her for the past few months. If she'd gotten a whiff of something corrupt, of course she'd be worried. And it would be entirely reasonable for her to ask for undercover help from other agencies — the Department of Public Safety, the Texas Rangers, the FBI.

But wouldn't she have told me?

My first thought: of course she would. We're friends, aren't we?

My second thought, a little unsettling: probably she wouldn't, unless she thought it was something I had a reason for knowing — a serious reason, I mean. Sure, we've been friends, good friends. We enjoy each other's company. We share a number of mutual interests and we've helped each other out of a jam more than once. But Smart Cookie is a cop's cop, and since she's been the chief of police, this part of her — the professional Sheila, hard as nails and tough right down to the core — has taken over. We used to talk a lot about what was going on in our personal lives: her sad breakup with Sheriff Blackie Blackwell, to whom she had been engaged for a couple of years, and my often frustrating relationship with my mother. But we don't do that very often these days. And we rarely talk about anything having to do with Sheila's turf or the internal workings of the Pecan Springs

Police Department — except, of course, when she's grousing about not having enough officers on the beat or the body armor to keep them safe and the radios to keep them connected.

My third thought was even more disturbing. Sheila might not know about an undercover investigation, especially if the situation in the department was out of control. If Hark's source had the story right, it was possible that Reid had been sent on the QT to get information that might lead to wholesale arrests in the department and a career-ending embarrassment for Sheila. There have been several instances in the state of Texas in which other agencies — the FBI, the Texas Rangers, even the DEA — were dispatched to do the housecleaning in a small community, and the chief was the last to know. And in this case, Sheila and Reid had once been lovers, which further complicated an already complicated situation. I didn't like this, not one little bit.

"Yeah," Hark said, appraising me with a newsman's eye. "Opens up all kinds of possibilities, doesn't it? In terms of who killed Reid, I mean. Could've been revenge for what went down in Dallas, if he was the one who fingered those cops. Could also have been connected with his investigation into corruption in our fair city, if somebody was afraid of getting fingered."

It was not a possibility I wanted to consider, for if it was true, Sheila was going to find trouble coming at her from all directions. It would be like being in the path of a very large and dangerous hurricane. There'd be nowhere to run for cover. But I needed to know more.

"You might be right," I said cautiously, "*if* it's true that Reid was here on an undercover corruption investigation. Maybe he was — and maybe he wasn't. Is your source reliable? Who *is* your source?"

"You know I can't tell you that," Hark said.

I gave a good facsimile of a nonchalant chuckle. "Well, I guess you can't expect me to get all hotted up about this, then. If I don't know who's trotting the tale around, I mean."

"I just thought you might know something you'd be willing to share," Hark said. He shrugged. "But if not . . . well, forget I brought it up. Okay?"

"I can't," I said seriously. "This might figure in Sheila's murder investigation. You can't keep it to yourself, either, Hark. That's legal advice. I'm giving it to you for free, but you'd better take it seriously, or you'll find yourself in trouble."

He looked glum. "Yeah. I guess I'll have to talk to her. She's not going to be happy to hear it."

"She's a big girl," I said. "She'll handle it like a pro."

He nodded. "Listen, China, there's something else." He slid me a wheedling look. "I wonder — you wouldn't be willing to give me the phone number where Ruby is staying, would you?"

"It wouldn't do you any good if I did," I said. "Her mother's moving to a new apartment today, and I don't have that number." Seeing his crestfallen expression, I added, "But I'd be willing to give you Ruby's cell phone number, as long as you promise not to bother her with questions about Colin Fowler's personal life. Or tell her that she shouldn't adopt his dog. It's none of your business."

"Oh, you bet." He smiled eagerly. "All I want to do is tell her I'm thinking of her. Gosh, China, thanks!"

"For you, Hark," I said generously, "I'd do anything. Well, almost anything." I wrote down the number and gave it to him, adding carelessly, "You've heard about the murder over at Sonora?"

"How'd you know about that?" he asked,

pocketing the number with a pleased expression. Without waiting for an answer, he said, "I was out there just before I came here. The victim was the bookkeeper. She was killed in the office. Robbery, apparently."

"Really," I said. "So that's what it was."

"Yep. Somebody grabbed the cash box. When she put up a fuss, he slashed her throat. With a dagger."

"A dagger?" I frowned.

"Yeah. The cops found it under the desk. The killer must've dropped it and failed to find it in the dark."

"Prints?"

"I don't know. Sheila never tells me anything." He pushed his lips out and in regretfully. "The Conrads are good folks. I interviewed them when they opened Sonora, for a story in the paper. Remember that?"

"Yes, come to think of it, I do," I said, smiling a little. It had been the standard *Enterprise* "On their way to the top" story, portraying the Conrad family — parents and kids — as hardworking people with a strong specialized knowledge of the plants of Mexico and the Southwest. The photo had shown all four of them in front of the just-completed fountain in the central garden, Betty and Allan standing with the two kids, Ricky and Jeannette, all four smiling proudly. "They're a nice family."

"And Allan is one of the hardest workers I've ever seen," Hark replied. "He and Betty have done wonders with that place in just a few years. Hope this doesn't set them back. They deserve a break. They don't deserve robbery and murder."

"Nobody does," I said softly. "Nobody."

CHAPTER TWELVE

The Zuni, Navajo, and Anasazi used the banana yucca (*Yucca baccata*) in a variety of ritual ceremonies. Before the ceremony, they washed their hair with yucca lather in a ritual cleansing, using special baskets woven of yucca. Participants in the ritual might carry decorated yucca stalks as prayer sticks and ceremonial staffs, or hoops and chant arrows. Ceremonial sandals were woven of yucca and hemp. And dancers impersonating the tribal gods wore bands of braided yucca around their heads and wristlets and anklets of yucca ribbon around their arms and legs.

At eleven thirty, Missy went next door to the Craft Emporium to buy some beads for her bead jewelry, and then to the restaurant across the street, for lunch. I kept an eye on both shops, waiting on customers while I grazed my way through a large plate of goodies — sandwiches, some salad, a couple of cookies — that Cass brought from the tearoom. At twelve fifteen, Leatha called, to apologize for leaving our dinner party so precipitously on Wednesday evening. "It was rude," she said contritely. "I felt sorry about it the minute I got in the car. And when I got home, Sam read me the riot act."

"Don't worry about it," I said. "To tell the truth, I'd almost forgotten. Quite a lot has gone on here in the past day or so." I started to tell her about Miles hiring McQuaid to investigate the circumstances of Dad's death, but stopped. It was a long story, and complicated. Then I opened my mouth to tell her about Colin. But I didn't get that out, either. She would have dozens of questions, and there were other things I needed to do. I'd call her tonight and let her know what was going on.

She took a deep breath, as if she were steeling herself. "I'm sure you're too busy to talk right now, China. But I'd just like you to know that I've had second thoughts about what your brother — about what Miles wants to do. If he wants to hunt down that old Cadillac of your father's, that's what he should do. I still don't understand why Laura Danforth would want to keep the old thing — just plain morbid, if you ask me. But if it's that important to Miles, he has my support. And you do, too. Whatever you children want to do is fine with me. Will you tell him that?"

"Sure," I said, feeling a little taken aback. Did this mean that Leatha had decided there might be something to Mrs. Danforth's suspicions about Dad's death and hoped an investigation would settle the issue?

But her next words suggested that she had decided nothing of the kind. "I still for the life of me can't understand why the car is so important," she added. "And I certainly hope Miles doesn't intend to turn it into a shrine. But surely he has more common sense than that. He ought to tow the old thing to a junkyard!"

"I'll be sure and tell him," I said. I brought her up-to-date on Ruby's mother's situation — that, at least, was something we could talk about, and we said good-bye. I went to wait on a man who had read a recent research report on saw palmetto berries and prostate health and wanted to know how to use the herb. I showed him Michael Jansen's booklet, which surveys the research and describes the herb's effects, and he bought several ounces of the dried berries.

Then Missy came back, and it was my

turn to take off. Big Red Mama and I were about to have an adventure. We were going to rescue a Rottweiler and keep him from being sent to the animal shelter.

But after listening to McQuaid, I was feeling a little more nervous about this mission. Howard Cosell was a member of the family and we all loved him dearly. If Rambo injured him, McQuaid would never forgive me. Heck, I'd never forgive myself. So I'd better make sure that didn't happen. Also, I was a bit concerned about riding around with an unrestrained Rottweiler, who might take it into his head to leap in my lap or bite my ankle just as I approached an intersection. It would be better if I crated him, and Big Red Mama, boxy girl that she is, is perfectly capable of toting a crate.

So my first stop was Beezle's Pet Shop, where Howard Cosell spends his weekly allowance on doggie treats. When I told Barbara Beezle about Rambo, she agreed that the dog would be safer (not to mention the driver) if he were confined, and generously offered to loan me a Rottweiler-sized crate. I also bought a leather leash that looked substantial enough to restrain a rambunctious rhinoceros, and — pondering the task ahead and thinking that success might depend as much on distraction as deterrence — several cans of pop-top dog food and a big package of bacon-flavored treats. I considered a muzzle, but muzzling a reluctant Rottweiler didn't fill me with enthusiasm, so I gave it up. Barbara, looking more apprehensive than I might have wished, helped me wrestle the crate into the back of Big Red Mama, and off I went.

Colin's small frame house was still wrapped in yellow crime-scene tape, but there were no cop cars out in front, or anywhere else on the quiet residential street. I parked Big Red Mama beside the curb, put a handful of bacon treats in my pocket, and took a can of dog food and the leash. I walked, whistling with as much bravado as I could muster, around the house to the back.

"Well, look at that!" I sang out in a cheery voice, trying to mask my apprehension. I approached the chain-link dog run. "Well, heck, if it isn't Rambo! Hey, Rambo, old boy. Nice to see you again, fella. Been a good dog while I've been gone? Hungry?"

Rambo ran to the gate and bounced up and down with enormous energy, barking in a vigorous, substantial voice. The muscles of his meaty shoulders rippled with the authority of a Dallas linebacker, and he moved with the muscular agility of Arnold Schwarzenegger skipping rope. His eyebrows, golden brown in a nearly-black face, were going up and down, registering some sort of extreme emotion. I studied him nervously, trying to decide whether he was offering to tear me limb from limb, or whether he remembered me as the giver-of-weenie-treats and was extending a warm welcome to his world.

There was only one way to find out. Taking a deep breath and muttering the mantra, "Nice doggie, good doggie," I let myself into the run, bracing for a quick exit if necessary. But Rambo only grinned and panted and made eager, whiny noises, so I popped the top of the dog food can and dumped the contents into the plastic dish I'd left there. As he wolfed it down, I snapped the leash on his chain-link collar. Sneaky, yes, but quick and effective.

Rottweilers are even faster foodies than bassets (which is saying something), and Rambo scarfed up a full can of dog food in about fifteen seconds. When he had licked the dish and then licked it again to assure himself that he hadn't missed anything significant, he noticed the leash in my hand, the business end of which was connected to his collar. I thought for an instant that he was going to object and tensed, glancing up quickly to be sure that I had latched the gate. If he decided to chow down on my arm, I didn't want him running loose around the neighborhood with my bloody hand in his mouth. It might scare the children.

But Rambo was looking up at me with the same goofy "Oh-boy-oh-boy!" grin that Howard Cosell always wears when we snap on his leash and he thinks we're going in the car. His eyebrows were up, his tongue was lolling, and his head was cocked.

I relaxed a little. In my experience, dogs with goofy grins are generally in a mellow mood. And why shouldn't he be? I was a well-meaning, good-hearted person, wasn't I? And his belly was full of dog food, wasn't it? No room for a piece of my arm.

"Go for a ride, Rambo?" I inquired brightly. In case these weren't the magic words, I added, "Wanna ride in the van?" I put my hand in my pocket, pulled out my keys, and jingled them.

With a gleeful abandon, Rambo barked twice and lunged for the kennel gate, nearly yanking me off my feet. Obviously, going for a ride in the van was something that appealed to him. But before we left the safety of the kennel, there were one or two things I needed to check out.

"Sit," I said.

Rambo looked at me over his shoulder, his eyebrows suddenly worried. Obviously, a Rottweiler who is sitting can't be going for a ride.

"Sit," I said again, more firmly. When I didn't see any immediate response, I put my hand on his butt and pushed. "Sit."

Rambo sat, under protest and with a plaintive look that said, plain as words, "I wish to hell you'd make up your mind. First you said we were going for a ride and now you're telling me to sit. Which is it?"

"Good dog," I said in a warmly congratulatory tone. "That's a very nice sit." I pulled on his leash and he sprang to his feet. "Heel," I said.

Rambo heaved a "well-if-you-insist" sigh and stood at attention beside my left thigh, humoring me. Bless you, Colin Fowler or Dan Reid or whoever you are, I thought warmly. You've raised a Rottweiler with manners. To the dog, I said approvingly, "Good boy, Rambo. You're a peach of a pooch. Now, we'll go out into the yard and you can show me how well you come when I call you. Got that?"

Beside me, Rambo suddenly tensed, pressing himself against my thigh, his muscles gathering. He stared fixedly toward the house, a low, menacing growl rumbling in his throat. I looked up. The back corner of the house was visible through the foliage screen of the photinia bush, and a man was coming around from the side. A cop, I thought, a member of the crime-scene team who had been sent to the house to pick something up.

He wasn't a cop.

The man was big, burly, and blond, and he had a clipboard in his big hands. His face was square-jawed and he held himself aggressively, as if he were used to giving commands and having them obeyed. He was wearing a brown khaki shirt and pants, a brown cap, brown gloves, and about ten pounds of keys on a large ring at his belt. It was the meter man, and — much to Rambo's consternation — he was intent on getting into the house.

"No barking," I cautioned in a fierce whisper, as Rambo tensed. I encircled his muzzle with my fingers, not wanting the man to glance toward the dog run and see me with the Rotti, who seemed to know him. Or maybe he recognized the figure as an intruder, and was preparing to do what Rottweilers are trained to do on such occasions, which is to scare the bejeebers out of the guy.

The intruder seemed to know what he was

doing. He didn't bother with the windows (I happened to know that the kitchen window was unlocked). Stepping around the yucca and agave pots, he headed straight for the back door, which still sported a strip of yellow tape. Ignoring the tape, he selected a key on his ring and tried it in the lock. No dice. He tried another. He was going back for a third when —

"Yoo-hoo!" cried a high-pitched voice. "Excuse me, but you really shouldn't be trying to get into that house!"

The man's head snapped around. A woman had just come down the back steps of her house and was standing at the hedge of clipped yaupon holly that separated her backyard from Colin's. She looked to be in her late thirties. Her bleached blond hair was swept up in the kind of towering bouffant do that you rarely see outside of Dallas, which is the Big Hair capital of Texas. She was wearing a skimpy red bikini that exhibited almost all of her bounteous Dolly Parton boobs, saucer-sized gold hoop earrings, and a sexily flirtatious smile. She had a blanket over her arm and was clearly bent on spending the afternoon worshipping the sun in the privacy of her backyard, wearing as little as was legal.

"Good afternoon, miss," the man said,

and tipped his cap politely. His voice was deep and husky, with no accent.

"I'm sure you're just wantin' to do your job," she said, in a voice honeyed with Southern sweetness. "But maybe you don't know that the guy who lived there has been murdered." Her voice quavered delicately on the last word.

"Murdered!" the meter man exclaimed, as if this were an enormous surprise. "Oh, gosh, that's horrible!"

"Oh, I know — isn't it just? But what I'm tryin' to tell you is that the police were all over the place, lookin' for evidence, and then they went away and locked everything up tight as a drum. Can't you see that yellow tape across the door? You shouldn't try to get in."

"So that's what that is," the meter man said, as if he couldn't read what was printed on the tape. He pushed up the bill of his cap with his thumb and drawled, in a fair imitation of Andy Griffith, "Well, darn." He left the door and went toward the hedge. I loosened my grip on Rambo's muzzle and the dog leaned against my leg, trembling slightly and making little whining noises. I couldn't tell whether he was excited or afraid.

The woman came close to the fence and

leaned against it, putting her cleavage on full display. "In fact, there was a policeman there earlier today — a very nice young guy." She smiled and fluttered her eyelashes, lowering her voice and giving it a resonant erotic trill. "Hey. I don't think I've seen you before, and I am posilutely, absitively sure I would've noticed. You're new on the job, huh?"

"Yes, ma'am, I sure am," said the meter man, and his Southern accent became more pronounced. "New in town, too. Say, that policeman — was he in uniform?" With a concerned look, he added, "My crew chief told us last week to warn folks to be on the lookout for impersonators — people pretending to be security officers. There've been quite a few reports."

Impersonators? I stifled a sarcastic chuckle and Rambo looked up questioningly. "Shh," I said, putting a finger to my lips.

"No, he wasn't in uniform," the woman said slowly, "but he was very, very nice. He didn't even seem to mind when I asked him to please show me his badge." Her eyes widened and she put her hand to her mouth in a gesture almost comically reminiscent of Marilyn Monroe. The meter man wasn't the only one doing impersonations. "You don't think — Perhaps I shouldn't of been so quick to let him use my —" She stopped, biting her bee-stung lower lip in exaggerated consternation.

"Oh, well, if he had a badge," the meter man said in a reassuring tone. He went closer to the fence. "I'm sure he was real glad for your help, Miss —"

"Sanders. But everybody calls me Zany." She giggled. "That's short for Zania. My mama named me for my great-grandma. She was some gal, let me tell you. Vaudeville, back in the early days. Dance?" She rolled her eyes. "Oh, my, could she dance! A real hoofer, she was."

The meter man's voice was warm and complimentary. "I'll bet you're some dancer, too, Miss Zany."

"Miss Zany, that's me." Another giggle. "Crazy Zany, my friends call me. Crazy Zany, always ready for a good time. And yeah, I do my share of dancin'." She looked up at him. "Hey, do you like to dance? I love dancin' with big men."

"Do I dance? Oh, you bet," the meter man said with enthusiasm. He paused. "You let him use your — was it a key, did you say?"

"Well, sure," Miss Zany replied. "He couldn't of got in otherwise, could he? How else could he do his job?" She pouted. "To tell the truth, I felt really sorry for the poor guy. I mean, wouldn't you think they'd of made sure he had the key before they sent him out here? But he was just dadgum lucky, because —" She smiled happily. "Because I had one. Colin gave it to me when he first moved in. He had to have the hot water heater repaired, y'see, and I said I'd be glad to let the repair man in. Well, one thing sorta led to another and I kept the key." She smiled again, with significance. "It was a good thing, doncha think?"

"I certainly do," the meter man assured her. "Did the officer get what he came for?"

"I believe he did. He was carrying something with him when he left, so I guess maybe he did." She leaned forward, smiling sexily. "Say, how about a cup of coffee? I've got the pot on in the kitchen. Doncha think you're about due for a break? I could clue you in on the best places in town to go dancin'."

"Oh, hey, that's a tempting offer," he said. He held up his clipboard. "But I'm afraid I need to check this place out. Seems to be an overloaded circuit." He put his head to one side. "I wonder . . . I hate to impose on your generosity, Miss Zany, but would you mind loaning me your key? I know it's a lot to ask, but —"

"I'd love to be able to help you out," she

said regretfully. "Honest, I would. But the police officer had to take it with him. Since the house is an official crime scene, see, they have to collect all the keys. He was very apologetic, and he hated to do it, but of course, I don't need the key anymore, now that poor Colin is dead." She batted her eyelashes, to simulate the blinking back of tears.

"I see," the meter man said, and became suddenly businesslike. "Well, I guess that finishes up my work here, then." He yanked his cap down over his eyes, the party clearly at an end. "Thanks for your help, Miss Zany. You have a good day."

"Don't go away mad!" she cried, but it was too late. The meter man was walking toward the driveway and around the house, his clipboard under his arm.

"Aw, shit," she muttered disgustedly. She stamped one bare foot and flounced back into the house, clearly out of the mood for sun-worshipping.

Now was my chance, and I'd better be fast. I pushed the gate open and, with Rambo tugging me along, ran as fast as I could into the alley, turned left, dashed past the next two backyards to the cross-street, and made another left. Just before we came to the corner I slowed to a fast saunter, snapped Rambo's leash, and said "Heel!" Thus paired, we made another left onto the street that ran in front of Colin's house. A girl and her dog, out for a pleasant mid-afternoon walk.

And sure enough, there was the meter man, just climbing into a nondescript blue Ford van parked across the street from Colin's house. He had a cell phone stuck in his ear, and he didn't look up as I walked past on the other side of the street, memorizing the license plate number and noticing that the right rear of the van sported a long scrape, and the rear bumper hung slightly askew.

Big Red Mama was parked on the other side of the street, facing in the opposite direction. I reached it, opened the rear door and the door to the crate, and unfastened the leash. "Okay, Rambo," I said. "Let's go for a ride."

With a delighted "woof," Rambo jumped in, pushed past the open crate, and vaulted into the passenger's seat with the assurance of long habit, the perfect picture of a pooch ready for just about anything.

There was no time to argue with him. I slammed Mama's back door, ran around to the driver's side, and climbed in, grabbing for my cell phone in my vest pocket. I punched in Sheila's direct number, praying she would answer.

She picked up snappishly. "Yeah? What? Who? I'm in the middle of an interview."

"It's China. Sorry to interrupt but this is important. I'm looking at the man who snitched the box from Ruby's house. He's driving a blue Ford late model van. Here's the plate number." I rattled it off. "There's a scrape along the right rear, and the back bumper is crooked."

"Where are you?" Sheila snapped.

"In front of Colin's house," I said. "Hold on a minute, while I plug you in." I put on my headset. That done, I added, "He tried to get into the house, but Crazy Zany from next door brandished her bazookas and he had to cease and desist."

"Bazookas?" Sheila asked, mystified. Her voice hardened. "And just what the hell were you doing at Colin's?"

I put the key in the ignition and started the van. Why did I feel so defensive? I was doing what she'd told me to do, wasn't I?

"I came to pick up Ruby's dog. I've got him with me now. In fact, I was in the dog run with Rambo when the meter man made a try at getting into your crime scene. Colin must have good locks, though. His all-purpose key wouldn't work." I looked at

Rambo, who was panting heavily, his tongue hanging out. Mama had been sitting in the sun, so I lowered the windows partway, to get some air. Rambo immediately stuck his head out. "The bazookas are . . . Oops, I can't explain now. The meter man is pulling away. Should I follow him?"

Sheila hesitated. "I guess, if you do it without being spotted."

"I'll try." I shifted Mama into reverse, backed clumsily into the nearest drive, and turned around, as the Rotti barked gaily at a mockingbird. "I'll have to hang back, though. I'm driving Mama, and Rambo's head is hanging out the window, so I'm conspicuous." On the other hand, nobody would ever think that somebody in her right mind would attempt to tail in a vehicle that maneuvers like a garbage truck and looks like a circus wagon, complete with performing Rottweiler.

"Just keep the guy in sight. I'll get a car to pick you up." Sheila was off the line for fifteen seconds, maybe half a minute. When she came back, she said, "Where are you, China?"

"Making a left turn off Hendricks, onto San Antonio," I said, suiting the action to the words. "He's heading east, a couple of cars ahead of me." I paused. "Did you send a plainclothes out to Colin's place this morning?"

"Who, me?" The response was so quick and natural that I knew it was the truth.

"Well, somebody was here, with a badge. You might want to talk to the neighbor and find out what kind of badge it was."

She was silent for a moment. "Tell me again what this guy looks like. The guy you're following."

"Tall, broad-shouldered, blond, buzz-cut. Square jaw, rugged face. Walks like he owns the world." I paused, waited. No response. "Anybody you know?" I asked.

"Nope, sorry," Sheila said. This time, though, I wasn't sure it was the truth. "Where are you now? Still have him in sight?"

"Just coming up on the light at Laramie. And yep, I can still see him." I was thinking about her reply. Why did it give me pause for concern? Or had my suspicion threshold, always pretty low, been lowered still further by what Hark had told me that morning? If Sheila was dealing with police corruption —

But there wasn't time to think about that now. The blue van was rolling through a commercial neighborhood, and there was more traffic. I had to pay attention. Staying in the right lane, we zipped through the green lights at Laramie and Toledo, Rambo barking gleefully at people walking along the street, like somebody shouting "Hello, I'm having a great day — hope you're having one, too!"

Sheila abandoned her interview and stayed on the line, and I kept her posted on our whereabouts. About four blocks later, at Hastings, the van hit a red light and pulled to a stop, a battered old pickup and a Harley with a sidecar between us. I looked to my left and saw a Pecan Springs black-and-white with two officers pulling out of a Circle K parking lot on the other side of the street. The squad car made a U-turn into the left lane of the two-lane street, pulling up just behind a green SUV, to the left of the blue van.

"Your boys just picked us up," I said to Sheila, as a Blazer towing a golf car pulled up behind the squad car, boxing it in. "But they stick out even worse than I do. I was hoping you'd send an unmarked car and a couple of plainclothes."

"Not available on short notice," she said shortly. "This isn't Houston PD, you know." She said something to someone else, then to me, added, "Glad the guys got there, China. I'm sure you've got things to do at the shop this afternoon, and if you've got

285

the dog, you're probably anxious to get him home. You can drop out now."

"Not on your life," I retorted. "I was the one who called this in, remember?" I paused. "Your boys aren't going to pull him over, I hope. Better to keep an eye on him until we figure out what's going on here."

"I told them just to keep him under surveillance," Sheila said. She didn't sound too happy with my reply. "They're not to stop him."

Surveillance in a black-and-white? Who was she trying to kid? That squad car was as obvious as a black mule riding herd on a flock of snowy white sheep. But Smart Cookie had to work with the police department she had, as somebody once said about an army. No good wishing for an unmarked car that isn't in your inventory.

"Well, I'll just tag along," I said comfortingly. "It doesn't hurt to have an extra tail. You never can tell what might happen."

Sheila didn't answer. The light turned green, I let out the clutch, and Mama rumbled forward as Rambo aimed a volley of complimentary barks at a red-haired girl wearing very short shorts. I kept my eye on the blue van and the black-and-white as they moved in tandem down the street ahead of me, wondering who the meter man was and what his role was in all this.

But wondering was all I could do, I thought as I drove. I had no confirmed facts, no firm ideas, just unfounded speculation. Darla had overheard the man tell Colin it was payback time, or words to that effect, which had led me to guess that he might be connected to the Dallas Dirty Dozen. That notion had been reinforced when I found out that he'd taken the box of photos from Ruby's house, and when I saw him trying to break into Colin's place. And revenge was definitely a prime motivator. If the meter man was part of that Dallas gang, I didn't have to look far for his reason to get rid of Colin.

But Lucita's murder was a complicating factor. Until she turned up dead this morning, it had seemed to me that any connection between her and Colin must have been business related, having to do with his account at the nursery or with a purchase. But now that she was dead — killed with a knife, as Colin had been — I had to admit the strong likelihood of a different kind of relationship. And Sheila, who is a smart cop with plenty of investigative experience, was no doubt thinking along the same lines, even if she wasn't ready to discuss it with me.

What kind of relationship? Not a romantic relationship, certainly. But there were other possible connections between Colin Fowler and Sonora Nursery's bookkeeper. For instance, she might have had some sort of ties to the Dallas Dirty Dozen. Lucita had come from Brownsville, according to Betty, and the chances were probably better than even that at least one of the Dirties had connections to that troubled town, which has a reputation as a convenient border crossing for drugs of every description.

But maybe there was another connection. I thought back to my earlier hunch about *Cannabis* and my speculation that maybe Dan Reid had decided to cash in on his law-enforcement experience in the underworld of Dallas drug dealing by becoming a dealer and reinventing himself as Colin Fowler, industrious shopkeeper and law-abiding citizen in small-town Pecan Springs. The lure of big money must be incredibly, perhaps irresistibly powerful for a guy like Reid, who understood the business inside out, upside down, and from both ends. He'd know every trick in the book for distributing the merchandise while keeping clear of the law — even the time-honored trick of the police payoff, the bribes that would keep the local gendarmerie off his back. If that was the story behind this story, there was certainly a role for Lucita, who might have been helping obtain the stuff. She had come here from Brownsville, a hub for dope traffic. A little digging into her background might turn up all kinds of dirt.

And in the midst of all this speculation, there was one thing I felt pretty sure of: the man driving that blue Ford van, whoever he was, understood the connection between Colin and Lucita, whatever *it* was. I shivered, thinking of the man's aggressive walk, his burly shoulders, his commanding style. In fact, maybe *he* was the connection. Maybe he was the killer.

Sheila came back on the line. "You still there, China?"

"I'm here," I said. "Have you got a fix on the license plate yet?"

"Stolen."

"Why am I not surprised?" I braked and shifted down as the car ahead of me slowed. "The van, too, probably."

"Nothing on that yet." She paused, and her voice lightened. "What was that about bazookas?"

I chuckled dryly. "You had to have been there. It was a masterful performance, on both sides. Tit for tat, so to speak." I pulled in my breath. "Hey!"

"What's happening?"

"The meter man has made a sharp right turn, without a signal, onto River Road. The patrol car's moving on, straight ahead. They've lost him." To give the officers credit, they might not have had a choice. They were stuck in the left lane behind that green SUV and a snazzy yellow convertible with the top down, and the right lane was occupied by a school bus — not the best place to be, if you're trying to keep your options open. But Pecan Springs cops probably don't get much training in how to do a tail.

"Don't worry, Sheila," I added reassuringly, glad that I could be of some help. "I'm staying with him." I swung Big Mama into a fast right turn. When she straightened up, the Ford was about a block ahead, heading south, and I slowed. "I'm on River Road. I've got him in sight, but I'll have to hang back some. No need to advertise." I checked my rearview mirror. The lane behind me was empty. "No sign of your boys. I wonder what's keeping them."

Sheila said something I couldn't quite make out. She didn't sound very happy, which I could understand. Her officers had lost the guy they were supposed to be following. I wouldn't like to be in their shoes.

Sheila can be very bitchy when she's displeased.

"Okay, we're heading down River Road," I told her. I was feeling pretty good, and who could blame me? I'd spotted the guy and successfully stayed with the tail when the cops flubbed it. "There's not much out this way but the park and the river. Wonder where he's going." I chuckled. "A shack in the country, maybe? A secret spot where he does a little cooking?" The Adams County deputies had busted a meth lab a dozen miles south on River Road the month before. Blackie says those damn meth labs are all over the place — close one down and two more open up.

"What makes you think of drugs?" Sheila asked sharply.

"Dunno," I said. "A wild guess." I looked around, getting a fix on exactly where we were. "Or maybe he's heading for the Pack Saddle Inn."

The Pack Saddle Inn is a family-style place with a decent restaurant and an acre or so of landscaped grounds beside the Pecan River. The grounds are especially pretty at this time of year, with sweeps of bluebonnets, bright patches of coreopsis and daisies, and lush green ruffles of ferns. And since it's out of the way, the place is private and very quiet, unlike the big motels along the interstate, where the traffic noise will keep you awake all night. If you're going to be in town for a couple of days and don't mind driving an extra couple of miles, the Pack Saddle is a good place to stay.

In fact, there's a specially nostalgic place in my heart for the Pack Saddle, which is where McQuaid and I spent our wedding night, and I thought about this as I drove across the low cement bridge over the Pecan River. We were planning to be married in the Thyme and Seasons garden, but Hurricane Josephine breezed into town, disrupting all the arrangements and forcing us to move the ceremony and the reception to the Pack Saddle's Garden Room. The wedding went off without a hitch, but the entire wedding party — including the bride and groom — was marooned when the Pecan River flooded and took out a couple of bridge abutments. (You can still see the pile of concrete rubble on the left side of the road just after you cross the bridge.) Of course, the event wasn't a total washout. Our guests stayed up long after McQuaid and I had retired to the Honeymoon Suite, enjoying themselves to the hilt. There were enough sandwiches and cake to feed a village of hurricane refugees, not to mention gallons of bubbly and spiked punch, and since Josephine had knocked the power out, there was nothing to do but eat, drink, and be merry. Our wedding was the rowdiest in recent memory.

Beside the road, a doe, brown eyes large and wondering, paused in the green shadow of a juniper. On the seat next to me, Rambo woofed happily at a blue jay perched in the lacy foliage of a mesquite. And ahead, I could see the meter man's blue Ford van, pulling into the Pack Saddle's parking lot.

"Hey, I guessed right!" I said to Sheila, feeling excited. "He's just turned in to the Pack Saddle. Looks like he's driving around back, where the guest parking is. I'll give him a minute or two, and then I can tell you what unit he's staying in."

"No, you won't." Sheila let her breath out and I wondered if she had been holding it. "Okay, China, you've done a great job, and I'm grateful. But this is the end of the line. You're getting off."

I frowned. The end of the line? "But don't you want me to stick around until your boys get here?" I slowed, letting my quarry finish making his turn around the main building and checking the rearview mirror again. There wasn't a squad car in sight. "And where the heck are they, Sheila? They must know they lost him. They had to've seen him peel off down River Road. They should have been here five minutes ago."

"Don't worry about it." There was a note of finality in Sheila's voice. "I'll take it from here, China."

I turned into the Pack Saddle parking lot. "If you're worrying about my safety, don't. I can take care of myself. And somebody ought to keep an eye on this guy until you can get some backup here. For all we know, he's just dropping in to pick up his stuff before he hits the road again."

"I said I'll take it from here." Her tone was flat and hard. "You're gone, Bayles. This is an order. Got it?"

Got it?

And then, in a flash, I got it, as you might get it when somebody smacks you, hard, with the flat side of a two-by-four. The oddly inept way the squad car seemed to lose the Ford van and the fact that it hadn't yet attempted to pick up the target. Sheila's earlier effort to get me to drop out and now, her flat-out order to leave. There was something strange going on here, some sort of business I wasn't supposed to be involved with.

And now that I had gotten myself involved

— inadvertently so, I could honestly say in my own defense — I was under orders to get *un*involved, in a hurry. Whatever the nature of this particular party, I wasn't a welcome guest. The hostess had just sent me home.

Well, okay. At least I knew where I stood, even if I wasn't especially happy about it. The trouble is, of course, that I've never been very good at taking orders. There's something about being told to leave that raises my hackles, makes me want to dig in my heels and hang in there. But in the face of an order from my friend Sheila Dawson, who is also the chief of police, what was I going to say?

"Got it," I replied, with cheerful ambiguity. "Have a good afternoon. I'll talk to you later, Smart Cookie."

I clicked off the phone and pulled into a parking space in the shade of a large pecan tree. "Hey, Rambo," I said, reaching for his leash. "You need to go pee?"

As Rambo was watering one of the Pack Saddle's shrubs, I looked over my shoulder in the direction of the road. A black-and-white was driving slowly by. The two officers were scanning the parking lot. My first impulse was to jump up and down and get their attention, then signal them that their quarry had driven around back.

But for some reason, I didn't do that.

CHAPTER THIRTEEN

Agarito (*Berberis trifoliolata*) is a species of barberry shrub native to Texas, New Mexico, and northern Mexico. Its yellow blossoms appear in the spring and red berries in the summer. Indians used the fruit, stems, and roots for a variety of medicinal purposes, primarily to treat liver and kidney ailments. Early settlers made a yellow dye from the woody stems. The berries have been used to make juice, syrup, and jelly.

The Pack Saddle Inn was built back in the forties and expanded in the fifties, at a time when families from the suburbs of Houston and Dallas couldn't wait to get away to the Hill Country for a cool, quiet summer vacation. The kids spent their days tubing down the rippling rapids of the Pecan River or hunting for arrowheads and spear points left behind by nomadic Indians. The dads fished for bass and crappies in the river's still, deep pools, and the moms fried fish, doctored sunburns and chigger bites, and caught up on their summertime reading.

The world has changed since those halcyon leave-it-to-Beaver days. Vacationing families are looking for thrills and spills instead of peace and quiet, and the kids would rather go to Sea World in San Antonio or Six Flags in Fort Worth. Nowadays, the Pack Saddle's chief clientele are retired snowbirds who migrate South during the winter, academic types who are attending conferences at CTSU, and guys who come for serious fishing in nearby Canyon Lake. But the snowbird migration is reliably steady, the university hosts a conference or two every month, and the fishing is good. The inn stays pretty full.

The main building, sided with dark brown shingles and roofed with red tile, is built like a large ranch house, with one- and two-story wings angling off in different directions. Individual cedar-shingled cabins, left over from the days of leisurely family-style vacations, are scattered among the trees in a haphazard arrangement designed for the maximum amount of privacy.

Rambo had other business besides peeing. He sniffed around for a bit, then turned his back with a don't-interrupt-me-until-I'm-finished look, and began to fertilize the flower bed. When he had finished that urgent chore, we took a walk around the main building and into the back lot. Since it was afternoon, most of the guests were out doing other things and only a few cars were parked in front of their owners' units. Because of the odd, meandering way the buildings are laid out, it took me several minutes to spot the meter man's blue Ford van. It was at the very back of the complex, down a narrow lane that led to a cluster of two or three cabins along the bank of the Pecan River. The Ford was half-hidden behind a group of spreading green junipers and a large clump of pampas grass, beside Cabin Number 37.

Rambo finished his job and we went back to Mama. I gave him the bacon treats to keep him busy, but he disposed of them in one gulp and thanked me by enthusiastically washing my cheek and ear with his rough tongue. Howard Cosell occasionally expresses his affection by licking my ankle, but I had never been laundered by a Rottweiler before.

As Rambo turned around a couple of times in the passenger seat and began to settle down for a nap, I sat staring out the window. My suspicious nature has been enhanced by my legal training. It was impossible for me not to suspect that something was going on and that Sheila was smack dab in the middle of whatever it was. I didn't know enough to make informed guesses about the man in Cabin Number 37 — who he was, what he was doing here, and how, or whether, he was involved in Colin's or Lucita's death. But I don't like feeling left out of the loop, and I'm not a happy camper when I'm asked to play go-along-and-get-along. Now that I had trailed the guy this far, I was inclined to invest a little more time in the project, if only to scratch the itch of my curiosity. If Sheila didn't like my sticking around, well, that was just too dadgum bad. She wasn't my boss, just my friend.

I frowned. Not my boss, just my friend. From that perspective, I had an obligation to stick around, didn't I?

I picked up the phone, tapped the speed-dial button for Thyme and Seasons, and told Missy that I had hit an unexpected snag. It might be another hour or two before I could deliver the dog and get back to the shop.

"Take your time," she said cheerfully. "We've been busy, but it's nothing I can't handle. Oh, yes — there've been a couple of cancellations for tomorrow's papermaking workshop. I went ahead and called the first two people on the waiting list." She paused. "One of them was Betty Conrad. I was a little surprised when she said yes, she'd come. I thought, under the circumstances, she might not want to . . ." Her voice trailed off.

"People have to get on with their lives," I said. "I'm glad Betty isn't letting it get her down."

"She said she wanted to talk to you," Missy added. "She left a number."

I wrote it down, then said, "Would you please check with Carole to make sure she's got everything she needs? Tell her I'll be there about eight in the morning to give her a hand. She'll need help, and Ruby will still be in Fredericksburg."

"I'll tell her," Missy said. "Oh, Ruby called here a little bit ago, looking for you. I told her you went to pick up the Rottweiler. How's he doing?" Her soft voice became anxious. "The dog isn't giving you any trouble, is he? I've been worried that he might be . . . well, a little aggressive. Hard to handle."

I glanced at Rambo, who was curled up on the seat with one paw over his eyes. "Aggressive?" I chuckled. "Not at the moment, anyway."

"That's good," she said. "One thing more. Has Wanda Rathbottom reached you? She's called the shop several times. She said she wanted to talk about what happened this morning at Sonora."

"No, she hasn't reached me. Not yet anyway." Wanda is nothing if not persistent. She is one of those people who will pester you to death when she has something on her mind. And there wasn't anything I could — or would — tell her about the Sanchez murder. "Don't give her my cell number, please," I added.

"I won't." Missy lowered her voice. "Have the police found out anything more? About who killed that bookkeeper, I mean."

"If they have," I said dryly, "they haven't confided in me." We said good-bye and I clicked off the phone. Then, remembering about Betty, I turned it on again and punched in the number Missy had given me. It must have been her home number, because there was no answering machine on the line. As the ringing went on, I had time to wonder why she needed to talk to me and wondered whether it had anything to do with Lucita Sanchez's murder. It must not be a very good day at Sonora.

No answer. I gave up after seven rings and dropped the phone into one of the pockets of my vest. It was time, as McQuaid says, to fish or cut bait. I had already decided to fish, but I had to find the right spot, so I started Mama and drove around the side of the main building, where I had spotted a trio of large metal Dumpsters, lined up like railroad boxcars, end to end. I backed between the Dumpsters and a fence — no mean feat, if I do say so myself. Mama isn't very agile, and she's not crazy about squeezing her bulk into snug-fitting places.

This one was a perfect hidey-hole. Mama was out of sight, but angled, so I had a clear view of the blue Ford van and Cabin 37, which had a wooden porch across the front, complete with a cozy couple of rust-colored metal lawn chairs, circa 1950. The green-painted front door was closed and green curtains were drawn across the front window. I took note of the fact that there was another, smaller window on the side I could see, about six feet above the ground, and closed.

The cabin was one of the older models. Likely, it had a kitchenette in the rear, where those fifties' moms could fry up the fish caught by the dads and serve them to the kids, who were so healthily tired from their outdoor exercise that they'd eat their suppers and trundle off to bed in one of the two tiny bedrooms. There was no way to tell from where I sat, but there were probably a couple of windows on the other side, and a back door facing the river. The cabin was surrounded by some sort of shrubbery — I couldn't tell what it was from this distance — and trees, mostly junipers, with spreading lower branches that offered plenty of handy cover. If I were inclined to do a little reconnoitering in the vicinity, it would be easy and relatively safe.

Rambo sighed and settled deeper into the seat. I settled back to wait, chewing on my cuticle. I wasn't sure why I was doing this. One of those hunches Ruby is always talking about, maybe. Or maybe I just didn't like the way Sheila had instructed me to butt out.

I wasn't sure what I was waiting for, either. A personal invitation to get out and have a look around? The sound of sirens? The sudden appearance of a team of stealthy sharpshooters with rifles at the ready who would silently surround the cabin and flush out their quarry with teargas? These thoughts filled me with nervous energy, and I chewed harder.

It was a good thing I didn't have to wait

long, or I wouldn't have had any cuticles left. Interesting things began to happen in fairly short order. Sheila's red Blazer — ah, the unmarked car, at last — with Smart Cookie herself at the wheel, sped smartly around the main building. I sat up straight, expecting the Blazer to be at the head of a parade of cop cars.

But it wasn't.

And it didn't stop or even slow down, as you might expect, if the driver was trying to get her bearings in what is basically a confusing and haphazard arrangement of buildings. Instead, she drove purposefully across the lot and up the little lane that led to Cabin 37, as if she knew exactly where she was going. This seemed strange, since as far as I was aware, Smart Cookie had no notion that the meter man was staying at the Pack Saddle until I tailed him here and reported back to her. But I hadn't told her that he was in Cabin 37. How did she know that?

Sheila pulled in beside the Ford van and got out. She had changed her clothes since that morning. Now, she was dressed in civvies, and very nicely dressed, too, in chic beige slacks and a lemon yellow pullover with the sleeves pushed up and a chunky gold bracelet on her arm. She didn't look anything like a cop, but if past experience was any guide, I knew that her sidearm was concealed in the handsome Gucci bag slung over her shoulder.

What was wrong with this picture? Well, for starters, while Sheila is certainly a woman who knows how to take care of herself, she was out here all alone. If there was an officer crouching in the Blazer to cover her pretty rear, he didn't show himself — and a fat lot of good he'd do her, anyway, hidden away in the vehicle. And where the hell was the rest of her backup? If there was a squad car anywhere in the vicinity, I hadn't spotted it. No army of stealthy sharpshooters deployed among the bushes, either.

As I watched, wondering nervously whether I should leap from the van and rush like Supergirl to Smart Cookie's defense, she rapped at the cabin door. Then she cocked her head, listening, and rapped again. The door opened a crack, on the chain. She leaned forward, saying something. I couldn't hear her, of course, but I could read her body language. She was watchful and wary but not especially tense, and she wasn't looking for trouble. What's more, she wasn't afraid of this man, and she wanted him to know it. The door opened, and she stepped inside. The door closed.

Whatever I had expected, this wasn't it. I sat very still for a moment, staring at that closed green door, processing what I had seen and putting it together with the other things that had happened that afternoon. It looked to me like Sheila had deliberately pulled her officers off the tail. She had tried to pull me off, too. She either knew the man or she knew who he was, why he was there, and what his connection was with the case.

All of which added up to one thing: the meter man, whoever he was, was not a killer — or at least, Smart Cookie didn't think so. Heck, he might even be a cop. But what kind of cop enters a house — Ruby's house — without a warrant and walks out with a box that might be crucial evidence? He'd attempted to enter Colin's house, too, even though it was marked as a crime scene. And what if Smart Cookie, for once in her life, was wrong? What if the meter man *was* a killer?

My frown turned into a scowl and I grunted and shifted in my seat, which was enough to wake Rambo. He lifted his head, sensing my quandary. So what was I going to do? Follow Sheila's instructions, like a good little girl, and leave her here, alone with whoever-he-was?

Heck, no. I pulled the keys out of the ignition and stuck them into my jeans pocket.

Rambo hoisted himself upright, cocked his head, and looked at me expectantly. *Time for another walk?*

"Stay," I said.

He grinned and leaned toward me.

"Sorry," I said, and showed him my empty hands. "All out of bacon treats. But you have to stay, anyway."

Do I have a choice? his resigned look said, as he settled himself back into the seat. I rolled down the windows a couple of inches before I climbed out and locked the door. It was only April and the sun wasn't quite hot enough to turn Mama into a toaster oven, but I didn't want to come back and find Rambo baked to a crisp.

Now that I was out of the van, I wasn't sure what I intended to do. But there was only one way to find out what was going on in that cabin, and that was to get as close as I could to the scene of the action. I walked quickly across the lot to the main building. Using one of the building's wings as cover, I strode jauntily along, as if I were a guest on her way back to her unit, or one of the hired hands taking a ten-minute break in the spring sunshine. Hands in pockets, whistling tunelessly with an air of casual nonchalance, I made my way through a patch of shrubbery, down a meandering path along the river bank, and hence to the rear of Cabin 37.

My heart lightened when I saw it. Like a lot of old-fashioned cottages, this one had a screen door, which was sheltered by a trellis covered with early roses. The shrubbery around the cottage proved to be agarito, a gray-green shrub with sharp-pointed, holly-like leaves, an effective barrier to an eavesdropper who might want to listen beneath a window. But I didn't have to. While the screen was shut, the back door itself stood open. I stopped whistling, abandoned the pretext of a stroll, and went up to the door as noiselessly as I could, on the alert for any sound.

Whatever was going on inside, it was going on quietly. If Sheila was in trouble, there was no audible sign of it, no cries for help. I could hear the murmur of voices, a man's voice, a woman's voice, low, urgent, intense. Hoping to get a better fix on what they were saying, I pressed my ear against the screen and held my breath.

"— don't care what you *think* you're doing," Sheila was saying disgustedly. "You jump-out boys are all alike. No supervision, no chain of command, too damn much discretion."

Jump-out boys? I sucked in my breath. So that was it! Well, it figured.

A jump-out boy is an undercover narcotics agent, named for the sudden habit of jumping out of an unmarked car and arresting the street seller and his small-fry customer. It's a tactic much used by the narcotics task forces that began national operation in the early 1990s under the Byrne grant, named for a New York police officer who was killed by drug dealers in 1988. In Texas, these task forces are notorious for their carelessness with evidence, their cavalier attitude toward the truth, and their eagerness to rack up arrests, especially after the Texas legislature, in its infinite wisdom, rewrote the state's asset forfeiture laws to allow the task forces to pocket money and other assets seized during drug arrests. The legislation — heralded as a way to make criminals pay through the nose for their crimes — turned the drug-bust business into a cash cow and corrupted a great many cops and politicians.

Corruption. I felt suddenly cold, remembering what Hark had said that morning. What if this man was —

"Hey," the meter man drawled lazily, "don't be so hard on a guy, huh? I'm only doing a job here."

"I should have been notified about your 'job,' " Sheila said, her voice flat and angry. "Why didn't somebody from your task force let me know that you were coming? Why didn't I hear from your DPS supervisor? Damn it, Tyson, you've stepped into the middle of two murder investigations. How was I to —"

"You might've been notified if you hadn't slept with the guy," Tyson said brutally.

Sheila's reply was so low and harsh that I couldn't quite make it out.

"Well, hell," Tyson said, soft and slick. "Can't say I blame him, now that I get a good look at you. Wouldn't mind having a little of that myself. Say, what'd'ya think? Maybe we could —"

There was the swift, hard sound of a slap, and I heard Tyson suck in his breath.

"How about it?" Sheila snapped, icy cold. "Want a little more of *that?*"

Way to go, girl! I said silently, clenching my fist.

Tyson's voice was hard and rough. "As I was saying, you might've been notified. But my task force commander thought it wasn't a good idea to involve you in the investigation, since you had a prior relationship with the subject. He —"

311

And at that moment, my cell phone rang. Without thinking, I had slid the damn thing into the pocket of my vest, and now "The Eyes of Texas" was tinkling merrily into the silence of the sunlit afternoon. I fumbled hastily for the phone, flipped it open, and broke the connection. Frantically, I looked around for a place to hide, but it was too late.

"China Bayles!" Sheila said sharply. She was standing in the doorway, her fists on her hips, wearing the fiercest scowl I had ever seen on her face. Over her shoulder, she said to the man, "Stay where you are. I'll handle this." To me, she said: "What the *devil* do you think you're doing, skulking around out here?"

"I . . . uh, I —" I could feel my face flaming. I'm sure I have been more embarrassed in my life, although I couldn't think when. "I only was trying to — I mean, I —"

Sheila came outside, closing the kitchen door firmly behind her. "I told you to *leave,*" she snapped angrily. "I told you to take that dog and go home. You disobeyed a police order, China!"

"But I thought you might . . ." I straightened my shoulders, struggling to recover my cool. "I thought you might be in trouble. You didn't bring any backup. For all *I* knew, this guy was a killer, maybe a two-time killer. I was worried about you."

Sheila regarded me, narrow-eyed, processing what I'd said. "But you're not worried now?"

"Are you kidding?" My cool was coming back. In fact, I was all fired up. "I know what a jump-out boy does for a living, Smart Cookie. I know how those guys deal with the local authorities. He could set you up. He could frame you. He could —"

"Yeah." Sheila's look said she had already thought about this. "We need to talk, China. But not here. Not now. Tonight. You going to be home?" A breeze shivered the roses and a shower of white petals fell on her hair and shoulders.

"Anytime after six," I said. "Come for supper. But listen, Sheila," I added urgently, in a lower voice, "I want you to watch your back. These jump-out jockeys can't be trusted. They're bad news. They —"

And then the damn cell phone rang again. The jingling tune of "The Eyes of Texas Are Upon You" pealed into the quiet air.

Sheila threw back her head and laughed, a genuine laugh. "China Bayles, as a detective, you are positively inept."

I had to laugh, too, as I grabbed for the phone, feeling about as dumb as dirt.

"You've noticed, huh? But as a friend I'm tops. You have to admit that."

"As a friend, you are definitely super," she agreed amiably, still chuckling. "Now get outta here, will you? I've got work to do, and you're keeping me from doing it." She went back inside and closed the door in my face. Then she opened it again and said, through the crack, in a tone of mock severity, "And if you don't get out of here, I'm going to call the police." She laughed and shut the door.

The phone was still ringing. I flipped it open. "Whoozzit?" I growled.

"Hey, China," a man's voice said. "Hope I haven't interrupted something important. I don't have your husband's cell phone number, and I need to talk to him. It's about the car. Your dad's car. Our dad's car. It's important."

It was my brother. Excuse me. My *half* brother.

Chapter Fourteen

Lemony Spring Green Noodles

2 cups minced dandelion greens, packed (use only unsprayed, washed leaves, or substitute fresh spinach)

2 eggs

1 teaspoon lemon juice

1/2 teaspoon salt

1 tablespoon fresh or 1 teaspoon dried dill weed

1 1/3 cups flour

Beat together dandelion greens, eggs, lemon juice, salt, and dill until smooth. Beat in flour, one-quarter cup at a time, continuing until dough is very stiff. (You may not use the full amount, depending on the moisture in the greens.) Turn dough onto a floured surface and knead for 5–6 minutes, until smooth and elastic. Roll into a sheet 1/16-inch thick. Allow to dry for about an hour, then dust with flour, roll loosely (like a cigar) and slice into strips of whatever width you like. Drop into boiling water; cook for about 8 minutes. Toss with butter and grated cheese and serve as a flavorful, colorful side dish, or add to your favorite seafood.

I took Rambo home and introduced him to Howard. The two circled each other, sniffing warily at front ends and back ends while they exchanged personal greetings in that silent code that all dogs, no matter what breed they are, understand. Howard (who is more aggressive than he looks) let Rambo know that he was the boss here and didn't intend to relinquish that position any time soon. Rambo (although he is much the larger dog) politely let Howard know that he got the message and was fully prepared to cooperate.

Introductions made, territorial negotiations completed, and the truce ratified, Howard sat on the back steps and watched with his usual aloof-basset expression as I put the Rotti into the backyard Puppy Palace, a securely fenced twenty-by-six-foot run, equipped with cozy doggie igloo, a doggie water fountain, and all the doggie toys any basset's heart could desire. Howard disdains the run, of course, preferring to spend his waking hours chasing squirrels and his naptime dozing under the porch swing, but Rambo settled in as if he had lived there all his life.

I left the two dogs observing each other across the neutral territory of the backyard and drove back to the shop. I was still smarting from my performance at the cabin, where I had come off looking and sounding like an idiot. Worse. A blathering idiot with a teenaged cell phone. I would have changed the ring-a-ding thingy if I could've, but that would have to wait until Brian got home. I hate to confess it, but I don't know how.

I spent the rest of the afternoon trying to improve my attitude. Cass had already closed the tearoom by the time I got back, and business was slow enough to allow me to go outside and weed the beds along the path to the front door, where I could keep one eye out for customers while I made sure that each weed I pulled was a genuine weed.

To some gardeners, of course, a weed is any plant that's growing in the wrong place. But in my garden, what looks at first glance like a weed may be a volunteer herb, and while I might not enthusiastically endorse its unexpected appearance or invite it to stay for the season, it deserves a certain amount of respect. The common dandelion, for instance, is a potassium-rich diuretic, a nutritive tonic, and a treatment for high cholesterol, as well as a tasty food. Chickweed has been used to treat kidney ailments, coughs, and even obesity. Plantain, one of the Anglo-Saxons' nine sacred plants, was called *waybroad,* for its ubiquitous growth. It was known as a powerful burn treatment and all-round wound-wort, especially potent in the case of mad-dog bite. I love this old recipe for a salve to treat "flying venom," which Brother Cadfael probably manufactured by the bucketful:

Take a handful of hammerwort [pellitory] and a handful of maythe [chamomile] and a handful of waybroad and roots of water dock, seek those which will float, and one eggshell full of clean honey, then take clean butter, let him who will help to work up the salve, melt it thrice: let one sing a mass over the worts, before they are put together and the salve is wrought up.

I don't sing a mass over the worts while I pull them, but I have found that this sort of work is a very good thing for the soul, particularly when you know that you've made a total idiot of yourself.

But while I might feel somewhat better about my idiocy, the central questions still remained. Who exactly *was* the guy in Cabin 37? A jump-out boy, Sheila had said — but what was a narcotics task force agent doing in Pecan Springs? What was Tyson's connection to Colin? Why did he want the box of photos Colin had stashed at Ruby's house? How was he connected with Lucita Sanchez? And did any of this have to do with that business about official corruption that Hark had mentioned?

But as Sheila had made abundantly clear, those questions were none of my business, and I wasn't going to get any answers — not right away, anyway. So I might as well stop thinking about them, and get on with my life and my business. I certainly had plenty to keep me occupied. Ruby had called to tell Missy that the psychiatrist was going to evaluate her mother on Monday morning, so she wouldn't be back until that afternoon, at the earliest. Carole had checked in to say that she had things pretty well set up for the next day's workshop and was headed to San Antonio for an evening with friends.

I looked down at a curling tendril of Texas bindweed, the bane of a gardener's existence and a notorious strangler that grabs every stem within its greedy reach. I was trying to remember where I had read that the plant was used by the Navajo to treat spider bites when I heard someone call.

"Yoo-hoo, China! China Bayles!"

It was Wanda Rathbottom, coming up the walk. Wanda is a large woman with broad shoulders, strong arms, and a perpetual frown. The former owner of what is now Sonora Nursery, she did not give up her business happily and I knew that she resented the Conrads for transforming her failure into a stunning success. She was writing a book, I'd heard, about how to succeed in the nursery business. It figured. Those who can, do. Those who can't (with a few exceptions), write about it.

"Hello, Wanda," I said, straightening up. "Sorry I didn't call you back." I was going to say I'd forgotten, but that wasn't very tactful. It wasn't very true, either. I hadn't called her back because she is so pushy. I avoid her as much as possible.

"No matter." She waved away my apology. Her spiky brown hair was unusually spiky today, and her nose was twitching. Wanda always reminds me of a rabbit, with that twitchy nose, and she has no natural eyebrows. Today, she had penciled upside-down brown Vs over her eyes, giving herself a clownish look. "I thought I'd catch you here," she added, looking around. "Is there a place where we can sit and be a little private?"

"How about that bench over there?" I asked, pointing to the wooden bench at the gate to the Peter Rabbit garden that we share with the children's bookstore next door. "If we sit there, I can keep my eye on the shop."

"Oh, right," she said, turning down her mouth with her usual sarcasm. "You wouldn't want to miss any customers, would you?"

I ignored that. "What's up?" I asked, as we sat down.

"It's about what happened at Sonora this morning." She looked around nervously, as if she expected somebody to pop up out of the rhubarb patch. Farmer McGregor, maybe. "Ronny — my son works in the greenhouse there — told me about it when he came home for lunch. He said you found the body and called the police."

I frowned. "Well, actually it was Betty who found the body. I just happened to —"

"Lucita Sanchez," she cut in darkly. "But I suppose you know who she was. If Betty had listened to me, this wouldn't have happened. I told her it wasn't a good idea to hire that woman. She'd been in trouble with the law down there in Brownsville, you know. She was in jail last year for dealing drugs."

Dealing drugs. "Really? You knew her, then?"

"No, of course I didn't know her," she said indignantly. Her nose twitched. "My son told me about it."

Now, Ronny Rathbottom is not what I would call a credible witness, since he has frequently been in trouble with the law. But perhaps, in this case, he could be trusted. He certainly had an insider's view.

"Tell me about it," I said encouragingly.

Wanda hesitated. Now that she had identified her son as an informant, she wasn't sure how much she wanted to involve him — or how much of the truth she wanted to tell. In a more tentative voice, she said, "You probably don't know about this, but Ronny has occasionally taken drugs." She coughed dismissively. "Lots of young people do these days, of course. Seems like every mother I talk to has a kid with a drug problem. But I always say that everyone deserves a second chance."

If Wanda thought I didn't know her son was a user, she was fooling herself. Everybody knew that Ronny had done jail time and treatment time, not once but twice. Still, Pecan Springs is a forgiving town, and

Ronny isn't the only one to forgive. There's a long lineup of kids with drug problems, all in need of forgiveness, all in need of a real second chance.

"But how did Ronny know about Lucita?" I persisted.

"I'm getting to that," she said. "Ronny was down in Brownsville about the time she got out of jail. Turns out that she's an aunt of his friend Woody, and Woody said maybe she could get them something. Ronny just said no, of course," she added defensively. "He's off the stuff altogether. He's clean as a baby. He's got a job at Sonora. That's where he saw her, you see, working in the office. He told me, and I told Betty what I thought about that."

"Yeah, right," I said softly. So much for second chances.

"Well, I didn't want her around where Ronny could be tempted, did I?" Wanda flared. "Of course, I know he wouldn't. He's sworn to me that he'll never do that again. But maybe Woody would. Lucita was his aunt, after all."

"Did she offer to get anything for the boys?" Anything like marijuana or cocaine, two herbs with nasty reputations.

"No, but the woman was trouble. That's why I alerted Betty to the situation. I like

Betty, you know, although I'm not too keen on some of the things she and Allan have done with the place. That fountain, for one thing. Makes the place look like a Hollywood set. Must have cost a fortune."

True enough, I thought. But Wanda's words had the tart tang of sour grapes, which I could definitely understand. The Conrads had turned her failed business into a major success story.

"But Betty has a good heart and she works hard," Wanda went on. "And she's crazy about Ricky and Jeannette. She'd do anything for those kids. I thought she ought to know that this woman — Lucita Sanchez — has been in trouble with the law over drugs, because I didn't think she'd want her around her children. Teenagers are so vulnerable these days. Boys, especially. They get into the wrong crowd, you know. And Betty has always been very grateful when I've given her a little advice here and there."

Yeah, I bet. "How did she take it?"

Wanda pursed her lips as if she were tasting something bitter. "She was shocked, of course, poor thing. Just devastated. But Allan had hired the Sanchez woman, and she'd been here since the middle of March. Betty said she hated the thought of having somebody on the premises who'd been dealing drugs, but she really didn't think she could just up and fire her."

It must have been a challenge for gentle Betty to deal with Wanda on her high horse, full of self-righteous disdain. And I knew it wouldn't be easy for her to tell what she knew to the police, especially if she hadn't yet told her husband that Sanchez had a record. I wondered if that was what she had wanted to talk to me about earlier that afternoon.

As if she had read my mind, Wanda went on. "That's why I thought I should discuss this with you, China. I mean, you found Sanchez's body. And you're a lawyer — you know about things like this. Ronny said he didn't think Betty had told the police about the woman's record. You have to tell them."

"But they'll run a check on her," I objected. "They'll pull up her record. They'll find out whatever —"

She leaned closer. Her rabbit nose twitched. "Ronny knows why she was killed. And it didn't have anything to do with a robbery, either, you can bet your sweet patootie on that." She folded her arms and regarded me with dark satisfaction.

I frowned. "Why was she killed?"

"Because she was mixed up in a dope deal with that friend of Ruby's. That man Ruby was running around with."

I felt the skin prickle across my shoulders. "Colin Fowler?" It was an unnecessary question. There was no doubt who she meant.

"Yes, Fowler. The one who got killed." A pitying smile curling at the corners of her mouth. "I know that this is a really bad time for Ruby, with her mother and all. And I certainly don't want to put her to any unnecessary grief by associating her with a drug dealer. But somebody ought to tell the police that Sanchez and Fowler were —"

"Where did Ronny get his information?"

She stonewalled me with a shake of her head.

"I have to know who his source is," I said firmly. "Otherwise, I am not going to get involved." Probably not even then.

She hesitated, weighing her options. "His girlfriend told him," she said grudgingly.

"Who's his girlfriend? And where did she get *her* information?"

Wanda leaned forward, her clown eyebrows pulled down, her nose twitching as furiously as a rattlesnake's rattle. "Ronny's girlfriend worked in Fowler's shop. She knew what he was up to, every dirty little bit of it."

My mouth dropped open. "Ronny's girlfriend is *Marcy Windsor?*"

"You know her?" Wanda asked, surprised.

"We've met." I could have said that I made Marcy's acquaintance when I caught her with her hand in the till at Colin's shop, but I didn't. I might have added that when I talked with her, I had the feeling that she knew more than she was willing to tell me. But I didn't say that, either.

Instead, I said sternly, "Let me get this straight. You're saying that Marcy Windsor told Ronny that Colin Fowler was dealing?" If that was true, it probably answered my question about what Tyson, the undercover drug task force guy, was doing in Pecan Springs. He was after Colin. And if Colin hadn't ended up dead, he might have ended up in jail.

"Well, I couldn't say whether that was the exact same word Marcy used," Wanda said, as carefully as if she were a sworn witness and I was a prosecutor. "I got it from Ronny, and I don't know if what he said was *exact*. But yes, that's the meat of it. That's what she told him. Dealing." Her face hardened. "Which is probably what got him killed. It's a dangerous world out there, if you're into drugs. That's why I keep telling Ronny he has to stay away from the stuff. One way or another, it'll kill you."

I couldn't argue with that, and anyway, there wasn't time. A couple of women had come up the walk and were pausing to admire the plants on the rack outside the door. I stood up. "Ronny has to go to the police and tell them what he knows," I said.

"But he's on probation!" Wanda cried, her clown eyebrows shooting high up under her hair. "If he goes to the police, they'll find an excuse to put him back in jail. They'll say he knew about it because he bought dope from Fowler, or something like that. They'll crucify him."

"I honestly don't think —"

"Of course you don't. You don't know what they're like. They never want to give anybody a second chance." She was working herself up now, her voice rising shrilly. "But you're good friends with that police chief. You can get her to check out this story without involving Ronny. You can, I know you can." She fixed me with her eyes and said, in a commanding tone, "I am depending on you to help him, China."

I made a noise low in my throat. "I am not a dependable person." And I do not like being pushed around, especially by Wanda Rathbottom. "Your son needs to find the courage to tell his story to the authorities. If he doesn't, he may find himself in jail. It's a crime to withhold important information in a murder investigation."

Wanda's nose twitched alarmingly. "You mean, you won't help us?" she cried. "You won't help Ronny?"

"Ronny has to help himself," I said, practicing anger management. "Now, if you'll excuse me, I have to go help my customers."

And with that, I stalked away. It was just like Wanda to expect me to wash Ronny's dirty laundry with the Pecan Springs police. But I must admit that my anger was somewhat dampened by the important bit of information, true or false, that she had passed along.

Colin Fowler had been dealing.

Marcy Windsor had known about it.

And Marcy Windsor owed me.

CHAPTER FIFTEEN

Coca was first used by the ancient Incas of Peru, where coca-induced trance states were part of their religious ceremonies. As time went on, the leaves of the herb were chewed by workers to reduce fatigue and promote a sense of well-being and the plant began to be cultivated. The Spanish conquistadors introduced coca to Europe, and in 1853, its active ingredient was isolated and named cocaine. The drug became enormously popular and was used by such notables as Sigmund Freud, Robert Louis Stevenson, and polar explorer Ernest Shackleton. It was sold over the counter in tonics, toothache cures, and patent medicines; in chocolate cocaine candies; and in cigarettes "guaranteed to lift depression." Cocaine was banned in the U.S. in 1914, and outlawed under the Dangerous Drug Act of 1920.

China Bayles' Book of Days

The phone rang several times before the girl picked it up. She was not the communicative type, and her mouth was so full of whatever she was eating that she could barely get the words out. No, Marcy wasn't home right now. When could she be reached? Maybe around seven, when she got back from work. Where did she work? Well, (giggle) she didn't work at the Good Earth anymore, now that the owner had gotten himself killed. She had a new job at some bookstore. Which one? Dunno. A place that sells kids' books, maybe?

Kids' books. Well, that was a piece of luck, for the Hobbit House, Pecan Springs' only children's bookstore, is right next door. If Marcy was working there, her new job involved a very nice promotion with an up-front bonus: the chance to work with Molly McGregor, the creator of the Hobbit House and one of my very favorite people.

I checked the answering machine and made a note of the calls I had missed while I was outside pulling weeds. Somebody wanted to know how much dried herb to substitute when the recipe called for fresh (an approximate answer: a generous teaspoon of dried herbs for one tablespoon of fresh). Somebody else wondered if there was anything she could plant instead of tarragon, which sulks in our Texas heat (a suggestion: Mexican mint marigold, with its bonus of pretty yellow flowers). And Betty Conrad had called again. This time, she said she needed to talk to me as soon as possible. She sounded urgent, so I tried both the house and the nursery. But there was no answer at the house, and all I got at the nursery was her voice on the answering machine, saying that Sonora was closed, due to the death of an employee.

I hung up, thinking that Betty had probably decided to cancel her participation in tomorrow's workshop, after all, and wondering whether I should phone the next person on the waiting list. But since I was only guessing about Betty's cancellation, there wasn't much I could do. Maybe she was concerned with something else, like Lucita Sanchez's criminal record.

I put out the Closed sign, checked out the cash register (noting with satisfaction that the afternoon was substantially more rewarding than the morning), and said good night to Missy, who was closing up Ruby's shop. Then I went next door.

The Hobbit House is located in the big frame house where Vida Plunkett used to live. Molly bought it with the settlement from her divorce and turned it into a treasure house for kids — and for grown-ups who haven't outgrown their childhood love of Pooh Bear or Jemima Puddleduck or Alice in Wonderland. Molly is not a woman who dallies. She gets around faster than a brush fire with a tail wind, as Pecan Springers like to say. Within three months after she bought Vida's ramshackle old house, she had converted the third floor into an attractive apartment for herself and remodeled the first and second floors to create colorful rooms with shelves full of books, cozy reading corners, lots of art on the walls, and child-size tables and chairs. On the second floor, a round green door with a shiny brass knob in the middle opens straight into the Hobbit Hole, a large room with green carpet and green walls, filled with toadstools and rock-shaped pillows, especially designed for children — although Molly's cat, Mrs. T (short for Mrs. Tiggy-Winkle, of course) has first pick of places for catnapping. Mrs. T is almost as large as Khat, so the kids respect her choice.

As the months have passed, Molly and her Hobbit House have made a name for themselves in Pecan Springs. Moms and grandmas adore the place, because it's such a rich source of interesting, family-friendly books and gifts, and the stock is always changing.

Children love to crawl into the Hobbit Hole for weekly story times, or gather in the back garden for an Easter egg hunt or a Halloween haunting or a Christmas-tree-for-the-birds party. Molly does most of the work herself, with only a couple of part-time helpers, so she is always very busy. But she insists that what she does is play, not work, and I don't doubt her. The evidence is right there in front of us. She has created successful work out of the things she loves most in life: books and children. What better definition of play do you want?

The bell over the door gave a cheerful tinkle when I went into the shop, and Molly looked up from the tower of fairy tales she was building, Grimm's at the bottom and the Flower Fairies on top, under a dancing Tinkerbell mobile. Molly has slimmed down quite a bit since she bought the store (it's all that running up and down those stairs, she says). Her clear, steady blue eyes are her best feature, and her short brown hair is brushed forward against her cheeks, giving her an elfin look. She was dressed in her usual colored jeans — pink, today — and a pink and yellow smock decorated with children's book characters.

"Hey, China!" she said happily, dimples flashing. "Nice to see you!" She lost her smile. "I heard about Colin Fowler. How's Ruby taking it?"

"About the way you'd imagine," I said soberly. "It's tough."

"It must be. Very, very tough. Give her my love." She added a book to the tower, eyed it, and moved it a half-inch. "Will I see you at the papermaking workshop tomorrow?"

"Oh, you're coming," I said. "I haven't looked at the updated list."

She nodded. "Missy called to tell me there was a place. I'm glad. I've been wanting to learn to make paper so I can teach it to the kids. Did I tell you? I'm turning the garage into a crafts workshop. It'll be a place where moms and kids can work together."

"Why am I not surprised?" I asked with a grin. Nothing that Molly did would surprise me — she barely gets one thing done when she's thinking ahead to the next project. I looked around. "I'm looking for Marcy Windsor. Is she working here now?"

She nodded. "That's how I knew about Colin Fowler. When she answered my ad, she told me she couldn't get a reference from her former employer because he was dead. She worked for him." She raised an eyebrow. "Or maybe you know that."

"I do. May I speak with her?"

"May I ask why?" Molly isn't nosy, just

careful. Having hired Marcy, she was already feeling responsible for her.

"Because she worked for Colin Fowler."

She tilted her head. "I hope she's not in trouble."

"So do I."

She thought about that for a minute. "Upstairs," she said at last. "I always start my kids out by asking them to straighten the bookshelves. They learn the stock that way."

Marcy had her own way of learning the stock. She was standing beside a window, reading a page of *Anne of Green Gables*. She turned guiltily as I came into the room.

"May I help you?" she asked, replacing the book on the shelf. "Are you looking for something special, or just browsing?"

"I came to talk to you. It was dark when we met last night, so you probably don't recognize me. I'm China Bayles, the person you ran into at Good Earth Goods."

"Oh, gosh," she said, flustered. Coloring, she pushed her plastic-rimmed glasses up on her nose and looked away. She was wearing a dark skirt and a white ruffled blouse and her blond hair was loose, caught behind her ears with a pink velvet ribbon. In spite of the acne, she was lovely. She seemed younger and more innocent than she had last night, but that might have been the afternoon sun gilding her hair and the ruffles at her throat. She was Alice in Wonderland, and I was the Red Queen.

I gestured to a table. "Let's sit down, shall we?"

The chairs were suited to seven-year-olds with very short legs, but we sat on them anyway. Marcy tried her hands in her lap, then on the table, and finally ended up by leaning on her elbows, her fingers clasped under her chin.

"What did you want to talk about?" Her gray eyes were wary, almost hostile. She was obviously wondering whether I had mentioned the circumstances of our meeting to her new boss, and if I had, how she was going to handle it. Lie? Tell the truth and throw herself on the mercy of the court?

"About what you told Ronny Rathbottom." This was not a time for beating around the bush. "That Colin Fowler was dealing."

I had caught her by surprise. Her mouth made an O and her eyes opened wide. "How did you — ?" She gulped. "Who told you that? Did Ronny tell you?"

"Never mind. Just tell me what you said to Ronny. Exactly."

She set her jaw. "I don't think I should."

Her soft young face tightened. "I don't want to talk to you at all, if you don't mind."

I looked straight at her. Time for another surprise. "I found Lucita Sanchez this morning. She was very dead." I made my voice hard. "Somebody slashed her throat, Marcy."

"Slashed her —" she whispered. Her face paled and her hand went to her mouth. "Oh, my God."

"Now there are two people dead," I said in a matter-of-fact tone. "Colin Fowler and Lucita Sanchez. Whether you're in danger depends on how much you know, and whether the killer is aware of it. I might be able to help — if you tell me what you told Ronny." With a heavy emphasis, I added, "Of course, you could tell the police. You're going to have to, sooner or later."

The police were the least of her worries. "You think the . . . the killer might come after *me*?" Her voice squeaked, a childish, frightened squeak.

I eyed her. I hated to see her frightened. But better scared than dead. And fear is a powerful motivator.

"He — or they — might," I said bluntly. "I don't know who the killer is, so I can't say. Do you?"

She picked up a blue velveteen rabbit from

338

the center of the table and turned it in her hands for a moment. Then she clutched it to her chest and looked at me, her lip trembling. "No." And then, "Not really. I mean, not exactly."

Something inside me went cold. I didn't know what game was being played, but the stakes were high enough to justify a pair of bloody murders. If Marcy knew, if she even suspected who the players were, she could be in a whole lot of trouble. "You'd better tell me," I said, and softened my tone. "I can only help you — and Ronny — if I know what you know."

"Ronny doesn't know anything," she said, very fast.

"But you do."

Shaking her head, she shrank back in her chair away from me, shoulders rigid, lips pressed tightly together to keep them from trembling. She was scared, scared of me. And why not? I was the stranger who had jumped out of the dark and scared her silly the night before. For all she knew, I might be the killer. I tried again, hoping to find a key that might unlock her fear, something that might allow her to trust me.

"Look," I said. "I've known your boss — Molly McGregor — since she opened this place. I own the herb shop next door. Before that, I was a criminal attorney, so I've seen what happens when drug deals go bad and people get killed. My husband used to be a cop, so I've seen it from the other side, too."

She swallowed. I tried another tack. "My best friend, Ruby, was Colin Fowler's girlfriend. She —"

She leaned forward a fraction of an inch, giving me a little with her body language. "Ruby . . . Wilcox?" she asked uncertainly.

This might be the key. "Yes. Do you know her?"

She shook her head. Her eyes had misted and her lips had gone soft. "No, but I know that Mr. Fowler . . . well, he cared about her. He was terribly upset when she broke up with him. Normally, he'd never say a word about anything like that — he kept personal things very much to himself — but I guess I caught him at a bad moment. He told me she'd said she had to get on with her life. He said she was a straight-shooter and that she had every right to kiss him off, but that didn't make it any easier." She stroked the rabbit. "He said it still hurt like hell."

Ah, romance. The key to so much of life. "If it's okay with you, I'd like to tell her," I said quietly. "She wasn't sure he cared, and she's having a tough time handling his death. Maybe this will make her feel better."

"I guess it's okay. Sure, if it'll help." Her eyes still on my face, she rested her chin on the velveteen rabbit, pondered for a moment, then decided to take a chance on me, since I was Ruby Wilcox's friend. "What I told Ronny was . . ."

She stopped, cleared her throat, started over again.

"I told Ronny I heard Mr. Fowler talking to Mrs. Sanchez about a drug deal they were involved with."

"When did this happen?"

She frowned, concentrating. "Two weeks ago. It had to be on a Saturday, because it was afternoon. The only afternoons I worked were Saturdays. I have afternoon classes."

"Where were you when you heard them talking?"

"I was in the shop, restocking the shelves along the back wall. They were in the back room. The wall is pretty thin."

"Was anyone else in the back room with them?"

"I don't think so. If there was, I didn't hear him. Or her. I think it was just the two of them. But I didn't see her, either. Mrs. Sanchez, I mean. She came in through the alley door when he was updating orders on the computer. I was restocking shelves and I overheard —" She looked at me as if she were expecting me to read her the riot act for eavesdropping. "I wasn't *listening,* if that's what you're thinking, Ms. Bayles. Not on purpose. I mean, I couldn't help but hear them. I —"

"That doesn't matter," I said. "What matters is what you heard, not how you heard it. How did you know it was Mrs. Sanchez, if you couldn't see her?"

"He called her Lucita. She phoned the store once, about some plants Mr. Fowler bought. That's how I knew who she was."

"Did she say which plants?"

"Over the phone, she did." Marcy frowned and fiddled with the rabbit's ear. "Yucky, or something like that. I'm not sure exactly. She said she'd drop them off at his place."

"Yucca?" Obviously, the pots in Colin's backyard.

"Yeah. Yucca. But that was over the phone. When they were talking in the back room, it wasn't about that. It was about —" She hunched her shoulders and held on to the rabbit as if it were a life preserver. "It's been a . . . awhile ago. I'm not sure I remember exactly." She swallowed again. "You're sure she's dead? You couldn't be mistaken?"

"I'm sure," I said gently. "There's no mistake. I saw her." Sprawled on the floor, in a pool of her own warm blood.

She bit her lip. "And the police don't know who killed her?"

"Not a clue. They don't have any leads in Mr. Fowler's death, either."

She stared at her knuckles. She was gripping the rabbit so hard they were white. Downstairs, Molly had put "Peter and the Wolf" on the CD player, and the melody wafted through the speaker over our heads. "I . . . I'm not sure I can remember the exact words."

"Just the gist of it, Marcy. It doesn't have to be exact."

She took a deep breath. "Well, Mrs. Sanchez said that the next delivery was going to be a big one. Mr. Fowler said he needed to know the details, like when and what and how much." She stopped, as if she had run out of breath.

"And she said?" I prompted.

She gulped for air. "She said it was . . . it was coke. It was supposed to arrive at night, but she didn't know exactly when. Any time in the next few weeks, she said. In an eighteen-wheeler, up the 'main road.' Three hundred pounds."

I nodded, understanding. Coke, cocaine,

coca, once a sacred herb whose ritual use was restricted to priests in trance states, now a killer, arguably the most dangerously addictive plant in the world. Three hundred pounds of it was being trucked up Interstate 35 — the main road between the border, Pecan Springs, and points north — in a tractor-trailer rig. About the same amount of cocaine had recently been seized in El Paso, where it was found hidden inside stereo speakers. The street value was something like three million dollars. DEA officers had arrested the driver and a couple of local drug lords, but the main ring was still out there, still in business.

"Where?" I pressed urgently. "Did she say where?"

"No." She frowned. "I think . . . Mr. Fowler seemed to know that already. He said he'd handle it, and that she should stay out of the way. She'd already done her part by delivering a sample. He laughed when he said that, but I don't think he thought it was funny. She didn't laugh. She sounded pretty scared."

A sample? Delivering a sample? I stared at Marcy for a moment, but I wasn't seeing her. I was remembering something, something that had struck me as odd when I first saw it. Something that hadn't seemed quite in synch with what I knew about Colin Fowler. And then, suddenly, I understood. I knew where that sample was.

She was looking at me strangely, and I brought myself back to the present. "Did either of them mention any names? How about a man named Tyson?"

"Tyson?" She shook her head. "No, not then. The name didn't come up when they were talking — at least, not that I heard. But later that afternoon, a guy came into the store. He said his name was Tyson. Scott Tyson. He came to see Mr. Fowler."

"What did he look like?" I asked, and was not surprised when she replied, without hesitation, "Like he'd just got out of the army. Tall, big shoulders, buzz cut. Strong face. But nice. He was really awfully nice."

Yes. Tyson, the meter man, the jump-out boy. "Did the two of them — Fowler, Scott Tyson — seem to be acquainted?"

"Sort of. But not friends. I got the idea that Mr. Fowler didn't think much of the way Mr. Tyson was handling something."

Handling something. Something like an undercover narcotics investigation for one of the task forces, no doubt. It sounded as if Colin had Tyson's number. "Did you hear the two of them talk?"

"Not really. They said a few words, and

then they went out the back way."

And across the alley into the First Baptist parking lot, where Darla had seen them having a heated discussion. Where Tyson reminded Colin that he "owed" him.

Tyson, who worked for a drug task force, notorious for slipshod dealings with evidence, for a bloodlust eagerness for booty. Was Colin playing Tyson for a fool, planning to make a big drug buy and ride off into the sunset, leaving Tyson holding the bag? Or was Tyson planning to make a big drug bust — the biggest of his career — and set Colin up to take a fall?

On a hunch, I said, "Did you see or hear from Tyson after that Saturday afternoon?"

She bit her lip. "Well, yes. Actually, I did. I —" Her eyes suddenly brimmed with tears. "He . . . he came into the shop. Tuesday morning."

Tuesday morning. "The day Colin was killed?"

She nodded. Her chin was trembling. "I opened at ten and was planning to stay until one, when I had to go to class. He was looking for Mr. Fowler, and I said he wouldn't be there until after lunch. He asked where he could find him, and I said I didn't know. But I knew that Mr. Fowler was meeting somebody at Beans at eight that night. I told him that. I said if he went to Beans, he could probably catch him there." She blinked fast, and the tears spilled over. "Did . . . did Mr. Tyson go there and . . . and *kill* him? Did I —"

"No, you didn't," I said gently. "You're not responsible for Colin Fowler's death, Marcy. Whatever happened the night he died had nothing to do with you. It would have happened, regardless." I wasn't sure of that, but I had to say it anyway. And hope she believed me. She had enough to carry around, without that burden of guilt on her young shoulders.

"I'd like to believe that," she said brokenly. "Maybe I will, later. Right now, I'm afraid I . . . Oh, God," she said to the rabbit, and put her head down.

"You said that Mr. Fowler was meeting somebody at Beans at eight. Who was that?"

She shook her head, still bowed. "No idea," she said in a muffled voice. She raised her head, her eyes still wet. "Listen, when you see Ms. Wilcox, will you please tell her that he really loved her? Deep down in his heart, I mean. I think he just didn't want her to get involved in his bad stuff. The drugs, the dealing." Her eyes brightened. "I think he gave her up to save her. Will you tell her that?"

She had found her fairy tale. Colin Fowler, a bad guy with a good heart, who surrendered the woman he loved rather than drag her down into the pain and darkness of his underworld. Colin Fowler, the mythic hero of Marcy Windsor's romantic story. But who am I to find fault with a good myth that explains a mystery, whether it's Marcy's myth or Ruby's, whether it's true to life or a total fiction? One myth is as good as another, if it will help to heal a broken heart.

I stood up. "I'll tell her," I said.

Marcy was going to have to go through all this again for Sheila, since her testimony would be crucial to any case in which the murders of Colin and Lucita Sanchez were linked, or in which Tyson somehow figured. But now wasn't the time to lay that on her. Anyway, I needed to talk to Sheila before Sheila talked to Marcy. I left the girl clutching her rabbit, said good-bye to Molly, and headed for my car.

It was nearly six. Brian wouldn't be home from his field trip until Sunday afternoon, so I didn't need to rush home and cook supper. I had another errand, however, and I was anxious to wrap it up before the same bright idea occurred to somebody else — somebody whose intentions were not as pure as mine.

CHAPTER SIXTEEN

Although the common names Spanish dagger and Spanish bayonet are applied to many yuccas, it is *Yucca faxoniana* that most deserves the name. This is an imposing, treelike yucca that regularly grows to twenty-five feet, with a sturdy trunk covered by a thatch of dead foliage and a dense crown of stiff, wide, olive-colored leaves. It is native to far west Texas, New Mexico, and the mountains of northeastern Mexico, where it grows in yucca forests, spectacular when the plants are in bloom.

The errand, important as it was, would have to wait. I was unlocking my Toyota when an old green Dodge pulled up to the curb in front of me and Amy Roth jumped out. Amy is Ruby's wild child, the daughter she gave up for adoption at birth (at Doris' insistence), the daughter who searched her out a few years ago. As you can imagine, it has been a stormy mother-daughter relationship, with Ruby's anguished guilt on one side, Amy's bitter resentment on the other. Having passed the quarter-century mark and given birth to Grace, Amy is settling into a quiet and apparently stable relationship with Kate Rodriguez in the comfortable house where they live together. As you might guess, this liaison has not won the approval of all of Amy's relatives. Doris has taken every opportunity to snort "lesbians" with a fiery contempt. Shannon, Ruby's younger daughter, pretends it doesn't exist. Ruby and Grammy, however, love Amy, adore Grace, and are fond of Kate, and so they accept it.

As far as I'm concerned, the ambiguous morality of the situation can be resolved into one single word: Love. Amy (who works part-time for Jon Green at the Hill Country Animal Clinic) and Kate (who has her own accounting business) are good parents. Grace — who might have been raised by a single mom struggling to make ends meet — has been welcomed into a devoted home. Lots of kids born into heterosexual families aren't so lucky.

Amy rushed up and flung her arms around me with a glad cry. She is a younger version of Ruby, tall and slender, with freckles plastered across her delicate, triangular face. She no longer has rainbow-colored hair (purple on one side, pink on the other, green between) and seems to have made a sort of peace with the naturally red, naturally curly mop she inherited from Ruby and passed down to Grace. But while motherhood might have matured the wild child a bit, she has not gone completely au naturelle. The gold rings still glitter in her pierced ears, nostrils, and eyebrows, her makeup would still be the envy of a Metropolitan Opera diva, and she still dresses like a punk rocker. But that's just Amy, in her own way as outrageously flamboyant as Ruby. I have learned to love her various weirdnesses. In fact, I confess to a serious fondness for the girl, who moved in with McQuaid and me last summer after she and Ruby had a fight and she moved out.

But that's ancient history. They made up before Grace was born, and now Ruby can never get enough of her baby granddaughter. Amy sometimes brings Grace — nearly five months old now — to spend a morning or an afternoon at the Crystal Cave. With her curly red hair (of course!), sky blue eyes, and sunshine smile, the baby is a hit with the customers and a delight for the rest of us. The only creature who can't tolerate her is Khat, who is bitterly jealous of the usurper. He can't understand why everybody makes such a fuss over her — she doesn't have fur and if she's got a tail, she's keeping it a secret.

Now, I could see Grace snugly settled in her car seat in the back of her mother's old green Dodge — the Gracemobile, we call it. I waved and made happy faces at her and she smiled back, bouncing a little with pleasure.

But Amy didn't look very happy. "Mom says you drove all the way to Fredericksburg just to break the news about Colin," she said somberly. "I came by to thank you for that, China. I can't tell you how much Shannon and I appreciate it." Shannon lives in Austin, where she teaches girls' physical education at Bowie High. "Bad as it was, it would have been a heckuva lot worse for Mom if she'd heard the news on the television or read it in the newspaper."

"I only did what I had to do," I replied. "Have you talked to her today?"

She nodded gravely. "She sounded harassed. Grandma Doris seems to have gone completely bananas. I hope Aunt Ramona gets there *soon*. It's not fair for Mom to have to do this all by herself." She made a face. "I'd go, if I didn't have to work —

although Grandma Doris doesn't like me very much just now. And Grace makes her nervous."

"It's a sad time," I agreed. "We need to give your mom all the support we can."

"And to think I saw Colin that very evening," Amy mused. "It must have been just a little while before he —" She shuddered and looked away. "God. What a horrible thing. I don't even like to think about it."

"You saw him that evening?" My ears perked up. "You were in his store?"

"No, we were at Beans. Kate and I and Sissy Conroy, our neighbor. We were having a Girl's Night Out. Sissy's husband babysat Grace and Sissy's boys, and we went hootin'." She grinned mischievously. "Of course, we don't hoot as hard or as long as we used to, now that we've got kids. It's just a chance to get out for a little while."

I remembered what Marcy had said about letting Tyson know that Fowler would be at Beans. "Was he alone when you saw him, or with someone?"

"Colin?" She glanced at her watch. "Oh, gosh, look at the time. I have to pick Kate up at her office."

"Yes, Colin," I said. "Was he alone?"

"When we first went in, yes. He was sit-

ting in that dark corner way at the back."
She tilted her head. "I knew he was planning to stop at Mom's to pick something
up, and I remember thinking that it was a
damn shame that they weren't together. It
would have been so good if they'd been able
to work it out."

"But he wasn't alone for long?" I persisted. "Somebody joined him?"

Amy nodded. "Some guy. They had a beer
and talked for a little while. And then they
left together." She smiled a sad little smile.
"He waved at me as he went out the door. I
figured he was on his way to Mom's house."

"What time was that?"

In the back seat, Grace began to whimper.
Amy went to the driver's door and opened
it. "Mommy's coming, sweetness," she said,
getting in. "I'm sorry, China. Grace is getting restless and I promised Kate I'd —"

"What time, Amy?" I repeated urgently.
"When Colin left with the man."

She put the key into the ignition. "Oh,
nine or nine thirty, I guess. A little later,
maybe. Sissy doesn't get off work until
seven, and she had to go home and give the
kids their supper before we could leave."
She frowned. "Why? Is it important?"

"It might be. What did the man look like?"
Big shoulders, blond buzz cut, I'd bet my

last dollar. The jump-out boy. But I was wrong.

"Short, stocky, dark. A mustache."

Dark-haired, a mustache. "Oh, Hark Hibler." But why hadn't he mentioned it?

"No, not Hark. I know him. He's sweet on Mom." She turned to check on Grace, who was working herself into a crying fit. "Hang in there, dumpling. We're going."

But she couldn't go, because I was holding on to the open door. "Wait, Amy. How did they seem? Were they friendly? Angry? Argumentative? What was the guy wearing?"

"Gosh, I don't know, China." She started the car and Grace immediately stopped crying. "I didn't pay that much attention, actually. I was having too much fun." She looked up at me, her eyes wide. "You're not telling me that he might've . . ." She gulped. "I thought Colin was killed later. Like after midnight."

"It was probably just before ten," I said. "That's when one of the kitchen helpers heard some hollering out near the tracks."

"Oh, Lord," Amy whispered, and shut her eyes.

"One more thing." I was pushing it. "Did you happen to notice a guy with big shoulders and a blond crew cut — sort of a military look? Maybe he was hanging out at the bar, or playing pool in the back room."

She opened her eyes and shook her head. "I don't remember. But I really wasn't paying attention. You might ask Kate or Sissy."

I would. I was betting that Tyson was there, killing time in the pool room or at the dart board, watching and waiting for Colin to leave. He had followed him out, waited until the other man had gone and —

Grace started to cry again, and I stepped back from the car. "Thanks, Amy." I blew a kiss. "Bye, Grace."

I watched them drive away with something close to envy. Grace — sweet-tempered, cuddly, smelling sweetly of baby lotion — is almost enough to make me want to add a little girl to the family. Almost, but not quite. Little girls grow up to be teenagers, and teenaged girls (as I remember from my own experience) are generally unhappy creatures. Anyway, I reminded myself, it's out of the question now. If I'd been interested in giving Brian a brother or sister, the time for that had all but ticked away on my biological clock.

And speaking of a clock ticking, there was my errand. I'd better hurry.

It was beginning to drizzle when I drove down Oak Street and parked in Colin

Fowler's drive. People were home from work, the driveways were filled with vehicles (mostly pickup trucks, of course), and Oak Street was crowded with the usual gang of kids, dogs, and skateboards, now beginning to scatter because of the rain. Crazy Zany Sanders, dressed in skimpy white shorts and a black top that were more substantial (but not much more) than the bikini she'd been wearing when I saw her last, was painting a chair on her front porch. She was pretending not to notice the man changing a tire on the Ford station wagon in the driveway across the street, who was ogling her eagerly. She watched as I got out of my car and walked up Colin's driveway.

The crime-scene tape had been removed from the front and back doors. I didn't have a key, but I didn't need one. The kitchen window was unlocked. However, I resisted the temptation. I didn't need to go through the house. The cops had been over it with a fine-tooth comb and had taken anything that even smelled promising. Anyway, I knew what I was looking for, and it wasn't inside the house. I opened my trunk, found a pair of dirty garden gloves, and put them on.

It took only ten seconds to find what I had come for, and another ten seconds to make sure that I was right. I stared at what I had found for a moment, then put it back. I straightened up. Of course, I knew exactly what I was supposed to do. I was supposed to whip out my cell phone, call Sheila, and tell her to come and get this stuff, pronto. I should not, under any circumstances, get myself involved with possession of —

I heard the sound of wheels on gravel and looked up to see a blue van prowling down the alley. No surprise, really. The meter man was after the same thing I was. If I gave him half a chance, he'd grab it. I glanced around. I wasn't eager to stand my ground here, like Custer, against a jump-out boy who was as big as a gorilla and armed, to boot — he'd be a fool to come after something of this value without bringing up the artillery. I was unarmed, having a serious aversion to guns and not having planned on being forced to use one. And like Custer, I knew that the cavalry couldn't get here fast enough to save my skin. But the cavalry (aka the chief of police) was coming to my house for dinner and —

I made a snap decision, not the wisest one, certainly, but the best I could come up with under the circumstances. I was closing the trunk lid when Crazy Zany, carrying a red umbrella, sauntered over to the hedge.

"Hi," she said, with a studied carelessness.

"Hi," I replied, very friendly. I opened the driver's door.

"Are you sure you should be taking anything from that place?" she asked dubiously. "The guy who lived here was murdered, you know."

I widened my eyes. "Oh, gosh," I said innocently. "Murdered? That's awful! Maybe that's why he didn't get around to paying for his stuff. I'll tell my boss. I wish she weren't such a stickler about slow pays — I always feel bad when I have to do something like this."

"I'll bet," she said sympathetically. "I couldn't do it."

"You get used to it," I said philosophically. "It's part of the job."

She frowned. "Those plants — they don't look like much. Are they all that valuable?"

"Oh, you bet," I said. "*Yucca faxoniana.* They'll grow as tall as a palm tree. Very impressive in the landscape." And then, on impulse, I made another snap decision, thinking that it might not be a bad idea to leave a trail of crumbs for Tyson. It might lure him into making a mistake. "Listen, I'm going to give you a business card, just in case there are any questions." I looked through my shoulder bag, found a slightly tattered Thyme and Seasons card, scratched out the shop address and scribbled my home address on it. "It's possible that somebody else may come looking for this stuff. A guy. If so, tell him I'm the one he wants to see."

"Thanks," she said, taking the card with a puzzled look. "I will."

"You have a nice evening, now," I said, and gave her a brisk wave as I got in the car.

I backed out of the drive. Crazy Zany was watching me, and the man across the street was watching her. The blue van was nowhere in sight, but I was betting that the meter man was also watching — from somewhere close enough to be tempted. He'd have that business card in his gorilla hands faster than you could say "Custer's last stand."

But I was barely around the corner before I began to regret my impulsiveness. I had given Tyson all the probable cause he needed. If he decided to stop my car and search it — task force agents have the authority to do that, in any jurisdiction in the state — there was enough cocaine to warrant a charge of possession with intent to distribute, a second-degree felony. Clearing myself would be tough, very tough. I could be up to my neck in some serious trouble. And under the forfeiture laws, I could lose my car.

And I had compounded this stupid error in judgment by leaving a trail to my house.

A trail to my *house?* When McQuaid was out of town — Brian, too — and I was there alone? What was I thinking? He might try to seize my home, too!

The only thing I could do was to dump Colin's stash, before the guy stopped me and searched my car. But I couldn't dump it just anywhere. I reached for my cell phone and punched in the speed-dial number for Sheila's direct line. She picked up on the fourth ring, long enough to make me very nervous.

"You're still planning to come over to-night, I hope," I said fervently. I checked the rearview mirror. No blue van. "If you're not, I've got something I need to drop off at your office, pronto." The sooner I got this stuff out of my car, the happier I would be.

"Hang on to it, China," she said genially. "I'll pick it up when I come over. It's been a helluva week, and I'm ready for an evening off."

I took a deep breath. I hate to admit I've made a mistake, but now was the time. "Listen, Sheila. I really think I should —"

"I'm getting ready to leave," she went on, in her peremptory, don't-interrupt-me-I'm-the-law tone. "All I have to do is change my clothes. Want me to phone Gino's and order a pizza? I can pick it up on the way out."

"Okay," I said reluctantly. "Anchovies and double cheese for me. I'll make a salad and find something for dessert." I paused, and added a heartfelt plea. "Come as soon as you can, Sheila. I have something important for you." Once Sheila was there, the stuff was all hers. I was off the hook.

"Show and tell in thirty minutes, then," she said briskly. "And make damn sure that Rottweiler is locked up. You know how I feel about attack dogs."

But an hour later, Sheila still wasn't there, and I was a nervous wreck. Feeling vulnerable and apprehensive, I had locked the doors, closed the blinds and drapes, and was pacing from one window to another, peeping out. We live in an isolated house off Limekiln Road, about eleven miles outside of town, and I was all alone in the place — unless, of course, you count the intrepid Howard Cosell (napping in his basset basket beside the kitchen stove) and the valiant Rambo (napping in Howard's doggie igloo). I had secured Colin's stash and now I kept a close watch on the driveway, checking for vehicles and beating up on myself for giving my address to Crazy Zany. What if Tyson showed up and demanded Colin's stuff?

Would I give it to him?

Would I try to keep him from taking it?

Would he attempt to arrest me?

My palms were sweaty. I was breathing hard. This was a fiasco, a catastrophic misjudgment. My stupidity was beyond belief. The sooner Sheila arrived and took possession of the stuff on the other side of the stone fence, the better I would feel.

My nervous pacing was interrupted by a call from McQuaid. I held on to the phone, wishing he were here. I wished I could tell him why, but instead, I told him that Miles had phoned. "He wants you to call him. It has to do with Dad's car."

"Maybe he's located it," McQuaid remarked. "He found something in his mother's papers that gave him an idea of where it might be." He paused. "What are you up to tonight, honey-bunch?"

What was I up to? I didn't want him to know. "Oh, not much," I said, and cleverly bounced the conversational ball back to him. "How about you? Finding anything interesting?" I lifted the curtain and peered anxiously out at the driveway. When was

Sheila going to get here?

"We just might have," McQuaid replied judiciously. "I'll be home tomorrow. I'll tell you all about it then. So what's new in the Fowler investigation? Has Sheila turned up anything?"

I don't make a regular practice of lying to my husband, but I am sometimes known to evade the truth, especially when the explanation will require at least two hours of face-to-face discussion, during most of which I will be on the defensive and inclined to be a bit short.

"If she has," I said, "I haven't heard about it. What are you doing this evening?"

"Having dinner with Hawk. How about you, babe? Going out?"

"Sheila's bringing a pizza." I frowned at the old Seth Thomas clock over the refrigerator. The hands showed eight thirty. Outside, twilight was falling and the drizzle had become a serious rain, complete with sound effects. I could hear thunder rumbling in the distance, and wondered if Rambo heard it, too. "I don't understand what's keeping her. She should have been here long ago."

"Maybe she had to nab a dope fiend. Tell her I said hi. And you girls stay out of trouble, you hear?"

"We will," I promised agreeably, but without conviction. I had invited trouble, and it might prove a little difficult to stay out of it, especially since I myself might be mistaken for a dope fiend. We exchanged kissy noises, said I love you and good night, and hung up. I went back to pacing and biting my nails and cursing myself for being all kinds of a fool.

Five minutes later, the phone rang again. This time, it was Ruby. Her mother was installed in her new apartment and she wanted me to have the phone number. She sounded tired and discouraged and ready to throw in the towel.

"Mom is so cantankerous that it's hard to do anything for her," she said. I could hear the tears in her voice. "You'd think she'd like a nice hot supper, but she refuses to eat a bite. She says it's poisoned. Even when I traded my plate for hers, she wouldn't touch it. And her language — really, China, it's obscene. I hate for other people to hear her."

"They'll know she's not herself," I said.

"But what if this *is* herself?" Ruby wailed. "What if she's going to be like this from here on out?" She stopped and took a breath, trying to calm herself. "One of the supervisors gave me an article on something called 'frontal lobe dementia.' Impaired judgment, inability to recognize the consequences of choices, lack of concern over personal appearance, irritability, confusion. The article doesn't hold out much hope for recovery. Once you've lost your frontal lobe, it's gone forever."

I made some soothing noises, but there wasn't much I could say to comfort her. "I talked to Amy this afternoon," I said. "And Grace gave me a big smile."

I could almost feel Ruby brighten. "My beautiful girls," she said happily. "Give them a hug for me." She paused. "Has Sheila found out anything yet? About Colin, I mean."

"Nothing very productive," I said. "I'll let you know as soon as I hear anything." I glanced at the clock. "Listen, Ruby, I have to get off the phone. I'm hoping Sheila will call and say she's on her way. I don't know what's keeping her."

"She'll be along." Ruby sighed. "I wish I were there with you and Sheila, China."

"So do I," I said.

But it wasn't true. I didn't know what was going to happen that night, but I had a very large hunch that it was just as well that Ruby was in Fredericksburg, taking care of her crazy mom.

CHAPTER SEVENTEEN

Landscape contractor Blair Davis was in his Houston-area home when the door flew open and he found himself held at gunpoint by some ten members of the Harris County Organized Crime and Narcotics Task Force. They had come to arrest him and confiscate his hibiscus, which (acting on a tip from a botanically challenged informant) they mistook for marijuana. Task force agents searched Davis' house for an hour, paying special attention to the red and gold bamboo growing in his window and the cantaloupes and watermelons in his garden. They left without apology.

Source: *Houston Chronicle,* July 29, 2004

Hibiscus sabdariffa, an herbal shrub that grows in tropical areas around the world, has antibacterial properties and has been shown to reduce blood pressure. It has also been used to treat indigestion, colds, respiratory ailments, and circulatory disorders. The edible flowers are used to make syrups, cordials, jam, and tea, and as a colorful addition to salads.

It was almost nine o'clock, full dark, and raining hard when Sheila finally showed up, still in uniform and managing to look beautiful even though she was clearly tired. She had two very good reasons for being late. She had been headed for the locker room to change when Hark Hibler came in. He had something important to tell her, he said, which turned out to be the same tale he had told me about Dan Reid's investigation into "official corruption."

There was one important addition, however: the name of his informant, who turned out to be — yes, you guessed it. Scott Tyson. Tyson had surreptitiously contacted Hark and offered him information about Dan Reid, aka Colin Fowler, and what he was doing in Pecan Springs. Hark didn't mention his conversation with me, nor the salacious tale Tyson had peddled about Sheila's relationship to Reid. Instead, he told her that although he wasn't able to corroborate the "official corruption" tip from other sources, he thought she ought to know about it, in case it had something to do with Reid's murder.

"Of course," Sheila said disgustedly, "it doesn't. The whole thing is a pack of lies, from beginning to end."

"You're sure?" I asked, eyeing her. If Sheila was giving me a line, I couldn't tell it, and I've had quite a bit of experience with liars. Sometimes when I look back on my life as a lawyer, it seems like most of it was spent sifting through lies to get to something, anything, that might approximate a truth.

"Absolutely. If Dan — Colin — had any official connection, it wasn't with the FBI, and it didn't have anything to do with a corruption investigation. This is another of Tyson's schemes."

"But why — ?"

"Because. Because he wanted to call attention to Colin. Wanted to muddy the waters any way he could. There's nothing to it, believe me."

And then she went on to tell me that after she'd spent thirty minutes dealing with Hark, she had driven over to Gino's to pick up our pizza. As she was leaving the parking lot, some college kid backed his mother's dump truck–sized SUV into the rear of her red Blazer, effectively rendering it undriveable. That would have been bad enough, but before the kid had driven over to Gino's to pick up pizzas for his frat buddies, he had polished off three beers. He was drunk as a skunk. An hour later, he was in the cooler, the paperwork was turned in, and Sheila had borrowed a car from one of the other officers. The pizza, of course, was cold. Smart Cookie, on the other hand, was well and truly steamed.

Feeling much better now that she was there, I heated the pizza in the microwave while Sheila told me about the Blazer. "Oh, and there's something else," she said. "I had old Wilford Mueller checked out. Seems he fell off his porch a week ago. The day Colin was killed; he was in surgery in Austin, getting a pin in his hip."

"Well, that scratches him off the list," I said, getting out the salad dressing.

We put our salads and pizza on the dining room table, and Sheila slumped into a chair.

"Why does everything happen to me?" she muttered dramatically. Howard Cosell threw himself at her feet, looking up at her adoringly. Hearing the tone of her voice, he gave her ankle a consoling lick. She bent over to scratch under his long, droopy ears. He replied with the basset equivalent of a purr.

"Because you're gorgeous?" I suggested helpfully, checking the drapes and blinds to be sure they were closed against a possible Peeping Tyson. "Because you're the chief of police and act in loco parentis for cops who misbehave? Because your Blazer was parked where some drunk kid could back into it?"

"I hate lawyers," Sheila growled.

"Me, too," I agreed. "They're rotten, through and through. Anyway, you're not the only one who's had a bad day." I finished pouring glasses of iced hibiscus tea and sat down. "Have a piece of pizza and pay attention, please."

Sheila helped herself. "Pay attention to what? Pass the salad."

"A complicated story. A tale of tales."

I pushed the salad bowl in her direction. And then, while we ate, I told her what Wanda Rathbottom had told me, which had led me to track down Marcy Windsor and talk to her, which conversation had taken place only a few minutes before I bumped into Ruby's daughter Amy. I held off telling her what I had found at Colin's house and my dumb stunt with the business card. I didn't feel quite so vulnerable now that she was here — there's safety in numbers, especially when one of you is the chief of police. And anyway, Tyson hadn't shown up yet. Maybe he wasn't coming.

When I finished my narrative, Smart Cookie shook her head. "Windsor was on my list," she muttered. "I just hadn't got to her yet." She narrowed her eyes. "How come she spilled this story to you?"

"I had some leverage. Ronny Rathbottom is Marcy's boyfriend." And Marcy is a romantic, whose heart was touched by the love story of Ruby and Colin. "Also, I might have suggested that Marcy could be in danger herself. Anyway, I told her she'd have to talk to you."

Sheila nodded. "Well, she's right about one thing. Lucita Sanchez has a record. She served two years for dealing in South Texas. She was released only six months ago." She paused. "So this girl thinks her boss was buying and Sanchez was his contact in the ring?"

"That's what she told me," I said cautiously. "It's probably what she would testify to in court — although there's more than one possible interpretation of what she overheard. The important thing is Sanchez's statement about the cocaine delivery. Three hundred pounds is worth something like three million dollars." And three million dollars is worth a couple of murders, in some people's estimation.

"An eighteen-wheeler," Sheila said thoughtfully. "The drugs could be hidden in just about anything. That's what makes this so hard. In Arizona, the Feds pulled over a cargo of bird supplies — the cocaine was concealed in bags of birdseed. In San Diego, it was hidden in a truckload of imported Mexican furniture. Sniffer dogs do a lot of the work."

But this particular truck wasn't carrying just about anything. It was carrying a specific cargo, and I knew what it was — or thought I did. In a minute, I'd show her.

"As far as what Amy told me is concerned," I went on, "I'm not sure it helps all that much. Whether she actually saw the killer or not is anybody's guess. And there must be thousands of dark-haired guys with mustaches in this area. I thought of Hark first, of course," I added. "But she said it wasn't him."

Sheila licked her fingers. "I haven't talked to Bob yet — he was in El Paso yesterday. But now that we know that Colin had dinner at Beans Tuesday night, maybe Bob will remember seeing him. He might even know the man he was with." Bob Godwin, who owns Beans, is acquainted with most of the people who frequent the place. He knows their names, what they like to eat and drink, and whether they're likely to get testy when they lose at darts or pool. He can even remember how many times he's had to kick them out.

I helped myself to another piece of pizza. Howard moved restlessly under the table and poked out his nose to ask whether he might have a bite of pizza. Outside, Rambo had waked from his nap and was barking at something — the raccoon that's been raiding our compost bin, maybe. Or the thunder.

"One thing I don't know is how Tyson fits into this picture," I said. "I got some hints this afternoon, but I was hoping you would enlighten me."

Sheila gave me a knowing grin. "This afternoon, when you were skulking around outside the cabin at the Pack Saddle, pretending to be V. I. Warshawski, on the case?"

"Yeah," I said, deadpan. "With my cell phone turned on. Swift, huh? V. I. would never make such a dumb mistake." V. I. would never give out her home address, either. I was a fool.

Sheila shrugged. "I've seen dumber. Remind me to tell you about the officer who was demonstrating gun safety to a bunch of school kids and blasted a hole in the blackboard. Nearly killed the teacher in the room next door." She took another piece of pizza. "Tyson says he works undercover for one of the West Texas narcotics task forces. Bitter Creek."

I raised my eyebrows. "*Says* he works?"

"He had identification. It looked okay, but I've learned not to trust those guys. There was some character out in Amarillo last year — he'd been kicked off the task force but kept on acting like one of the agents. Caused all kinds of trouble."

"Ah," I said thoughtfully. Impersonating an officer is a third-degree felony in Texas, but the potential benefits might outweigh the liabilities, if there's a strong incentive. And in this case, there was plenty of incentive. Three million dollars' worth. "West Texas. If Tyson's legit, he's pretty far out of his territory. Aren't they supposed to notify DPS when they're working extrajurisdictionally?" The Department of Public Safety has been supervising the task forces, not with entire success, for the last couple of years. "Wouldn't DPS notify you?"

"They're supposed to, but it doesn't always work that way. This afternoon, while I was on the phone with you, I got a call from somebody who identified himself as a task-force agent, saying that they had an undercover man in the area and giving me his location. Cabin 37, at the Pack Saddle."

So that was how she knew where Tyson was staying. "Did you pull your guys off his tail because of that phone call?"

She shook her head disgustedly. "No, they managed that cute little trick all by themselves. I guess it's time we had a refresher course on surveillance."

I gave her a questioning look. "Think maybe Tyson himself made that call?" It would make sense. He'd spotted the tail and figured he'd better give himself some cover.

"Could be. I tried to verify Tyson's status before I headed out to see him, but I hit a snag. The DPS captain responsible for this particular task force is out sick. I couldn't reach the Bitter Root commander, and nobody in their office seemed to know anything about Tyson being here. Which isn't unusual, I suppose. Those cowboy outfits are pretty loosely organized, without much command and control."

"So we're not sure whether Tyson is who he says he is."

"That's how I read it. He's been here in Pecan Springs for about ten days. He said he got in touch with Colin because Colin was here on a similar assignment from the Drug Enforcement Administration. Said he wanted to compare notes." She coughed.

"So he told me, anyway. Obviously, he fed Hark Hibler a different line. He told Hark it was the FBI."

"Colin was with the DEA?" I asked sharply. "Have you been able to confirm that?"

If true, it straightened out Colin's twisted back story, suggesting that his jail time was a cover designed to legitimize him for another job. It also challenged Marcy's reading of the situation. Maybe. Things are not always what they seem. There's nothing except good sense, good training, and a strong personal ethic to keep an undercover narc — a DEA officer, task-force agent, or deputy sheriff — from working both sides of the street.

She shook her head. "I put in some calls right after we found Colin's body, but I haven't heard anything back yet. Now that I've heard Hark's story, I'm inclined to discredit both versions. Tyson doesn't have any credibility at all, as far as I'm concerned."

"Did you ask him whether he had any ideas about who might have killed Colin?"

"I did. He said no." She frowned. "But I think he's lying. Some of the guys who sign on to work with these task forces are no better than mercenaries, and some are bad actors with sticky fingers. They deal with large amounts of cash and drugs. And the assets they seize —"

She gave me a questioning look. "Am I telling you something you don't know, or is this old stuff for you?"

"After Tulia, most Texans know something about it," I said.

Tulia is the tiny West Texas town where a 1999 drug task force sting netted forty-six alleged dealers and users. Forty were black, nearly 20 percent of the town's black population. A single officer's uncorroborated testimony — no audio or video surveillance recordings, no supporting testimony from other officers — resulted in sentences up to ninety-nine years. But the whole thing was bogus, from beginning to end, and eventually, the governor pardoned almost all of the defendants. The rogue cop — who was under indictment for theft in another county when he was hired as a narc — was convicted on a charge of aggravated perjury. And the counties and cities belonging to the Panhandle Regional drug task force had to collectively cough up a six-million-dollar civil rights settlement, to be shared among the forty-six defendants. The scandal, which made headlines all across the country, focused national attention on narcotics enforcement in Texas. Whether it changed any questionable practices is debatable, although it's had one stunning effect: cities and counties are now on notice that they can be held financially liable for the malfeasance of the regional task force to which they belong. In Texas, mention Tulia and watch everybody shudder. It's a true tale that no one wants to see repeated.

"I know that the assets a task force seizes during a drug bust go into its pockets," I went on, "rather than into the city or county general revenue funds. Remember the instant soup bust?" In the late nineties, a task-force agent interdicted a truck loaded with instant soup. It was loaded with ten million dollars of contraband drug cash, too. The task force got nearly eight million of it. "This kind of thing obviously creates some friction between the local authorities and the task force," I added.

"Who could forget the instant soup bust?" Sheila replied ironically. "Yes, of course there's friction. Over in East Texas, one of the regional task forces withheld information about a drug ring from the county sheriff — a man I knew and respected. They staged a bust, the neighbors called the local cops, and in the confusion the sheriff was shot and killed. It wouldn't have happened if the task force had brought the local officials into the loop. Instead, they did it all on the QT. They wanted to make the arrests and seize the assets without splitting the take with the county authorities." She shifted uneasily. "Something like that could be coming down here."

And that was assuming that Tyson was a legitimate task force agent, which might or might not be the case. This whole thing was so twisted that it was impossible to know what was true, what was false, who was crooked, who was straight. All we had were plenty of suspicions — and two dead bodies.

I tilted my head, listening. Outdoors, Rambo was barking again, a note of urgency in his voice. Under the table, Howard had raised his head, too.

"So you think Colin was killed because of Tyson?" I asked.

"You bet I do," she said bitterly. "I think Tyson blew Colin's cover, inadvertently or deliberately. Which amounts to the same thing in the end. Either way, Colin is dead."

"Why? Why would he do that?" I thought I knew what she was going to say. I was right.

"If Tyson's legit, he could've wanted to keep the DEA from participating in the bust. If he's not legit, he did it to further his own criminal interests. But this is just a hunch. Nothing I can prove — yet."

"You have witnesses who will testify that Tyson illegally entered Ruby's house and took evidence pertaining to a murder investigation," I pointed out. "And that he attempted to enter Colin's house." Ordinarily, you wouldn't expect a law-enforcement officer to do such things, but undercover narcs don't always observe the niceties.

"Yeah." She smiled grimly. "I'm saving those. I intend to surprise that joker with a search of his cabin just as quick as I can get a warrant. I would've had it tonight, but Judge Porterfield is out of town. I want that box. I want to know what's in it, and how it bears on Colin's murder."

"And what about Sanchez? Do you think Tyson had anything to do with that?"

"Not directly, probably. But once Colin's cover was blown, it would've been easy for anybody to figure out how Colin and the Sanchez woman were connected."

"Which was how?"

"I suspect that Sanchez was a member of the drug ring. What Marcy Windsor overheard confirms that Sanchez was making her own private deal on the side. She could've been killed because somebody was afraid she was going to turn informant."

"She already had."

Sheila looked at me. "How do you know?"

"Because Marcy said Sanchez mentioned leaving a sample with Colin. Didn't you pick up on that?"

"Of course. But Marcy heard wrong, or Sanchez lied, or Colin got rid of it, or somebody else beat us to it. There was no dope in that house. No pot, no crack, no cocaine, nothing. The place was searched top to bottom."

"It was there. I found it."

A silence. Then: "You found . . . what, precisely?"

"Precisely, I found three pots of yucca and one of agave. Right where Sanchez left them. You'll probably find her fingerprints on those pots."

"Yucca?" She stared at me, uncomprehending.

"Spanish dagger, although it goes by other names as well. You know, those spiky plants that Carole and I were harvesting when we found Colin's body. There were three pots of yucca in his backyard, not to mention a beautiful agave. You were standing right beside them when I showed you that note. They —"

"I know what yucca is, damn it," Sheila

said crossly. "You're not trying to tell me it's some sort of drug, I hope." She eyed me. "It isn't one of those weird herbal things you're always talking about, is it? Can you smoke it? Do you mainline it? Does it —"

"No. Stop. I'm telling you. It's not the yucca, it's what's *under* the yucca. There's a Baggie of cocaine — maybe three, four grams — inside one of those five-gallon plastic pots. Tip out the plant and you'll find it. Although," I added sternly, "if I'm ever asked about this outside this room, I will lie. I will swear I never saw anything in those pots. The penalty for perjury is a lot less than the penalty for possession."

"Possession?" Sheila was aghast. "You didn't actually *take* that stuff, did you?"

I blushed. "Well, I —"

"China Bayles, have you lost your freakin' mind? What kind of a damn lawyer are you?" The dumb kind, I wanted to say, but Sheila was going on, her voice rising. "Are you trying to get yourself arrested for possession? You should have left that shit where it was and called me. I would have sent an officer to get it. Hell, I would have come myself!"

"I know, I know. It wasn't very smart. But if I hadn't taken that stuff when I did, your buddy Tyson would have it in his hot little hands at this very moment. I was checking out those pots to confirm my guess when I happened to look up and see his blue van cruising down the alley. I had every intention of calling the cops, and I certainly didn't have any desire to get busted. But I figured that keeping Colin's stash safe from rogue jump-out boys had high priority."

She gave me a hard-eyed look. "Did anybody see you?"

"Crazy Zany, next door. The one with the bazookas. I told her I was repossessing landscaping materials that hadn't been paid for." I omitted the bit about leaving my address. The less said about that stupid stunt, the better, especially since Tyson hadn't shown up.

"Crazy Zany? Bazookas? *Re*possessing?" Sheila shook her head darkly. "I'm not believing this," she muttered. "I am flat not believing it."

"I'll show you." I pushed my chair back. "Let's go outside."

Her face was tense, her mouth compressed into a thin, hard line. "You've got it *here?*"

"Well, not here, exactly. That is, if by 'here' you mean in the house at this address or on the real property at this physical location. But —"

"Cut the lawyer talk," Sheila growled, low

and level. "I want to see it."

"Well, come on, then. I'll show you." I led the way down the hall and into the darkened kitchen and put my hand on the backyard light switch. But I didn't turn it on. I didn't open the door, either. Beside me, Howard lifted his nose, sniffed twice, and growled deep in his throat, the thunderous basset growl he summons to warn unauthorized persons and other beings who might be invading his territory. Rambo was going crazy, barking up a storm.

"What's happening out there?" Sheila asked uneasily. "Why is that dog barking?"

I took a deep breath. "Might be Tyson," I conceded.

"Tyson?" she exclaimed incredulously, peering at me. "What the hell would *he* be doing here?"

"He's probably looking for that cocaine," I said sheepishly. "I left my business card with Zany Sanders. Not a very smart idea, I admit, but the best I could come up with under the circumstances."

"Huh!" Sheila snorted. "If that's your best, I'd hate like hell to see your worst."

I frowned. "You said Judge Porterfield is out of town. Even if Tyson is a legitimate task-force agent, he can't have a warrant."

"Yeah," Sheila said, "but if he saw you taking those pots or thinks that they're in your car, he's got probable cause to search the vehicle. That is, if he's an officer." She squinted at me. "Are they?"

"There are . . . pots in my car," I admitted.

"Hell's bells, China. You are in serious trouble, and there's nothing I can do to help. If Tyson finds that cocaine in your car, he's going to charge you — if he's for real. If he isn't, he'll just try to take it."

"Sounds like a pretty good test to me," I said cheerfully. "Are you armed?"

"I will be, if I can find my bag. Turn on the kitchen light. No, don't," Sheila corrected herself. She glanced around the kitchen, saw her bag on one end of the counter, and took her gun and a pair of handcuffs out of it.

"We'll split up," I said. "I'll go out the front door and around the house to the dog run and let Rambo out. He doesn't seem very aggressive, but maybe he'll distract the man. Give him something to think about, if nothing else."

"Sounds damned aggressive to me." Sheila was checking her gun, all business now.

"Ruby says his bark is worse than his bite. Turn on the yard light and come out when you hear me yell."

"No way." Sheila scowled and put her hand on the doorknob. "You're staying here, China. This is my job. I'll handle it."

"Yeah, but it's my territory. You'll put your foot through a flower pot or something. And with Rambo loose —"

That gave her something to think about, but it didn't stop her. "This guy is probably armed," she protested. "You're a civilian. You could get hurt. You could —"

"Forget it, Smart Cookie," I said firmly. "My house. My rules."

I didn't give her any more opportunity to object. I turned on my heel and went down the hall to the front door. I was opening it when I saw McQuaid's newly purchased antique Remington shotgun, standing in the corner. It wasn't loaded, but it looked mean as hell. I wanted very much to take it with me — I felt vulnerable going out, unarmed, into the dark. But McQuaid's ammo is always locked up in his workshop with his gun collection. And it's dangerous to carry a gun you don't intend to fire. Reluctantly, I left it behind and went out onto the porch.

The rain had stopped and the air was cool and April-sweet. A fugitive sliver of moon flirted with luminous clouds and the trees smelled of freshly washed leaves. Rambo had momentarily stopped barking. In the silence, I could hear the soft, inquiring *whoo-hoo-hoo* of a great horned owl, far down by the creek, and something small and fleet of foot scampered through the flower bed. I could hear the beating of my heart, too, much louder than usual. On another night, I would have found the darkness irresistible, the scents and sounds and sights enticing. I would have sat down on the porch steps and leaned against the pillar and looked up at the moon. Now, I was wishing for broad daylight and McQuaid, who is a very big guy and doesn't take backtalk from anybody, especially an armed undercover narcotics agent who may or may not have a warrant.

I stood on the porch for a moment, peering through the shadowy darkness. Our house sits at the end of a long gravel lane that leads to the county road. The car Sheila had borrowed, not a squad car but a nondescript black Ford two-door, was parked in the circle drive in front of the house. I couldn't see my Toyota — it was around back, on the kitchen side of the house. There were no other vehicles, but I thought I could see the dark shadow of a truck or van just beyond the curve in the lane, about thirty yards away. Tyson, if that's who was sending Rambo into violent paroxysms, had parked and walked.

I stepped off the porch and made my way to the left, around the corner of the house on the side away from the driveway, then toward the back. Since I'd had the foresight to close all the blinds and drapes, only an occasional glint of light shone through the windows. I had weeded the flower beds along the house often enough to know every inch of them by heart, which was a good thing. It was very dark, with only a fleeting peek-a-boo glimmer of moonlight to light the way.

I swallowed. The cloud shadows were disorientating. The owl called again, nearer now: the voice of impending death, many think, although of course that's only a superstition. Nobody really believes that stuff anymore. But still, maybe this hadn't been such a good idea after all. Maybe I should have stayed in the kitchen and let Smart Cookie go out and arrest Tyson for trespassing, before he could try to arrest me for possession. Or maybe it wasn't Tyson at all, but somebody with an even more sinister motive, although I couldn't at the moment think who that might be.

Rambo was barking again — growling, snorting, threatening noises that made him sound meaner than a junkyard dog and as unstoppable as a Sherman tank. His bite didn't need to be very bad, I thought — his bark was terrifying enough to give most prowlers pause. Inside the house, inspired by Rambo's uproar, Howard Cosell had lifted his throaty basset bass to join the chorus. Together, they sounded like a dozen devil dogs in full voice.

I crept to the back corner of the house and peered around it. The backyard was very dark, although I could see Rambo's menacing, fast-moving shadow in the dog run. He was racing back and forth, rattling the chain-link fence, barking maniacally. The fur was stiff along his spine. He sounded totally wild, flat-out fierce, and utterly dedicated to the task of tearing an intruder, any intruder, limb from limb. If I'd been the intruder, I would've been quaking in my Birkenstocks. I wasn't, but that didn't mean I wasn't scared. The fact that Ruby believed this dog was a cream puff or that he had treated me with civility this afternoon didn't mean very much. Excited as he was, it was entirely possible that Rambo would tear *me* limb from limb.

I looked in the direction of the driveway where my Toyota was parked. I saw a dark figure open the driver's door, saw my trunk lid pop open, heard steps on the gravel as he went around to the back of the car. Sonuvabitch, I thought, suddenly fired with an unreasoning anger that drove out my fear. Tyson didn't have my consent to a search, and I hadn't seen any warrant. I grinned maliciously. Yeah. His prints would be all over my car. Sheila could charge him with attempted grand larceny auto.

I slipped through the shrubbery and scurried across the grassy yard to the dog run. The fence was shaking with the force of Rambo's lunging, and the night rang with his frenzied barks. "Hello, Rambo," I crooned. "Nice Rambo, nice doggy. Want to catch a car thief?"

Cream puff? Hardly. As I lifted the latch on the gate and swung it wide, Rambo launched himself through the opening like an exploding bomb, a hound of hell.

"Go get him, Rambo!" I shouted. "Get that guy! He's stealing our car!"

And at that moment, the yard light came on, flooding the entire rear of the house and garden with bright light. Tyson, dressed all in black, was caught in the act of reaching into my opened trunk.

Rambo caught him, too. With a demonic snarl, the dog hurled himself furiously at Tyson, catching him off-balance and knocking him flat on his back. Tyson screamed and tried to roll over, flinging his arm up to protect his face and throat. Rambo's teeth snapped on to the man's right forearm and held it in a viselike grip. Tyson flailed and kicked desperately, trying to break free, but it was no use. Rambo stood firm, all four feet planted on the ground, jaws clenched, a threatening growl rumbling in his throat. I stared at him, frozen with admiration. Wow. This was a disciplined dog, trained military-style to attack and hold a prisoner until his handler released him.

"Call off the dog, China," Sheila commanded, jumping down the steps and running out to the car. "I've got him covered." She had her gun in her hand. Behind her, in the house, Howard was baying, frantic to come outside and join the party.

Call off the dog? I gave myself a shake and stepped forward. I hadn't thought that far ahead. What the hell do you say to a Rottweiler to make him let go of somebody's bloody arm? What if he likes the taste of blood? What if he'd rather chew than —

"Off, Rambo," I said. Rambo cast a questioning glance at me, but he didn't move. If anything, he clenched his jaws harder.

Tyson moaned and writhed. "Get this dog off me," he cried shrilly. "He's killing me."

I came closer. "Hey, Rambo," I said, louder. "You can quit now, boy. Time to go home."

Rambo gave Tyson's arm a hard shake. Blood was dripping between his jaws.

I leaned forward. "Release it, Rambo," I roared. "Leave it! Drop it! Let it go! Knock it off!"

One of these phrases — I have no idea which one — apparently contained the magic words that unlocked Rambo's jaws. Agreeably, he opened his mouth and released Tyson's arm. He turned and looked at me, cocking his head to one side, a goofy "didn't-I-do-good?" look on his face. He strutted over to sit on his haunches beside me, the picture of triumphant conquest, of a job well-done.

"Yeah," I said, rubbing his ears. "You did great, guy. Really great. So you're a cream puff, huh? Scared of cats? Afraid of thunder? I don't think so." I looked down at the dog, wondering where Colin had gotten him and just what else was included in his training. I wasn't sure I wanted to find out. As an afterthought, I added, "Okay, Rambo. You stay. Hear me? Stay."

I stepped away. With a satisfied grunt, Rambo dropped onto the ground, put his muzzle on his paws, and prepared to stay.

Tyson had struggled to a sitting position, and Sheila was standing over him. "I need a doctor," he groaned. He was gripping his arm, the blood spurting between his fingers.

"You sure do," Sheila agreed. "That's some dog bite. Got you good, didn't he? Guess he figured you were doing something you shouldn't." She flipped open her cell phone and hit the speed dial.

"This is Chief Dawson," she said crisply. "Can you send a deputy out to 3199 Limekiln Road? We've had a little problem out here. Everything's under control now, but we'd sure appreciate a hand."

A deputy. She was calling the Adams County sheriff's office to pick Tyson up and book and jail him. Our place is well outside her jurisdiction, and the town and the county have always played fair on who does what.

She paused, listening. "Yeah, that's right. One will do the job, most likely." She cast an appraising glance at Tyson. "He's not too fierce at the moment. In fact, he needs some sewing up, so your deputy will need to transport him to the ER." Another pause. "Good. Thanks." She clicked off the phone and closed it up. "So tell me, Tyson. What are you doing here, and why were you messing around with that car?"

"I told you this afternoon. I'm an under-cover narcotics agent," Tyson said, gritting his teeth. "I'm here on a case." He looked down at his arm. "Can you do anything to stop the bleeding?"

"I'll see what I can find," I said.

"Got any identification?" I heard Sheila ask as I went toward the house. When I came back with a length of webbing strap to use as a rough tourniquet and a towel to wrap Tyson's arm, he was on his feet, searching clumsily through his pockets with his left hand, his right arm dangling help-lessly at his side.

"Can't locate it, huh?" Sheila remarked with a dry smile.

"Must've left it in my cabin," he muttered, taking the rope and the towel from me. He wound the rope around his upper arm and pulled it as tight as he could, then wrapped the towel around his forearm.

"Not a problem," Sheila said agreeably. "We can handle that tomorrow. By then, your task-force commander and the DPS captain who's supposed to be overseeing your work should be able to give us some of the details of the case you say you're work-ing on. In the meantime, the county will get you sewed up and find you a cell in their jail for overnight. Their accommodations aren't as palatial as the Pecan Springs lockup, but —"

"A cell!" Tyson squawked.

"Yeah, right. A cell." Sheila smiled frostily. "You're under arrest, Tyson."

He stared at her. "You can't arrest me! No way! I have to be at —" He stopped and licked his lips with a desperate look. "You can't arrest me," he repeated. "I'm working a case. You can't —"

"Be where?" Sheila asked evenly. "You've got a hot date tonight, Tyson?"

"I'm . . . I'm on assignment."

"Oh, yeah? Where's the rest of your team? How come you're here by yourself? How come I can't get anybody to verify you?"

He drilled her with a look, but he didn't answer her question. "I work alone," he muttered. "You saw my damn identification. This afternoon. You saw it this afternoon."

"Be *where*, Tyson?" Sheila repeated.

He raised his voice angrily, his face tight. "You know who I am, by God. And you know what kind of shit you'll be in if you don't let me do my job. You —"

"I know who you say you are," Sheila said in a quiet voice, "which is not the same thing." She narrowed her eyes. "And before you start threatening me, you can show me the warrant for your search of this vehicle."

His lips went tight.

She held out her hand. "The warrant. Let's see it."

He looked away.

Sheila grunted. "Yeah, that's what I thought." She raised her voice. "I don't give a rat's ass who you are, Tyson, you're under arrest for trespass. And since you won't tell me what you want with this vehicle, I have to assume that you were here to steal it, so I am adding attempted grand theft auto to the list of charges. And when I've finished checking you out — as I intend to do personally — you may be charged with impersonating a police officer, as well. Let's have your weapon."

"I'm not armed," he said sullenly.

"Bullshit," she snapped. "Bend over from the waist. Take the gun out of your right boot and drop it on the ground." With a practiced assurance, she rattled off Miranda. It was music to my ears.

Slowly, unwillingly, Tyson bent over, took out the gun, small but businesslike, and slid it onto the ground. He straightened up.

"The knife in your left boot."

If looks could kill, Smart Cookie would've been a dead duck. He snarled something, but obeyed.

"I wasn't stealing this car," he gritted,

tossing the knife at her feet.

"Turn around. Hands on the car." Sheila patted him down, very professionally.

"What the hell would I want with a four-year-old Toyota with dings in the doors?" he said, over his shoulder. "She's concealing drugs." He nodded grimly at me. "This woman. She took the plants from Reid's yard."

"Plants?" I asked innocently. "You mean, those plants Mr. Fowler didn't pay for? Sure, I picked them up. Those are rare yuccas, from Mexico, and one pretty nice *Agave zebra.* As I told Miss Sanders, Mr. Fowler's neighbor, they're worth plenty of money." I grinned congenially. "You've met Miss Sanders, I guess."

"You bet those plants are worth money." He laughed in a nasty way. "You know exactly what's in those pots, lady. Cocaine. Four ounces of pure cocaine." He glared at Sheila. "You're so hot to arrest somebody, Dawson. Arrest her." He jerked his head in my direction.

"Shut up." Sheila's eyes were unblinking and her voice was as hard as granite, but she cast a nervous glance in my direction.

"You think you're so friggin' smart, don't you?" Tyson said, and laughed a little. He pulled the belt tighter. The wrap-around towel was already stained red. "Some hot-shot lawman, I guess. Big brass balls, huh? Got everybody in this little town scared shitless? Well, go on then, do your job, Dawson. Arrest her, damn it! Charge her with possession. You want to throw the book at somebody? Throw it at her. Second-degree felony. Two to ten."

Hearing the threat in Tyson's voice, sensing that it was directed at me, Rambo scrambled to his feet and came to stand behind me, all four feet planted firmly, defensively on the ground. "It's okay, boy," I said quietly. To Tyson, I said, "What makes you think there's cocaine in my car?"

"I'll show you," he snarled. "Let's have a look in those pots."

The trunk of my Toyota was still open. I saw Sheila glance toward it. There was just enough light to see the pots inside, where I had pushed them far toward the back, and the green leaves.

"In the pots?" I said, and laughed a little. "I haven't the faintest idea what you think you're looking for. But you can check them out if you want to. I have no objection, as long as you don't damage the plants. As I said, they're rare. They're valuable."

I could feel Sheila's startled eyes on me, but I didn't look at her. "Go ahead, Mr. Tyson." I folded my arms. "Since you're making such a fuss about it. Have a look."

There was a gotcha smirk on his face. Holding his injured arm against his side and working with his left hand, he dragged one of the heavy five-gallon pots out of the trunk. He tipped it onto the ground without any regard for the plant itself.

"Hey, careful," I warned. "Don't snap those leaves! Those plants are valuable!"

Tyson gave a sarcastic chuckle. The second pot followed, and the third. He stared down at the piles of soil and naked roots. In a grating voice, he muttered a string of curses.

"Well, are you satisfied?" I knelt down and scraped the loose soil into the pots, then picked up the plants and settled them in tenderly. I'd need to repot and water them, but I didn't think they were badly damaged. "There's nothing in these pots but plants, roots, and soil," I said, in an injured tone. "Just what did you think you were looking for?"

Tyson made a growling noise in his throat, then staggered a little. The exertion had cost him something. His face was the color of a snake's belly.

If Sheila was surprised or relieved not to see the cocaine she had every reason to expect in those pots, she didn't show it. "What *were* you looking for, Tyson?" she asked.

"You know as well as I do, damn it," he snapped. "And if you don't, you're not going to hear it from me." He sagged against the car. "I've got to get out of here," he muttered. "I've got work to do. You can't keep me from —"

"You've lost a quite a bit of blood," Sheila said gently. "You'd better sit down before you fall down."

And when the county mountie pulled his brown and silver sheriff's car into the drive and shone his headlights on the scene, that's where Tyson was sitting, his back to the right rear tire of my Toyota, a look of confusion and bewilderment on his face. From the look of it, I guessed that his arm was going to require several dozen stitches. Rambo's bite was even worse than his bark.

The door opened and a heavyset man climbed out. "Got trouble out here, Chief?" The question was asked in a deep voice, courteously, and the deputy, Carl Martin, tipped his cap. "Evenin', Miz Bayles. Good to see you, ladies."

"Evenin', Deputy," I said. "Thanks for coming. Hope we didn't take you out of your way."

Carl Martin is another of McQuaid's fishing and hunting buddies, a good ol' boy in his late thirties. His belly hangs out over his belt, testifying to an excessive indulgence in Lila Jennings' jelly doughnuts and Bob Godwin's barbecue plate specials. But he's still a very fair first baseman for the Posse, the sheriff's office softball team. He's faster than he looks, and he uses his bulk to good advantage to block the base paths.

"Glad you could give us a hand, Deputy," Sheila said. Her smile was beguiling. "Figured you'd like to have this man in your custody, seeing that this is county turf."

"Sure, we'll take him." He squinted at Tyson, still sitting on the ground, shielding his eyes from the headlights' glare. "What we got here?"

"Trespass and attempted auto theft, for starters," Sheila said. "He's got a pretty fair dog bite on that right forearm, though. Needs to be sewn up before he's booked."

Martin pulled out a ticket pad and started writing. "Name?"

"Book him as Scott Tyson," Sheila said. "Says he's an agent of the Bitter Creek Narcotics Task Force, but I haven't been able to confirm that."

Martin grunted skeptically. "Task-force agent, huh? I ain't heard nothin' 'bout no

402

jump-out boys 'round here. Leastwise, not lately. A couple of 'em give us a hard time when we went to bust that meth lab out on River Road last month, though. Seems like they got a habit of gettin' in the way."

I bit back a smile. Tyson was not going to get a warm reception at the jail tonight. There's enough bad blood between local law-enforcement agencies and the task forces to fill up Canyon Lake.

Martin handed the ticket pad to Sheila for her signature, and pulled out a pair of cuffs and snapped them on Tyson. "Got chewed up by a dog right good, didn't ya, fella?" he asked, as he grabbed Tyson under his left elbow and hoisted him to his feet. He glanced at Rambo. "Looks mean enough to've done it, that's for sure."

Rambo grinned and lifted both eyebrows. Tyson grunted. To me, Martin added, "That your dog, Miz Bayles?"

Sheila cleared her throat. "When the doctor asks about the dog bite, tell him that the prisoner was apprehended by a police dog."

Martin gave her a sharp glance. "Didn't know you had a dog on the force."

Sheila returned the look. "You just tell him what I said."

Martin nodded, put Tyson into the sheriff's car, and they drove off. I turned to

Sheila. "Why did you tell him to say that Rambo is a police dog?"

But the minute I asked the question, I thought of the answer — a lawyer's answer. "Because if he was my dog," I said, "that jerk could sue me."

"Right," Sheila said. "And if he was your dog, the court might tell you to put him down." She looked at Rambo, who was watching us with interest, his tongue lolling, his eyes bright and alert. "He's too good a dog for that."

We had no idea.

CHAPTER EIGHTEEN

¡CARAMBA! CAFÉ

1 1/2 cups cold strong coffee
6 ounces tequila
4 ounces coffee liqueur
1/2 teaspoon vanilla extract
1/2 teaspoon ground cinnamon
1 pint coffee ice cream
cinnamon sticks for stirring

Combine all ingredients except ice cream and cinnamon sticks in a blender container. Refrigerate. Prior to serving, add ice cream and blend. Pour over cracked ice into glass coffee mugs. Add a cinnamon stir stick.

After the deputy had driven off with his prisoner, Sheila and I, accompanied by Rambo, searched Tyson's blue van. We turned up an assault rifle, two handguns, and a knife, plus a six-pack of beer and a bottle of tequila. Rambo sniffed everything thoroughly as we took it out of the van.

"Were you able to get any prints off the dagger that killed Sanchez?" I asked, remembering what Hark had told me earlier in the day.

Sheila gave me a quick look. "How'd you know about that?"

"Hark." I grinned. "Hot-shot reporter. You can't keep the press away, you know."

Her grunt expressed her feelings about the press. "Yeah, we found a print. Just one, a partial." She loaded the weapons into a box she found in the van and straightened up. "Okay, China. It's time for you to come clean about those plants in your trunk. You really had me going there for a minute, you know." She picked up the box and gave me a hard look. "I figured Tyson would find the cocaine in one of those pots and I'd have to call the sheriff to arrest you, damn it!"

"Those weren't the right pots," I said, as we went toward the black Ford Sheila had borrowed, Rambo at our heels.

"What do you mean, not the right pots?" Sheila demanded. "Those yuccas were in your trunk. They —"

"Don't get your panties in a twist, Smart Cookie," I said, grinning. "Stash those weapons, and I'll show you."

But as Sheila was loading the weapons into her car, a pair of vehicle lights swung down the lane, catching us in the glare. It was another of the county's brown sheriff's cars, and the man who got out of it was the sheriff himself, Blackie Blackwell.

Blackie's face was taut when he looked at Sheila, and she was instantly tense. I felt an immediate compassion for both of them. Blackie and Sheila had been engaged for nearly two years, in an off-and-on fashion. Sheila loved him, but couldn't make up her mind whether she cared enough to exchange her freedom for commitment, a dilemma I fully understood, having experienced it for myself. And she had another reason, a good one: a pair of enforcement careers in the same family makes for a difficult balance, especially when one person holds an elective office and the other is appointed.

Last October, Blackie got tired of the uncertainty. He came to the conclusion that it was a lost cause — that Sheila was not going to marry him, and it was time to call it quits. "I'm a marrying man," he'd said to me. "I want a wife. I want a home. I want Sheila, but if she doesn't want me, I'll find somebody who does." He thought he had — the woman who was hired to develop the forensic anthropology program at CTSU. But that didn't work out, either. The "bone doctor," as people called her, is gone, and

Blackie is still looking. Sheila, on the other hand, remains married to her job. It's hard to say whether she's happy. As I said, she keeps her feelings to herself.

Blackie was looking around. "Everything okay here, China?" he asked. "I picked up the dispatch. I knew that McQuaid was over in Houston, so I thought I'd better stop by and see if you needed anything." He touched the bill of his cap. "Evenin', Chief."

"Hello, Sheriff," Sheila said quietly.

"Everything's fine," I said. "Carl Martin just picked up Tyson. You heard what happened?"

"Martin called it in," Blackie said. "Man claims to be a narcotics task-force agent, undercover." He looked at Sheila, his tone neutral. "That right?"

"I'm checking it out," Sheila replied, "but I have my doubts. I don't know how, yet, but I figure he's connected to both the Fowler and the Sanchez murders. Sounded to me like something might be coming down tonight, but he wouldn't say what. I'd appreciate it if you could keep him in custody until we find out what's going on."

"Yeah, sure. Whatever you need. Happy to help."

"I'm glad you're here, Blackie," I said. "I was about to show Sheila something. You'll probably find it interesting, too."

"Oh, yeah?" Blackie said.

Blackie Blackwell is a careful, by-the-book lawman who wears his uniforms neatly pressed and his sandy hair cut regulation-style. He has a sense of humor, but it's buried so deep under his sheriff's persona that it's sometimes hard to find. His intelligence, care, and compassion, however, are all right there on the surface. I'm glad to report that he was reelected last fall, defeating a militia-type challenger who wants to see armed citizens riding around the county in unmarked cars to defend the homeland against terrorism. The margin of victory wasn't as comfortable as those of us who worked on his campaign might've hoped. But Adams County is safe from the militia for another four years.

With Rambo tagging at my heels, I led Sheila and Blackie to the place where I had stashed the yucca pots on our neighbor's side of the stone fence that borders our lane, about twenty yards from Tyson's van. For obvious reasons, I hadn't wanted the pots on the property. As I drove up the lane on my way home that evening, I had stopped, taken them out of the trunk, and lined them up on the back side of the fence, well out of sight. Our neighbor has a couple of thousand acres and lives in Austin. He'd never know that he'd been temporarily guilty of possessing enough cocaine to get him put away for twenty years.

I retrieved my garden gloves from behind the fence, put them on, and hoisted the pots back over onto our property. As I did, Rambo came suddenly alert. His eyes brightened, his nose twitched, his whole body tensed. As we watched, bemused, he sniffed the air, then got down to business, sniffing first one pot and then the other three. And then, with a final, definitive *whuff*, he put his nose to one of the yuccas and lay down beside it. He looked up at me alertly, as if to say, *Pay attention now. This is important.*

"I'll be damned," Sheila said softly. "A sniffer dog."

"That's what it looks like, all right," Blackie said admiringly. "Where'd you get this guy, China?"

"He belonged to Colin." Still wearing my gloves, I reached down and tipped the yucca out of the pot. "Okay, Rambo. Let's see how good you are."

He was good. We were looking down at the Baggie half-hidden among the fibrous roots of the yucca. "Super dog, Rambo," I said, bending over to ruffle his fur. He lifted his head and licked my ear.

"Amazing," Sheila said, hands on hips. "Rambo, I take it all back. You are one damn fine dog."

"Sure looks like dope," Blackie said, kneeling down for a better look. "You never know, though, until it's been tested. Could be gypsum, talcum, chalk."

"Rambo thinks it's dope," I said. "But maybe somebody had better test him. Just to see what he's capable of." I gave him an appraising look and he grinned at me, eyebrows up, eyes shining, the picture of smug Rottweiler achievement. "Attack dog, drug-sniffing dog, who knows what else. Cross-trained as a cadaver dog, maybe?"

I was joking, but Sheila took me seriously.

"You think? Yeah. Let's get him tested. If Ruby would part with him, and if he's as good as he seems, I could put him to work for the department. We need a K-9 program, but we don't have the money."

"Ruby?" Blackie asked, straightening up. "How did she get into this?"

"She says she's going to adopt him," I said. "But Rambo might be happier if he had a job to do. If he lived with Ruby, he'd have nothing to do but lie around all day, waiting for her to get home."

The yucca was evidence in Sheila's investigation into Colin's murder, so we loaded the pots into the black Ford. "I know you're going to explain what those other yuccas were doing in the trunk of your Toyota," she said. "The ones Tyson was looking at." To Blackie, she added, "I thought for a minute you might have to arrest China for possession."

He raised his eyebrows. "Oh, yeah?"

"Those weren't yuccas," I said. "They're tequila agaves. When Sonora first opened, I bought —"

"Tequila agave?" Blackie asked, frowning.

"The plant that produces tequila. It's been throwing off pups. When I got home this evening —"

"Pups?" Sheila stared at me, then down at Rambo.

"Not that kind," I said patiently. "Agave offshoots are called pups. I've been potting them up for sale, in five-gallon black plastic pots. When I got home this evening, I stashed the yuccas behind the stone fence, and put the agaves in my trunk. To an experienced eye, agaves and yuccas look nothing alike, but if Tyson showed up, I thought the agaves might fool him."

"Fooled me." Sheila looked at her watch. "Ten twenty. If I want to get this stuff processed tonight, I'd better be going." She scowled. "Damn it, I wish I could have forced Tyson to tell us what he had on tap for tonight."

"You guys have ten minutes for a cappuccino, don't you?" I said. "Caramba café." This is the frothy, frosty after-dinner Mexican coffee that McQuaid and I like so much. We always served it to Blackie and Sheila, back in the days when they were together.

"Sounds great," Blackie said heartily. "I'll take you up on that." When Sheila hesitated, he slung his arm around her shoulders. "Lighten up, Chief," he said in a tone of friendly camaraderie. "You can spare the time for a cappuccino with old friends, can't you?"

Sheila gave him a game smile. "Sure," she said, subdued. "Yeah. Fine."

I shut Rambo into the dog run and went inside to explain to Howard Cosell, whose nose was badly out of joint, why he hadn't been allowed outside to join in the fun. I was lighting the burner under the kettle when I saw the blinking red light on the answering machine. I hit the button and heard a woman on the other end of the line. She sounded out of breath. She sounded scared.

"China, it's Betty," she said. "I need your

help. Please." She lowered her voice to a whisper as if she was afraid of being over-heard, but I could still hear the desperation. "It's about . . . it's my son. Ricky. I'm afraid for him. So afraid."

She stopped, sucked in her breath, and was momentarily silent, as if she had turned to listen to something. "They're coming tonight." The words began to tumble out raggedly, faster and faster. "I'm in the office here at the shop. I was cleaning up after — The police told me I could clean up the blood and straighten things out. Somebody called, a man. He thought I was Lucita. He said the truck was coming at eleven thirty tonight, here. And Ricky is . . . Allan has — I don't know what to do."

There was a sudden fearful intake of breath, and then a click. The connection was broken.

Sheila and Blackie had come into the kitchen just as the message began. "Play it again," Sheila commanded tersely.

I hit the Replay button. The three of us listened in silence, Sheila with a fierce concentration, Blackie with puzzlement, and I with a cold certainty in my stomach.

"What's this about?" Blackie asked, frown-ing, when the tape was finished.

"A drug delivery," I said bleakly, "coming

to the Sonora Nursery. Tonight. The caller is one of the owners, Betty Conrad. Ricky is her son. Allan, her husband, is the other owner."

I thought of the Conrads' hard work, of the way they had remade Wanda's failing business from nothing into something special, successful, admirable. I thought of the way they worked together, of Allan's skilled plantsmanship, of Betty's pride in her children. I thought of the pots in Colin's yard, and where Sonora's specialty plants were coming from, and understood, or thought I did, what was happening here. Understood, and was swept by a wave of sadness so strong that it nearly knocked the breath out of me.

Sheila turned to Blackie. "I don't have the manpower to handle this. Can you give me some help?"

He considered briefly. "Let's divide up. You interdict the truck. I'll handle the situation at the nursery."

"That'll work," Sheila said. She frowned, going over the steps in her mind. "I'll set up a roadblock at King and Feldman. Three cars ought to do it. But what we really need is to identify —" She looked at me. "Think Rambo can handle this?"

She didn't have to spell it out. I turned off

the burner and took down the leash hanging beside the door. "If he can, he'll save us a lot of work." As an afterthought, I reached for my poncho.

Sheila gave me a dry look. "I suppose you think you're riding along as his handler."

"You got it," I replied. Seeing the leash and hearing the word *ride*, Howard scrambled excitedly to his feet. "Howard, old buddy, you're staying here," I said. "This is a job for a trained nose." I gave him a dog biscuit. He took it grudgingly — biscuits are good, but a ride is better — and retired to his basket beside the stove, grumbling that his nose was trained: he could smell a squirrel halfway across the county.

"You'll have to waive liability," Sheila said, as we went out the door and I locked it behind us.

"Yeah," I said. "Sure. I waive liability."

She appealed to Blackie. "You heard that, right? Civilian waives liability, insists on being involved in police business."

"I heard it," he said over his shoulder, already headed for his car. "But don't let her get shot up, or McQuaid will have your hide. Let's roll."

And then I went to get Rambo, who had just been attached to the K-9 Unit. Pecan

Springs PD's only drug-sniffing attack dog, on his first assignment.

I hoped that Colin Fowler would have been proud.

I hoped that Betty Conrad would not regret what she had done.

There's only one road to Sonora. With Rambo in the backseat, panting with happy excitement at the idea of yet another ride, I drove Sheila's borrowed car while she got on her cell phone, setting up a roadblock at the corner of King and Feldman. Feldman is a main feeder road that heads east off I-35, and King is the north-south road to the nursery. The intersection is about two miles east of the interstate.

There has never been much after-hours truck traffic in the Pecan Springs area, but things are changing. In fact, a warehouse depot recently opened up on the east side of King. We saw five or six trucks — eighteen-wheelers and smaller delivery trucks — as we drove along Feldman. I could hear Sheila on the phone, sketching out the plan. Three squad cars, two officers each — with Sheila and me, we'd be eight. Nine, counting Rambo.

The first squad car, a lookout, would be concealed behind a sign on the east side of

King just past the warehouse depot, watching for trucks heading north on King. Since Sonora was the only commercial business out that way, the traffic should be minimal. When an eighteen-wheeler was spotted, the first car would radio ahead to the second, which would pull out and block the road. The officers would flag down the truck, while the third car would pull in behind the stopped vehicle and apprehend the driver and anyone with him. The officers in the second and third cars joined Sheila and me — and Rambo — for a search of the truck.

I had raised my share of challenges against police searches of vehicles in my career as a criminal defense lawyer, but this was the first time I'd been on the other side of the legal fence. I knew the rules. The Fourth Amendment requires that searches and seizures be "reasonable." A search or seizure is ordinarily reasonable when there is individualized suspicion of wrongdoing.

And individualized suspicion was exactly what we had. Lucita Sanchez had told Colin that the shipment was coming in on I-35, in an eighteen-wheeler, and had left him the pots of yucca, to show him how it would be packed. Betty had said it was due in at eleven thirty. Whether we stopped two trucks or twenty, any court would uphold tonight's search and seizure as legal. Once a vehicle was stopped, we wouldn't have any trouble determining whether it was carrying contraband — that is, if Rambo's earlier identification of the cocaine had not been a fluke. If Rambo did his job, and if there was no trouble with the driver, the bust should go down smoothly and without incident.

Things didn't turn out quite that way, of course. It started to rain hard just as we set up the cars. Even though it was late, there were plenty of vehicles coming off Feldman and heading north on King. A number of cars went past, three or four pickups, and several SUVs. Then we got a heads-up from the first squad car and flagged down a tractor-trailer rig whose driver said he was on his way home at the end of a long day on the road. He was not happy about being asked to stand beside his truck while Rambo circled it, sniffing. The dog didn't act as if he was on to anything, but Sheila ordered the driver to open up the trailer anyway, just to be sure. It was empty. The driver, muttering a curse under his breath, rolled on.

The second truck that came along was not an eighteen-wheeler, but Sheila ordered it stopped anyway, just in case. It turned out to be a rented vehicle loaded with the driver's furniture, headed for a new house a couple of blocks away. Rambo gave it an all-clear. Sheila confirmed to her own satisfaction that it looked to be filled with furniture, and radioed a warrant check against the driver's license. He came up clean, too, and she sent him on his way.

At eleven forty-five, Sheila looked at me, her face taut in the light reflected from the dash. "Fifteen minutes late."

"Yeah," I said comfortingly. "But they're coming up from the border, and it's raining. It's hard to fix a time of arrival with any precision."

She punched in Blackie's cell number. "All set?" she asked, when he answered.

"All set. Seven deputies, stationed around the perimeter. Got anything yet?"

"Negative. I'll let you know."

"Roger. Out."

I sat back against the seat, thinking about Sheila and Blackie. They had been intensely involved for almost two years, romantically, sexually. But to hear their voices, flat and expressionless, you'd think they were two strangers. They were pros, both of them. It was a shame they couldn't work out their differences.

The radio crackled to life at eleven fifty-five, the cop in the first squad car reporting an eighteen-wheeler just passing the ware-house depot, moving fast on the rainy street. The flagman stepped off the curb swinging his flashlight, and after what seemed like a very long time, the truck slowed and stopped. The driver, in his twenties, got out and stood, shielding his eyes against the glare of the squad car's headlights. The tractor was licensed in Arizona, the trailer in New Mexico, the driver in Mexico. He spoke broken English. He was alone.

Rambo got to work, and if I'd had any doubts about his credentials, they were immediately erased. He was halfway around the rig, at the left rear wheels, when he began to whine, low in his throat, and the fur stood up along his spine. He pulled at the leash, tugging me to the back of the truck.

The driver was brought around to the back and told to open the double doors. "Only plants," he said, frowning. "Only plants in here. Yuccas. Inspected when I crossed the border, all legal."

"Right," Sheila said softly. "If it's all legal, there shouldn't be any problem, should there?" Her voice hardened. "Open up, sir. Now."

The driver complied. The doors swung open and three powerful flashlights illuminated the load. Tiers of metal shelves, three feet wide, were stacked floor to ceiling on either side of a narrow aisle. On the shelves were rows of five-gallon pots. I couldn't see all of them, of course, but those I could see were filled with yuccas, closely packed and kept from sliding off the shelves by restraining metal bars. There were hundreds of pots, and Rambo was going nuts. I dropped the leash, an officer gave the dog a boost, and he scrambled into the trailer. He sniffed at one pot on the bottom row, then another, and then, with a *whuffle* and a grunt, dropped flat to the floor and put his muzzle on his paws.

"Check it out," Sheila said to the officer, who leaped into the truck and tipped a yucca out of its pot.

"Yeah," he said with satisfaction. He held up a plastic-wrapped package. "This is it."

"Way to go, Rambo!" I exclaimed.

"Some dog," Sheila said quietly. "That is some dog." She clicked her phone. "We hit pay dirt," she said to Blackie. "Get set. We're on the way."

Fifteen minutes later, the truck was pulling into the utility drive that led around to the back of the Sonora Nursery. Four men materialized out of the darkness and converged on the rear of the trailer. The doors were opened. But instead of finding the truck filled with potted plants, the crew was startled when a half-dozen armed officers spilled out — and even more startled when another half-dozen deputies closed in on them from behind, firearms raised and ready.

"Down," Blackie barked. "Facedown, flat on the ground. Now!"

There was no resistance. Within several minutes the four were frisked, handcuffed, and lined up alongside the truck trailer. Two of the men I recognized as Sonora workers.

The third was Ricky Conrad. He was trying not to cry.

The fourth was his stepfather, Allan.

CHAPTER NINETEEN

Betty Conrad couldn't come to the paper-making workshop on Saturday morning, because she was still in custody. The investigation was only hours old. It wasn't yet clear what role she had played in the drug smuggling operation, or whether she had known, when she telephoned me the evening before, that her husband was a murderer.

For it was Allan Conrad who killed Colin and Lucita. He fit the description Amy had given me of the man she'd seen leaving Beans with Colin, not long before Colin's death. And the dagger that had killed Lucita — a deadly weapon with a six-inch blade, two-edged and shaving-sharp, that folded neatly into a grooved aluminum handle — would convict him. It bore Lucita's blood and a partial print of his right thumb.

And that was what broke him. Faced with the knife and the very real possibility that his stepson and his wife might be charged as accomplices to murder, he had confessed, and the whole story came out. He'd gotten involved with the drug-smuggling ring when he was working in Brownsville. His purchase of Wanda's failed nursery was bankrolled by drug interests in Matamoras, and even though he may have had illusions of earning his way out, it doesn't work that way. With these people, once in, you can never get out. You know too much. You're a threat to too many people. Even if Allan wasn't addicted to the drugs, he was addicted to the income they provided. When Sonora didn't do as well as he and Betty hoped, there was always the drug money, keeping the business afloat.

And then Tyson came along, eager for his own cut. But Tyson discovered that Colin Fowler and his colleagues in the DEA were about to beat him to it, so he tipped Conrad off. Frightened for himself, his family, and his business, Conrad put a dagger into Colin. And then, discovering that Lucita was involved, he'd had to kill her, as well. A bloody, bloody business.

Myself, I didn't feel much like getting out of bed on Saturday morning. Rambo and I hadn't gotten home until after midnight and I wasn't firing on more than a couple of cylinders. I'd dreamed restlessly through most of what was left of the night, one long, bad dream in which I was Allan Conrad's attorney. My defense depended on shifting Conrad's guilt to Scott Tyson, arguing that he had put Conrad up to the killings, which he committed out of desperation and fear. It was a weak defense that got exactly what it deserved: the inevitable guilty verdict. But in my dream, Tyson also got the conviction he deserved, on two counts of conspiracy to commit murder.

Dragging myself out of bed early that morning, I wasn't looking forward to the day. But after I'd managed to get up, zip myself into my jeans, and pour a couple of cups of hot coffee down my throat, I knew I'd make it. I had to. Carole was counting on me, and even though I might not feel like dancing the Texas two-step, I could summon enough energy to fake it. Which was probably more than Betty Conrad could say that morning.

The papermaking workshop was a terrific success. With her usual resourceful thoroughness, Carole had prepared a great many different plant fibers for people to experiment with. At the end of the day, all our happy campers went home with samples of a dozen different papers made from a wide variety of plants: yucca, of course, but also hollyhock, okra, cattail, iris, Joe-Pye weed, mugwort, willow, and thistle — not to mention the herbal flowers and leaves they'd added to the paper pulp they had made. Thanks to Carole's excellent teaching, they also took with them some valuable new skills, an eager desire to explore an exciting new way of working with plants, and a growing appreciation for "weeds." Who would have imagined that you could walk out into your garden and gather leaves and blossoms for beautiful handmade paper? And even if you don't have a garden, you can collect plenty of material during a neighborhood walk, a drive in the country, or even a trip to the local grocery.

As I said earlier, papermaking is a messy process. Carole, Cass, and I spent a couple of hours cleaning up spills, sweeping up bits of plant fiber and leaves, packing supplies and equipment, and loading Carole's van. While we worked, I told them what had happened the night before, to a chorus of incredulous oohs and ahhs.

"I cannot believe how much serious trouble you managed to get into while I was here," Carole said as she put her van in gear. "Killings, dope smuggling, drug-sniffing dogs — it's all utterly amazing." She lifted her hand in a good-bye wave. "Give Ruby my love when she gets back," she added, and drove off.

Ruby didn't get home until nearly four on Monday afternoon, by which time I was feeling somewhat better. The shop is closed on Mondays, but I had come in to catch up on some record keeping. I was sitting in the tearoom with a glass of iced tea, my calculator, and all my paperwork spread out on the table, when Ruby breezed in.

"Whew!" she said, flinging both arms wide and taking a deep breath. "I am so glad to be home!" She flopped into a chair, stretched out her legs, and let her arms dangle in a sign of extreme weariness. "I would've been here a couple of hours ago, but I had to return all those scarves. You wouldn't believe the explanations I had to make. A couple of the stores acted like I'd stolen the blasted things myself."

I got up, circled behind her chair, and gave her a long hug. "I'm glad you're home, too," I said feelingly. "When you're not here, this place goes to the dogs. How's your mom?"

"More ornery than ever. She gave the psychiatrist fits this morning. No doubt about it. She's three chipotles shy of a salsa."

I took a glass off a table and poured it full of iced tea, laughing in spite of myself.

"I know, I know." Ruby took the glass with a grimace. "It's wretched to make jokes about your mother losing her mind. That, on top of Colin's murder. But it's like M.A.S.H. If I couldn't find a way to laugh, I'd go nuts, too."

I nodded. Each of us deals with tragedy in her own way, and Ruby had a lot to deal with. I had given her a sketch of events over the phone on Saturday evening, when I was finally able to tell her that Sheila had charged Allan Conrad with Colin's murder, and Lucita's as well. But we hadn't been able to talk very long because her mother had put up a fuss, and now she wanted the full story, with all the details. I started at the beginning and told it all the way through to the end, including the information I had heard from Sheila earlier that morning: the Drug Enforcement Administration had confirmed that Colin was one of their undercover agents. When I had finished describing Rambo's exploits, she clapped her hands.

"You see, China? I told you Rambo was a wonderful dog!"

"You told me he was a cream puff," I said sternly. "Cream puffs don't chomp down on somebody's arm like a turkey drum-stick."

"You're right about that." Her face clouded. "Actually, I'm having second thoughts about adopting him. The way he attacked Tyson —" She bit her lip. "I'd be afraid to trust him with Baby Grace. I don't think he'd hurt her, but I'd be on edge every minute."

"You don't have to be," I said. "Sheila wants him."

Ruby's eyes widened. "Sheila? But she has a phobia about attack dogs!"

"Sheila knows an opportunity when it barks at her. The Pecan Springs PD is ready to adopt Rambo as its first K-9. She's already made inquiries about sending him to school with one of her officers." I grinned. "Rambo knows what he's doing. It's the officer who needs training."

Ruby breathed out, relieved. "Well, then, that's settled." She frowned. "What about Colin's box of photos? And the meter man? What's going on with him?"

"Sheila got a warrant to search Tyson's cabin at the Pack Saddle and found the box. It contained a couple of dozen photos taken on one of Allan Conrad's plant-hunting treks through the mountains of Mexico. But Conrad was after more than just yuccas and agaves. Three of the photos showed Allan at a staging site in northern Mexico, where cocaine is brought in from Bolivia or Colombia. The shipments are broken down and repacked for smuggling across the U.S. border. On the back of one of the photos were the map coordinates, showing the location of the staging site. With that evidence, the Mexican police and the DEA could raid the site and shut it down."

"But how did Colin get the photos?" Ruby asked wonderingly.

The door opened and Sheila came in, still in uniform, her gun on her hip. "Having a party?" she asked, taking off her hat and running her hands through her hair. "Hey, Ruby — glad you're back!" Her face darkened. "I can't tell you how sorry I am about what happened to Colin."

"Thanks," Ruby said softly. "I just wish I had known. About Colin's real work, I mean."

Sheila sat down. "Why? Would you have felt differently about him if you had known?"

Ruby thought about that. "I would have understood why he couldn't be straight with me. I might have been more patient. I might have hoped for less, might have —"

Her eyes filled. She picked up a paper

napkin and blew her nose. "No, forget all that. I'm only fooling myself. Colin's job was only part of the problem. The other part was — We didn't want the same things. I wanted security and love. He wanted freedom, excitement." She blew her nose again. "Danger. He loved danger more than he cared about me."

"Danger is a hard mistress," Sheila said, her face tight.

I appropriated another glass, fished some ice cubes out of the pitcher, and poured tea for Sheila. "Ruby was asking about the photos of Conrad's Mexican trip, Sheila. How did Colin happen to have them?"

"They were taken by another undercover operative who went along on the trek," Sheila said. "Turns out that Colin and several other agents had been working for the past three years in a DEA project called Operation Spanish Dagger. They were targeting a drug smuggling network with ties to Colombia, operating out of Matamoras." She looked at me. "That guy who flashed his badge at Colin's neighbor? He was DEA, coming to check up on his agent. Of course," she added with some bitterness, "he didn't bother to check with me."

I nodded. It was all making sense. "Then Colin's jail time was part of his investigation, I suppose," I said.

Sheila nodded. "He was assigned to a cell with a man who had had some important information. Colin gained his confidence and got the information out of him. What he learned made it possible for the DEA to infiltrate the ring."

Ruby let out her breath. "I hope Colin gets a medal. He deserves it."

"I don't know about a medal," Sheila said with a shrug. "But the DEA will give him some sort of recognition. There'll probably be a ceremony. I'll stay on top of it, Ruby, and let you know."

I leaned forward. "And Tyson? Got anything more definitive on him?"

Sheila made a disgusted face. "He's still a paid agent for the Bitter Creek Narcotics Task Force, although he's on administrative leave while he's investigated for bribery. But he's in far worse trouble here. Conrad will testify that Tyson blew Colin's cover and fingered Sanchez as an informant. Bastard. If it hadn't been for him, Colin and Sanchez might still be alive."

I shook my head sadly, thinking of all the hard work that had gone into Sonora, all the family pride in the family endeavor, all the pleasure in the family success. "I didn't know Allan Conrad well, but it's hard for me to figure him as a killer."

Sheila's face was hard. "There was a lot more riding on this than just one drug shipment, China. Both Colin and Sanchez had information vital to the continued operation of the ring. There was also a weapons-for-cocaine deal in the works with a paramilitary organization that the Feds have designated as a terrorist group. Conrad seems to have been in the middle — and he'd recruited his stepson. He had a powerful motive."

"But it was the stepson that did him in," I said thoughtfully. "When Betty Conrad found out that Ricky was involved, she couldn't take it."

Ruby frowned. "How is Betty involved in all of this? Did she know what was going on?"

"Not until Ricky told her," Smart Cookie replied. "At least that's what she says. Ricky got scared when Sanchez was murdered — although he doesn't seem to have known that his stepfather was the killer. And then she got the phone call saying that a shipment was due in on Friday night. To protect Ricky, she felt she had to put a stop to it, even if it meant that her husband would be arrested. That's when she left the message on China's answering machine."

"She called me a couple of times during

the afternoon," I said. "I tried to get back to her, but we kept missing one another." I paused. "It makes sense to me that she'd blow the whistle on the drugs. She loves both her kids. She'd do anything to keep them from going bad." His mother's love hadn't kept Ricky from going tragically wrong, but a prison term might teach the boy a lesson in consequences.

Sheila nodded. "She didn't know her husband had anything to do with the killings. That's her story, anyway. Of course, she should have phoned the police, instead of calling you."

"Sure, she should've," I said. "But she was afraid for Ricky. She was scared of going to the police. She did the best she could." I slanted a look at Sheila. "Are you going to charge her?"

"She's still under investigation," Sheila said. "But probably not. There's no evidence that she was a part of the smuggling conspiracy. She'll lose Sonora, though. Her house, too."

"Lose the nursery!" Ruby exclaimed. "Lose her *house?* But how? Why?"

"Asset forfeiture," I said darkly. "The government has the right to seize any property connected to illegal activity."

"But if she wasn't in on it —" Ruby appealed anxiously to me. "How can they do that?"

"Because her husband was involved. When he's convicted, the state will seize his part of their joint property, including bank accounts, cars, and furniture under criminal forfeiture law. They'll try to seize her half — and they'll get it, too. They'll argue that Betty enjoyed the benefits of her husband's criminal activities and that it can be inferred that she knew the money didn't come from legitimate sources."

"That's grim!" Ruby exclaimed.

"Hey," Sheila said defensively. "It's the *law*. The money will come to the Pecan Springs Police Department — and the county sheriff's office, too, since they took part in the raid. I don't know about Blackie," she added, "but we can sure use whatever we get. It's a huge windfall. The cocaine in that truck is worth nearly a half million dollars, in addition to the Conrads' property and any cash that was seized. It'll hire new officers and get us better equipment."

Ruby turned to me. "The cocaine I understand. I can even understand why the government could take Allan Conrad's property as part of his punishment. But if Betty is innocent —"

I shrugged. "The government doesn't have to convict you of a crime to confiscate your property. In fact, it doesn't even have to charge you with a crime. In civil forfeiture, all it has to do is establish probable cause to believe that the property was involved in a crime. That it was used to facilitate a crime or represents its proceeds."

"Probable cause?" Ruby asked dubiously.

"Yeah, right," I said. "The same minimal standard the cops need to justify a search. And once they've established probable cause that your property is subject to forfeiture, you have to prove — by preponderance of the evidence — that it isn't. That's a high standard, and tougher than you might think. I've put in a call to Justine," I added. Justine Wyzinski, aka The Whiz, is a friend from my law-school days, who practices in San Antonio. "She took a civil asset forfeiture case a couple of years ago and won it. She might be willing to take Betty's case."

"You lawyers are all alike," Sheila said, sounding irritated. "The cops catch a passel of crooks, bust up a drug-smuggling ring, and you want to pick the case apart." She finished her tea and stood up. "But I won't let that come between us, China. It was your involvement in this business that allowed us to conclude it so speedily. Thanks." She grinned. "I'm glad it's over. Thanks a lot."

"You're welcome," I said, and gave her a hug.

We left it at that, but both of us knew that the matter wasn't settled, Betty Conrad's part of it, at least. It would be a long time before justice was done — or before anybody had any clear idea what justice might look like.

"Well," McQuaid said, handing me a glass of red wine, "I hope you see Sheila's side of it. Forfeiture revenue helps fund law enforcement. Police departments need the money."

"I don't dispute that. In fact, it just might be the reason Colin died."

McQuaid sat down on the porch swing beside me. "Yeah?" He pushed with his foot to set the swing in motion.

"Yeah. Tyson wanted Colin out of the way so he could make that bust himself. He figured that if he took those seized assets back home to the Bitter Creek Task Force, they'd forget about that puny little bribery investigation. He'd be back in their good graces. That seizure would fund task-force salaries for three or four years — until the next big bust came along."

"My, my." McQuaid shook his head. "Cynical, aren't we, counselor?"

"You bet I'm cynical. The forfeiture laws invite corruption. They need to be reformed." I sipped my wine. "But my guess is that Betty Conrad is going to lose the nursery, her house, and all her assets. And you and I aren't going to change the law by arguing about it."

McQuaid slipped his arm around me and pulled my head against his shoulder. "I agree," he said mildly. "So let's don't."

We rocked in companionable silence for a few minutes. A hummingbird, whizzing and whirring, visited the honeysuckle blossoms. A cardinal, with a flash of bright red wings, called from the cedar tree, and from the back porch, Brian called Howard Cosell. Somewhere in the distance, a chain saw buzzed. A quiet afternoon in the country.

"Hawk and I made some progress," McQuaid said finally, his lips against my hair. "And your brother thinks he has a line on your dad's car, down in Victoria."

I sat up straight. "I thought I wasn't supposed to get involved in your cases," I said. "Wasn't that what we agreed when you hung out your shingle?"

"Well, yes," McQuaid said. He put his hand on my back and began to rub. "But

Miles is your brother. And this case is about —"

"Half brother," I said firmly, and got to my feet. "I am pleased as punch that he's paying you a decent fee for your investigative work. You are very good, and Miles is damned lucky that you were interested enough to take the case. But I have had just about enough crime to last me for a while, if you don't mind. It's time to put dinner on the table, and Brian's due at the soccer field at six thirty."

"I know, I know," McQuaid said, getting to his feet. "But —"

I stood on my tiptoes to kiss him. "Come on, babe. Leave it for a while, can't you?"

"Yeah, sure," he said. "But I predict you'll want to know —"

I kissed him again, and this time, it worked. He straightened up and sniffed.

"Hey," he said happily. "Is that meat loaf?"

HERBS OF THE
AMERICAN SOUTHWEST

The landscape around Pecan Springs, across the Hill Country, and west and south through the arid regions of Texas, New Mexico, Arizona, and Southern California, is rich with an enormous variety of native herbs — herbs that indigenous peoples used in cookery, in medicine, as fiber and dye plants, and in their community rituals. On my own small acreage in Burnet County, Texas, I see dozens of wild herbs as I walk through the meadows and fields: from familiar plants like cattails and echinacea to the less familiar squaw weed, buffalo gourd, and prairie parsley. And herbal knowledge is not a thing of the past, either, for a lively tradition of wild gathering still exists and respected herbal practitioners can be found in many communities of the rural Southwest.

For a comprehensive survey of Southwestern herbs, you might want to consult one of the books listed in "Further Reading." And here, in addition to the plants I have mentioned in the text of *Spanish Dagger,* are a few of those I find interesting. I hope these very different plants will give you some idea of the diversity of the native herbs of this region.

Chile peppers (*Capsicum*) range from mild to hot, hotter, and hottest. Capsaicin, the phytochemical that causes the chile's searing heat and pain, is used in ointments to treat arthritis and joint pain.

Cilantro (*Coriandrum sativum*) is to cooks in the Southwest what parsley is to everyone else. The green flecks of fresh cilantro show up in soups, salads, and salsas, and the dried seeds (called coriander) are essential in curry and chili powders, and are a widely used digestive aid.

Creosote bush (*Larrea tridentata*) can be found in arid places from West Texas to California. A shrubby bush about five feet high with yellow flowers (after a rain), it is remarkably enduring. One study found that an average age of a clump was 1,250 years! It is antibacterial, antioxidant, and is often used in the treatment of joint pain and allergies.

Epazote (*Dysphania ambrosioides* formerly *Chenopodium ambrosioides*), kin to lambs-quarters and goosefoot, has a well-earned reputation for improving the social lives of bean lovers. Its camphorous fragrance and resinous taste partner perfectly with black beans, pork dishes, and chicken soups. Medicinally, it is an effective vermifuge (one folk name: wormseed) and has been used to treat fungal infections, athlete's foot, and ringworm. Toxic in large doses.

Mesquite (*Prosopis glandulosa*) was a staple herb for the native people of the Southwest. They processed the tree's dried beans into flour, which was made into flatbread and fermented in an intoxicating drink. Mesquite honey has its own distinctive flavor, and mesquite beans (gathered green) can be processed into juice, jelly, syrup, and wine. The gluelike gum exuded from the bark was used to mend pottery and to produce a black dye for weaving and basketry. The leaves and bark are astringent and antibacterial; a tea was used to treat bladder infections and diarrhea.

Mexican mint marigold (*Tagetes lucida*), native to Mexico, is the answer to the Southwesterner's inability to grow tarragon. This pretty, yellow-blooming perennial is used in place of tarragon in teas, vinegars, and pestos, and with chicken, pork, and vegetables (especially cabbage). Medicinally, the herb has been used to treat digestive ailments, reduce fevers, and as a diuretic. Shamans are said to have used a strong tea to induce trance states.

Prickly pear cactus (*Opuntia sp.*) is another staple Southwestern herb. Both the pads and the ruby-red fruit were used in cookery (There's nothing quite like prickly pear jelly!). Research suggests that the plant's nutrient-rich fiber helps to reduce cholesterol. A pad with spines removed was split and warmed for use as a poultice to relieve chest congestion. A warmed pad was placed over the ear for earache, or over rheumatic or arthritic joints. The gelatinous sap was a soothing skin lotion for rashes and sunburn, and a poultice made of the mashed flesh of the pad was used to heal wounds and burns. Taken internally, the plant treated many gastrointestinal disorders. And like most native plants, prickly pear served many other domestic purposes. In the rural Southwest, it was used (with water, lime, and salt) to make a waterproof paint for walls, and as a formidable fence — just try getting through that dense, thorny wall! Its fibers were used to make paper and its thorns as needles and pins, while the insect that feeds on its pads and fruit (the cochineal) made red dye.

FURTHER READING

American Indian Food and Lore, by Carolyn Niethammer, MacMillan, 1974.

Gathering the Desert, by Gary Paul Nabham, University of Arizona Press, 1985.

Handbook of Indian Foods and Fibers of Arid America, by Walter Ebeling, University of California Press, 1986.

Medicinal Plants of the Desert and Canyon West, by Michael Moore, Museum of New Mexico Press, 1989.

¡Tequila! Cooking with the Spirit of Mexico, by Lucinda Hutson, Ten Speed Press, 1994.

RECIPES AND CRAFTS

CHAPTER ONE:
CASS' GINGERBREAD WAFFLES
WITH AGAVE SYRUP

3 eggs
1/4 cup sugar
1/2 cup molasses
1 cup buttermilk
1 1/2 cups flour
1 teaspoon ground ginger
1/2 teaspoon ground cinnamon
1/2 teaspoon ground cloves
1/2 teaspoon salt
1 teaspoon baking soda
1 teaspoon baking powder
6 tablespoons butter, melted and cooled

Preheat waffle iron. In a small bowl, beat eggs until light and fluffy. Add sugar, molasses, and buttermilk, and beat. In a large bowl, sift together flour, ginger, cinnamon, cloves, salt, baking soda, and baking powder.

Add to batter and stir until smooth, then add butter and combine. Pour 1/2 to 3/4 cups of batter into very hot waffle iron and bake 4 to 5 minutes. Serve hot with agave syrup.* Makes 6 waffles. To freeze, cool baked waffles on a wire rack. (Do not stack.) When completely cool, layer between sheets of wax paper, pack in a zipper-lock bag, and freeze. Reheat in a toaster, or in a conventional oven at 300°F for 10 minutes. Do not use a microwave oven.

AGAVE SYRUP*

Often called agave nectar, this is a delicious golden syrup a little thinner than honey. It is the processed juice of the agave plant (fermented, the juice becomes tequila). Agave nectar, which has a low glycemic index, is made up of natural fructose (90 percent) and glucose (10 percent) sugars, as well as iron, calcium, potassium, and magnesium. Natural fructose is processed and absorbed slowly by the body, thus avoiding the highs and lows of glucose. Because agave nectar tastes sweeter than table sugar, you'll use less. Agave nectar dissolves readily and can be substituted for other sweeteners in cooking and baking. Use as a syrup on pancakes and waffles, or as a sweetener in lemonade, smoothies, in vinaigrettes, and on cereals. In a recipe that calls for one cup sugar, substitute three-quarters cup agave nectar and reduce the amount of liquid by about one-third. The darker syrup has a stronger flavor than the lighter. Agave nectar is approved for use by the American Diabetes Association.

CHAPTER TWO:
A DILLY OF A GRILLED SALMON

1/4 cup white wine vinegar
1/2 teaspoon garlic powder
1 teaspoon salt-free "almost beau monde" herbal seasoning
2 tablespoons fresh dill weed
4 tablespoons olive oil
juice of two lemons
2 pounds salmon fillets

Combine vinegar, garlic powder, seasoning, dill weed, oil, and lemon juice. Place the salmon in a shallow glass dish and pour the marinade over it. Cover and marinate in the refrigerator for at least 1 hour, turning occasionally. Preheat the grill for medium-high heat and spray the grate with cooking spray. Grill the fish for about 3 to 4 minutes per side, or to desired doneness. Serves 4.

Salt-free "Almost Beau Monde" Herbal Seasoning

1 tablespoon ground cloves
1 1/4 teaspoons ground cinnamon
1 tablespoon ground bay leaf
1 tablespoon ground allspice
2 tablespoons ground black pepper
1 teaspoon ground nutmeg
1 teaspoon ground mace
1 teaspoon ground celery seed

Mix all ingredients. Store in a tightly closed jar away from heat. Good with fish, poultry, pork, vegetables, potatoes. Makes about 6–7 tablespoons.

Chapter Three

If you want to try cooking your yucca flowers, here's an easy, tasty recipe developed by well-known herbalist Susan Belsinger, who teaches and writes about food and gardening. This recipe first appeared in *Flowers in the Kitchen: A Bouquet of Tasty Recipes,* which includes wonderful recipes for favorite herbal flowers such as rosemary, lavender, chives, and nasturtium. You can learn more about Susan's work and find a list of her available books at http://www.susanbelsinger.com. The recipe is reprinted here by permission.

Braised Yucca Flowers with Peas

About 24 yucca flowers

2 cups peas, freshly shelled or thawed if frozen

2 tablespoons unsalted butter

1 clove garlic

Salt and freshly ground pepper

Wash the yucca flowers and remove the stamens. Pat them dry. Steam the peas until just barely done, pour the water off, and keep covered. Melt the butter in a skillet over medium-low heat. Cut the garlic clove into slivers. Sauté them in the butter for about 2 minutes. Do not allow the garlic or the butter to brown. The butter should just barely begin to turn golden. Remove the garlic from the butter and discard. Add the yucca flowers to the skillet, stirring well so that they all are coated by the butter. Cook them until they just begin to wilt, about 2 minutes or so. Add the peas to the skillet, season with salt and pepper, and toss well. Cover for about 1 minute, taste for seasoning, and serve immediately.

Chapter Four:
Nopales Salad

2 pounds nopales (cactus pads), spines removed

2 quarts water
1 medium onion
3 medium tomatoes, chopped
1 cup sweet corn, drained
1 cup black beans, drained
2–3 serrano or jalapeño peppers, chopped
2–3 sprigs cilantro, minced
1 cup shredded yellow cheese
dressing

Bring water to a boil in a large pan. Add chopped nopales and simmer for 20 minutes. Drain, rinse, and chill. Place in salad bowl with chopped onion, tomatoes, corn, beans, peppers, and cilantro. Toss with dressing and cheese.

Dressing: Mix 1/2 cup red wine vinegar, 1/2 cup olive oil, 1 teaspoon oregano, and salt and pepper to taste.

CHAPTER SEVEN:
SLEEPY-TIME HERBAL TEAS

Many herbs are valued for their ability to calm anxiety and soothe ruffled spirits. Here are three recipes for bedtime teas that will help you slip gently into sleep. Each recipe makes enough for four cups of tea. Mix all ingredients; store in a cool, dark place. To brew one cup: pour 1 cup of boiling water over 3 teaspoons dried herbs. Steep for 8–10 minutes. Sweeten with honey.

Sweet Dreams Tea: 4 teaspoons each of dried lavender flowers, chamomile, and catnip

Calming Tea: 4 teaspoons each of dried passionflower, skullcap, and peppermint

Pillow-Time Tea: 4 teaspoons each of dried lemon balm, chamomile, and oatstraw

CHAPTER EIGHT:
DAMIANA APHRODISIAC TEA

1 tablespoon dried damiana leaves
1 tablespoon dried chamomile
1 tablespoon dried lemongrass
1 tablespoon dried spearmint leaves
1 teaspoon dried passionflowers
1 teaspoon crushed cinnamon bark
1 teaspoon dried orange peel, grated

Combine herbs, cinnamon, and orange peel. Pour one cup of boiling water over one tablespoon of mixed herbs and let steep for 5–7 minutes. Sweeten with honey.

CHAPTER SEVENTEEN:
HIBISCUS SYRUP

Hibiscus flowers have a cranberrylike flavor with citrus overtones. This syrup is tasty over ice cream, pudding, pancakes, and French toast.

10 large hibiscus flowers
1/4 cup lemon juice
1 cup water
1 cup sugar

Detach petals from the calyx; discard calyx. Cover petals with lemon juice in a deep bowl. Microwave for 2 minutes. Combine sugar and water in a saucepan and heat until water boils and sugar is dissolved. Add cooked flowers and lemon juice and mix well. Simmer over low heat until reduced by one-third (about 45 minutes). Strain and refrigerate. Other ways to use hibiscus:

Place a large flower on a clear glass plate and fill with your favorite dip. Surround with small crackers.
Sprinkle petals over salad greens.
Float a flower in a tropical punch bowl.
Use the inner bark (called *bast*) to make paper.

CHAPTER NINETEEN

You'll find clear directions for making yucca paper in *Papermaking with Plants: Creative Recipes and Projects Using Herbs, Flowers,*

Grasses, and Leaves, by Helen Hiebert (Storey Books, 1998), which also provides an excellent introduction to papermaking and directions for making paper from mulberry, hibiscus, milkweed, thistledown, hosta, and mugwort. Another book I've enjoyed: *Grow Your Own Paper: Recipes for Creating Unique Handmade Papers,* by Maureen Richardson (Martingale, 1999). On the web, Gin Petty's helpful discussion, with photos, takes you step-by-step through her adventure with yucca: http://ginpetty.com/archives/2003_06.htm (scroll down the page to the entry for June 20). Gin manages the Yahoo! papermaking list, where papermakers share their creative ideas for using plant fibers to make paper: http://groups.yahoo.com /group/papermaking/. And for more of China's experiments with papermaking, you can read "The Collage to Kill For," in the mystery anthology *Murder Most Crafty,* edited by Maggie Bruce (Berkley, 2005).

ABOUT THE AUTHOR

Susan Wittig Albert grew up on a farm in Illinois and earned her PhD at the University of California at Berkeley. A former professor of English and a university administrator and vice president, she is the author of the China Bayles Mysteries and a family-friendly mystery series set in the early 1900s featuring Beatrix Potter. She and her husband, Bill, co-author a series of Victorian-Edwardian mysteries under the name of Robin Page. The Alberts live near Austin, Texas. Visit their Web site at www.mystery partners.com.

We hope you have enjoyed this Large Print book. Other Thorndike, Wheeler, and Chivers Press Large Print books are available at your library or directly from the publishers.

For information about current and upcoming titles, please call or write, without obligation, to:

Publisher
Thorndike Press
295 Kennedy Memorial Drive
Waterville, ME 04901
Tel. (800) 223-1244

or visit our Web site at:

www.gale.com/thorndike
www.gale.com/wheeler

OR

Chivers Large Print
published by BBC Audiobooks Ltd
St James House, The Square
Lower Bristol Road
Bath BA2 3SB
England
Tel. +44(0) 800 136919
email: bbcaudiobooks@bbc.co.uk
www.bbcaudiobooks.co.uk

All our Large Print titles are designed for easy reading, and all our books are made to last.